SHATTERED PROMISES

BOOK THREE IN THE SHATTERED TRILOGY

PHOENIX WOLFE

PHOENIX WOLFE PUBLISHING

CONTENTS

DEDICATION

TO ANYONE WHO'S EVER FELT BROKEN OR DAMAGED,

WHO'S STRUGGLED WITH BODY IMAGE ISSUES OR DEPRESSION,

WHO'S LISTENED TO THE LIE THAT YOU AREN'T GOOD ENOUGH –

THIS BOOK IS FOR YOU.

YOU ARE MORE THAN ENOUGH!

TRIGGER WARNINGS

THIS BOOK CONTAINS REFERENCES to physical injuries, physical assault, sexual assault, kidnapping, PTSD, depression, anxiety, suicidal thoughts, infertility, loss of pregnancy, and graphic violence.

Please read the note from the author and a sample of the first chapter for free on my website at **www.phoenix-wolfe.com/sample-of-chapter-one** to see if this book is a fit for you.

CHAPTER ONE

CHARLIE

No. No! No!

This isn't real. This can't be happening.

Mark wouldn't do this to me. He loves me.

He promised he'd never leave. He said nothing could make him leave me, nothing.

He promised me.

He promised.

But here I am. Alone.

All alone.

I'm on my knees in the hall outside Mark's room, envelopes scattered across the floor where I dropped them when I realized he was gone. My phone lies on the floor beneath the wooden foyer bench. My fists are clenched beside my ears, my head tucked down so my arms shield my face. My heart slams erratically in my chest. Iron bands surround my ribcage, squeezing ever tighter, making it difficult to breathe. I'm gasping, my breaths coming fast. Too fast. Black spots crowd my vision, and my hands and forearms tingle.

Somewhere inside my head, I hear a gentle voice. *Slow, deep breaths. Slow your breathing down. You're hyperventilating. You're safe. Slow your breathing. Nice deep breaths.*

Lila's voice.

I focus on slowing my breathing, trying to block the stark reality crashing over me. I have to close my eyes to concentrate, to stop seeing the truth.

That I'm alone.

That Mark left me.

That my best friend, the man I love, walked out on me.

Worse, he waited till I was *at work* to pack up his belongings and leave, sneaking away like I was *a mistake*, a mortifying one-night stand. No phone call. No text. No note.

Just an empty house and my shattered heart.

Lila called to tell me he was staying with her and Tucker at their house. She said not to worry, that they'd talk to him. I'd lied and said someone was at the door and hung up. My phone has buzzed more times than I can count, but I can't talk to her. I can't talk to anyone.

She and Tucker can talk to Mark all they want, but it won't make him love me, and that's what it all comes down to.

He doesn't love me.

How could he? I'm too fucked up for anyone to love.

The sky grows dark as hours pass. Shadows crawl across the floor, reaching for me with long claws, threatening, menacing. My heart thunders in my chest again.

I can't be alone in the dark. I can't handle the darkness.

Somehow I get to my feet, turning on every light downstairs before returning to Mark's room.

To the floor.

His floor.

I remember with startling clarity the night we discussed taking our friendship to the next level. I was afraid I'd lose my best friend if things didn't work out between us. Mark had stared at me with intense blue eyes from across my dining room table, his large hands gripping mine.

You won't lose me, Charlie, not ever. You've been the best part of my life for as long as I can remember, and nothing would make me walk away from you. Nothing.

Yet here I sit, crumpled in the floor, because he discarded me and walked away.

I drag his pillow off the bed, clutching it to my chest, hoping to dull the sharp pain slicing through me. It doesn't work. Instead, his scent assaults me, reminding me of the perfection of mere days ago, when he made me feel cherished. Loved. Like I was important to him. Like I mattered.

He said he doesn't love me.

He insisted I deserve someone better. Someone whole.

He said people who are broken and scarred don't deserve love, referring to his own war wounds. His amputation. His scars.

I'm still flabbergasted he said those words to *me*, a woman whose entire back is a web of interlacing scars from razor wire, leather strips, and an Arabic-script brand that declares me to be a "stupid cunt whore". He made his declaration to a woman whose breasts and upper thighs bear scars of mutilation, a woman whose insides are scarred and ruined from repeated rapes and violations from a rusty knife and filthy metal pipes. A woman whose psyche is most definitely broken.

People who are broken and scarred don't deserve love.

So he took his love away.

When I could breathe again after his harsh words, I'd recognized he wasn't talking about me. My wounded expression left him confused until I removed my shirt. When comprehension dawned, he was horrified I'd thought he was talking about me. He's seen my scars so many times that he'd stopped seeing them, the same way I don't see his. I only see him. I only loved him.

But it wasn't enough.

I gave him all of me. My trust. My body. My heart. It still wasn't enough.

I'm not enough.

I still don't understand what I did wrong. Sunday night was the most tender, beautiful, perfect night of my entire life. His kisses, his touches, were reverent. He made me feel cherished. Treasured.

And I knew with complete certainty that he loved me.

The next evening, I came home to find him waiting for me in the hall, telling me we needed to see other people. His sudden one-eighty was a knife in my heart. I told him I loved him, but it didn't matter. I fled the house and got drunk, ending up at a bar until my friend Tom came to my rescue. He took me back to my hotel room and stayed at my side, keeping me safe.

Tom and I attempted to make Mark jealous by having dinner together and being affectionate where he would see us. We needn't have bothered. Mark was already emotionally gone. He had been for weeks. Telling him I loved him only made him more desperate to end things between us.

Last night I thought I'd finally gotten through to him after his scar comment. We made love urgently, frantically, unable to get enough of each other. Our bodies said what our words couldn't. I thought we'd fixed things, that he'd realized how he felt about me.

I was peacefully curled up against his chest when he called our lovemaking "closure".

Closing the door on us.

On me.

I begged him to admit he loved me. I was positive he did. He just needed to let go of his fears and say it. He said he couldn't tell me what I wanted to hear. I argued it wasn't that he couldn't, but that he wouldn't.

He didn't deny it.

Instead, he left me.

Telling Mark how I feel about him has destroyed the most important relationship in my life.

It might destroy me.

This pain is unbearable, ripping through my chest, shredding me to ribbons from the inside.

I can't take this pain.

I can't take this.

I can't.

Make it stop.

I just want the pain to stop.

I spend the night on the floor, knees drawn to my chest, clutching his pillow for dear life as though it will bring him back to me.

MARK

I'm facing a furious Lila, trying to explain things. It's not going well, not that I'd expected it to. She and Charlie are like sisters.

"Let me get this straight," she says, the heat of her violet stare searing me. "You told Charlie you needed to see other people less than twenty-four hours after going out of your way to make her feel more loved than she had in her entire life." My face burns with shame, but I don't look away. I don't trust Lila not to slap the shit out of me, especially since I've earned it. "Then you tell her she deserves someone whole. You tell her people who are broken and scarred don't deserve love." I swallow hard. "You used those *exact* words, knowing the hell she's been through, knowing that's the shit Blake told her, and knowing that's exactly how she views herself — as broken and scarred." I wince. "Then you two make love, and just when she thinks that means things are okay, you tell her it was just 'closure'. Then you call *my husband* —" she turns to glare at him before whirling back to me, blond curls flying over her shoulder with the speed of her movement, "— to come and help you sneak the fuck out of her house, the house she remodeled to accommodate your disabilities after you were released from the hospital, the same hospital where she stayed by your side for three months when you were injured. You treated her like shit after claiming she was your best friend, after you swore to her nothing could ever come between you." Her voice has steadily gotten louder, and a big vein throbs in her forehead. "Did I miss anything?"

"Lila —" I begin, but she cuts me off.

"Don't," she says, holding up a hand and pressing her lips so tightly together they turn white. "Just don't. I love you, Mark, but you're a fucking asshole, and if you say one more word, I swear to God, I'll knock every one of your teeth out and shove them down your sorry throat." She rounds on Tucker. "And you? Helping him do this to Charlie? What the fuck, Tucker?"

"He didn't know what was happening, Lila," I interject quickly. "All I told him was that I needed help."

Lila mutters something that sounds suspiciously like, "you're both gonna need help when I'm done." Then she holds up both hands, fingers splayed and shaking with rage. "Take your shit to the guest room at the end of the hall. It has a bathroom, but there aren't handrails in the shower, so use your fucking walker." She turns to Tucker. "You can stay on the couch or with Mark, I don't care which. I can't stand the sight of either one of you right now." His blue eyes widen and he opens his mouth to protest, but reconsiders at her murderous expression.

Tucker waits until her door slams upstairs before he sighs heavily. "Sorry about that. The hormone shots and the ectopic pregnancy – it's been hard." His voice trails off. Lila and Tucker have been trying to conceive, and Lila's been taking hormone shots. Just a couple of weeks ago, they rushed her into surgery for a tubal pregnancy, resulting in the loss of one of her fallopian tubes and effectively halving their already-slim chances of conception.

I shake my head. "No, I'm sorry. I didn't mean to get you in trouble."

He shrugs. "She might calm down in a couple of hours. Sometimes once the anger fades, she gets a little weepy. I might not have to spend the entire night on the couch." He frowns. "Or it could go the other way, and I'll be down here long after you and Charlie have patched things up." He steals a hopeful glance in my direction.

But that won't happen.

It can't.

Charlie deserves someone better. Someone who doesn't have a fucking metal peg sticking out of his stump of a leg for a prosthetic to attach to. Someone whose body isn't a goddamn patchwork of scars from burns, shrapnel, and surgeries. Someone who isn't half a man.

She deserves someone as beautiful and as perfect as she is. Someone who sees her true worth and loves her more than life itself. Someone who would die for her without hesitation. Someone who can do anything she wants, like dancing in the kitchen or going horseback riding or making love without having to worry about skewering her with his fucking peg leg.

Someone like Tom.

The thought makes my chest burn, even though I know he'd be perfect for her. He's strong, good-looking, kind, hard-working. They're already good friends, and his daughter Maya worships Charlie. The three of them hang out together regularly. One small nudge in the right direction is all it might take. The burning in my chest gets worse, and I force the image of the three of them as a happy family out of my mind.

I remember the two of them lying together on the couch a few days ago, his hand just beneath her left breast. Entwined in the dark beside his car. Slow dancing in the kitchen.

The pain in my chest becomes a searing, raging monster, and it takes everything I have to force it down.

Despite my jealousy, I can admit Tom is the perfect man for Charlie.

When I said decent people deserved better than to be stuck with someone who's broken and scarred, I was talking about Charlie deserving someone better than me. Her scars and self-described brokenness never entered my mind. I don't see her as scarred or broken. It's true that she has scars, but they don't even register with me. If I do notice them, it only makes me appreciate her strength even more. She's always been beautiful to me. No matter what those bastards in Afghanistan did to her, Charlie could never not be beautiful to me.

She said last night that she knew I loved her. That it wasn't that I couldn't tell her I loved her, but that I wouldn't. I didn't bother to deny it, because she's right.

I do love Charlie, more than life itself.

And that's why I had to leave.

Charlie wasn't supposed to fall for me. It wasn't supposed to be like this. We've been best friends for most of our lives. We kissed once, in her kitchen, and it ignited an insatiable fire between us. Once we accepted our mutual attraction, we agreed to explore a no-strings-attached physical aspect to our relationship.

I never stood a chance.

Unbeknownst to Charlie, I fell hard for her when we were teens. I never acted on it because I was afraid her parents would freak out. After all, we lived in the same house. Those buried feelings never disappeared. They simply went into hibernation, and at the first opportunity, they consumed me. I fell for her all over again, and I fell hard. I knew when things ended between us, I'd be crushed, but I wanted to savor every second for as long as I could.

But that love can't be mutual. Charlie can't be stuck with me. She deserves someone better. Someone healthy. Someone whole.

I realize Tucker's still waiting for me to respond. I shake my head. "This isn't something that can be patched up, Tucker."

He studies me. "Give it a few days. Things will look different after a little time and space."

A door upstairs opens long enough for a pillow and blanket to sail over the banister before slamming shut. Tucker sighs and retrieves them, tossing them onto the couch.

"Sorry," I apologize again.

"I'm not the one you should apologize to," he says. "I need a beer. Do you want one?"

TUCKER

It's two am. Mark's gone to bed. I'm on the couch. Lila's still awake. I can hear her pacing back and forth across our bedroom. I reach for my phone and text her.

"Can I come talk to you?"

Little dots dance on the screen as she types her reply. "Not without physical injury."

Well, it's not a no.

I try for humor. "Open or closed hand? Face or body blow?"

A solid minute passes before the little dots appear again. "Fine."

I collect my blanket and pillow from the couch, but have enough sense to stash them in the hall. If I take them in with me, she'll think I'm assuming I've won this round, and she'll toss me out again and keep my pillow and blanket. Been there, done that. Twice, actually. Sometimes I'm a slow learner.

I open the door and enter, my hands raised in surrender as I study her expression. She's upset, but not ready to erupt.

"Hi, Sweetness. Thanks for letting me come up."

She frowns. "Charlie won't answer any of my calls or texts."

At the moment, Lila seems more worried than mad. I can work with worried.

"Where's your laptop?" I ask, and she gestures to the small desk by the window. "I can still remotely access the camera in her foyer. We might be able to see her, depending on where she is, or you can try to talk to her through the mike."

Last year, Lila and I persuaded Charlie to let us install a camera system that feeds directly to our laptops and phones. Charlie battled severe night terrors, reliving the horrors of her kidnapping. She'd awaken terrified and disoriented, often firing her gun. The system would alert us via motion and noise sensors so we could talk to her and reorient her from here. On rare occasions, we'd have to go to her house to intervene. Thankfully, that didn't happen often, because startling a panicked, paranoid sharpshooter is something I'd strongly advise against.

Lila's face relaxes. "That's a good idea." I sit down at the desk and open the security program, and she crosses the room to peer over my shoulder.

The fish eye camera comes to life, looking down into her foyer. All the lights are on, but the area is empty. I frown. "She's not on the bench." I'd assumed that's where she'd be. Charlie used to stay on it every night so she could monitor all entrances to her home. She believed hypervigilance would protect her from ever being victimized again.

"Can you see into the living room?" Lila leans closer, and her blond curls fall forward and brush my cheek. I inhale her subtle cherry blossom scent.

I swivel the camera and zoom in. "You smell incredible," I tell her, not taking my eyes off the screen.

She ignores my compliment. "Do you see anything?"

Her tone isn't overly friendly, but it's not angry, either. I'm close enough to kiss her, and she hasn't mauled me yet.

I scan what I can see of Charlie's living room. One couch and the loveseat are empty. I can only see the back of the other sofa because it faces away from the camera. "She might be lying here," I point to the screen, "but if she is, she's out of view."

She purses her lips thoughtfully. "How about Mark's room?"

I look up in surprise. "You think she'd be in there?"

Her eyes grow sad. "It's the one place she'd feel close to him."

I pivot the camera again, turning it toward Mark's room. "There," I nod, pointing to the screen. Charlie's knees are drawn to her chest and she's rocking, her arms wrapped around something with her face pressed into it.

"She's holding his pillow," Lila says, her expression pained.

I drag my hand down my face. "Should we go over?"

She considers, pressing her fist to her mouth. "I don't know. I wish she'd answer her phone."

I reach for Lila's fist and tug her hand down. "She may want to lick her wounds in private. You know she hates for anyone to see her struggle."

Lila scowls. "There wouldn't be a struggle if Mark weren't being such a dumbass." She yanks her hand out of mine. "I can't believe you went along with this."

"What did you want me to do? Let him take an Uber to a hotel? Leave town and disappear? This was the best option. He's safe, and it gives us a chance to talk some sense into him. He's stubborn as a fucking mule. He's not going to change his mind easily."

Her frown shrinks but doesn't disappear. "I guess."

"You know I don't agree with him. This was the best alternative I could come up with."

"Fine," she mutters, "you don't have to sleep on the couch."

I slide a hand behind her neck and pull her down for a quick kiss, followed by a longer kiss until I feel her smile against me.

"Just because you're a good kisser doesn't mean you're off the hook."

I grin. "Of course not." Then I wink cheekily. "Feel free to punish me."

"I have the perfect idea," she says, leaning closer, her breath tickling my neck as her lips graze my ear. My grin deepens as possibilities race through my mind, but our minds are on very different tracks. "You're doing the dishes for as long as Mark stays here."

LILA

I doze off and on the rest of the night, curled against Tucker's chest with his arm around me. Every time I glance at the laptop, Charlie's still sitting there, clutching Mark's pillow. She's stopped rocking, but other than that, nothing's changed. Every time I raise my head to check on her, Tucker rubs my back and murmurs for me to go back to sleep, because he's keeping an eye on her.

Shortly after daylight, I fall into a deep sleep, not rousing until ten-thirty. I jump out of bed. I never sleep this late. I glance over, but Tucker's gone, probably downstairs. When I look at the laptop, Charlie still hasn't changed position.

My heart aches as I watch her. I don't know how she'll cope without Mark.

I've known Mark for years. He's the big brother I always wanted. I've never seen him behave this way. Him acting this horribly – with Charlie, of all people – has rendered me speechless.

Well, almost speechless. I gave him quite an earful last night.

And even though I'm appalled by his conduct, I know exactly what's driving it. Mark has loathed his body ever since the explosion.

Nine months ago, he was leading a mission in Afghanistan when an IED blew up, killing half the men on his team and leaving him critically injured. The explosion ripped his right lower leg off and caused flash burns to both thighs. He had massive internal hemorrhaging, a head injury, damaged lungs, numerous broken bones, and a body full of shrapnel. His doctors were worried about permanent brain damage, cautioning us that he might not remember anyone or anything. He spent over a week unconscious and on a ventilator. More than once, we nearly lost him.

Most of his physical injuries healed with time. The doctors stopped the bleeding and treated his sepsis. His burns healed with hyperbaric treatment and skin grafts. Broken bones eventually fused after multiple surgeries. Shrapnel punctures slowly closed, leaving his body peppered with scars. Thanks to his determination, intensive physical therapy with Tom, and strength training with Tucker, he's regained his strength.

But he's still an amputee.

That particular psychological wound continues to plague him. Mark can't accept his changed body. He views himself as half a man. I thought we'd finally gotten through to him, but when he and Charlie took their friendship to the next level, he reverted to calling himself a "useless cripple", a phrase he hadn't uttered aloud since he'd first come home from the hospital. Two months ago, Mark had osseointegration surgery, a goal he'd been working toward since his initial injury. A titanium rod was drilled into his remaining lower leg bone. The rod protrudes from his residual limb, allowing a prosthetic to mechanically attach with a simple Allen wrench. As his bone continues to fuse to the titanium rod, he can bear more weight on his prosthesis, and by Christmas, he'll only need his crutches when he removes the prosthesis to sleep. By then, as long as he's wearing pants, no one will have any idea he's an amputee, which is why he'd been looking forward to the surgery for months.

But Mark's mindset worsened dramatically following the surgery. He was quieter, more reserved. He began withdrawing from Charlie. She was concerned his depression was returning. Like many soldiers, Mark struggled with depression following his injury. With the help of medications, a psychiatrist who specialized in wounded warriors, and an amputee support group at the hospital, he'd improved. When he moved home with Charlie, the combination of meds and friends to keep him grounded seemed to return him to his previously healthy emotional baseline.

That healthy emotional state vanished following his long-anticipated osseointegration surgery.

I hear the front door close, followed by feet jogging up the stairs. Tucker opens the bedroom door, sweat trickling from his light brown hair, his gray tee shirt clinging to his muscled chest.

"Morning, Sweetness." He stops in front of me, pulling me close for a kiss, lightly running one hand over my healing abdominal incision. "How are you feeling?"

"I feel like you need a shower," I tease.

"I think we both do," he grins. "Wanna join me?"

"It's too soon for us to get pregnant yet." My response is automatic, and I cringe inwardly as hurt flickers in his dark blue eyes.

He masks it quickly. "Then I guess this will have to be just for fun." His lips graze mine lightly. I slide my arms around his neck and pull him in for a longer kiss, a wordless apology for my thoughtless remark.

When we pull apart, I peek up at him from under my lashes. "I like your kind of fun."

He links his fingers with mine and walks backwards, tugging me toward the bathroom with twinkling eyes. "C'mon, sexy lady. I'm gonna make sure you have fun again and again."

That's an offer I definitely can't refuse.

CHAPTER TWO

CHARLIE

A NOISE INTRUDES ON my pain. Rhythmic thumping, over and over. I close my eyes, wishing the noise would stop. Wishing everything would stop.

But the pounding continues. When I hear Lila's voice, I realize she's knocking on my door.

I don't want to see her. I don't want to see anyone.

All I want is for the pain to stop.

"Don't make me use my keys and the bolt cutter, Charlie." Her determined voice is muffled through the door.

For someone so delicate-looking, she's awfully pushy. But Lila is anything but delicate. She won't hesitate to unlock the door and cut my chain lock to check on me. She's done it before. I'm cold and stiff when I stand, and I don't know if the chill is coming from my house or my spirit.

"I'm coming," I mutter, and though my voice isn't loud, the knocking stops.

I unlock all three locks and open the door. Lila's arms are full of bags. I raise an eyebrow. "What's all that?"

"Carbs and booze. I have ice cream, cheesecake, cookies, chips, and wine. We'll work our way through them while we talk smack about his dumb ass."

I sag against the door. "I'm not sure I'm up to this, Lila," I say wearily.

I was awake all night for the... I think the fifth night in a row? The last time I slept was when I passed out drunk for three hours Monday night, and it's Saturday afternoon. But despite my exhaustion, I can't sleep. Every time I close my eyes, Mark's cold expression as he insists he doesn't love me scrolls like a movie in my mind, haunting me.

I just want the pain to stop.

Lila closes the front door as she pushes past me on her way to my kitchen. "I wasn't up to it when Tucker was being a dumbass a few years ago, and you wouldn't take no for an answer. Remember the three-day drinking binge where we talked shit about him until he came to his senses?"

"Not really," I admit.

Lila smiles. "We did get pretty drunk. But Tucker realized he was making a mistake, and so will Mark."

"I don't know, Lila. He's pretty stubborn."

Lila waves a hand dismissively. "All men are until reality bites them in the ass."

Lila spends the entire day with me on the couch, the TV on but neither of us watching it. She offers me food repeatedly, but I can't. She doesn't bombard me with questions or ask how I'm feeling. She's comfortable sitting silently with me in my anguish, and I'm grateful. She pulls me against her side, and by some miracle, I finally fall asleep. I wake up in tears once, and she rubs my back and lets me cry on her shoulder until exhaustion finally claims me for good.

She's still there when I awaken, shocked to find it's morning.

"You stayed with me all night?" I ask in surprise.

Lila grins. "I did."

"Awake?"

Lila nods. "I didn't want you to go back to the bench."

My eyes sting, and I struggle for words. "Lila," I begin, but she shakes her head.

"We'll help you through this, Charlie, whatever that means. And if it means standing guard so you can sleep, I'll do it."

"I haven't had night terrors in a while," I protest. The last time was right after Mark had his surgery.

"And I'd rather you kept feeling safe enough that you don't," she says gently. She yawns and stretches. "I'm going home to sleep for a few hours, but I'll be back tonight."

"What about Tucker?"

Lila shrugs. "He can curl up with Mark if he gets lonely."

TUCKER

Lila texts me Saturday evening around eight. "Charlie's finally dozed off. She's not in a good place. I'm staying tonight."

Mark and I are in the living room watching college football. "K. We'll order pizza here. Want me to send one your way?"

"No, but thx. I don't want to wake her. I have cookies and wine."

I open an app on my phone to order pizza, glancing over at Mark. He's been quiet all day, sitting on the couch with an untouched beer beside him, staring at a game he isn't paying any attention to. I'm hoping it's an indication he's miserable enough to reconsider his decision. "What kind of pizza do you want?"

"Whatever." He doesn't look at me.

"Sausage, olives, and mushrooms?"

He shrugs, and I place the order.

After our sexy shower-for-two this morning, Lila and I talked. We've decided our best approach is for me to remain as neutral as I can with Mark. If he feels like we're all against him, there's no way we'll be able to rationalize with him. Lila's going to focus on Charlie until Mark's dumb ass comes to his senses.

Charlie isn't weak – not even close – but she's emotionally weighed down by her demons. These last few years have been like watching her swim against a powerful current with a sack of massive stones strapped to her back. Every time her pain tried to pull her under, she'd grab a lifeline and drag herself forward. Unfortunately, her primary lifeline is Mark, and currently, he's the cause of her pain. Lila and I need to bolster her until she gets back on her feet, especially if Mark is slow to come around. One of his greatest strengths is his determination. It's what made him a great platoon leader. Unfortunately, under the wrong circumstances, it's simply pigheadedness.

When the pizza arrives, I bring it and a couple more beers back to the living room. I open the box between us. "Dig in."

He glances over. "Shouldn't we wait for Lila?"

I shake my head. "She's not coming home tonight."

He winces. "You still in trouble?"

I shake my head. "Lila and I are fine. Charlie's in a bad place, so she's staying with her."

Mark's jaw tightens, and he puts down the pizza slice he was holding.

Good. I hope he considers the bullshit he's needlessly putting her through.

Of course, I don't say that. I sit beside him, my eyes on the game as I munch my way through half the pizza before pushing the box toward him. "Come on. It's getting cold."

Instead, he reaches for his crutches and gets to his feet, his shoulders hunched. "I'm going on to bed." His voice is gruff, and he won't meet my eyes.

I affect an innocent expression. "But it's only nine o'clock."

He keeps moving toward the guest room. "G'night, brother."

"See you in the morning."

I'm silently pleased by the guilt he's radiating. Maybe it'll make him think about how his stupidity is hurting Charlie. The sooner he admits he's wrong, the sooner this nonsense ends. I reach for my phone and update Lila with a smile.

I'm still watching football when he returns just before midnight. I glance up. "I put the leftovers in the fridge if you're hungry."

He just shakes his head. "I need your help with something."

I sit up straight. I can make the five-minute drive to Charlie's house in three if he's ready to apologize. "Sure. What do you need?"

"I need you to help me find a handicapped-accessible apartment."

MARK

Tucker stares, speechless, when I tell him I need help finding an apartment to fit my disabilities. The silence goes on long enough to be awkward.

"Look, you and Lila are trying to get pregnant, and I don't want to be in the way."

"Why don't you give this a few weeks before you make any rash decisions?" His words are measured, but I can hear what he isn't saying.

He's asking me to change my mind about Charlie.

But I can't.

I can't be with Charlie. God knows I wish I could, but I can't. Charlie deserves someone better than me. Someone whole, someone as perfect as she is, who will love every part of her and treat her like a goddess.

There isn't anyone as perfect as she is, nor will there ever be anyone as good as she deserves. But there are definitely better candidates than me. Tom's face once again floats into my head, and my hands tighten into fists on the handgrips of my crutches.

I shake my head. "This is something I need to do, Tucker."

"Why?"

"I told you. You and Lila —"

"No. That's why you feel you shouldn't stay here. What I don't get is why you won't go back to Charlie. Hell, I'm still not sure why you left."

I exhale sharply. "She deserves better, Tucker."

Tucker narrows his eyes, glaring at me. "Why? Why does she deserve better than her best friend? Why does she deserve better than the man she loves, the man who loves her, too? Don't bother denying it, and don't give me any bullshit about having one leg, or I swear to God, I'll ram one of those crutches right up your ass."

I flatten my lips in annoyance. "Why ask if you don't want to hear my answer?"

"Because your answer is stupid," he snaps. "We've spent months telling you the same things over and over, but you don't listen to a goddamn word we say. Your only limits are the ones you place on yourself, Mark. Stop focusing on what you don't have and appreciate what you do."

My temper flares. "That's an impressive speech from someone with two working legs."

Tucker jumps to his feet and holds out his cell phone. "You're right. Let's call Joey. You can tell him he's only half a man, too, and that Natalie deserves better."

Joey is Tucker's younger brother, another vet disabled after a spinal injury left him paralyzed from the waist down. When Joey first came home, Tucker told him the loss of his legs didn't mean shit. He kept pushing Joey until he learned he could do pretty much anything he wants, including finding his beautiful red-haired sweetheart.

I clench my jaw. "That's different."

His dark blue eyes flash. "You're right. Joey was strong enough not to let his injury define him, and he was smart enough to work with his strengths instead of whining about his losses."

"I've never whined."

"Maybe not, but you're sure as fuck running like a scared rabbit."

I close my eyes briefly, anger coursing through me. When I open them, he's still glaring. I shrug. "Fine. I'm a coward. I'm running away. And you know what? Charlie deserves someone who wouldn't do that to her." Tucker grits his teeth, but I keep talking. "I've registered on a couple of apartment-finding websites, but there aren't any available that meet my needs right now. Give me ten minutes to pack and get an Uber and I'll be out of here. I'll send for the rest of my stuff when I find a place."

Tucker rubs his hand over his jaw, shaking his head before stopping with the heel of his hand pressed into one brow and exhaling sharply. "No," he finally says. "Stay here. I'll help you find a place." He won't meet my gaze, and he's balled both hands into fists.

He's furious, but I don't care. He doesn't understand. He can't.

I nod curtly. "I'll see you in the morning." I turn and amble back down the hall. As I close my door, I hear glass explode as Tucker hurls his beer bottle into the fireplace.

CHARLIE

Despite sleeping on Lila's shoulder for several hours, I'm in a numb fog. I stay busy with basic tasks, forcing my mind elsewhere every time it drifts toward Mark. I can't let myself think about him, or I'll shatter into a million pieces. I let the television run in the background, something I never do because I prefer the quiet. Today, the hum of voices keeps me from drowning in the overwhelming silence.

Tucker shows up at my door in the afternoon with a sheepish expression. "I feel bad letting Mark stay with us when he's being so stupid."

I shrug. "It's fine. He's safe, and he's with people who care about him."

I cared. But I ruined everything by telling him I loved him.

I lead Tucker into the kitchen to get him a drink. When I hand him a glass of tea, he thanks me, but doesn't meet my eyes. My spine stiffens at the discomfort suddenly radiating from him.

"Listen, I have a friend who installs alarm systems," he says, staring at the glass in his hand. "I looked through his stuff, and he's got a really nice setup he'll install for you at cost. He's a veteran, and he's dealt with PTSD. He can set up alarms for every door, every window, even perimeter alarms, and you can dial the sensitivity up or down, depending on your stress level. I asked him to come by. I'll stay with you so you're not alone with a stranger."

I study his expression. "What aren't you telling me?"

"Nothing," he replies quickly. "I just thought this way you'd feel safer being by yourself. I don't want you shooting holes in the walls again because you think you might have heard something. This way, if there's something actually there, you'll know."

He's stumbling over his words, his face flushed. My gaze sharpens. "Bullshit." Tucker looks away. "You didn't randomly decide I need a state-of-the-art alarm setup. What's going on?"

He's silent for so long I'm about to ask again when he finally speaks, looking miserable. "Mark's asked me to help him look for an apartment."

The words slash my battered heart, and it's all I can do not to drop to my knees. I grip the edge of the counter for dear life.

Please, just let this pain stop.

"Charlie, he'll come to his senses eventually. Besides, there aren't many apartments in this area that are disability-friendly, so it's not like he's going to find something quickly."

It doesn't matter. He's not coming back.

"He's had his surgery, Tucker. Pretty soon, he won't even need crutches. He won't need a handicapped-accessible apartment."

Tucker shakes his head vehemently. "Not true. He's not fully weight-bearing yet, and even when he is, he'll have to remove the prosthetic at night, so he'll need the bathroom to be disability-friendly. He's struggling with the shower in his bathroom at our place."

If Mark falls and ruins that abutment and his chance to walk normally, it will destroy him.

Be the bigger person.

I swallow hard and gesture down the hall. "When I'm at work, you guys can use the weight room for his training sessions. All that equipment was for him, anyway. He can shower here afterwards if it's easier for him. But – but not after I get off work. I can't –"

A huge lump forms in my throat.

I just want the pain to stop.

Tucker reaches for my hand. "Charlie, he'll figure things out. Don't give up."

Tears fill my eyes. "He's the one moving on, Tucker, not me."

"He's just being stupid," Tucker insists. "It will pass."

"It doesn't sound like it if he's looking for an apartment. Besides, he's convinced I need someone 'whole'. He keeps saying he can't be with me because I deserve better."

"Lila deserved someone a hell of a lot better than me, and look at us. Mark will sort himself out in time," he assures me.

True to his word, Tucker stays with me all afternoon while his friend Mike installs the security system. I've chosen one with sensors for every window and door, perimeter sensors, motion activated lights, and a large monitor so I can view the cameras.

I turn to Tucker. "Can you stay with Mike? I need to run to the hardware store."

"Do you want me to go pick something up?"

"No, I just need to look at a few things." I grab my purse and keys and pat my waist, reassuring myself my gun is in its holster, a move Tucker's eagle eyes don't miss.

I return less than an hour later with two heavy bags. "Do you feel particularly handy?" I ask Tucker. "I need extra door locks installed."

He takes out one of the packages and examines the lock. "I doubt you have the tools for this. You'll need a hole saw for this one."

I pause. "Give me a minute."

I call Tom, who answers immediately. "Hey. What's up?"

"Can you help me install some door locks?"

"Sure. Gimme a few minutes to get some things together."

"Thanks, Tom. And Tucker says we need a hole saw."

Tom arrives a short time later carrying a duffel bag filled with assorted power tools. Tom is the physical therapist at my and Lila's wellness clinic, more brother than friend. He's built like a cross between a bulldog and a bear, with a broad chest, muscled arms, and huge paw-like hands. He's a boxer, too, fast and strong, and his nose has the requisite crook to prove it. But his brown eyes are kind, and his boyish grin keeps him from looking menacing, at least to me.

"I really appreciate this," I tell him as I let him in. Tucker throws a hand up in his direction, studying one of the locks.

Tom glances at Mike, up on a ladder installing my security system. "Upgrading things?"

I hesitate. "With Mark gone, I need to feel safe."

Tom turns, his eyes widening. "Gone? He left?"

"He moved out Friday," I admit. My eyes fill with tears and I look away, trying not to cry but failing miserably.

Tucker and Tom surround me immediately, with Tom pulling me against his chest as Tucker rubs my back. "He'll come to his senses, Charlie. Just give him some time," Tom says as my tears soak his black tee shirt.

An image pops into my head, as though I'm looking down on myself from outside my body, watching myself being consoled by two large men. A year ago, I'd have had a panic attack and broken out in hives at the very thought, even though I trust both of these men with my life. Today, their touch brings comfort.

"I'll try to be patient with Mark," I say finally. "But in the meantime, I can't deal with night terrors and panic attacks, so I need this place to be a fortress."

"Whatever you need," Tom agrees. "Show me the locks."

I've bought additional deadbolts and two vertical slide bolts that extend into the floor for the front and kitchen doors. There's also a wedge lock for the glass door leading to the clinic.

Tom kneels at the front door, pulling tools from his bag. Tucker squats next to him, sorting parts. They work steadily as I watch from my perch on the stairs. In under an hour, they've mounted both new locks on my front door. It now boasts a chain lock, two deadbolts, a regular locking doorknob, and the bolt that slides into the floor. No one's coming through that door uninvited. Even with keys and a bolt cutter, the floor lock can only be raised from inside. Some of the tension drains from my body.

An hour later, they've put the new locks on the kitchen door. They're reading the installation instructions for the wedge lock when Mike comes to find me.

"I've got everything installed. If you'll come with me, we'll set up your codes and I'll teach you how to program everything."

I spend a long time with Mike, wanting to be sure I understand the system. He works patiently with me, testing multiple sensors and settings and running me through the paces until he's satisfied I know what to do.

"My suggestion is to tape a cheat sheet by the alarm pad until this becomes automatic. If this thing goes off in the middle of the night because of a deer, and you can't remember the code because you're half asleep, well," he grins, "your eardrums will be sorry." I thank him profusely, writing him a check more generous than our agreed-upon price.

When he leaves, I find Tucker and Tom. "I'm ordering pizzas. Who wants what?"

"Pepperoni and sausage," Tucker announces.

"Hawaiian," Tom says with a grin. He knows it's my favorite, and his sweet gesture coaxes a small smile from me.

After we eat, Tucker and Tom walk me through the house, making sure I'm comfortable with the new locks and the alarm system. I stop with both of them near the front door.

"I've got to pick up Maya," Tom says, "but you're always welcome to stay at my house. I've got a spare room."

I smile faintly. "Thanks, but I need to get used to being alone again."

He pulls me close for another hug. "He'll figure things out, Charlie. He's a smart guy."

After he leaves, I turn to Tucker and hand him the spare keys to the new deadbolts. "You and Lila will both need copies of these." I've already put color-coded rubber caps on both of them. "The green is for the front door, and the red is for the kitchen door."

I hesitate. "I'm usually out of the house by eight during the week, so come by after that for your training sessions with Mark. If it looks like you're going to be here during lunch or after work, text me so I can stay away until he's gone."

Tucker's discomfort is evident. "Charlie, I'm really sorry."

"Don't be. I'm the one that screwed everything up."

He shakes his head. "Telling Mark you love him isn't screwing up. Jesus, the first time I ever saw you guys together, I knew you two loved each other. He picked you out of a crowd from a hundred yards away and yelled your name. You spotted him like that –" he snaps his fingers "– and you two took off running for each other. When he picked you up and swung you around, he held onto you like he never wanted to let you go."

The memory makes me smile, but it fades as reality intrudes. Mark's not only let me go, he's shoved me away and bolted in the opposite direction.

"Charlie, Mark's been in love with you all along, and you've been in love with him, too. Lila and I have seen it for years. The only ones who didn't know were you and Mark. We knew sooner or later you'd both figure it out. It's just taking him longer because, as Lila's always reminding me, boys are stupid." He smiles gently. "Don't give up on him."

Tucker's words make me remember the pleading text Mark sent me in San Antonio after he'd raged at me during his darkest days.

Please don't give up on me.

My chest tightens. I didn't give up on Mark then. I won't give up on him now.

"I'm not giving up hope, Tucker, but he's made up his mind, and he's stubborn."

Tucker cups one side of my face in his big hand. "He'll come to his senses. I'm sure of it." He pockets the keys. "I'm going home for a while. Either Lila or I will be back later to stand guard."

I shake my head. "It's okay, Tuck. I kind of want to be alone. Tell Lila I'll see her at work in the morning, okay?"

"Are you sure? I don't mind staying up. Plus, it'll make Mark feel guilty," he adds.

"I don't want Mark to come back because he feels guilty. I want him to come back because he's in love with me."

He nods slowly. "Okay. But text Lila. She'll accuse me of misreading your cues."

When he's gone, I gather the empty pizza boxes and trash. I hesitate in front of the television before turning it off. The silence is deafening.

The painful chatter in my mind picks up, and I turn the television back on to muffle the sound.

CHAPTER THREE

CHARLIE

I ARRIVE AT WORK on Monday morning to find a fax from another rehab center in town. Mark has requested a transfer to their practice, so they've sent a medical records request. When I see Mark's signature on the release form, I inhale sharply.

Apparently, he's cutting off all possible interactions with me.

One more knife slashes through my heart.

I'm not even sure what's holding me together at this point. I keep finding myself with my arms wrapped around my body. I don't know if it's to keep myself from falling apart or to shield myself from any more pain. Maybe both.

But the hits keep coming. Lila looks at me later with stricken eyes and says she's agreed to do Mark's daily massages at her house.

"I'm sorry," she apologizes, but I numbly shake my head. Lila's caught in the middle just like Tucker, and Mark needs his massage therapy.

"It's fine," I assure her automatically.

She bites her lip. "Can you teach me the mirror trick? His phantom pains have started again."

He's hurting.

So am I. But his physical pain takes precedence over my emotional pain, so I bring Lila the angled mirror and talk her through the basics of mirror therapy.

My life becomes a blended haze of unending anguish, day after day, night after night, week after soul-crushing week.

Please. I just want the pain to stop.

Make it stop.

I survive weekdays by throwing myself into the clinic, going in early and working late, taking extra clients to keep busy. The busier I stay, the less time I have to think. I can't let myself think.

Nights and weekends are a different story. With nothing to distract me, all I do is ruminate.

I'm not struggling with night terrors, but I'm spiraling rapidly into a dark depression, one so dark that even I can recognize its lethality. Losing Mark is more than a simple breakup with a boyfriend. Mark was my best friend. He's been with me since I was nine, and his absence has struck every area of my life – my home, my work, and my small circle of friends.

I've lost everything because I told him I loved him.

The hardest part to accept is his utter abandonment. Since my early teens, I've known with certainty that he'd be there for me, no matter what. He always has been.

Until now.

Because I said those three little words.

I told Mark I loved him, and he walked away without a single backwards glance, surgically cutting me out of his life.

Maybe I misread him all along. Maybe I only saw what I wanted to see. Heard what I wanted to hear. Believed what I wanted to believe.

My depression spirals deeper and deeper, and everything requires more and more effort. Simple tasks like getting up, showering, going to work, running errands – all of these become weighty as basic survival demands all my energy. I have nothing left over for anything, least of all other people. I withdraw deeper into my shell, sidestepping my support system.

Linda, my psychiatrist, is in Japan again, and I'm secretly glad. I hadn't discussed the change in my and Mark's relationship from friends to lovers with her when it was happening, and I'm not up to baring my soul to her about its downfall now. Considering how often she and I have openly discussed my tortured past, that says a lot.

I avoid spending time with Lila and Tucker. Individually, they're fine, but it's excruciating to be around a happy couple. Steel knives shred my heart every morning when I wake up in my room upstairs and remember Mark is gone. Seeing Tucker and Lila together makes me wonder what he's doing. A small, irrational part of me feels like they chose his side by taking him in, leaving me as the lone outsider as our four became three. I know they're trying to make him realize he's in love with me. Still, letting him move in with them has essentially forced me out.

Stubbs has called repeatedly. I can't talk to him on the phone, because he'll hear my misery, and I can't discuss this with him. Skyping is definitely off the table. I settle on texting him early in the morning or late at night, keeping my answers vague. *I've been swamped at work... The weather's cooling off here. I bet it's still steamy in Texas, though... No, Mark hasn't talked to me about his self-image, but I'll see if he's let anything slip with Tucker... No, I haven't located a good amputee support group yet...*

I evade Tom's frequent invitations to do things with him and Maya, too. I still text Maya almost daily, because I can't bear the thought of hurting her. I can fake cheerfulness via texts, but I can't be openly dishonest with her, and my current state isn't something she should see.

I'm at my most-wrecked ever, and that includes the horrible time immediately following my trauma in Afghanistan.

Without my support system, the darkness threatens to drag me under.

I just want the pain to stop. Please. Just make it stop.

To dull my pain, I revert to my old standby: alcohol. After Afghanistan, I became a functional alcoholic. I went to massage school and worked as a bartender, kept up my responsibilities, and hid my drinking from everyone, including Lila, who was fighting her own emotional battles. It's easy for me to resume my learned behaviors, spending the long nights with a bottle.

But alcohol doesn't numb this pain.

It blunts the sharp edges, but it doesn't relieve it, something that doesn't seem possible given the volume I'm consuming. How could alcohol suppress the horrors of rape and torture, yet fail to ease the loss of the man I love?

Please. I just want this pain to stop.

Please.

The thought crosses my mind with increasing regularity that maybe I don't want to keep fighting this fight, that maybe I should just... succumb. Give in. Give up.

My pain would stop.

Each time, I dismiss the idea, but it lingers in the back of my mind as a viable option, waiting for a moment of weakness to try to persuade me again.

Between the drinking and the depression, there's a noticeable decline in my health. I'm constantly exhausted because I can't sleep. I rarely eat. My weight plummets like a 747 falling out of the sky. I'm gaunt and pale, with huge shadows beneath my haunted eyes.

The stress, alcohol, and gallons of coffee to prop me up and knock back my hangovers combine into an acidic blend that makes my stomach hurt constantly. I'm consuming antacids by the handful several times a day. But hey, at least I'm getting calcium. That's something, right?

The burning ache in my stomach gets so bad that I'm forced to stop drinking. Without the alcohol, I'm in more agony than ever, with no way to dull or forget it.

I can't do this anymore.

Please. I just want this pain to stop.

Make it stop. PLEASE.

LILA

It's been just over seven weeks.

Seven weeks since I lost my baby. Seven weeks since they had to remove my ruptured right fallopian tube.

I guess it wasn't technically a baby. Not yet, anyway. It was an embryo that implanted in the wrong place. But it would have been a baby. If our little embryo had traveled a few more inches before attaching, it would have grown into a baby inside my uterus.

But it didn't.

A few inches made the difference between life and death.

Dr. K – her name is actually Dr. Krakowskyvych, but she has her patients call her Dr. K – says I shouldn't give up hope. My hormone shots have been put on hold. At my two week post-op visit, we talked about in vitro fertilization. She said we could try after the first of the year. I mentioned it to Tucker, but when I reached the part about him providing fresh semen during the visit, he refused. He said there's no way he'd do *that* in an office full of people, especially not with them outside the door waiting for him to "perform". I tried to explain it wasn't like that, but it was a hard pass from him, with no further discussion.

Dr. K said to give my body two to three months to recover from the ectopic pregnancy before trying to conceive again. Without the shots to increase mature egg production, and with my body only able to transport eggs from one ovary, my chances of getting pregnant without medical assistance are slim. But I can't stop myself from trying. I'm still tracking my ovulation and pouncing on Tucker repeatedly on those days.

He knows why I'm relentless, ambushing him again and again over that four or five day period when my chances of conception are higher than other days of the month. His expression changes, and I can almost hear his thoughts. That I'm only interested because I want a baby. That it's only about his sperm and my egg, and not about us.

It's not true, but admittedly, I'm more prone to initiate marathon sexcapades when I'm most likely to get pregnant.

Sex with Tucker is good. *Really* good. After what happened, I wasn't sure I'd ever be able to say that. When he first came home, I had a lot of difficulty being intimate. Kissing was always enjoyable and didn't stress me, because it wasn't tainted. My rapists didn't waste time kissing – they had much darker things in mind. That meant I could kiss Tucker without fear, at least until things started to progress. That's when it would get dicey. One minute I'd be fine and engaged, and the next, I'd fall apart or detach and shut down.

I had a lot of triggers. One of the worst was having Tucker – or anyone, really – behind me. One day I was at the sink rinsing dishes. Tucker came up behind me and slipped his arms around my waist. I panicked, dropped a glass, and sliced my hand open in my scramble to escape, brandishing a large shard of glass at him while he stared in shock.

Seven stitches later, I accepted Linda's recommendation to meet with Willow.

Dr. Willow Entwein is an intimacy specialist. She encourages intentional vulnerability as a path to deepening relationships. Tucker and I already had a deep emotional relationship. We were engaged to be married before I was taken, and we already had a trust bond. My sessions – *our* sessions, because we attended together – revolved around determining my triggers and finding ways to delay my automatic fight-or-flight response long enough to allow me to respond rationally. The first thing we addressed was Tucker approaching me from behind.

I knew exactly why it triggered me. I killed the first man who came to my cell to rape me. As a result, they chained me facedown, spreadeagle over a table. Over the next eleven days, I was raped more times than I could count, always from behind. The day I divulged that to both Willow and Tucker was the first time I ever saw Tucker cry.

That was the first and most difficult trigger we had to work through, but I refused to marry Tucker until I was certain we could have sex without me freaking out. We worked through my triggers one at a time. He was patient and gentle and loving in a way I can't imagine anyone else would have been. It took the better part of a year for us to reach the point where sex was something I looked forward to and wanted again, but we got there.

Sex with Tucker is still something I want and enjoy. I just wish it wasn't all tangled up in my desperate desire for a child, because my compulsion to conceive muddies the waters of our sex life, and I hate it.

I'm ovulating now, and my urge to drag Tucker off to the bedroom again is palpable. But so is my anger, and it isn't directed toward Tucker – it's toward Mark.

Seeing Mark at the dinner table reminds me of the hell Tucker and I fought through to achieve intimacy after my trauma. Charlie fought through many of those same challenges to reach that point with Mark. It was painful, terrifying, and indescribably difficult.

And Mark just fucking threw it away, like her struggles meant nothing. The only thing that mattered to him was his goddamned amputation.

The more I think about the hell Charlie went through to be sexually vulnerable with Mark, the more my temper builds, like a seething volcano, ready to blow at the slightest infraction from him.

Like, say... breathing.

TUCKER

Lila and I watch helplessly as Charlie slips further and further down.

It's all so pointless. Mark is miserable without her, but he stubbornly refuses to change his mind. Lila and I have talked to him gently, coaxingly, and reasonably until we're blue in the face, and we've made no progress. When their separation hits the six-week mark, Lila explodes on him.

"I can't believe you're still being such a stupid jackass," she snaps unexpectedly at Mark one evening.

I look up from my plate. The three of us are eating dinner, one of many silent dinners we've had lately.

"You're really going to ruin both of your lives over your bullshit, aren't you?" she demands.

Mark lays down his fork. "I'm not ruining her life. I let her go to find someone as good as she deserves."

"So you think she deserves to be treated well?"

"Of course I do."

"Then why did you fucking abandon her?"

"I didn't abandon her."

"Really?" Lila explodes, slamming both hands on the tabletop. Her violet eyes flash with fury, and Mark's eyes widen. I wisely keep my mouth shut.

"You tell Charlie that a romantic partnership could never destroy your friendship because your relationship is too strong for that. When she tells you she loves you, which you've said to each other for as long as I've known the both of you, you backpedal away from her like she has some contagious disease. Then you have the bright idea to tell her you should start seeing other people and imply you're already seeing someone just to hurt her, so she'll 'know you're serious'." Her small fingers make air quotes as she glares at him. "Then you get your panties in a pucker when she tries to make you jealous enough to realize you're in love with her. You wait till she's at work to sneak away in secret, like a fucking coward, like she's a horrible drunken hookup that you never want to see again." Mark pales at her harsh words. "You've promised Charlie for her entire life that no matter what, you'd always be there, but because you got scared of your feelings for her, you walked out the goddamned door and never looked back at the woman who dropped *everything* for you and upended her world to help you, a woman who would take a bullet for you in a heartbeat, who loves you more than anything else in this world. You never even fucking hesitated to crush her heart beneath your shiny new prosthetic heel." He flinches, though I'm not sure if it's due to her words or her snarling reminder of his prosthesis. "Stop me at any point if I'm wrong," she challenges, pinning him with her ferocious gaze. She shakes her head when he doesn't speak. "Mark, you were one of my heroes, and I love you, but you're an asshole."

I reach for her hand, my voice soft. "C'mon, Lila."

She shoves her chair back from the table. "I'm going for a run." She slams the door on her way out for good measure.

I sit silently with Mark after she storms out of the house. Lila was right about every single thing. Brutal – *Jesus*, she was brutal – but right.

Mark never says a word. Not one word. Not, "What the hell?" or "She's got it all wrong," or "She's right, I fucked up."

After twenty minutes without making a sound or taking another bite of food, Mark gets up. "I'll see you in the morning, brother," he says, making his way down the hall and quietly closing his door.

I sit alone at the empty table, utterly disheartened.

Maybe Mark really is going to throw everything away because of his bullshit.

CHARLIE

Despite giving up alcohol, my stomach hurts all the time. It burns when my stomach's empty, but my appetite has completely disappeared. I rarely eat, and if I do, I vomit almost immediately. Lila stops by one Saturday with chicken salad croissants, but I can't eat them.

"Charlie, I can count your ribs through your shirt," Lila says. "You have to eat."

"I can't. My stomach constantly hurts, and I'm always bloated, and eating makes it hurt even worse."

"Then make a doctor's appointment. It's probably an ulcer. Are you throwing up?"

"When I try to eat," I admit.

"If you don't, you're going to start passing out again." Lila holds my gaze. I can tell she's remembering how I was after Walter Reed, when my depression had similar effects on my appetite and weight. "Make the appointment."

I know she won't let up, so I call. Dr. Oaks' first available appointment is in two weeks.

I maintain a steady routine in the meantime. Go to work early. Stay late. Drink a lot of coffee and eat a lot of antacids. Force myself to eat a few bites of food every day. Have work-related chats with Tara, Tom, and Lila so they don't realize how dark things really are. Send a quick text or funny meme to Stubbs and Maya so they don't worry. Monitor my video feed from the security cameras most of the night. Rage at the walls occasionally. Doze off briefly, only to wake up sobbing when I remember Mark left me because he doesn't love me.

Rinse and repeat.

By the time the Friday morning of my appointment rolls around, I'm so nauseous I can't even get out of bed. I text Lila to tell her I can't make it in to work. She quickly answers that she and Tara will cover my clients.

I lay in bed a few minutes longer before bolting to the bathroom and vomiting repeatedly. I'm still in there when I hear Mark and Tucker's voices downstairs.

Mark's here!

My heart leaps with hope before it hits me. *They're here for Mark's training session. He's not here for me.*

Tears fill my eyes and I lower my head, burying my face in my folded arms. Mark won't ever be here for me again.

TUCKER

I've just pulled into Charlie's driveway with Mark when my phone rings. "I need you to check on Charlie," Lila says. "You have to physically lay eyes on her."

"What's up?"

"She's throwing up again. She must be really bad today because she said she won't be in."

"I'll check on her," I promise.

"She has a doctor's appointment later. If she's too sick to drive, let me know and I'll figure something out."

"Will do."

Mark and I have just walked in when I hear the unmistakable sound of retching upstairs. I glance sideways. "I'll be back in a minute." I grab a bottle of water from the mini fridge in the weight room and jog up the stairs.

I knock quietly on her bathroom door. "Charlie, it's me. Are you alright?"

Her voice is barely more than a croak. "I'm okay."

I hesitate. "I'm under orders from Lila to see for myself. Can I come in?"

I'm horrified when Charlie opens the door for me, reaching for the door-knob from her spot on the floor. She's kneeling beside the toilet, her head resting on its closed lid. Although we've talked by phone and text, I haven't actually seen her in several weeks, and I'm stunned when I see her back. Her spine protrudes in sharp knobs where she's lost so much weight. I squat beside her. Her face is ghostly white and spattered with blood.

"Jesus, Charlie, you're throwing up blood?"

I grab a washcloth and dampen it, lifting her head and wiping her face like I would a small child's. She doesn't reach for the cloth to do it herself; she sits there numbly, and that terrifies me. Charlie's always been fiercely independent. For her to allow me to see her this way and accept my help is completely out of character.

That son of a bitch has destroyed her.

"C'mon. I'm taking you to the hospital."

She shakes her head. "It's just an ulcer. I have a doctor's appointment in a couple of hours."

"Fine. I'll drive you."

"I can manage," she argues weakly.

"I wasn't asking your permission, Charlie. What time is your appointment?"

She surrenders far too easily. "Eleven."

"I'll finish up with Mark and cancel my morning clients."

"Tucker, you really don't need to." Her voice is barely a whisper.

I ignore her feeble dissent. She looks terrible. She's gaunt, and her color is awful. And her eyes... Her normally vibrant green eyes are dull, and they have that same flat, dead look they did the night we rescued her.

But this time, all this shit is on Mark. She's not haunted by assholes who hated her. No, this pain is from someone who loved her. My temper rises.

I stand and lift her into my arms, and when she doesn't flinch or protest, it scares me even more. Her ribs and hipbones dig into my arms. I carry her to the bed and tuck her in. "Try to sleep. I'll call at ten to make sure you're awake."

"You're as bossy as Lila," she mutters.

I brush her hair off her face and force a teasing tone. "Yeah, but her washboard abs aren't as hot as my six-pack." I'm rewarded with a ghost of a smile.

This bullshit with Mark has gone too far.

As I'm coming down the stairs, Mark smacks the foyer table with the palm of his hand. He looks pissed. I ignore it. I'm barely holding my temper with him as it is.

"I need to rearrange my morning to take Charlie to the doctor. She's not feeling well."

Mark snorts. "I'll bet not."

His aggressive tone startles me, and my temper surges. "What's that supposed to mean?"

"She's hung over. She's drinking herself into oblivion. It's fucking pathetic."

He did *not* just say that.

He did *not* just call her pathetic after what he's done, turning her into little more than a shell.

I glare at him. "Charlie quit drinking weeks ago, asshole. She's vomiting blood. But you wouldn't know, since you fucking bailed on her."

Mark freezes. "Vomiting blood? How much?"

My temper boils over. "Get your stuff and let's go. Charlie's dealing with enough. She doesn't need to overhear your bullshit." I fish out my keys and move toward the front door.

"Is she alright?"

I spin around. "She doesn't matter to you anymore, remember? Now get your shit."

Mark stands there silently, then retrieves his backpack and makes his way to my truck.

"Is she alright?" he asks again quietly.

I'm silent until I've pulled out onto the road. "After the way you fucking deserted her, you don't get to ask. I've tried to stay neutral because I love you both, but you've treated her like shit you scraped off the bottom of your shoe.

Lila and I will take care of her, but I won't discuss her with you. If you want to know how she is, grow some balls and ask her yourself."

"She's got Tom to help her," Mark says dismissively.

That's when I explode. "Jesus, you really are a fucking dumbass! Charlie and Tom wanted to make you jealous. They were hoping you'd figure out how you really felt about her. Instead, you dropped her like a used tissue the second you got tired of fucking her. She's not with Tom. She was never with Tom. For some dumbass reason, she loves you, even though you've been a complete asshole." I shake my head, livid. "I mean it, Mark. No more questions about Charlie."

Both of us are silent for the rest of the drive. I stop the truck in front of my house to let him out. He's barely closed my truck door before I peel off down the street.

MARK

That's what he thinks?

That I left because I got tired of fucking her?

Bile rises in my throat.

I'd waited downstairs after Tucker heard Charlie vomiting up everything she's eaten for the last month. That's when it occurred to me. I'd have bet my last dollar she'd been drinking. When Charlie's really upset, she drinks to numb the pain.

I'd assumed that was the reason she was puking her guts out. I'd stormed through her kitchen and out into the garage to check her recycling bin. Sure enough, there were a ridiculous number of empty liquor bottles in the bin.

And it pissed me off.

Two months. I left her two months ago.

Jesus. Deal with it already.

I had a brief pang of guilt, knowing I'm the cause of her misery, but I shoved it back down and let my anger take control. Anger is easier to handle than guilt.

Or pain.

Rage fired through me. It's time Charlie got her shit together. Wallowing in self-pity like that is just pathetic. People break up. Relationships end. That doesn't give you a free pass to drink until you pass out and puke your guts out every morning, too fucking hung over to function.

My temper flared as soon as Tucker came downstairs to tell me we were rescheduling the session. I mouthed off, and his gaze hardened. When he told me she was vomiting blood, time stopped.

She's not hung over?

She's really sick?

Is she hurting? Is she okay?

My stomach had lurched when I asked him how much blood, unable to contain the panic in my voice. He didn't answer directly, and I'd asked if she was okay.

That's when he spun toward me, his expression icy. "She doesn't matter to you anymore, remember?"

That's what he believes. That she doesn't matter to me.

That's what they all believe.

Because it's how I'm behaving.

I'd asked him again in the truck, and he'd blown up. His words gutted me.

You deserted her.

You treated her like shit you scraped off the bottom of your shoe.

His final blow decimated me, because Tucker's always straight with me. He doesn't mince words or pussy-foot around. He's direct and honest.

You dropped her like a used tissue the second you got tired of fucking her.

Is that what they really think?

Is that what *Charlie* really thinks?

That I took advantage of a woman who'd been brutalized? That I got her to trust me enough so she'd offer me her body? That I used her for sex and threw her aside when I'd had my fill?

Her words from our final night together echo loudly in my head. She'd said it had only been about sex all along for me. I'd felt sick, hoping she didn't really believe that. I'd told her not to cheapen what we had. She'd asked why I called her mine if I didn't love her. I lied and said I'd wanted her to feel special. The pain in her eyes when she spoke ripped me in two.

I really was nothing more than another piece of ass to you. I hope I was at least memorable.

Fuck.

That's *exactly* what Charlie thinks. That I used her for sex and tossed her aside because I got tired of her.

I could never, *ever* have enough of Charlie, not in a thousand lifetimes.

Why can't anyone else see the truth? That Charlie deserves someone worthy, someone better?

Someone whole?

CHAPTER FOUR

CHARLIE

AFTER TUCKER LEAVES, I try to sleep but can't, tossing and turning under my white comforter. I pull the pillow over my head to block out the sun filtering through the sheers, but it doesn't help. Finally, I get up and shower, studying myself in the mirror afterwards, something I usually avoid.

I look horrible, and it has nothing to do with my scars.

My color is somewhere between pasty and grey. My face is hollow and sunken, and huge purple shadows bruise the area under my dull green eyes. Even my light brown hair is limp and lifeless. My weight has plunged much too low, and my ribs, collarbones, and hips jut out in sharp points. My bloated midsection protrudes in sharp contrast to my bony form. It's the same look I've seen in tragic photos of starving children in third world countries.

I suddenly see myself through Tucker or Lila's eyes.

I look like I'm dying.

The epiphany hits me like a bullet train.

No. I *am* dying.

I'm killing myself. Not actively, but passively.

Loving a man who doesn't love me back is literally killing me.

Hot tears fall, blazing trails down my cheeks. I can't keep doing this. Either I have to let Mark go and move on, or I need to surrender to the pain. And despite my emotional exhaustion from dragging myself through each day, I'm too damn stubborn to quit.

It takes all the strength I can muster to comb through my damp hair and put on clean clothes. I go downstairs and curl up on the couch to wait for Tucker.

While I wait, I place a long overdue call for an appointment with Linda, my psychiatrist.

The early December air is blustery and cold when Tucker arrives, and despite my coat, I'm shivering, wishing I'd dried my hair. He helps me into his big truck and turns the heater on high. "Here," he says, passing me a cup. "I know coffee is bad for ulcers, so I brought you hot chocolate. Thought it might warm you up."

"Thanks." Tears sting my eyes at his kindness. "You really don't have to do this, you know. You've been a huge help through everything."

He nods dismissively. "I know. You're more than capable. You are woman, hear you roar, yada yada yada. But you're having a rough time, and you're family."

He's never said that before, though I've thought of him like a brother for years. "Thanks, Tucker," I murmur. "That means a lot."

Tucker offers to go back to the exam room with me, but I decline, leaving him in the waiting room. Dr. Oaks is a kind woman in her late fifties or early sixties, with fluffy gray curls and a calm bedside manner. She's been my doctor since I moved to Cedar Ridge. I describe my symptoms, and she has me lie back on the table while she examines me, studiously checking my throat and ears, listening to my heart and lungs, and carefully pressing all over my abdomen while asking about the pain in my stomach and how often I'm vomiting blood.

"Let's start with some blood and urine tests," she says. "We'll run them while you wait. That will give me a clearer idea on how to proceed."

I provide the required samples and wait in the exam room in my skimpy gown, my hardback chair pulled over to rest my head on the padded exam table. It's a half hour or so later when Dr. Oaks returns.

"I'm very concerned about you, Charlie." She takes a seat across from me and studies my face. "You look exhausted. How much sleep are you getting?"

"Not much," I admit. "Maybe an hour or two a night."

Her voice is gentle. "You know that's not nearly enough. Are you still seeing someone for your night terrors?"

"I have an appointment, but it isn't from nightmares right now. I, well –" I struggle to find the words. "A long-term relationship ended recently and I'm having trouble coping."

Dr. Oaks nods. "Are you drinking?" She knows I struggled with alcohol after my trauma.

"I was for a few weeks," I confess, "but it made my stomach hurt worse, so I stopped. It didn't help the abdominal pain when I quit, though, and my bloating and nausea got worse."

"You're barely over ninety pounds, Charlie. You've lost far too much weight." She flips back through my record. "Twenty-five pounds. Are you eating?"

I shake my head. "Just bites, mostly. I'm constantly nauseous, and when I eat, it makes my stomach hurt worse or I throw up, or both."

"You're extremely malnourished." She passes me a printout of my labs. I scan the sheet as she continues. "Your electrolytes are dangerously unbalanced and your protein levels are critically low. We've got to address that immediately, Charlie, or I'll have to hospitalize you. You're a medic. You know electrolyte issues can cause serious cardiac and neurological problems. I'm starting you on multiple medications for your stomach. It's critical that we get you eating right away. I'm relatively certain you have a stress-induced stomach ulcer, so I'm going to start you on medication to help with that, and I'm adding something for nausea so you can keep food down. I'm also prescribing supplements and something mild to help you sleep. But you've got to do your part and take the medications and eat. Can you do that?"

I nod. "I can't keep going like this."

"There's something else we need to discuss," she says. "I ordered additional labs to be sure after I palpated your abdomen." She pauses before continuing. "Charlie, you're pregnant."

I hear her words, but they don't compute.

The room spins, and all I see are black spots. For a moment, I can't breathe. When my vision finally clears, I stare at Dr. Oaks in stunned silence. "I can't be," I whisper. "It isn't possible."

She lays a soft hand on my thin one. "I know this is difficult to hear in light of your relationship ending, but it's true. Based on your hormone levels and the size and feel of your uterus, I'd estimate you're about sixteen weeks pregnant."

"No, you don't understand," I say in disbelief. "The men who took me captive, they mutilated my vagina and cervix with a rusty knife and metal pipes and broken glass. I nearly died from the infection. The gynecologist at Walter Reed said my cervix was too scarred and damaged for me to ever get pregnant. They said it was impossible." My pulse flutters in my throat like a hummingbird's wings. "That's the word she used – impossible."

Dr. Oaks smiles and cups her other hand beneath mine, gently sandwiching it between both of hers. "Then perhaps this baby is your miracle," she says quietly. "I'd like to do a pelvic exam and an ultrasound, if you'll consent."

I nod woodenly, too shocked to object.

Tucker is waiting for me in the lobby half an hour later. "What did you find out?" he asks on the way to the truck.

I laugh numbly. "More than I expected."

"Do you have an ulcer?"

"Most likely. She's prescribing medications. Can we stop by the pharmacy?"

"Sure. We can drop off your prescriptions and grab lunch. What are you in the mood for?"

"Something that won't make me sick."

He thinks for a second. "There's a place around the corner from the pharmacy that has really good potato soup. How about that?" Suddenly starving, I nod my agreement.

We drive in silence to the pharmacy. "I can run those in for you," he offers.

I'm not ready to explain why I need prenatal vitamins yet, so I shake my head. "I've got it. Be right back."

While we wait for the pharmacy to get the medications ready, we hurry around the corner to the restaurant. An icy breeze blows, but Tucker automatically pulls me against his side, wrapping his jacket around me and sheltering me from the wind. My chest tightens as I remember his earlier words. *You're family.*

I'm not alone.

I've been feeling alone, but I'm not, not really.

And in a few more months, I definitely won't be.

The restaurant is warm and cozy, the windows steamy. I order a cup of potato soup and a chicken salad sandwich, and Tucker gets the same. I'm lost in thought.

Pregnant.

"Spit it out," Tucker says, a worried expression furrowing his brow. "What else did she say?"

"What?"

"You wouldn't be this distracted if it were just a damn ulcer, Charlie. You knew you had one before you ever went to see her. What else did she say?"

I push my plate back. "She said a lot of things. She said I'm not sleeping enough. She said I've lost twenty-five pounds. She said I'm malnourished and that she'll have to hospitalize me if I don't start eating."

Tucker scrutinizes me. "What else?"

I swallow hard. "She said I'm sixteen weeks pregnant, and did an ultrasound, and I'm having twins."

Tucker stares at me in stunned silence before jumping to his feet and grabbing me up in a huge bear hug, picking me up high enough that my feet dangle above the floor. He squeezes me tightly before setting me down and gripping my shoulders. "But I thought you couldn't –"

I laugh sadly. "So did I. That's what they told me at Walter Reed. Dr. Oaks called them my miracle babies."

Tucker helps me back into my seat and sits across from me. "They *are* miracles," he says gently. "You thought those bastards stole your chance to be a mother. They didn't win, Charlie." He grabs my hands and squeezes them. "They didn't win."

Tears spill down my face. "Tucker, I don't know how I'm going to do this. Look at me! I'm barely holding myself together. How am I going to manage colic and midnight feedings and earaches and doctor's appointments and diaper changes for two babies all alone?"

He squeezes my hands again. "You're not alone, Charlie," he says firmly.

I shake my head. "This isn't like Lila spending the night or you helping me get a security system. This is a twenty-four seven, lifelong commitment."

He leans forward, driving his index finger into the tabletop for emphasis. "I swear to you, if Lila and I have to move in and help you raise our nieces or nephews, we'll do it. Besides, this might be exactly what Mark needs to straighten his ass out."

I turn ferocious in an instant. "No. You cannot tell him. Swear to me, Tucker."

"But they're his babies," he says, startled at my sharp response. "You have to tell him."

"I'll tell him when I'm ready. But pregnant or not, there's no way I'm letting his sorry ass come strolling back in because of some crisis of conscience or misplaced sense of duty. I refuse to be with a man who doesn't love me wholeheartedly." My fierce tone surprises me even as it rings with truth.

A slow smile spreads across his rugged face as he leans back in his seat. "There she is." He tips his head at me, admiration in his voice. His deep blue eyes twinkle.

I stare at him. "Who?"

"The old Charlie. The fearless fighter. The one who doesn't take shit from anybody. The badass who fights for what she deserves." He takes a sip of his tea. "I'm glad to see her making her appearance again. It's been too damn long."

"Swear to me you won't tell him, Tucker," I insist.

"I won't tell him. It's not my news to tell. But please tell Lila. I'm already on thin ice for bringing Mark to our house. I've had to do the dishes every night since he moved in. If you make me keep this secret and she finds out I knew, she'll throw me out."

I smile. "I have a bedroom downstairs that's not being used. You can crash there." His eyes widen, and I laugh. "I'll tell her," I promise. "But not today. I need to sit with this for a day or two. It's a lot to absorb."

He nods slowly. "Alright. What do you need? Do you even have food in the house?"

"Not really," I confess. "I haven't been eating, so there wasn't any point in shopping."

"Fine. We're buying groceries after we pick up your medication. What else?"

"That's it, I think. She's giving me stuff for the ulcer and nausea, something to help me sleep, and vitamins. I need to eat more, gain weight, rest, and take care of myself. And I have to start seeing a high-risk obstetrician. I'll have to have a cesarean when it's time to have them."

He hesitates, holding his breath. "So you're keeping them?"

There was never a question, especially once she called them my miracle babies.

I nod. "She's right, Tucker, they are miracles," I say slowly. I take a deep breath. "And even if Mark never comes around, I'll always have proof that once upon a time, he loved me."

"He does love you, Charlie. He's just hung up on his idiotic conviction that he can't be the man you deserve because of his injuries. He'll figure it out sooner or later."

"Maybe. Maybe not. But waiting for him to love me back is literally killing me. Me sitting around drinking or crying or raging at the walls doesn't affect Mark in the least. The only one it affects is me. I'm the one not sleeping and throwing up blood and so malnourished my doctor is threatening to hospitalize me. Mark is comfortable with how things are. I'm the one who's miserable. I can't keep doing this. I have to take care of myself and these babies. It's time to move forward. I can't spend the rest of my life waiting for him to come around."

Tucker studies my face silently before nodding.

We finish lunch and pick up the medications before Tucker drags me grocery shopping. He fills a cart with everything imaginable, waving me away when I grumble.

"You're channeling Lila again," I mutter.

He laughs. "I've been told worse things." He tosses another bag of baby spinach in my cart.

He drives me home and insists on carrying my groceries in. "Tucker, I'm not an invalid," I protest. "Hell, I'm barely pregnant."

"I picked you up off the floor this morning, so that qualifies you as an invalid. And there's no such thing as barely pregnant. There's pregnant or not pregnant, and you're pregnant. Besides, these puny little girl arms –" he reaches over and squeezes my too-thin bicep through my jacket, "– are too skinny and bony. My little nieces or nephews need you to rest up and grow them nice and big. So shut up and get your malnourished ass out of my way," he says affectionately, kissing my forehead. He unpacks the bags, but when I protest again, he lets me put the food away.

After he leaves, I think about how he and Lila have been there for me. Tom and Maya, too. We're a family in our own right.

I thought I'd lost everything when Mark left.
The truth is, I have far more than I realized, even without him.

TUCKER

Charlie's four months pregnant.

With twins.

Holy shit. And only five months till their arrival. Maybe less. Don't twins usually come early?

I consider Charlie's words about Mark all evening, about how their breakup hasn't really affected him.

She's right. His life hasn't really been disrupted. He has a place to live. We take him to appointments, cook his meals, keep him company, and help with his massages and exercises. Lila and I have become his substitute for Charlie in every way, with one obvious exception.

Anger races through me again. How could he turn his back on her like she never existed? The two of them were as close as Lila and I are, yet he walked away without ever looking back.

Guilt consumes me when I realize the role we've played in the situation. We've ensured Mark is fine while inadvertently leaving Charlie to struggle along on her own. We're enabling his bad behavior. Now her already-difficult life has become infinitely more challenging.

Mark's life is perfectly comfortable.

It's time to change that.

I stay up late, working out a plan to make Mark come to his senses. I wake up to a notification on my phone that couldn't have come at a better time, and Saturday morning, I'm all smiles.

Last night, I located a handicapped-accessible van that will meet Mark's needs. It only has twelve thousand miles, and it's in great shape. There's also a handicapped-accessible apartment that just came available, and as soon as I got the notification, I booked an appointment to go see it. I also stopped at a bookstore yesterday and snagged two copies of the famous "what to expect" book for pregnant women. One is in my truck to give to Charlie; I left the other on the coffee table. I saw Mark glance at it and raise an eyebrow. Lila raised one, too, but I'd whispered it was part of my plan to make Mark come to his senses, and she'd been all for that.

I enact my plan during breakfast. "Great news, Mark. A handicapped-accessible apartment just came available, and I made an appointment for us to look at it this morning. They're hard to find, so it won't last long, you know?"

He looks up in surprise. "Really?"

I nod. "And I saw a great deal on a van that we should check out, too. It has everything you need, and it's low miles with only one owner."

Mark grins. "If I didn't know better, I'd swear you were trying to get rid of me."

I feign surprise. "You said you wanted help looking for an apartment, and this is the first disability-friendly one I've seen." I pull out my phone. "I'll call and cancel the appointment."

"No, don't do that," he says hastily. "I'm just messing with you. I definitely need to get my independence back."

"Great." I clap my hands together. "Our appointment to see the apartment is in an hour, and then we can drive up and look at the van."

The apartment isn't much to look at, which thrills me. It's ground-level, with wide doorways to accommodate wheelchairs, and the bathroom has rails and a fold-down shower bench. It's furnished, which is good since Mark has no furniture, but everything is outdated and reeks of cigarettes. The living room has a hideous plaid ruffled sofa and loveseat and a small television on a battered stand. The kitchen is sparsely stocked with cheap cookware and a limited selection of plates, glasses, and bowls. The bedroom holds a bed, a bedside table, and a low dresser with another small television, and the closet is missing its bi-fold doors. It has a washer and dryer, but no dishwasher, and the heater rattles noisily when I flip the switch to test it before shutting it off.

It's small, dingy, and nicotine-stained. I'm really going to enjoy making Mark uncomfortable.

Mark nods approvingly as he looks around. "It'll do."

"You sure? Kinda looks like it's seen better days," I say, sounding doubtful.

Mark shrugs. "I've been in worse places. You have, too."

"Okay. Let's go talk to the landlord."

After Mark hands the landlord a check and signs a six-month lease, we ride north to take a look at the van. It belongs to an older gentleman who's also a right lower leg amputee, so the pedals have been modified to be controlled with his left leg. He rides with Mark to test drive it, and while it will take a bit of getting used to, Mark's confident he can master it. He writes the man a check and follows me home in his new-to-him black van, ready to load it up and move into his apartment the following day.

Lila's pissed off, whisper-shouting at me upstairs. "Seriously? What happened to making him uncomfortable? You're moving him into a new apartment with his own van."

"Calm down. First of all, it's a crappy apartment. Keeping him trapped here while hoping he'll come to his senses isn't working. Charlie said yesterday that he's not been uncomfortable yet, and she's right. He went from her taking care of him to us taking care of him. He never missed a beat."

"That's what friends do," she argues.

"I agree, but we freed him from facing any consequences for his choices. If he's never forced to deal with being alone, he won't realize what he's giving up."

She looks at me doubtfully. "I'm starting to wonder if he ever will."

I think about Charlie's secret. "He will, Lila. Trust me."

Lila spends the evening shopping for Mark's apartment, purchasing towels, laundry detergent, and kitchen staples. We fill his van with the non-perishables. She leaves the cold items bagged in the refrigerator to send with him in the morning.

"You know I'm only a couple of miles away, right?" Mark teases. "There are stores nearby."

"What I'm hearing you say is, 'Thank you for taking care of me, Lila, even though I'm a monumental jackass sometimes'," she says loftily.

He grins. "Thank you for taking care of me, Lila."

She raises an eyebrow. "You forgot the last part."

"No, I didn't." He grins again, and she swats him with a kitchen towel.

Sunday afternoon, Lila and I follow Mark to his new apartment and help him get settled. Lila frowns as she unpacks boxes, but holds her tongue until we're back in my truck.

She glares as I crank the ignition. "It's a dive, Tucker."

I shrug. "We've lived worse places."

"This isn't the military. He has options," she snaps.

"He only signed a six-month lease," I point out as I pull back onto the highway. "Besides, this is to make him realize what he's giving up."

"You keep saying that, but it doesn't make any more sense now than it did yesterday."

"Being alone might make him realize how much Charlie means to him."

I pull off the road a short time later at a roadside Christmas tree lot. I pick two beautiful eight-footers and load them in the truck. "Charlie needs a tree, too," I explain.

We stop for lights and ornaments, and Lila oohs and aahs over decorations. My eyes land on a special one, and when Lila isn't looking, I sneak it into the basket. It's perfect.

I can't wait to give it to Charlie.

MARK

I sit alone in my crappy little apartment, drinking warm beer. When I check the refrigerator settings, the lettuce Lila put in there earlier is frozen, though the beer above it isn't chilled at all. I eat bland canned soup for dinner after eventually finding one working burner on the stove.

Anxious to relax, I take a shower and discover the hot water heater provides roughly two minutes of barely-lukewarm water, despite the fact that I haven't used any hot water before then. Shivering, I turn on the ancient heater and find that not only does it rumble like a jet engine, it also emits a smell reminiscent of dead rats. I yank on thick sweats and head to the living room.

I sit down on the ugly couch in the living room before immediately jumping back up. The blue plaid bastard has a broken spring guaranteed to turn me into a eunuch if I sit in the most obvious spot to view the tiny television.

I drag out my mirror and attempt to massage my left leg like Charlie and Lila have while pretending it's my right leg, but I can't get the mirror positioned properly, and I know damn well which leg I'm rubbing, so it doesn't work. Finally, I give up and settle on the lumpy loveseat with a book, reaching toward the shabby end table to turn on the navy lamp.

The bulb is burned out.

And I don't have a spare.

Frustrated, I hurl my book across the room. It careens off the wall and splays open on the floor, taunting me. Swearing under my breath, I hobble across the room without my crutches, attempting full weight-bearing on my prosthetic leg for the first time ever.

I'm still not sure exactly how it happened.

One second, I'm leaning over to pick up the book; the next, I lose my balance and topple to the floor, landing face-first.

Fuck.

I lay there for a minute, letting fly a string of colorful curses while I assess myself for injuries. Though I may end up with a bruise or two, it seems the thing I've wounded most is my pride.

"Dammit," I mutter, rolling to my side and slowly getting to my feet. I check myself over again, carefully inspecting my stump and the abutment protruding from it for any damage. That's all I need – an injury on my first night alone. Thankfully, the prosthetic, the abutment, and my leg all seem to be okay. I give up on my exciting evening and limp down the hall to the bedroom, carrying my crutches.

Lila's already made the bed with fresh sheets, and I settle onto the uncomfortable mattress after removing my prosthetic for the night. A musty smell rises from the mattress, and I stifle a sneeze, followed by a second and a third.

I desperately need a distraction. I sit up, reaching for the remote control for the television and turning it on.

Or rather, I try to turn it on.

But nothing happens when I press the button. Whether it's the television or the controller, I'm not sure, but it's not working.

Goddammit. I launch the remote across the room. It clatters against the wall and falls behind the dresser.

Perfect. Just fucking perfect.

I roll onto my back and throw my arm over my eyes. Unwanted images flood my mind, images of Charlie, her smile, her laughter, her kisses, and later, the anguish in her eyes.

God, I miss her.

I miss her so much, there's a constant physical pain right through the center of my chest.

Pain and anger. That's all I feel now, all the time – overwhelming pain and anger.

If only that damn IED hadn't ruined me.

I could have been happy with Charlie, truly, completely happy. I could have been the man she deserved. Whole, not broken.

If only.

But the IED *did* ruin me, destroying my leg, my body, and all chances of a normal life. Of happiness. Of love.

I love Charlie. I always will.

But sometimes, loving someone means making heavy sacrifices for the good of the other person.

No matter how much it hurts me, for Charlie, I will make this sacrifice.

Because Charlie deserves nothing less than perfection.

CHAPTER FIVE

CHARLIE

SUNDAY AFTERNOON, I DECIDE to make a pot of chili. It's the perfect cold-weather food, and I make a huge pot, enough to last several days.

Tucker and Lila show up as I'm eating. "That smells amazing," Lila inhales deeply. "And you're eating!" she exclaims, looking at my half-eaten bowl.

I shrug. "I need to take better care of myself," I reply with a quick glance in Tucker's direction. "I made plenty. Help yourselves."

We sit at the table and enjoy steamy bowls of chili with all the toppings. It's so good, I have a second helping, much to Lila's delight. When we finish, Tucker informs me he's brought me a Christmas tree. He goes to his truck and returns with lights and ornaments.

I used to love Christmas, putting up a tree and covering every inch of it with ornaments. I loved to sit there at night, just staring at the lights, feeling peace wash over me. I loved the classic kids' Christmas movies and hot cocoa, carols and wrapping gifts, baking cookies and sharing holiday dinners with friends. But these last few years, it hasn't been the same. It's one more joy depression stole from me.

Not this year.

This year, with their help, I'm taking it back.

"I appreciate you picking me up a tree, but it really wasn't necessary," I tell Tucker, but he waves me off. He and Lila have wrestled the huge tree indoors, and I watch with amusement while they both try to take charge before eventually securing it in a stand.

Tucker smiles as he straightens up. "It's a time for celebrating, and you needed a tree."

I smile, catching his not-so-subtle hint. "Does that mean you're stringing the lights for me?"

"Of course," he replies. "They're new, so they won't be in one giant tangled ball. That's next Christmas. They'll be your problem then."

I lean back on the couch while Tucker and Lila wrap an obscene number of white lights around my tree. Twice I attempt to assist them, but Tucker shoos me away so insistently that even Lila raises an eyebrow at him.

"You didn't see her Friday," he says defensively. "She was lying on the bathroom floor covered with blood. It scared the hell out of me. Besides, her doctor told her to eat and rest."

"I am eating," I remind him. "I just ate two bowls of chili."

"What about resting? Did you sleep last night?" Lila asks.

I nod. "Dr. Oaks gave me something to help, and I slept almost eight hours."

"No night terrors?"

"No. The security system and extra locks make me feel safe. And I leave my gun on the dresser. I'm making progress."

"I know you are," Lila says. "I just worry."

I try to keep my voice casual. "I scheduled another appointment with Linda. I should have done it weeks ago." Lila glances up. "It's time for me to move forward."

Her expression is cautiously neutral. "What do you mean?"

"I've made a lot of progress this year. I can hug Tom and Tucker now without anxiety. I've become more comfortable with men, and I've chosen to be vulnerable when I wouldn't have before. But after Mark left –" I pause, choosing my words carefully. "When I got knocked down, I gave up. Things got really dark for me, and I can't continue to stay mired in the darkness. It's okay to have setbacks, but at some point, I have to get back up and move on."

"Does that mean you've given up on Mark?" she asks quietly.

I draw a deep breath. "What it means is that I'm done sitting here every night crying or drinking or raging at the walls. None of that has any effect at all on Mark, but it's killing me. Maybe one day he'll realize he can't live without me. Maybe not. Either way, I have bigger things to focus on." I smile faintly at Tucker, who crosses the room to wrap me in a bear hug.

When he pulls back, he takes something from his pocket and presses it into my hand. Lila watches curiously as I examine what he's given me.

It's a silver heart-shaped ornament with two tiny pairs of baby footprints engraved into it, strung on a red ribbon.

I start to cry, one hand over my mouth. Lila rushes to comfort me, but Tucker holds her back. "She's okay. Just give her a minute."

I clutch the ornament to my heart and chuckle through my tears. "Lila, you'd better sit down."

Tucker smiles encouragingly as Lila and I sit down on the couch. I look into her worried violet eyes. "Dr. Oaks did a full workup the other day, and there was a lot. The ulcer, the exhaustion, the weight loss, the malnourishment." I stop for a minute, then tears start to fall even as I smile again. "And I'm pregnant, Lila. Four months pregnant, with twins." I open my hand and reveal the ornament from Tucker.

Lila's mouth falls open. "But you can't – they said –"

Her expression of stunned disbelief matches my own when Dr. Oaks broke the news to me. I nod. "She called them miracle babies."

"Does Mark know?"

I shake my head. "I'll tell him. I needed to come to grips with it before I could tell anyone else."

Lila turns accusing eyes on Tucker. "You knew and didn't tell me?"

I grab her hand. "Lila, I made him promise to let me be the one to tell you. I just had to wrap my head around it. Please don't be angry at Tucker."

"Pregnant," Lila whispers in wonder. "Oh, Charlie," she says, grabbing me in a tight hug, "this is amazing." She starts crying, and I start crying again. Tucker kneels in front of us and suddenly we're all hugging.

"Twins," I say weakly when we pull apart. "I'm having twins."

"That's why you're doing this with Mark," Lila says, eyeing Tucker. He nods.

"Doing what?" I ask.

"Kicking him out of the nest."

I look at Tucker in surprise.

"You were right when you said he was comfortable. He went from you taking care of him to us taking care of him, and the only thing that changed for him was the scenery. He still had someone to talk to and have dinner with and work out with and do his massages and everything else. Well, except the sex part," he grins. "He's pretty, but not that pretty." He winks, and I smile. "But your entire world changed. I decided he needed a reality check. I found him an apartment and a vehicle, and we helped him move out today. He's just down the road," he adds, "and to quote Lila, his apartment is a dive. He'll come to his senses pretty quickly once he has to adjust to life on his own."

My smile fades. "Unless he really has moved on."

"He hasn't," Lila encourages me. "Besides, when he hears about the babies–" but I interrupt her, shaking my head.

"No, Lila," I say firmly. "I'll tell him about the babies, but I won't take him back because of them. I won't accept a man who's only with me out of obligation. I deserve someone who loves me with his whole heart. Either Mark comes back because he can't live without me, or we'll find a way to co-parent. I'm not letting him waltz back in like nothing happened simply because I'm pregnant."

"But he does love you," she protests.

"Then he needs to figure that out, and he needs to do it soon. And I already told Tucker," I glance at him, "but I'm telling you as well. Neither of you can tell Mark. I'll tell him when I'm ready, but you guys cannot say a word. Swear to me."

"I already promised," Tucker says. "It's not my news. I didn't sleep with him."

"I won't say anything," Lila promises. "When are you going to talk to him?"

"I have to see a high-risk obstetrician in Pueblo this week. Maybe I'll stop by his new place on my way home."

Lila nods. "I'll text you his address."

I hang the footprint ornament on my tree, and Lila and Tucker help me decorate it with red and silver ornaments. We find a channel playing Christmas music, and I turn on the gas fireplace while we sit around the living room in our sock feet. When it grows dark, we light candles on the mantle and make cocoa. My tree shimmers with the abundance of white lights, the red and silver ornaments sparkling in their glow.

Tucker eventually looks over at Lila and takes her hand. "We need to get home. We still have to drag our tree inside."

"Take some chili," I offer. "There's plenty."

Lila scoops spicy chili into a container while Tucker goes to his truck, returning a moment later with a thick book. He holds it out to me, and my eyes get misty when I read its title. "Thank you, Tucker." I stand on tiptoe to hug him. He kisses my forehead, and Lila hugs me as well.

"I can't believe you're pregnant," she says with a soft smile. "Your life is changing in ways you never expected."

She's right.

None of the big things that happened this year were on my radar, yet their occurrences all had a massive impact. These two tiny babies will have the biggest impact yet.

Now I just have to figure out how to break the news to Mark.

LILA

Long after Tucker's fallen asleep, I'm awake.

Twins.

Charlie's having twins.

Tears stream from my eyes, dripping onto my shirt, but I don't bother wiping them away.

God... I'd give anything to be pregnant.

It's not that I'm not happy for Charlie. I'm *thrilled* for her. She's been given a gift she'd believed impossible, stolen from her forever by brutal, hate-filled savages.

Miracle babies, her doctor called them, and that's the truth.

Mark was with her when the gynecologist at Walter Reed delivered the news. She cried for days. I sat with her the next day, and the day after that, and the day after that, watching her grieve for the loss of what could have been, silently thankful they hadn't uttered those words to me, though until very recently, I couldn't grasp how much it hurt her to hear them.

I'm not upset that Charlie's pregnant.

It's just... because she'd been told she couldn't get pregnant, she's never tried to conceive.

She doesn't know the agony of hoping month after month that this time, we'll be successful, only to have my hopes dashed with that horrible bloody stain.

She doesn't know the emotional roller coaster caused by hormone shots and the unspontaneous, pre-scheduled sex that needs to occur in a specific window of time.

She'll never know the physical or emotional anguish of a tubal pregnancy that ends with the removal of a fallopian tube, rendering one ovary completely useless and cutting my chances of pregnancy even further.

I'm glad she'll never experience those things. I'd never wish any of that on her. She's been through too much already, and I love her. She supports me each month when my pain inevitably hits, sitting with me, holding my hand, asking how she can help.

I'm not upset that Charlie's pregnant.

I'm upset that I'm not.

Because of course, that goddamned red stain of failure had to happen *tonight* after I got home. Another month of trying down the drain. And ever since I began taking hormone shots, my monthly cramps have gotten consistently worse, like even my own body is punishing me for failing again.

I'm not upset that Charlie's pregnant.

I'm honestly, truly, unreservedly happy she's getting her miracle, because her life has been hell for so long now.

I just wish I could have a miracle of my own.

TUCKER

I awaken to the sound of quiet sniffles beside me. I raise my head just as Lila adjusts the covers, hiding her face because she doesn't want me to see her cry.

I snake a hand beneath the blankets, wrapping my arm around her waist and drawing her against my body. I bury my face in her neck. It's damp with her salty tears.

"Do you want to talk about it?" I murmur against her skin, nuzzling her with my stubble, and she shivers before shaking her head no. I inhale her warm cherry blossom scent, and my body tightens immediately.

"Do you want to forget about it?" I graze my lips over her collarbone and lick and nibble back up her neck to the hollow beneath her ear. She shivers again, this time arching her back. My hand leaves her waist, drifting lower before she captures it with hers.

"I can't," she whispers.

I slide my hand up instead, reaching for the buttons of her satin night shirt as I ease her onto her back. I kiss every inch of her soft skin as I expose it, button by button, until her lush curves are bared but for a scrap of lacy panties. She moans softly as I trace my way back up her body with my lips and tongue.

I shift to kneel above her, settling down to lavish attention on her breasts, suckling one and teasing the other between my thumb and forefinger until her nipples are perfectly peaked. She moans again before sliding her hands between us to push at my chest.

"I can't," she repeats.

I slip my arms under her and roll us both over so she's lying on top of me, chest to chest, then immediately release her. I won't hold Lila tightly, not even in play, not after what she's been through. I lift my head and find her mouth with my own, kissing lightly, licking along the seam of her lips until she cups my face between her hands and deepens the kiss. She tastes like honeysuckle on a warm summer morning. My fingertips caress up and down her sides and thighs, barely touching her, and she sighs softly before pulling away.

"I started my period."

I stroke her cheek with my thumb and gaze into her sad violet eyes. "Do you want to talk about it or forget about it?"

"Make me forget, Tucker." Her voice is almost a plea, tugging at my heart.

I slide a hand behind her neck and pull her closer. "Then come here," I mutter against her lips.

It's instantly explosive between us, whether from hormones, her grief, or my need to help her forget the pain. Our kisses turn scorching, my mouth claiming hers, my hands everywhere, and she can't get enough. Somehow I scoop her up and take her to the shower, the only place she'll have sex when she's bleeding, and we make love twice. The first time she's braced with her back against the wall, her calves hooked over my forearms, moaning my name with her hands fisted in my hair as we come together. The second time is slower, gentler, but every bit as exquisite as she straddles me on the shower bench, taking control and driving me wild. Her release triggers my own, and the intensity of our orgasms leaves both of us trembling.

She collapses against me, her face in my chest, both of us breathing hard. "Wow," she breathes.

I turn her face up to mine and capture her mouth in another fiery kiss. "You're so fucking sexy," I say when we finally break apart.

She chuckles, trailing her fingers through my chest hair. "You're not so bad yourself."

We take a leisurely shower before returning to the bedroom. I'm surprised to find it's not even three in the morning. It feels much later. Lila drags a comb through her wet curls. I feel the sadness radiating from her again as the glow of our lovemaking fades. I take the blow dryer from her hand and tug her to the bed, where I sit behind her and dry her tresses for her, occasionally sweeping them aside to nuzzle her neck. When her thick blond curls are dry, I tuck her into my chest and pull the covers over us both, holding her until she falls asleep.

Lila doesn't cry often. Following her trauma there were tears, of course, and there have been a few occasions when she's been so angry that she's cried, a phenomenon I don't fully comprehend but definitely have a healthy fear of. Aside from that, she's not really the weepy type. This year has been more emotional than most. Much of that stems from the hormone injections and from grieving each month when her pregnancy hopes are dashed. A few months ago, she'd be depressed for a day or so when her period would start, but the ectopic pregnancy has heightened her tension. Losing one fallopian tube means that although she still has both ovaries, only one can send her eggs where they need to go so my swimmers can do what they need to do. The hormone shots help produce more mature eggs, but if only half of them reach their intended destination, it's still an uphill battle, and she blames herself.

As long as I live, I'll never forget the heartbroken expression on her pale face when she woke up after emergency surgery a couple of months ago. When she learned they'd had to remove her ruptured fallopian tube after a successfully growing embryo had implanted in the wrong location, she'd stared into space with unseeing eyes, too distraught to cry. Her hollow whisper gutted me. "It's my fault."

"No, Sweetness, it's no one's fault. These things just happen," I'd hurried to assure her, turning her face to me to capture her attention.

But she'd shaken her head. "Maybe the only baby I was ever meant to have is the one from – from them."

My heart dropped into my stomach at her words.

When we'd finally found where the bastards had taken Lila and Charlie, Mark and I blazed in with our teams to rescue them. The bastards came out firing, and we were all too happy to engage. We showed no mercy, eliminating every one of those sadistic fuckers. Fifteen men were in their compound that night, *fifteen* vile monsters who'd repeatedly raped them, beaten them, and starved them. And in Charlie's case, they'd tortured and mutilated her, too.

On her arrival to Walter Reed, Lila was diagnosed with internal trauma from the repeated sexual assaults as well as a severe infection that had spread up into her uterus. When she called, she told me through tears they'd had to do a D&C. I was still in Afghanistan and didn't know exactly what that entailed. I'd looked it up, and from what I found online, they'd opened her cervix to repair the damage the infection had caused to her uterine walls. She later told me that in the course of performing the D&C, the doctors had terminated a non-viable pregnancy resulting from her assaults. The embryo had barely had time to implant, and the heavy-duty antibiotics saturating the uterine walls would have caused her to lose it anyway. Lila hadn't had any idea she was pregnant, but she was understandably relieved when the doctors told her they'd had to terminate the pregnancy, as was I. How could she have carried a baby sired by any one of a number of ruthless bastards? Enduring the constant reminder of a torment she was struggling to recover from would have destroyed her.

Since her tubal pregnancy, Lila's harbored fears that she unknowingly eliminated her only possibility of motherhood. Some part of her worries she's being punished for something she didn't choose, but didn't object to afterwards. Another part of her feels guilty for being relieved that the worst experience of her life didn't result in a baby fathered by her rapists.

I'm not religious, but I can't believe a higher power would strip away Lila's chance at motherhood because she was abused and mistreated by vicious savages.

Until tonight, it never crossed my mind how Charlie's unexpected pregnancy would affect Lila. I was too excited for Charlie, who'd believed she could never conceive because of what those bastards did to her.

Watching Charlie progress through this pregnancy is going to rip Lila's non-pregnant heart to pieces. Every milestone Charlie hits – her growing abdomen, feeling the first kicks, buying baby clothes, childbirth – each one will twist the knife in Lila's soul a little bit more.

I'd give anything for Lila to conceive.

Would you really?

Sudden shame sucks the air from my lungs.

After her ectopic pregnancy, Lila mentioned in vitro fertilization as an option. The doctor would use ultrasound to guide a long, thin needle into her abdomen to remove a few of her eggs. The eggs would then be combined with my freshly-produced sperm and placed in an incubator. I'd immediately encouraged her to give the shots and scheduled sex a few more months before making such a hasty decision.

The truth was, I'd balked at the idea of jerking off with people waiting outside the door to collect my "sample" and dash down the hall to create a test tube baby. The thought of masturbating with an audience nearby mortified me. My singular focus was on how the experience would affect me. God forbid I should have to pleasure myself and do a walk of shame with my cup of semen. Never mind that Lila was more than willing to undergo hormone injections, a large needle stabbing into her belly, numerous blood tests, pelvic exams, ultrasounds, the eventual implantation of the test tube tots, and, oh yeah, all the discomfort of pregnancy and the pain of childbirth. No, by all means, let's focus on my one brief moment of humiliation.

I stare down at the gorgeous, amazing woman curled up in my arms, a woman I love more than life itself.

If a few moments of embarrassment can ease her pain, I need to research IVF.

CHAPTER SIX

CHARLIE

On Wednesday, I sleep in an entire extra hour. Tara's going to cover my clients today since I have two doctor's appointments. I eat a real breakfast of oatmeal, toast, and fresh berries and drink two steaming cups of green tea instead of my beloved coffee. Before leaving the house, I drop diced chicken and sesame sauce into my slow cooker. When I come home, all I'll have to do for dinner is steam broccoli and make rice.

I'm doing my part to inch forward, and even though it feels like I'm slogging through knee-deep mud, it's still progress.

My first appointment is with my psychiatrist. The petite blonde meets me in the waiting room and leads me back to her office.

"I'm glad to see you again, Charlie." Today, Linda's dressed in a black fitted blazer and a matching skirt that lands just above her knees. Her consummate-professional business attire contrasts sharply with her four-inch leopard-print heels and matching blouse, its plunging neckline barely visible beneath the tailored jacket. Linda loves the sexy librarian look, and she pulls it off quite well, right down to the glasses perched on her perky nose.

"I appreciate you working me in." The soft blues and warm woods of her space have an instantly soothing effect.

"Why don't you fill me in on what's been going on?" She settles on her couch, patting the opposite end for me to join her.

Linda knows all about my past. She's heard the horrible events and emotions I've never voiced to anyone else, and she's never flinched or judged me, even as she'd gently nudge me in a healthier direction. I'm comfortable with her in a way I never believed I could be, though to be fair, the first two psychiatrists I spoke with were at Walter Reed. Though both men meant well, I couldn't bare my soul to them. They were males, and my trauma was too fresh.

With her mild encouragement, I unload everything, holding nothing back. It took a while for me to learn the value of full disclosure in our sessions. I wasted a lot of time candy-coating things and beating around the bush early on because I wasn't comfortable opening up. With time, I've learned that keeping secrets and downplaying the severity of things won't help me get better.

Linda is well aware of my history of night terrors. It was her suggestion that since Mark was standing guard to help me feel safe, he should wake me half an hour before they normally began. Interrupting my sleep cycle and having Mark at my side had relieved most of my nightmares. I'm not having night terrors currently, but until the last few nights, I've barely slept since Mark left, so despite her assertion to the contrary, I'm not sure it's a victory.

I tell her my anxiety around men continues to improve. I tell her I can hug both Tucker and Tom without hesitation, a definite victory which she makes me acknowledge.

Then we move into my dating life.

Linda already knows about my numerous online dating disasters from past sessions, and she knows about my experience with Blake. She sees my response to his horrible behavior as a victory because I'd chosen to be vulnerable with him to further my own healing, and when he reacted poorly, I walked away with my head held high.

Today, I discuss Mark. She knows our history and how he came to live with me, but the fact we'd started dating is new to her. I describe our rapidly intensified relationship and its unexpected demise, and I bluntly detail my vivid downward spiral following his departure. I lay it all out for her – my drinking, my utter despondency, and my newly-discovered pregnancy. She lets me talk without interruption, giving me her complete attention.

"You've had quite the year," Linda observes. I smile at her understatement. "Tell me what you want to focus on."

"I went to a really dark place after Mark left me, and I don't want to go there again," I admit.

"By dark, do you mean you had suicidal thoughts?"

I shake my head slowly. "Not exactly. I would never intentionally kill myself because of how it would affect the people I care about. Kip's suicide made me realize how my death would impact them." Linda frowns. She and I had discussed Kip and his situation in a prior session, one where we drew comparisons between the Japanese art of kintsugi – mending broken pottery with gold to emphasize its cracks, rather than hide them – and accepting one's own flaws. I haven't seen Linda recently, and she wasn't aware Kip had killed himself, so I take a moment to tell her about him before continuing with my own story. "Lila and Tucker would be devastated if I did that. Tom, too, because his sister committed suicide, and he blames himself for being unable to help her. And his daughter and I are close, and I couldn't do that to her. Hurting other people irreparably because of my own pain wasn't a step I could take. But there were a lot of days that I wished I were dead because it would hurt less, and knowing I didn't have suicide as an option left me feeling trapped in my pain with no escape," I confess. "I made reckless choices without any regard for consequences."

"What changed?" Her dark eyes probe gently, watching my response.

"I saw myself in the mirror. Literally," I add. "I was vomiting blood, so weak I could barely stand. I wasn't eating, wasn't sleeping. My skin was gray. My body was skeletal. I finally saw what Lila and Tucker and Tom were seeing when they looked at me, and I had a moment of clarity. I realized I was killing myself passively, clutching my pain and letting it drag me under instead of releasing it and moving forward. For years, fear ruled my life. All I did was exchange fear for pain. I can't keep doing that. I'm too stubborn to surrender, so if I'm not going to give up, I need to get busy getting better."

"That's very brave of you, Charlie."

Her gentle smile disarms me. "I'm not sure it's brave, but letting the darkness determine my path wasn't working. It's time to try something different."

"How do you feel about an antidepressant? In the past, you've been resistant to the idea."

"Mark's depression after his injury taught me that medication can be a tool in my arsenal," I reply. "As long as it's safe for the babies, I'm in."

"Do your babies factor into your decision to work through your pain?"

"Absolutely. I'm not sure what role Mark will play in their lives, so I've got to get my act together before they show up in a few months."

Linda smiles. "You don't need to be completely together when they show up. New babies just want to be held and loved and cared for. You'll be wonderful at that. You have plenty of time to work on yourself. You'll grow and change as they do."

We talk a while longer, with Linda closing our session by giving me simple ways to combat my depression. "Go for a walk every day, preferably in the morning," she says. "Even just a few minutes releases endorphins that improve your mood, as does exposure to morning sunlight, so morning walks produce twice the benefits. Make time to do things that relax you. Listen to music, take a bubble bath, watch flames dance in the fireplace. Anything that soothes you helps with anxiety and depression. When you do have a difficult day, analyze what's different. Did you have a bad encounter? Was the date significant? What was it that affected your mood? Determining the cause can help you learn how to avoid or prepare for that trigger in the future."

She hands me a prescription and an appointment card for my next visit. "Remember, what your babies need most is for you to take care of yourself."

I eat a banana on my drive north to the obstetrician's office in Pueblo. It's a three-story building full of modern white cabinetry and greyed splashes of dusty mauve and steel blue, rather than the traditional pale pastels. After stepping on a scale and providing the requisite blood and urine samples, I'm ushered to a room with an uncomfortable paper-lined table. Dr. Rose is a tiny woman with dark hair, dark eyes, and a warm smile. She sits down with me to discuss the records Dr. Oaks sent. When she asks about my cervical scarring, I hesitate only briefly before squaring my shoulders. "I was kidnapped when I served in Afghanistan. My captors raped and mutilated me with a rusty knife, metal pipes, and broken glass. They tortured me for eleven days before my platoon found me, and by then, they'd inflicted a lot of damage."

Her expression changes from horror to anger to sympathy as I speak. "I'm so sorry."

I nod, then plunge ahead with a topic that's been worrying me for a couple of days. "I'm worried I won't be able to breastfeed after – after what they did."

"They mutilated your breasts as well?"

I can only nod a second time. A hint of tightness begins in my chest, but I flex my hands and focus on breathing slowly, deeply.

I'm safe here.

Breathe.

She senses my anxiety and changes course. "I'll take a look when I examine you. Formula is always an option. I've had cases where a mother nursed her baby with just one breast. That would certainly be more challenging with twins, but not unmanageable if you alternated formula and breastmilk. The more you nurse, the more milk your body produces." She studies my face. "Are you comfortable having a pelvic and breast exam? My nurse will be present to assist me, unless you'd prefer I perform the exam without her."

"I'm okay. It's talking about what happened that's difficult."

She nods, then reaches into an upper cabinet and passes me a soft gown. "Slip into this, and remove your bra and panties. Take a seat on the table when you're done. I'll be back in a few minutes."

I'm poked, prodded, and thoroughly examined. Dr. Rose spends a long time on my pelvic exam, but she distracts me with questions about Cedar Ridge and my favorite hiking spots. After she examines my breasts, she places a small hand on my upper arm.

"I don't think breastfeeding will be a problem for you, Charlie. The scarring doesn't travel directly through the nipples. They focused their cuts on your breast tissue and areolas. Your nipples themselves are undamaged."

I can't keep the excitement from my voice. "Really?"

One more victory over those bastards.

She nods. "I'd like an ultrasound to get a better look at your babies. I'll walk you to our ultrasound suite. I'll rejoin you later to review the images and talk with you more."

I climb up onto another paper-lined table down the hall. The technician covers my lower body with a sheet, then lifts my gown and folds it just beneath my breasts. She squirts warm gel on my rounded belly. "I love twin studies," the cheerful redhead confides, sliding the probe over my abdomen. "You can see personality differences even in the womb."

Dr. Rose returns during my ultrasound. "Your babies look healthy and beautiful," she says with a smile, looking at the screen. I tilt my head to look too, and the technician angles her screen toward me.

In the space of a single breath, they steal my heart.

There they are, both of them moving and wiggling, and as I watch the screen and feel the internal wriggles, I realize the butterfly sensations in my stomach that I've been blaming on anxiety have actually been coming from two very specific tiny butterflies. She adjusts the picture, zeroing in on what is clearly a baby sucking its thumb. I stare in amazement at the tiny face, watching in silent awe. A moment later, she moves the probe and zooms in on the second baby kicking and squirming as it, too, turns to face us. She takes a picture of its face with a clenched fist beside it. The detail on the screen is astonishing.

I hesitate before turning to Dr. Rose. "I drank a lot," I blurt anxiously. "I had a really bad month or so and I didn't know I was pregnant and... I drank a lot."

Please don't let me have hurt my little miracles.

"How long ago?" Dr. Rose asks.

I think back. "Probably mid-October to mid-November."

She lays her hand on my leg. "The third week until about the eighth week of pregnancy are when heavy alcohol consumption can most deeply affect organ development and cause serious damage. You were already past that stage." Her smile reinforces her reassuring words.

I stare at her, my heart in my throat. "Really?"

"Really. Now, you should still avoid heavy drinking," she adds, "because your babies are still developing, but an occasional glass of wine with dinner won't hurt."

"So I'm really sixteen weeks pregnant?" I'm still wrapping my head around seeing the babies on the screen.

No. Not "the" babies.

My babies.

"About eighteen and a half, actually, based on the babies' measurements and your dates," she corrects me. "A normal pregnancy is forty weeks, but with twins, it's about thirty-seven or thirty-eight. You're almost at the halfway point, Charlie."

"Halfway?" I repeat faintly. I can't tear my eyes from the screen as the ultrasound technician starts printing pictures.

Dr. Rose smiles. "Halfway. Your bloodwork and exam look good, but you've got to gain weight, Charlie. You're seriously underweight even if you weren't pregnant, and these little babies need extra calories to properly develop. You need to be eating more nutrient-dense foods. A lot more," she emphasizes. Then she smiles. "Would you like to know their genders?"

I glance up in surprise. "You can tell?"

She nods. "They were showing off."

Too overcome to answer, I simply nod.

She smiles kindly. "You're having fraternal twins. A boy and a girl."

My eyes well with tears. "One of each," I whisper, resting my hand on my stomach.

"You'll need a cesarean section when it's time to deliver because of your cervical scarring," she cautions me. "And because you're high-risk and so malnourished, I'll need to check you every two weeks, and after you reach thirty or thirty-two weeks, I'll need to see you weekly."

I nod, but all I can think about are my babies.

A boy and a girl.

"Do you have any questions for me?"

I shake my head.

The cheery redhead hands me two envelopes filled with printed pictures, smiling. "A set for you, and a set for Dad to show off at the office."

A set for their dad.

For Mark.

I flip unseeing through the stack of pictures, still dumbstruck by the proof of their existence. Even though it's sunk in that the fatigue and rounded belly I'd attributed to bloating and malnourishment were actually caused by my pregnancy, seeing their tiny faces has been a shock.

No. A miracle.

In the parking lot, I sit in my car with the photos, unable to stop smiling.

A boy and a girl.

I have to tell Mark. Today.

Regardless of the demise of our relationship or how badly he's hurt me, he deserves to share in this incredible moment. I tuck the pictures carefully in my purse and drive back to Cedar Ridge. I find his apartment easily, and the black van Tucker described is out front.

Good. He's home.

I pick up the envelope with his pictures and walk to the door, knocking lightly. There's no answer. I knock again, more firmly this time. Still no answer.

"Mark?" I call, knocking again. "Open the door, please. I really need to talk to you." I press the doorbell, but don't hear a corresponding ring. I press it again, but it remains silent. I resort to knocking again. "Please, Mark? This is important."

I wait, but he never comes. Maybe he's in the shower. I knock again, a steady stream of firm knocks. I press my ear to the door, listening. What if he's injured, unable to get to the door? I dial his cell phone and hear it ringing. The tone is silenced mid-ring. I dial it again, and the same thing happens.

Son of a bitch.

He's in there, and he knows I'm out here.

He's ignoring me?

The man who swore he'd never leave me, who promised he'd always be there for me, is fucking *ignoring* me when I'm six feet away and telling him it's important.

"Seriously?" I yell through the door. "You won't even talk to me?" I dial again, hear half a ring, and hear him silence it, and I'm equal parts frustrated and angry.

"Dammit, Mark, I really need to speak to you. I wouldn't be here otherwise." I knock again, but there's no response.

Hurt and rage boil inside me, and I pound his front door with the side of my fist for a full minute, determined to annoy him until he either opens the door or calls the police. When his neighbor peeks out to see what all the racket is about, I stop hammering and start yelling instead.

"You know what, fine! Ignore me! But if this weren't important, I wouldn't be here. I didn't need yet another reminder of how little I meant to you. If you ever decide to pull your head out of your ass, you know where to find me."

I get in my car and leave in a rush, acutely aware his neighbor is still staring at me. Fury pours off me like a duck shedding water. I'm so angry, I'm shaking.

I've barely driven a block when my anger evaporates, replaced immediately by humiliation and soul-crushing pain. This is the most life-changing news I've ever gotten, the highest high I've ever experienced, and Mark just shattered it with his blatant rejection.

I can accept that he doesn't want to be with me, but refusing to speak to me at all? Especially when it's about something so crucial. Granted, he doesn't know what I wanted to talk to him about, but he damn well knew it was important, and it didn't matter.

I didn't matter.

He doesn't care.

He doesn't love me.

Maybe he never did.

Tears stream from my eyes as I choke back sobs. I pull over in a deserted parking lot, aware I'm not safe to drive. I allow myself to ugly-cry for a few minutes, dropping my head onto the steering wheel. It doesn't eliminate the pain piercing my heart, but it does vent some of it, like steam slowly releasing from a pressure cooker.

Slow your breathing.

Nice and easy.

Slow and deep.

Instead of wallowing in my pain and spiraling back into the darkness, I make the conscious choice to reach out.

I choose to move forward.

I dry my eyes and drive to Tucker's gym, Press On, where I'm relieved to find him in his office. When I knock on his open door, a huge smile spreads across his face and he springs from his chair, bounding toward me. "How was your appointment?"

I'd give anything for that kind of excitement from Mark.

"Good. I'm actually eighteen weeks pregnant. Almost at the halfway point."

His face lights up. "Halfway! How are my nieces? Or nephews? Or do you know what they are?"

"Dr. Rose said they're both healthy," I smile.

"Of course they are," he declares. "But will I have nieces or nephews?"

I reach into my purse and pull out the pictures. He takes them from me eagerly, scanning the photos with great interest. "They look like babies," he says, poring over them. "They're definitely babies, but I don't see any giblets. What are they?"

I laugh aloud. "Fraternal twins. And I'm having one of each."

"A boy and a girl?"

I nod, and he lets out a whoop as he picks me up, spinning me around. I laugh again and he puts me down, reaching for my shoulders to steady me. "I didn't hurt you, did I? Or them?"

"We're all fine," I assure him.

"Did you tell Mark?" His eyes search my face, halting on my puffy red eyes.

My smile fades. "I went by his apartment. He was home, but he refused to come to the door, no matter how many times I knocked or rang the bell. I know he was home because his van was there, and I heard him silence his phone each time I called him from his doorstep."

His face falls. "I'm sorry, Charlie."

I shrug as though it doesn't matter, then realize it's pointless to pretend I don't care. This is Tucker. He knows better. "I really wanted to share this moment with him. It was important to me. Really important." My words are choked by the growing lump in my throat.

"He'll come around," he insists, squeezing my shoulders with firm hands.

I shake my head. "He left what, ten weeks ago? He's not called, texted, driven by, nothing. Not once. He's moved on, Tucker. He's not coming back, and he doesn't care. Honestly, I'm starting to wonder if he ever did."

"He does care, Charlie, I promise." Tucker looks sad, but I can't tell if it's about everything Mark's missing or because he knows Mark really has moved on.

"Yeah, well..." I trail off. "I just wanted to share my news. Don't tell Lila yet."

He grins. "I heard your big news first again?" Then he pales. "Please don't tell her I already know. She still hasn't forgiven me for finding out you were pregnant before she did."

I smile and zip my fingers over my lips. "Not a word."

I drive home, but instead of going inside, I walk next door to the clinic. Lila's in a massage for another thirty minutes, but Tom comes out of the rehab gym and makes a beeline straight for me, smiling broadly.

"Lila told me," he says, pulling me in for a bear hug. "Congratulations, Little Mama."

"Thanks, Tom." I pull out my pictures, and he tugs them from my hands to study them.

"They're beautiful," he pronounces. "Or handsome. Which is it? Are they beautiful or handsome?"

I smile at his enthusiasm. "One is beautiful, and one is handsome. Fraternal twins."

He hugs me again. "A boy and a girl? That's fantastic!" His brows furrow as he scrutinizes me. "How do you feel? Are you eating?"

I nod. "The meds are helping, so I've stopped throwing up. My stomach hurts when I eat, but not as bad as before. And I'm still exhausted, but from what I've been reading, I should get some sort of energy burst soon."

He nods. "Seems like it was around the twenty-week mark for Chele."

"That's right, you've done this before." Then I laugh. "I mean, of course you have, since you have Maya, but I didn't think about you being involved in the pregnancy. Well, aside from the obvious."

He chuckles. "I loved it when Chele was pregnant. I went to all her appointments, rubbed her back, painted the nursery, went to Lamaze classes. I was even her birth coach. Not to brag, but I earned a certificate. It has a gold stork on it," he says loftily.

I grin. "Very impressive."

He hesitates uncertainly before meeting my gaze. "Listen, if Mark doesn't come around in time and you need someone with you for birthing classes and stuff, I'd be honored to help."

I'm not alone.

I stand on tiptoe to hug him, moved by his kindness. "Thanks," I say quietly, leaning my head against his broad chest. "I may take you up on that. I went by to tell him and show him the ultrasound pictures." I swallow hard. "He wouldn't even answer the door."

He squeezes me tightly for a second longer. "Look, Mark can only be a dumbass for so long. He's a good guy who thinks he's doing the right thing, even if it's completely boneheaded. He'll figure things out."

People keep telling me that, but his behavior indicates otherwise.

Tom returns to his clients, and I tape a note outside Lila's massage room for her to come over. I go home and stir the concoction in my slow cooker, then pull out leftovers for lunch.

Twins.

A boy and a girl.

I put down what I'm holding and walk to the half bath down the hall, turning sideways and lifting my shirt to view my belly. It looks significantly bigger than it did even a week ago. The rounding is definitely more pronounced, and this morning I had to button my jeans below the curve and wear a long top because of my changing shape.

I'm eating tomato soup and a grilled cheese sandwich when I hear Lila entering through the glass door. "It's me," she calls. "Don't shoot."

I smile. I've stopped wearing my belly-band holster and carrying my gun in the house, not because of the babies, but because I'm becoming comfortable in my home. I'm finally moving out of my hypervigilant combat mode. "In the kitchen," I answer.

Lila hurries in with a huge smile and immediately hugs me, then pulls back, frowning. "I smell Tom's cologne," she says, leaning in and sniffing me again. "You've been hugged. Don't tell me you've seen him already. Did he get to hear your news before me?"

I smile sheepishly. "You were in a massage, and he saw me come in."

"Dammit!" Lila smacks the counter. "Tucker finds out you're pregnant first, and Tom hears about your appointment first."

I don't volunteer that I stopped by to see Tucker before going to the clinic. "How was the appointment?"

I grin. "Apparently, I'm pregnant." Lila swats me, but stops when I pull out the ultrasound pictures. She snatches them from my hand and gazes at them in awe.

"Oh, Charlie," she says, her voice soft with wonder. "They're beautiful. Tiny and perfect and beautiful." She glances up. "Boys or girls?"

"One of each."

Lila gasps and hugs me again. "A boy and a girl! Oh my God! Did you tell Mark?"

Pain rockets through my chest. I describe my visit to Mark's apartment and his refusal to come to the door. "Everybody keeps saying he's going to come to his senses, but I'm starting to feel like we've passed the point of no return. He won't even speak to me. He let me stand on his doorstep in the cold, begging him to come to the door, and he completely ignored me. It was as infuriating as it was humiliating and hurtful."

Lila sighs heavily, considering her words for a long time. "I don't know what to say, Charlie," she finally admits. "I was positive he'd come around within a few days. Maybe Tucker's right. Maybe having to fend for himself will be the kick in the balls he needs. But maybe not." She hesitates, her eyes sad. "I love Mark, and I'm not telling you to give up. Whether you choose to wait for him or let him go, Tucker and I support you all the way."

After she's returned to work, I sink onto the couch, staring out the window at the snow-topped mountains.

Mark's not relented in any way since he left. He's given no indication that his final statement, that we couldn't be lovers or even friends any longer, isn't what he really wants. My few remaining shreds of hope are based on things he said in years past, before our failed romance, and that hope is sputtering like a struggling flame, about to die out completely.

Maybe I was wrong. Maybe the last thing he said to me really *is* what he wants. Maybe he really doesn't love me.

I wish I knew.

One way or the other, knowing would be easier than hanging onto false hope.

MARK

I'm alone in my crappy little apartment, sitting on the lumpy loveseat in the darkening twilight, utterly despondent.

I watched Charlie through a narrow sliver between the edges of the blinds and the window frame when she was here today. I haven't seen her since I left her seventy-five days ago.

She looked amazing, her long hair blowing in the wind, bundled against the cold in a black thigh-length coat with a deep red scarf around her neck.

Even from inside, I could see the fire in her beautiful green eyes when she got angry. She started knocking relentlessly, and I knew she wasn't going to quit. My resolve had finally shattered, and I'd gotten up to let her in, knowing I'd admit I love her, knowing I'd beg her to still love me, knowing I don't have the strength to fight it anymore.

But just as I started across the living room, she'd yelled at me one last time and stomped back to her car. I opened the front door in time to watch her peel out of the driveway, half-hoping she'd see me in the rearview mirror and come back.

No. Not half-hoping.

Praying with all my heart.

I'm in love with Charlie, completely and madly in love with her, and I'm unspeakably miserable without her.

I shut my eyes against the unfairness of it all.

I'm in love with an incredible woman, and because of some asshole with an IED on the other side of the world, I can't be with her, because she deserves more than being saddled with an amputee. I thought this burden would get easier to bear with time, but it's only getting worse, and I have absolutely no idea how to make it stop hurting so much.

The weight of it all overwhelms me, and a single tear trickles down my face.

I've lost everything, and there's not a damn thing I can do.

CHAPTER SEVEN

CHARLIE

DESPITE HIS OUTRIGHT REFUSAL to speak to me, I have to tell Mark I'm pregnant. I can't handle another humiliating in-person rejection, so I opt for the least invasive contact I can think of – texting him. "We need to talk face to face. It's really important. Please." I press send before I can change my mind, and though I'm not surprised when he doesn't respond, it still hurts.

I copy and send the same text to him every single day, first thing in the morning. Sooner or later, he'll get sick of it and either answer me or block my number, which, I suppose, would also qualify as an answer. But he doesn't block me, nor does he reply or call. He simply ignores me.

I've just sent my daily text to Mark and laid down my phone when it rings. My mouth goes dry. I snatch it up and answer without looking. "Hey," I say, suddenly shy. *How do I say something so important to someone who's cut me out of his life? Do I just blurt it out? Surprise! I'm not infertile after all! How do you feel about twins?*

It turns out to be completely irrelevant.

"Green Eyes!" booms a deep voice, startling me.

It's not the man I'd expected, but I'd recognize that voice anywhere. I don't know anyone else with such a rich timbre in his tone. "Stubbs?"

The big man laughs heartily. "Who else? I hope I didn't wake you. How have you been?"

Horrible. Completely and utterly horrible.

But I don't say that. "Working a lot," I reply, which is true. I buried myself even deeper in the clinic when I quit drinking. Without alcohol to numb my pain, I was desperate for a distraction.

"Funny you should mention work," he says cheerfully. "That's actually why I'm calling. I accepted a job offer from the VA yesterday afternoon. The medical director will call you today to work out the details."

My mouth falls open. "You get to work with us?"

"Yep," he says proudly. "The feds are paying me to set up shop with you since you're in an under-served rural area."

"Congratulations! When do you start?"

"As soon as I can get an apartment, I'm headed your way. I was hoping you could help me find a place."

"Sure. Tell me what you're looking for."

"Disability-friendly with two bedrooms, so one can double as a guest room and office."

"Tucker knows a guy for just about everything. I'll send you any information we come up with. You're welcome to stay with me in the meantime."

"I don't want to encroach on Mark's turf," he says.

I still haven't told Stubbs that Mark and I aren't together now. I couldn't. I've avoided him, much like I've avoided Maya, because I won't lie to either of them, nor can I be honest about my struggles of late. That's why I've limited myself to text messages. I can send funny pictures and deflect questions with humorous responses from a distance. Admitting aloud that Mark left me would have been too painful, especially because with Stubbs, it wouldn't be a short conversation.

"I wouldn't worry about that," I say, then change the subject. "We have an empty office at the clinic. What do you like? We can get the furniture for you."

He laughs. "I'm a simple guy. I just need somewhere to sit and talk to people and a place to write down what we talk about."

"I'm glad you're coming, Stubbs. We have a lot of clients who need you."

When I get to work, I grab Lila and Tom. "Stubbs got the job! He called me this morning."

Lila squeals excitedly. "When does he start?"

"He said he'll be here as soon as he can find an apartment. I told him he can stay with me until he finds something. Will you ask Tucker if he knows anybody with a place for rent? His only requirements were disability-friendly and two bedrooms." She nods, and I look between her and Tom. "In the meantime, we should talk to our clients and look over our rosters. Start a list of anyone we think could use his help, even if we're not sure they'd be willing to talk to him. He has a gift for drawing people out."

Tom nods, and a shadow passes over his face. "Damn, I wish he could have met Kip. He could have done that kid a world of good."

We all fall silent, remembering the sweet kid with dark blond hair, dimples, and beautiful blue-green eyes. Kip was a soldier who'd struggled with depression after losing his leg. His despondency was compounded when his girlfriend dumped him, apparently citing his amputation as a major factor in her decision. We'd set him up to see a psychiatrist, but he committed suicide before his appointment. None of us had realized his depression was that bad. He'd kept up a steady stream of cheerful chatter that masked his darker feelings. Kip's death had left all of us shaken.

"To no more fallen soldiers on the home front," Lila says soberly, raising her coffee cup in the air, and Tom and I do the same.

Thinking of Kip reminds me of not only my failure to help him, but to help Mark with his body image issues as well. After a moment, I sigh. "I don't have a client until ten. I'm going to start apartment hunting. The sooner we get Stubbs here, the better off our clients will be."

"Let me know what you come up with," Lila says, pulling out her phone. "I'm putting Tucker on it too, so between all of us, we'll find a place for him."

By lunchtime I've found several vacant apartments, but none of them are disability-friendly. Tucker calls around four to tell me the owner of Mark's apartment building recently passed away, and his granddaughter is taking over. She's renovating all the units to make them disability-friendly, but she doesn't have an immediate opening.

"There are two vacancies right now, but she's temporarily moving two of her current tenants into them so she can renovate their apartments. She has someone moving out next week, though. If Stubbs can be patient, she'll let him have that apartment once it's renovated."

"What is she doing?"

"It sounds like the full works," he says. "Ripping out carpeting, replacing old appliances, installing new heating and cooling units, remodeling the bathrooms, updating the furniture, painting. The non-disabled tenants have been notified that as their leases expire, they'll need to move elsewhere, but she's willing to give them a three-month grace period to find something. I honestly don't think she'd kick anybody out who really needed the place," he confides, "but she's making an effort to create living quarters for people who struggle in standard-built homes."

"Impressive," I murmur. "So when does it sound like Stubbs' apartment will be available?"

"Before the end of January, I think," Tucker says. "I'm going to get the paperwork from her and email it to him."

"You really do know a guy for everything, don't you?"

He chuckles. "Of course. Wanna buy a cheap Rolex?"

I spend Saturday doing something I loathe: shopping. Lila and I drive to Pueblo while Tucker goes to Mark's to watch football. My pants-situation has quickly turned critical. My rapidly rounding belly is creating wardrobe issues, and apparently, I need maternity clothes ASAP.

My day with Lila starts off as the best I've had in ages. Instead of one of her full-on Acquisition Expeditions, we're focusing on maternity clothes, which is more of a niche, so I'm expecting a much shorter outing. Because it's Lila, she still finds a surprising number of boutiques. I allow her to usher me through display after display of clothing. She pulls items off racks, holds them against me, then either returns it to the rack or sends me to try things on while she waits, handing the pieces that meet her expectations off to the pleased commission-based salesgirls trailing after us. She's ecstatic that, for once, I'm actively participating. The fact I don't have much choice given my ballooning waistline is irrelevant.

We linger over lunch. I have a glass of white wine with pasta and salad and eat every bite. We even share a slice of cheesecake for dessert. She smiles happily at my empty dishes but doesn't comment. Neither of us mention Mark at all, and it's a relief.

After lunch, we keep shopping, finding things she insists I need, though I do place a limit on how many outfits I'm willing to purchase for a short-term situation. Unlike Lila, I don't need closets and dressers exploding with clothes. I end up buying several pairs of black leggings, an assortment of cute tops, ballet flats to accommodate puffy feet, and a handful of wrap dresses.

Baby stores are next, where we examine cribs, car seats, strollers, and changing tables. I had no idea there were so many options for such seemingly simple things. I turn to ask Lila a question, but my words die in my throat. Lila's stroking a delicate pink baby blanket with her fingertips, tears welling in her eyes. Her pained expression is like a blow to my chest.

Oh God.

Lila.

I've been completely focused on myself, on how these babies are changing my world. I never once considered how my pregnancy would affect Lila. She's been desperately trying to conceive, and I go and pop up pregnant without any effort at all. Not only did I get pregnant, but I'm having twins. Now I'm dragging her through aisle after aisle of maternity clothes and mannequins with baby bumps and posters of beautiful infants with huge toothless smiles. How could I have been so insensitive?

Lila hasn't noticed me watching her. I turn away, frantic to get us out of here. "This is a lot to take in," I say to the nearest salesgirl. "Do you have a catalog I can look through instead?"

"Absolutely," she gushes, filling a bag with multiple volumes. "These should get you started."

Get me *started*? The bag weighs as much as a gallon of milk.

Lila's silent on the drive home. Even the radio volume is low, and I feel worse by the second. When we're nearly back to my house, I can't take it any longer.

"I'm sorry, Lila," I blurt, my voice loud in the quiet car.

She glances over. "What?"

"I'm sorry. I never meant to be so insensitive."

Lila looks genuinely confused. "What are you talking about?"

"The pregnancy stuff. I'm sorry. I didn't mean to upset you. I won't drag you to any more stuff like this, I swear."

Lila swallows hard, her eyes fixed on the winding road. "You have nothing to apologize for, Charlie. You didn't upset me. If anything, I upset myself."

"What do you mean?"

She shrugs lightly. "I allowed myself to imagine the possibilities, what it would feel like. When reality intrudes, it hurts, but I have no one to blame but myself."

I shake my head. "Wanting your dream to hurry and come true isn't wrong. I know in my heart you and Tucker will have a baby, Lila. I can feel it. I shouldn't have asked you to come baby shopping with me. It was thoughtless, and I apologize."

Lila frowns. "You weren't being thoughtless or insensitive. Who else are you going to take? Tucker?" She rolls her eyes. "I'm sure he'd be super helpful at picking out maternity clothes."

"I don't want to hurt you, Lila."

She shrugs again. "You aren't hurting me, Charlie. My inability to get pregnant? That hurts. But supporting you through this isn't hurting me. If anything, it helps."

I reach for her hand on the gear shifter. "It looked pretty painful to me."

She sighs. "Honestly, I'd probably have had the same reaction to a diaper commercial. I'm hyper-aware of everything baby-related right now. The more I try not to think about it, the worse it is. But I'm not upset about you and your miracle babies. I swear to you, Charlie, I'm thrilled for you, even if it might look otherwise sometimes." She squeezes my fingers.

"Promise you'll tell me if it gets to be too much," I tell her, and she laughs. "I'm serious. Tom's offered to be my birthing coach. He's been one before. I'm positive he'd look at baby furniture with me. I don't want to make things harder on you." God – it's bad enough she's having to watch my belly grow bigger by the day, taunting her flat one. No way will I intentionally make things more painful for her.

Lila pulls into my driveway and shuts off the engine. She shifts in her seat to look at me, her expression serious.

"Charlie, I hope with all my heart that one day soon, I'll be the one picking out baby furniture and maternity clothes, but there's a very real possibility that won't happen. There's no way in hell I'm missing even one minute of your pregnancy. These miracle babies of yours may be the closest I ever get to having my own, and I'm going to savor every second of this for as long as you can stand me."

I examine her violet eyes. There's not a hint of insincerity in them. "Promise me you'll tell me if it gets to be too much," I repeat.

She nods. "As long as you promise to tell me if I start getting on your nerves."

I nod my agreement, but I can't suppress the feeling that my pregnancy will be an increasing source of pain for Lila.

TUCKER

Saturday afternoon, I go to Mark's apartment to watch football. I arrive with a pair of footlong subs, chips, and beer.

"Hey, man," Mark greets me. "How's it going?"

I grin. "Great. Lila and Charlie went shopping in Pueblo, and I didn't have to go."

Mark nods. He's seen Lila's closet and the armload of shopping bags that magically appear with "just one or two new things."

We head for his living room and turn on the small television to watch the game while we eat. Mark sits on the loveseat. I eye the hateful plaid couch with its eunuch-spring and opt to sit on the floor instead.

I wait until halftime before turning to Mark.

"Charlie said she stopped by the other day, and you wouldn't even come to the door."

Mark doesn't answer, not meeting my eyes as he takes a long sip from his beer bottle.

"She knew you were here. She heard you silence your ring tone each time she called to ask you to open the door. She said you wouldn't answer her knocks or the doorbell, even though she was yelling through the door that she needed to talk to you about something important."

"The doorbell doesn't work." He won't meet my eyes.

I raise an eyebrow. "But knocking does, and so did your cell phone."

There's a long pause. "I can't see her, Tucker," Mark finally says.

I shake my head. "I don't understand you, man. You'd have taken a bullet for her. You've literally killed for her. Now you won't have anything to do with her. Is this some game to you, to see how much more you can hurt her?"

Mark drops his head. "I never wanted to hurt Charlie."

I'm intentionally harsh, twisting the knife to provoke a response. "You've got a weird way of showing it. Of everyone I know, you're the one person I was certain would always be loyal."

I can tell my words hit home because he flinches, but remains silent.

I watch him carefully. "Mark, I'm telling you this as your friend. Talk to Charlie, and do it soon. If you don't, you'll regret it for the rest of your life." I get up from the floor and collect our trash. "Come on. I need to run an errand."

"What about the game?"

I shrug. "It's halftime. Grab your jacket."

I don't volunteer where we're going, and Mark doesn't ask. He's startled, however, when we arrive at the local VFW. "What are we doing here?"

"Going inside," I answer curtly. "We have a meeting."

Mark keeps peppering me with questions, but I ignore him. A dozen or so veterans, mostly men, sit in a circle in one corner of the room. I lead the way and Mark follows. He glances questioningly at me, his expression hardening as he realizes these veterans are all missing a limb, and in some cases, multiple limbs.

"We're here for the support group meeting," I say to the group by way of introduction. "I'm Tucker, and this is Mark."

Several group members greet us as we find a pair of empty seats.

"Most of us know each other," says a man in his fifties. "I'm Bill. How did you find us?"

"I was looking for an amputee support group for vets to help my friend here pull his head out of his ass," I say conversationally. "He's a below-the-knee amputee from an IED earlier this year. He recently broke up with the woman he loves because he told her that people who are scarred and broken don't deserve love."

You could hear a pin drop as Mark swivels his head to stare at me. I smile broadly.

"Why would you say that here?" he hisses.

I shrug. "If you're going to ruin two lives, you ought to be willing to stand by your beliefs in front of others who are in the same boat."

Mark holds up his hands defensively. "I wasn't speaking about anyone but myself. I certainly don't mean any of you." His guilty expression hints that he's bracing for angry responses.

A woman speaks first, an attractive redhead with a prosthetic arm. "So what is it that makes you think you don't deserve to be loved?"

He drags a hand through his hair, rubbing his head. "I just feel like she deserves someone whole."

"Didn't you tell her someone with two legs would be better?" I press him.

"I swear to God, Tucker," he growls under his breath.

"That *is* what you said, though, right? That she needed a real man, one with two legs. You said having half a leg made you half a man, right?"

Mark drops his head into his hands before raising it again to meet the curious eyes around the circle. "Again, I'm only speaking of myself and my relationship with this woman. I would never say any of you who are missing a limb aren't real men. Or women," he adds quickly.

"But you believe it about yourself." The redheaded woman speaks again, and it's a statement, not a question.

Mark glares silently at me.

An older fellow with white hair looks Mark up and down. He's in a wheelchair, both legs absent below the knee. "What is it about the bottom half of that leg that was so damn special?"

Mark glances up as though he's not sure he heard him correctly.

"Name's Buck," the man offers. "And if you were good enough for this woman if you'd still had both of your legs, I want to know what was so damn special about the bottom half of that one." He gestures toward Mark's legs.

"There wasn't anything special about it," Mark says. "It's just... I was different before."

The man nods knowingly. "Plumbing doesn't work now?"

I choke back a snort.

Mark's eyes widen. "My plumbing works fine," he says quickly. "I was just different, that's all."

Another man turns, studying him carefully. He looks to be about forty. His face is heavily scarred on one side, and he's missing his left arm below bicep-level. "I was different before, too. I'm David. I was a high school quarterback. Good-looking, athletic. You'd never know it now. I was on an Apache helicopter that went down. I got pretty charred, lost my arm. Thought my life was over when I came home. I mean, look at me." He shrugs. "But then I met Val." He smiles. "She saw me. The real me," he emphasizes, "not what I look like on the outside, back then or today. She saw my soul, who I am. We've been married ten years, and we have three kids."

"This woman," the redhead says, "did you meet her before or after your injury?"

"Before, but we didn't start dating until after my injury."

"They were best friends for over twenty years before that," I chime in.

Mark mutters something under his breath. I grin. This is going better than I'd hoped.

"So is it fair to say that this woman – what's her name?" Bill asks.

"Charlie. Her name is Charlie."

"Is it fair to say she knows you pretty well?"

He swallows. "Yes."

"And you didn't start dating until after your injury," Bill continues. Mark nods. "Were you concerned she didn't fully understand the extent of your injuries?"

"Oh, no, she knew all about them," I pipe up. "She was a battlefield medic, so she understood more than most. She dropped everything to go stay with him in Texas for three months when he was hurt. Never left his bedside. She moved him home with her to recover. She even remodeled her house to accommodate his physical needs."

"You know, you don't have to be quite so helpful," Mark grumbles through gritted teeth.

"That's where you're wrong. I'm betting I'll never get you to set foot in here again, and I'm trying to get you to see what a colossal dumbass you're being, so full disclosure is critical."

The redheaded woman looks at him. "I'm Carrie, by the way."

"Hi, Carrie," Mark says, looking more unsettled by the second.

"So what would be different in your relationship with Charlie if you still had both legs?"

He stares at her like she's crazy. "I beg your pardon?"

"What would be different? You have a prosthetic, right? So you can functionally do the majority of the things you could before. So what can't you do?"

"If I still had both of my legs, I wouldn't look like a damn cyborg when I wear shorts. I wouldn't go to bed with a metal peg sticking out of my shin. I wouldn't need rails in the bathroom or a bench in the shower. I wouldn't be self-conscious because there wouldn't be a roadmap of scars all over my body. I wouldn't have to feel like a freak for not being like everyone else."

She studies him, her piercing blue eyes round behind tortoiseshell glasses. "And these things bother Charlie? She's so shallow that your scars and prosthetic leg bother her? Because if they do, then you're better off without her."

He shakes his head. "She wants me to get to the point where they don't bother me."

"So you feel she can't understand what it's like to feel broken and scarred."

He swallows hard and closes his eyes.

Fadeaway three-pointer at the buzzer for the win.

I look at him expectantly. "Are you going to tell them, or am I?"

Mark rubs his hand over his face. "Her scars are worse than mine," he admits. "Physically and emotionally. She was kidnapped and tortured in Afghanistan. They whipped her, branded her, beat her. Mutilated her. Raped her, with knives and pipes and God knows what else."

"Do her scars bother you?" Buck asks.

"What she went through breaks my heart," he answers immediately. "She was brutalized, and I'm glad we killed every one of those fuckers. But when I look at Charlie, I don't see her scars. I just see her."

"Then why don't you trust her to just see you?" David asks quietly.

He pauses. "I do, but she deserves to be with someone she doesn't have to look past."

"So the problem isn't that Charlie's shallow," says a statuesque African-American woman with a prosthetic leg. "I'm Sheila," she adds. "The problem is that you're shallow."

Mark gapes at her, his mouth falling open. "Excuse me?"

"You said if you had two legs, you could wear shorts and not look like a freak, and you'd still be with her. If you'd throw away your relationship because you don't like the way you look in shorts now, you must not have loved her very much."

"I loved her more than life itself," he says quietly. "I still do. I love her enough to let her go."

I hold my breath. It's the first time he's admitted that he's in love with Charlie.

It really sucks that the first time he says those words, it's to a group of strangers.

"Let her go? Go what?" Buck demands. "What is it you want her to go do? Spend her life alone after the man she loved dumped her because his 'special leg' had a boo-boo? Settle down with some douchebag just because he has two legs? What exactly was your goal here?"

The silence is deafening. Mark drops his head into his hands for several seconds before raising his eyes to find every single person watching him.

"It sounds stupid when we say it out loud, doesn't it?" Carrie asks, scrutinizing him with those penetrating blue eyes.

He sighs heavily. "Charlie is amazing. She deserves someone equally amazing."

"Does she deserve happiness?" Sheila asks intently.

"Yes."

"Does she deserve a man who loves her?"

"Yes."

"Even though she's scarred and broken?" she asks pointedly.

"Especially because she's scarred and broken. She's been through hell already. I want her to be happy and loved."

"Mark, Charlie was happy and loved with you," I say quietly. "The only person making an issue of your injuries is you."

Buck leans forward. "Son, battle wounds don't change who you are on the inside. Your body is just the outer shell for your mind, your spirit, your heart. You could lose every one of your limbs and still be you. You'd just be you in a different shell. If this woman is as wonderful as you say and she loves you, you'd be a fool to let her go."

The drive back to Mark's apartment is silent. I pull up and leave the motor running, grabbing his forearm when he reaches for the door handle.

"You can be pissed if you want, brother. I know I blindsided you, but you'd never have gone if I'd asked. You need to stop and think before you throw away the best thing that's ever happened to either of you, all because of some dumbass notion you've got stuck in your head."

"I'll see you Monday, Tucker," Mark says wearily, climbing out of the truck.

I watch him slowly walk inside and close the door before I pull out of his driveway.

CHAPTER EIGHT

CHARLIE

AFTER LILA DROPS ME off from shopping, I shower and run a comb through my damp hair. I examine myself in the mirror again, surprised again by how quickly my shape is changing. I dress in sweatpants and a baggy shirt and put away my new clothes. I smile as butterfly sensations spiral through my abdomen. "I'll feed you guys in a minute," I promise.

I settle on my overstuffed sofa in front of the television with a grilled ham and cheese sandwich and creamy red pepper soup, watching a movie by the glow of my Christmas tree. The movie is a sappy Christmas romance where two people fall madly in love and find their happily ever after over the holidays.

They don't make Christmas movies about lives like mine.

I nestle deeper into the couch as another movie begins. This one shows a man shopping, talking to the saleswoman destined to become his love interest.

My thoughts turn to Mark, and I wonder what he'll do for Christmas. Probably sit alone in his apartment. He knows I spend the holidays with Lila and Tucker, and he sure as hell won't want to see me.

The thought of him alone at Christmas saddens me. Regardless of how things stand between us now, Mark deserves to be with people who care about him, and even though he's written me out of his life, there's one gift I still owe him.

I go to the bookcase below the window, retrieving my photo album. I flip through it until I locate the photo I want. It's the picture of Mark with his mom, taken a month or so before she died of cancer. She's wearing her pink scarf on her head and smiling at Mark with so much love, it's palpable even through the camera lens. It's his favorite picture, but he doesn't have a copy.

He deserves one.

My eyes land on my favorite picture of us, the one Tucker snapped when I first arrived on base, when Mark picked me up and spun me around.

I pull it from the album, scrutinizing it. I'm holding Mark's face between my hands, and we're looking at each other like we've each found cool water in a scorching desert. Our expressions are nearly identical to those in the photo Tucker took of us kissing in the woods this past summer. Looking at our faces now, I can clearly see what he and I missed all along. We were in love with each other, even then. We were just too blind to see it.

My thoughts turn reflective, a common occurrence since I found out about the babies.

I'm almost nineteen weeks pregnant, and Mark has been gone for eleven weeks. I count back and realize I got pregnant shortly after we became intimate. I'm glad, because the most critical window for my drinking to damage my babies' development was before he left me. Miraculous protection for my miracle babies – protection from me and my destructive coping mechanisms.

I was angry at Mark when he left – angry, hurt, and confused. Angry because he betrayed my trust. Hurt because he rejected me. Confused because I didn't understand his abrupt one-eighty after that night he made me feel cherished. Alcohol was my automatic response because it dulled my pain. But it didn't relieve my anger, and I never directed my anger at its true source: Mark.

I did the same thing after Afghanistan. I didn't direct my anger at its true source then either, although in fairness, the offenders were dead. Instead, I turned my anger inward, condemning myself for not being strong enough to fight off my attackers. It was only this past summer, years later, that I realized I'd fought back in every way I could. I finally understood that although they'd physically bested me through brute strength and numbers, I still triumphed because I never stopped fighting. I'm learning I can let that battle go. I can step out of fight mode and claim victory because I survived. I'm learning that it's okay to move forward.

When Mark left, I didn't direct my anger at him, either.

Sure, we argued the night before he moved out, and I'm glad, because at least I verbalized part of what I felt before he ghosted me. But after he left, I didn't speak of my anger toward him. Perhaps I was afraid acknowledging it might prevent him from coming back. And in some ways, it felt disloyal to be angry with him after everything he'd done for me in the past.

Once again, I directed all my anger, blame, and condemnation inward. Even before he left, I was blaming myself. In our final conversation, I told him

I didn't understand what I'd done to drive him to end things with me. He'd insisted I'd done nothing wrong, but I didn't believe him.

My default mode seems to be self-blame and self-anger. But anger can only carry you so far, and slowly, I'm healing.

It isn't my fault Mark left.

I can say that now with certainty. It isn't my fault Mark left me.

Time has given me perspective. Mark left me because he's wrestling his own demons. Body insecurities that he's never dealt with drove his decisions. Because of his self-loathing, he believed – and likely still believes – that he was doing what was best for me, however faulty his logic. His actions stemmed from his inability to recognize his own self-worth. He'd seemed better for a while, but once he had his osseointegration surgery, he reverted to hating his changed body.

Not only has time given me perspective, it's healing my wounds.

The feelings of intense loss have faded. When I stopped drinking to numb my pain, I was forced to face it. The babies have helped tremendously with that because I've had to shift my focus. Wallowing in pain is no longer an option. I have to get better so I can be the mother they deserve.

I haven't given up hope Mark will come to his senses. I'm not sure I'll ever completely extinguish that hope, because I know I'll always love him. But the jagged wound in my heart is slowly scarring over, becoming less raw with each passing day.

I turn off the television and make my way to bed, still thinking about Mark. I wonder how he is. I wonder if he feels the loss of our relationship now that he's living alone. Like me, he tends to bottle up his feelings. I doubt he discussed them when he lived with Lila and Tucker. He probably suspected they wouldn't have been terribly sympathetic, given the circumstances. Now he's isolated, with no one to discuss them with, even if he wanted to.

I don't want Mark to be miserable. I want him to heal his emotional wounds, to be healthy and whole. He deserves to be happy, even if he doesn't find that happiness with me.

I roll onto my side, praying for one brief second that he's just miserable enough to realize he loves me before it's too late.

MARK

When I was sixteen, I was crazy about Charlie. I loved everything about her – the sun-kissed golden brown hair that fell to her waist, the scent of vanilla body wash that clung to her and hung in the air after she left a room, and the short denim shorts she wore that bared her long, colt-like legs. I loved the way she bit her lip when she'd struggled to balance equations in chemistry and furrowed her brow when she'd erase an algebra error and try again. I loved the way she'd sing off-key with the radio and dance her heart out in the basement with me where no one could see. I'd have done anything to make her mine.

But I was an orphan, living with her family, and that made it impossible.

Looking back now, I don't think her parents would have kicked me out if they'd known I'd fallen for Charlie, but they'd certainly have had reservations about having us under the same roof – especially if they had any idea of the thoughts I entertained about their daughter.

So I hid my infatuation with their innocent green-eyed beauty and instead, worked my way through an astonishing number of high school girls. I was on the football team, and there was no shortage of females who desired the status of dating a star athlete.

I distinctly remember the night my secret obsession with Charlie turned into private drama.

It was my junior year, and I was in the basement with my latest conquest. The Emersons had turned their furnished basement into my own little apartment. They respected my need for both family and privacy. It wasn't fancy, but it had everything I needed. It was late, way past curfew, and I'd snuck my current girlfriend in. I can't remember her name – Lacey, Stacy, Casey – something like that. We were making out on my couch, and things were getting hot and heavy.

Then I moaned Charlie's name.

I remember getting the shit slapped out of me. It took me a minute to figure out what I'd done to warrant a face-numbing smack like that. Then Lacey/ Stacy/ Casey/ whatever her name was straightened her clothes and stomped out of the house. By Monday, everyone knew we'd broken up, but she never told anyone why. Presumably, admitting I'd called her another girl's name in the heat of the moment would have been humiliating. I certainly didn't tell anyone, least of all, Charlie. Lacey/ Stacy/ Casey moved on to another football player, and I moved on to my next flavor-of-the-month, careful to call all of them "Babe" from that day on.

All because I couldn't admit out loud how I felt about Charlie.

Nineteen years later, I still can't.

CHARLIE

My phone rings the next morning as I'm sipping hot tea after breakfast. It's Tom. "I have a forty-pound problem. Can I come over?"

"Of course." I hang up, meeting him at my door when he knocks a few minutes later.

"What's wrong?" I ask. My eyes fly to the emaciated dog cowering as far from Tom as her leash will allow. She's medium-sized, with silky white and brown fur, copper-colored speckles scattered across her chest, and brown eyes that quickly scan my entryway for danger.

"This is Penny," Tom says. "Her previous owner abused her. I brought her home to foster, but she's terrified of me. The shelter owner's a friend of mine, and she warned me Penny was skittish around men, but I've fostered abused dogs before. She's fine with Maya and Bella, but she hides from me and cowers whenever I speak. Maya had to leash her up and put her in the car just so I could bring her over. I was hoping she could stay with you until the shelter reopens tomorrow."

"Come on in." I take the leash from him. "I wondered what you meant by a forty-pound problem. Go hang out in the living room while I meet her."

I take Penny to Mark's old room, his lingering scent assaulting me as soon as I walk in. I close the door behind us and sit in the floor a few feet from the trembling dog, speaking softly.

"Hi, sweet girl." My voice is gentle as I tuck her leash under my leg, keeping my hands in plain view. Her discomfort gradually fades, and she sits, maintaining her distance but no longer openly terrified. I speak quietly to her, and after several minutes, I place my hand flat on the floor for her to sniff. The dog hesitantly leans forward, ducking back a couple of times before snuffling me. She gives me a quick lick before flinching and darting away, her head low.

Anger rises inside me as I recognize her fear of being hit. I fight the urge to find her asshole owner and make him quail in fear.

"Good girl," I say softly instead, encouraging her forward again. Penny inches closer, crawling on her belly, and I reach forward and unclip the leash, then very lightly stroke her neck beside the collar. "Such a pretty girl." I pull my hand away, not wanting to frighten her, and continue to speak soothingly as I text Tom to bring puppy treats. I hear him outside the door a moment later. Penny watches warily, but I open it just far enough to grab the package. I return to the floor, opening the package and holding it out for her to catch the scent. She lifts her head, sniffing curiously.

"Food motivation makes this easier for both of us." I hold out a treat in my palm, frowning at her knobby spine and bony hips. I have no tolerance for people who mistreat animals or children.

"We're a lot alike, Penny." She cautiously takes the soft biscuit and wolfs it down, looking back toward the bag. "Too skinny and in need of healing. Think you could hang out here?" I give her another one.

I open my hand closer to me with each successive treat, convincing her to step nearer for each one until she stands directly in front of me, solely focused on the snacks. I feed her one final treat and close the package. She eyes it expectantly.

I smile. "No more," I tell her, holding out my empty hand. Penny sniffs it, then rewards me with a lick and lays down, thumping her tail once. I stroke her side with gentle fingers, then take a picture of us and text it to Tom.

After another minute, I get to my feet, and Penny gets up as well. "Sit," I tell her, and she obeys. I slip into the hall and close the door.

Tom's pacing back and forth in my living room. "She's really okay?"

I grin. "She's fine. She can stay."

"I can get her tomorrow morning, or I'll get Liz to come pick her up."

"Is she available for adoption?" I ask impulsively.

Tom beams, and I narrow my gaze suspiciously. "You planned this."

He chuckles and raises his hands. "Yes and no. I did think Penny would be perfect for you, but I'd planned to foster her first before seeing if you wanted to adopt her. I wasn't expecting her to panic every time I opened my mouth." He frowns. "I'd like to beat the hell out of her former owner."

"You and me both."

"I have her stuff in the car. Can I bring it in?"

I nod. "I'll help."

Tom glances over and chuckles as we walk down my steps. "Your baby bump is growing."

I look down. "I don't understand. It went from looking like I was bloated to looking like I'm smuggling a volleyball in less than two weeks."

He grins. "Give it a couple of months."

"Wonderful," I say glumly. "Because what's better than looking like you've shoved a basketball under your shirt when you're hoping the man you love will realize he loves you, too?"

"There's nothing more beautiful than a pregnant woman to the father of her baby. Trust me. It's..." Tom pauses. "Breathtaking."

I glance at him dubiously. Stretch marks and swollen ankles might indeed be breathtaking, but probably not in a good way. "If you say so."

Tom brings in Penny's belongings, not letting me carry anything except her bowls and a plush bed. I roll my eyes. "What is it with you and Tucker? I'm not an invalid."

"Of course not," he says kindly. "I'm just being respectful of your motherly state."

I snort. "Motherly state?"

He grins his boyish grin. "Would you prefer I call it your 'knocked-up condition'?"

We both laugh before he shoves his hands in his pockets. "I need to get back. Maya's waiting for me to take her Christmas shopping for her mom."

I tilt my head as I look up at him. "What do you buy a supermodel for Christmas?"

"Usually jewelry or a scarf, something one of a kind. She's impossible to please, though. Whatever we give her, she says, 'This would be perfect if it just blah blah blah– ', meaning, it's not good enough as it is." He sighs. "It doesn't bother me, but it hurts Maya's feelings."

The more I learn about Chele, the less I like her. "Why don't you tell her it upsets Maya?"

"I have. Repeatedly. She and I fight about it every visit. She insists she should be able to be honest. I say she should be gracious because Maya puts a lot of effort into trying to find the perfect gift. It's like arguing with a brick wall. She's never going to change." He sighs again. "Maybe we should just get some mass-produced crap, since she's going to complain anyway."

"Give her a jar of wrinkle cream. A really big jar. Make sure it says something in bold letters about minimizing crow's feet," I suggest, and he bursts out laughing. "Hey, if she's going to bitch either way, give her a good reason."

"I'll keep that in mind for a stocking stuffer."

When he leaves, I open the door to Mark's room. Penny's lying exactly where I left her. "Good girl." I pat my leg, and she trots after me as I lead her through the house, introducing her to her new surroundings and putting out food and water. She freezes at the foot of the staircase when I start upstairs. I look back and return to the main level. "We'll save the upstairs for another time. You've had a pretty big week."

I sit down to make a grocery list with my new furry friend perched atop my feet. Sundays are when I shop and cook a few things for the week ahead. That way, if I'm too tired to cook, dinner's already taken care of. I jot a few things down and get up to poke through my cupboards and fridge. When I'm finished, I text Lila. "Headed to the store. Need anything?"

"Wait for us. We're going too," she replies.

I grab my coat and take Penny out to explore the backyard while I wait. She's completely different outside. No longer timid, she bounds around the fenced-in yard, investigating every corner before finally squatting to pee. I'm relaxing in a chair watching her when Lila drives up. "I'm around back," I call.

Lila and Tucker appear from the side of the house, and Penny pauses uncertainly. "It's okay," I soothe her.

Lila gasps when she sees her. "She's beautiful," she breathes.

"Tom dropped her off this morning," I explain. "He took her home to foster, but she's been abused, and she was terrified of him."

Both Lila and Tucker stay outside the fence, with Tucker squatting down and turning his side to her, making himself seem less threatening.

"Hi, Beautiful," Lila coos. Penny perks up her ears. "What's her name?"

"Penny."

"She's gorgeous," Tucker says, his voice intentionally soft.

Lila kneels and places her open palm against the fence. "Such a pretty girl," she says in that same sing-song voice.

"You never talk that sweet to me," Tucker replies, imitating her tone.

"You haven't been mistreated," Lila says, keeping her tone consistently light.

Tucker grins, a sarcastic comment at the ready, but Lila continues, "Not yet, anyway. Isn't that right, Pretty Girl?"

Penny makes her way to the fence, hesitating several times, studying them both. Tucker places his hand flat on the ground near the fence but avoids eye contact. After several minutes, Panny nervously moves in, giving Lila's hand a quick sniff before jumping back. Lila continues to speak in her reassuring tone, as does Tucker, and a few moments later, Penny returns, sniffing Lila's hand for a longer time before nosing against it through the fence. She leans over and gingerly snuffles near Tucker's hand as well, lingering longer. He slowly edges his hand closer, and she continues sniffing before finally lifting her head and trotting back to me.

I reward her with a head rub. "Good girl. Come on in." Tucker and Lila open the gate as I lead Penny back inside. She pads down the hall to Mark's room and curls up beside his bed, right where she'd waited for me before.

"I see she's claimed her spot," Tucker says.

"That's where I took her when Tom arrived. I guess she feels safe there. She wouldn't go upstairs."

"Maybe she's never been around steps," Lila says. "She'll get used to them."

I follow Tucker and Lila to the grocery store, where we shop side by side, chatting and filling our carts. Lila keeps sneaking things into my buggy.

"I see where Tucker gets it from," I mutter.

"What?" she asks innocently.

"After he took me to the doctor, we stopped for groceries, and he kept adding things to my cart. I told him he was channeling you."

Lila makes a face. "I still can't believe you told *him* you were pregnant before you told me," she grumbles, glaring at Tucker.

"Don't be mad at Tucker. It's not his fault. Or mine, really." I lay a hand over my heart and affect a pious expression. "I was following Willow's advice — you know, the therapist you encouraged me to see. She advised me to share important things with people I trust. So really," I muse, "it's your fault for sending me to her. I was merely trying to further my recovery."

Lila rolls her eyes. "You did not just play the therapy card."

Tucker jumps on board. "I could tell that's what Charlie was doing. You know, sharing and being vulnerable. Frankly, as her sister-from-another-mister, you should be more supportive."

Lila scowls at him. "You don't really think I'm buying that crap, do you?"

"Did it work?"

"Not even remotely."

I glance at Tucker. "I tried."

He grins. "Admirable effort."

We finish our shopping and check out. I'm putting my groceries in my car when I recognize a figure out of the corner of my eye.

It's *Mark.*

The bag slips from my hands, its contents spilling out into my cart.

He's walking up the parking lot, *walking*, without crutches. My hands fly to my mouth as I stare, transfixed. He's wearing faded jeans and his black leather jacket, and his sandy hair curls slightly at the nape of his neck.

He's never looked better.

Unable to stop myself, I abandon my cart and walk toward him.

He raises his eyes when he notices me moving his direction. I see the instant he recognizes me, because he stiffens and halts abruptly.

I stop, too.

He's close enough for me to see the expression in his eyes. It's the same look Penny had when she first saw Lila and Tucker, trying to decide whether to flee or move closer.

I wait silently. The choice is his, and no soothing words from me will help.

"What about the rest of your stuff, Charlie?" I hear Lila ask behind me. Then she sees Mark and gasps, recognizing the magnitude of this moment.

Mark stands rooted in place, thirty feet from me, our eyes locked. I'm afraid to breathe. Afraid to hope.

I raise my right fist to my chest and thump twice over my heart, my eyes never leaving his. It's our sign for I love you, a signal we've used for over twenty years.

Mark lifts a fist toward his own chest and takes a half step toward me.

Then he stops. A shadow falls over his eyes, and he tightens his jaw. He drops his hand to his side and turns, stalking to his van and racing out of the parking lot.

The vicious wrenching in my heart is so painful, it nearly brings me to my knees. My intense pain is followed by an excruciating realization.

Mark's never coming back.

Never.

TUCKER

I watch Mark from across the parking lot, his gaze focused on Charlie. Tension radiates from his posture. I'm praying he's come to his senses, that the wounded vets we talked with yesterday got through to him.

Then he turns away, leaving Charlie standing there, shattered.

Again.

Her shoulders slump. I want to chase him down and shake him until he comes to his senses. Instead, I load her groceries into her car. She stands unmoving, staring at the spot where Mark had stood. "Charlie?" I place my hands on her shoulders. "Give me your keys. I'll drive you home."

She hands me her keys wordlessly, climbing into the passenger seat of her own vehicle. I tell Lila what I'm doing before sliding into Charlie's car. I pull out of the parking lot and turn toward her house before resting my hand on her shoulder.

"I spent all day yesterday with him, Charlie. He's miserable without you."

Her voice is quiet. "No, Tucker, he's not, but I have been. Miserable. Angry at his betrayal. Hurt by his rejection. Confused about what I did to make him abandon me. I know he's fighting his own demons. I know he truly believes he's half a man. I was willing to overlook a lot because of that, but the way he's treated me... even if he didn't want to be lovers any more, he should have at least been civil after everything we've been through. He knew I was barely hanging on, knew I was drinking, even knew I was vomiting blood, but he never once checked on me. He won't come to the door, won't answer my calls, and won't respond to my texts. He won't even speak to me in a parking lot. He couldn't be any more clear about his feelings, and I'm done."

I glance at her resigned expression. "What does that mean?"

"I'm letting him go. I'm going to file for sole custody. I'll have an attorney draw up the papers. He won't have the liberty of ignoring them."

My heart sinks at the finality in her voice. Mark's fucked up the best thing he ever had and lost her forever.

I carry Charlie's groceries into her house without a word of protest from her. She follows me silently, sinking onto a barstool at her counter, staring into space. She's pale, her eyes haunted, and I'm powerless to help.

Lila arrives in a spray of gravel, having dumped our grocery bags on our counter to race back to Charlie. I meet her outside. "I'll take care of the groceries and be back later." She nods, heading straight to Charlie.

At home, I put away our food, growing angrier by the second. I was positive yesterday's visit to the VFW would bring Mark to his senses. Apparently not.

It's been hit after hit after hit for Charlie, and she doesn't need his bullshit, especially not now. I recall her lifeless expression, and my temper boils.

Charlie's not the only one who's done.

I speed down the road, tires squealing as I whip into Mark's driveway and skid to a halt. I knock firmly and see him glance out, hesitating before opening the door.

"Look, Tucker," he says wearily, "I don't want to talk about it."

I shove past him, back-kicking his door closed.

"Good, because I'm not here to listen to your bullshit." I grab the front of Mark's shirt firmly in my left hand. He looks down in surprise right before I throw one solid punch, connecting hard with his left cheekbone. His head snaps back, and he stumbles, but I maintain my grip on his shirt to keep him from falling, releasing him only when he's fully regained his balance.

"I've tried to stay neutral," I growl. "I've tried to let you work shit out for yourself. I've tried to push you in the right direction, even when you obviously didn't want to be pushed. But I'm done, Mark, and so is Charlie. Today was the last straw. You took something beautiful and rare and precious, and you threw it away. You rejected her, not just once, but every time she's reached out to you. You were everything to each other, and you fucking abandoned her because she told you she loved you?" I shake my head in disbelief. "She would have forgiven your sorry ass until that stunt you just pulled. I want you to remember this day for the rest of your life, Mark, because *today* is the day you lost everything, not the day you left her. And the saddest part is, you have no goddamn idea how much you've lost, because you can't be bothered to talk to her."

I spin on my heel and walk out, slamming the door behind me and leaving Mark with a rapidly swelling face and a desolate expression.

CHARLIE

I stand in my kitchen, putting groceries away with Penny pressed against my leg. Lila takes a package from me and puts it down before reaching for me. I stand frozen as she hugs me, unable to move and unwilling to feel. Feeling hurts too much.

"Talk to me, Charlie," Lila says worriedly, pulling back to look at me.

"I'm done," I say softly. "Mark won't answer my calls, reply to my texts, or come to his door. He literally fled a parking lot to avoid me. Every time I reach out, he slaps me away." I square my shoulders. "I'm getting a custody lawyer. They can tell him about the babies."

"Charlie, no," she protests. "Not like that. He needs to hear it from you."

"I've tried, Lila, and every single time, he rejects me all over again."

"Then let one of us tell him," she pleads.

I shake my head firmly. "No. I won't have you guys stuck in the middle any longer. He can find out from a neutral third party."

"At least think about it for a little while," Lila begs. "Don't make any rash decisions. Please, Charlie." She grabs my hands and squeezes them until I look at her.

"Fine," I relent. "I'll wait a few days to see an attorney, but it will take a miracle to change my mind at this point."

"They're miracle babies. Maybe you'll get another miracle."

But my decision is made. I'm done waiting for Mark to pull his head out of his ass. When I'm finally alone, I research local family law attorneys and download the necessary forms.

CHAPTER NINE

MARK

I SIT ALONE ALL afternoon and evening on my lumpy loveseat in my crappy little apartment, getting drunk. Not just a little drunk, either. I want to be so drunk I can't remember my name.

Because if I can't remember that, maybe I can forget the rest of it, too. There are so many things I want to forget.

Like Charlie's look of stunned disbelief when I told her I was ending things, all because she'd fallen in love with me.

Or the anguish in her broken voice when she said she didn't understand what she'd done to drive me away.

Or the agony in her beautiful green eyes when she pleaded with me to tell her I loved her, and I remained silent.

And then today, the gut-wrenching pain on her face as I rejected her again.

I didn't want to. When she'd made our sign for "I love you," and thumped twice over her heart, I'd automatically started to respond in kind, because I do love her, more than life itself. But my brain jerked a knot in my ass, reminding me sharply that Charlie deserves a man who is whole, and that's not me.

That'll never be me.

So I'd turned and walked away, but not before her stricken expression gutted me.

Maybe if I get drunk enough, I'll be able to forget the way the memories of her smile and her touch haunt me nearly as much as her tears.

I'd thought the physical pain following my injury was bad. The phantom pains were even worse. But this emotional anguish is a neverending torment of my own making, because I walked away from the only woman I'll ever love.

At the time, I thought my reasoning was sound. I wanted Charlie to have the best. God knows she deserves it after everything she's fought through. I was convinced she deserved to be with someone who didn't have to bolt on an artificial leg every morning, someone able-bodied, someone who could physically do anything she wanted.

It wasn't that I didn't love her. It was *never* that I didn't love her.

It was that I loved her enough to want what was best for her, and I thought that meant an able-bodied man. I only told her I didn't love her because I knew she'd never accept my able-bodied argument.

Now I'm not sure my reasoning is as airtight as I'd believed, especially after meeting with the amputees at the VFW. If anyone should have agreed with me, it would have been other amputees who could truly understand my perspective. Instead, they basically told me I was a dumbass. Tucker and Lila have called me one outright, and Charlie – well, I don't recall her using that specific word, but the takeaway message was the same.

In the military, I'd occasionally see desk-jockey officers create grand plans that were doomed from the start. They were too disconnected from the reality of the front lines, but no amount of polite disagreement or calm logic could dissuade them. They taught me a valuable lesson. When multiple intelligent people reach a conclusion that completely contradicts your own, perhaps it's you who's mistaken, not everyone else.

Maybe I'm the one that's wrong.

Maybe I've been wrong all along.

And now I don't know what to do.

What I want to do is go straight to Charlie and beg her forgiveness. But I've waited too long, and I've hurt her too much. That door is closed.

So in my drunken state, I do the next best thing.

I glance at my phone and realize it's just past eight at night, though it feels much later. At least, I'm pretty sure it's nighttime. I frown and pull the blinds away from the window, seeing a darkened sky.

Yep, still night.

I text Lila. "I need help. Can you come over?"

That's what I'd intended to type, anyway, but when I blearily reread it after hitting send, it has several more letters than it ought to.

She answers quickly, apparently able to decipher my gibberish. "OMW."

She arrives minutes later, and I stagger to the door when she knocks, far more intoxicated than I'd realized. "Hang on," I mumble, trying to maintain my balance using walls and furniture that mysteriously keep shifting. I eventually reach the door and unlock the deadbolt, but I can't get the chain to cooperate.

"Close the door before you unlatch the chain, dumbass," comes Tucker's voice.

He's right. I am a dumbass.

"Hey, Tucker," I say, tripping over my words. "I didn't know you were coming."

"You said you needed help. We thought you might be hurt. Do you want me to leave?"

I push the door shut and fumble with the chain, shaking my head no. Then I remember Tucker can't see me through the door. "You can stay," I say, finally unchaining it and yanking the door open. The momentum causes me to lose my balance, and I stumble backwards. Tucker rushes to catch me before I hit the ground.

"Jesus, Mark," he mutters. "How much have you had to drink?" He hoists me upright, gripping my arm to steady me.

"Not enough." Even I can hear the slurring of my words.

Lila closes the door and turns, gasping when she sees my face. I sort of saw it in the mirror earlier. Reddish-purple bruising mars my left cheekbone and eye socket. My cheek is puffy, and my eye is swollen shut.

She beelines straight to me. "Did you fall? Do you need to go to the hospital?"

I shake my head. "I didn't fall. Tucker caught me."

"Not just now. Did you fall earlier?" She sounds exasperated.

"He caught me then, too. Didn't you tell her?"

"Tell me what?" she asks, turning to Tucker.

"I did that," he admits. "Charlie was devastated, and I lost my temper. I came over and... well, I held onto his shirt so he wouldn't fall, but I did punch him once in the face."

Charlie was devastated.

All I do is hurt her.

Lila whirls back around to examine me, her movement so fast it leaves trails in my vision, and I blink. "Let me check," she says, palpating my cheek and eye socket with her fingers. Pain surges at her touch, and I pull back. "Stand still," she scolds. "I'm feeling for fractures."

"It hurts," I complain.

"That was the point," Tucker mutters, still holding me upright.

Lila glares at him. "I'll deal with you later." She turns back to me. "I don't feel any broken bones. How's your vision?"

"It was fine before my eye swelled shut."

"Can you open it enough to make sure it's still alright?"

I pry it open a bit, wincing, but nod. "I can see."

"Then go sit down before you fall. I'm getting you some ice."

"The icemaker doesn't work," I mumble as Tucker steers me across the room.

"Then you can make do with frozen peas," she says, wrapping a bag in a clean kitchen towel and pressing it to my face. I wince again. "Hold it there."

"You're bossy," I tell her grumpily.

She shrugs. "Tough shit. You're the one who drunk-texted a medic."

Tucker helps me to the loveseat before sitting cross-legged on the floor. "I'd avoid the couch," he warns her. "There's a rogue spring." She chooses a spot beside me on the loveseat instead, turning sideways to face me.

"How drunk are you, Mark?"

"Pretty damn drunk," I answer, "but not drunk enough, because I still hurt." I turn to look for my whiskey bottle, but Lila spots it first and moves it out of reach.

Damn, she's quick.

"You said you needed help," she reminds me.

I nod. "Yeah. I need help."

Lila waits for me to say more, but I just sit there. She looks helplessly at Tucker.

"Let's start with coffee. If that doesn't work, I'll throw his ass in a cold shower," he says, heading for my tiny kitchen.

"The shower's always cold," I grumble. "The hot water only works for two minutes."

"Perfect," Tucker replies as he brews coffee. "Then Plan B for sobering up your sorry ass is fully operational."

Lila turns back to me. "What kind of help do you need, Mark?"

I sit there for a long time before dropping my head into my hands. "I've fucked everything up, Lila," I say quietly. "And I don't know how to fix it."

She studies me carefully. "I'm not sure how much of what you're saying is drunken regret and how much is actual insight. What do you want?"

"I want Charlie," I say despondently. "It's always been Charlie. It always will be."

"Then why did you throw it away?" she demands. "You had Charlie. You both had everything you ever wanted, and you ripped it apart with your bare hands."

I shake my head in despair. "I wanted her to have the best. She deserves the best. And that's not me."

"It was you," she says sadly. "She's never loved anyone but you."

"But she deserves someone able-bodied. Someone who can do whatever she wants. Someone who doesn't have to screw on a fake leg every morning."

"Didn't you listen to anything those guys at the VFW said?" Tucker returns, handing me a cup of black coffee. "Don't spill it. It's hot."

"The VFW?" Lila asks.

He sighs. "I found an amputee support group and dragged him to it yesterday while you and Charlie were shopping. I told them I was there so they could help him pull his head out of his ass. Clearly, it didn't help."

"You said more than that," I mumble. "He told them I said people who are scarred and broken don't deserve love."

Lila's eyes widen.

"You did say that," Tucker points out. "It was your bullshit reason for throwing away the best thing that ever happened to you."

"I was talking about me, not her. And I told them that, too. And then they all told me I was a dumbass for about an hour. But in a nice way," I add.

"You are a dumbass," Tucker says.

"You're not helping." Lila glowers at Tucker.

"But he's right," I tell her. "I was sure I was right, but I was wrong. And I've fucked everything up, and I don't know how to fix it."

"Drink your coffee," Lila orders. "I want you sober enough to remember this conversation later."

I meet her determined gaze. "I'll try, but I'm pretty drunk."

"Mark, if you don't come to grips with who you are, you'll never be the man Charlie deserves. It's not about your leg. It's about how you view yourself."

I close my eyes. "Easy for you to say. You don't know what it's like to be damaged goods."

Lila's temper blazes, and Tucker gives me a now-you're-in-for-it look.

"I don't understand being damaged? *I* don't understand it?" she snaps. "You do remember what I went through, right? Tied up and raped day and night for eleven goddamn days by more men than I could count? You think that doesn't damage someone? I was terrified, *terrified*, for the man I loved to touch me. Tucker deserved a woman who didn't flinch at his touch or try to stab him for putting his arms around her. He deserved someone who was sexually able-bodied. But Tucker chose me because he loved me, and Charlie chose you because she loved you. Your wounds may be more visible, but I was damaged, too. The difference is, I was smart enough to accept Tucker's love and get help. You should have been smart enough to do the same."

Lila's royally pissed, flinging her arms wide as she gestures wildly. She's right to be angry. I just diminished everything she fought through.

Fuck. I can't do or say anything right where the people I care about are concerned.

I sit silently with my head in my hands, then drain my coffee and hand the cup to Tucker. "Can you get me another one?" When he stands, I look at Lila.

"I'm sorry, Lila. I forget because you seem normal now. I'm sorry," I repeat.

She looks at her hands, her anger melting away. "I still have bad days. But I was willing to get help. If I hadn't, my relationship with Tucker couldn't have survived. I talked to two different people, one to deal with the trauma and another to help me accept intimacy again. Tucker and I saw her together so he could learn how to help me." She hesitates briefly. "You need to talk to someone. You saw a psychiatrist at Brooke, but you've been home for eight months, and your body image issues are destroying your life.

"Listen to me, Mark, because this is critical." She waits for me to focus on her. "If you don't find a way to fully accept yourself, the parts you like and the parts you don't, things will never work out between you and Charlie. The broken part of you that's destroying everything isn't your leg. It's that you fixate on what's missing and ignore everything that's still there."

"How does that help me with Charlie?" I ask, accepting more coffee from Tucker.

She pauses. "You and Charlie will be connected in some capacity for the rest of your lives. If you want any shot at repairing things, you have to be the best version of yourself. That means becoming emotionally healthy, because that's what she deserves."

"I don't even know how to start."

"Charlie and I discussed this months ago. I found a psychiatrist who specializes in wounded veterans with body image issues. He has a solid reputation."

That gets my attention. "You and Charlie talked about this?"

She nods. "When you went back to seeing yourself as a useless cripple again after your surgery. She thought it would help you deal with your self-loathing."

I sit quietly for long moments before turning to Tucker. "When you came by earlier, you said Charlie was done. What exactly did she say?"

He studies my expression. "You're sure you want to hear this?"

Whatever she said must be really bad. I hesitate, but nod anyway.

Tucker scrutinizes me. "She said even if you didn't want to be her lover anymore, you should have at least been civil. She said you knew she was barely hanging on, that she was vomiting blood, and you didn't care enough to check on her. She said you've ignored every call, every text, every knock. She said you'd made your feelings very clear, and she was done."

Lila quietly says, "Tucker," but Tucker shakes his head.

"No. I'm not going easy on him anymore." He turns to me, his eyes hard. "When I said you lost everything today, I meant it. I don't think you can undo the amount of damage you've done."

I lean back and rest my head on my lumpy loveseat, laying my arm across my eyes. The knot in my throat grows bigger by the second, and I fight back tears, knowing everything Tucker said is true, and I have no one to blame but myself.

"Give me the name of the psychiatrist."

LILA

I have no idea what to do.

After months of trying to get through to Mark, Charlie's surrendered. When he first left, she held out hope, trying to see him, calling, texting, but he flatly refused. It's hard for me to comprehend his behavior. From the first time I saw them together, it was obvious that they loved each other, and not just as friends. Neither of them realized it, though, and one of them is too fucking stubborn to admit it.

Mark's persistent cold-shoulder nearly destroyed Charlie, and nothing Tucker or I said or did helped. The only one who could've helped her refused to pull his head out of his own ass. Honestly, if she hadn't found out she was pregnant, the darkness might have won this time. It almost did once before, when we first came home, and the only thing that pieced her back together was Mark. Losing him might have been the only opening her darkness needed.

Those babies are miracles in more ways than one.

Today was the last straw. She'd have forgiven him until today. I'd never have shown as much faith in Tucker as she's shown in Mark. I'd have told him weeks ago to take his self-pity and go fuck himself. Not Charlie. She still trusted Mark, even when he kept proving he didn't deserve it.

The parking lot incident today changed that. She's done. Completely, totally done.

I heard a marriage counselor on a talk show say that men often leave a marriage impulsively. Not women, though. He said women will put up with their spouse's crap over and over. They ignore their pain and let things go and forgive and overlook until one day, they're done. Their absolute limit for bullshit has been reached, and no amount of desperate apologies, promises, or sweet words will change their minds.

Charlie's hit her absolute limit for Mark's bullshit.

When we left her house this evening, she was calm. Tucker and I stayed with her all afternoon. I roasted two chickens with new potatoes and cooked fresh green beans and a creamy bacon-tomato soup for dinner, and she's got plenty of leftovers for the next few days. Her shock at seeing Mark faded as the day went on, and she's resigned herself to moving forward alone.

Her haunted expression had eased before we left. "I'm going to take a shower and go to bed, Lila. I'm okay," she'd assured me, and though her eyes were still sad, there was quiet strength in her voice.

She's going to be okay. As harsh as it was, today gave her the closure she needed.

Not five minutes after we leave her, just as Tucker and I pull into our driveway, my phone buzzes with a drunk-text from Mark. "i meeeed hepp can y comne overt".

"Come over? Are you fucking kidding me? He'll be lucky if I don't knock his teeth out," I'd sworn when I'd showed Tucker the jumbled text. His jaw had tightened, but he'd turned around and driven to Mark's.

Mark's complete dumbassery has been particularly hard for Tucker. Mark was our platoon leader, and he was one of the best. We all knew we could trust him to make the right calls, to always have our backs. Watching him betray Charlie has left a sour taste in Tucker's mouth.

I didn't realize how sour until I saw Mark's face.

Tucker's punch didn't break any bones, but Mark's face looks terrible. His left eye is completely closed, and the entire socket is bright purple, all the way down his swollen cheek. If he weren't drunk off his ass, he'd be in a lot of pain, and Tucker's not the least bit sorry.

But Mark hasn't called me because he's injured and I'm a medic.

Nope. He called because he wants my help to get Charlie back.

It's all I can do not to punch the other side of his face.

First of all, he's so drunk, he's literally falling down. Tucker practically had to carry him to the sofa. In all the years I've known Mark, I've never seen him drunk, not once. He's rambling about how much he loves Charlie, but for all I know, he's just another weepy drunk who swears he's willing to do absolutely anything to make amends – until he sobers up.

No fucking way will I risk letting him anywhere near Charlie.

Instead, I put the ball squarely in his court. He's the one who fucked everything up. If he's serious about wanting to fix things, he needs to do the work. I tell him to see a psychiatrist and work out his body image issues. I tell him he needs to get emotionally healthy and be the best version of himself if he wants a chance at any relationship at all with Charlie.

Because there's the rub.

Mark doesn't know it yet, but they're always going to be connected because of their babies. Even if Charlie does file for sole custody, he's still going to be part of their lives, so he needs to get his shit together. She's got enough to deal with without worrying about his delicate male ego.

Because that's exactly what all his bullshit boils down to.

Mark needs to take responsibility for his actions instead of blaming everything on his leg. He's the one making crappy decisions. He may say it's because of his leg, but the truth is, it's all about his dainty little ego. Mark was comfortable being the perfect alpha male. Now that his body doesn't fit that image in his head, he's let his fragile ego destroy everything.

When he asks Tucker what Charlie said, Tucker tells him, and he doesn't soften the blow.

Every drop of color drains from Mark's face. He looks as agonized as Charlie did earlier. For the first time, I think it finally sinks in how badly he's fucked up. When Tucker tells him he can't undo the damage he's done to Charlie, Mark looks as though someone has died.

He asks for the psychiatrist's card, and though I'm afraid to hope, I wonder if hearing Charlie's words has finally broken through his shell of self-loathing.

He lays the card beside him and leans his head on the back of his horrible loveseat, his arm across his eyes. Right about the time I think he's finally grasped the magnitude of his actions and is ready to do whatever it takes to fix the mess he's made, he snores.

Loudly.

Goddammit.

He fucking passed out.

I shouldn't be as livid as I am. I knew he was drunk off his ass when we got here. The nearly empty bottle of whiskey can attest to that. But I'm so angry, I want to hurl it into the wall and shatter it into a thousand pieces.

What if he wakes up tomorrow and doesn't remember any of this?

What if he goes right back to his "half a man" nonsense?

I exhale sharply, looking at Tucker. "We need to put him to bed, but I don't think he should be alone. He'll fall if he tries to get up during the night."

Tucker's dark blue eyes are humorless. "I'm not staying in this rat hole."

I sigh. "Fine. I'll help get him in the truck."

"Perfect," Tucker mutters under his breath as we drag an unconscious Mark to his feet and haul him outside. "But if he pukes in my truck, I'm leaving his sorry ass on the side of the road."

CHARLIE

I'm lying in bed, emotionally and physically drained. But I have a new feeling: acceptance.

Mark's chosen a different path, and I'm moving forward alone.

It's not ideal, but I'll be okay. I've dealt with far worse. I can deal with this, too.

Soft cries filter up the stairs, intruding on my thoughts. I settled Penny in her plush puppy bed in Mark's old room, but she's whined incessantly since I came to bed. I've tried repeatedly to coax her upstairs, but she balks at the steps, and no amount of cajoling can persuade her. I'd hoped she would calm down, but her whimpers are intensifying, not easing.

I sigh and throw back my warm blankets. "Hang on, girl." As I descend the stairs, she darts into Mark's room, where his faint scent assaults my battered heart again.

Dammit. As soon as I smell his warm pine smell, pain pounds inside me like a war drum.

Penny wags enthusiastically at my arrival. I steel my heart as I glance around. Mark's neatly-made bed still stands untouched since his abrupt departure, and the sliding door to his bathroom is still ajar. I haven't cleaned in here since he left, and a thin layer of dust covers the surfaces. In the bathroom, cloudy drip lines mar the shower door and mirror.

I step back into his bedroom and pause.

No. This isn't Mark's room anymore.

He's moved on.

This is my house, and it's time to reclaim it.

I don't allow myself to dwell on Mark or the memories we made in this room. Instead, I strip the linens from the bed and run them through the washer twice, determined to erase all traces of his scent. I scrub the bathroom with citrus-scented cleaners, then do the same in the bedroom, polishing and dusting and vacuuming until all I smell is soothing orange oil. When my eyes fall on the chaise lounge, I feel a stab of anguish as I recall the times we made love there.

That chaise has to go.

Unfortunately, it's much too heavy for me to safely move in my condition.

I'd planned to sleep in here, but I can't look at that chaise. It holds too many memories. Since Penny won't climb my stairs, we end up in the living room.

I spend hours tossing and turning on the couch. Every time I change position, Penny noses my hand or face until I give her a reassuring pat. I'm up long before daylight, taking her outside before going upstairs to shower. I've made a decision during my sleepless night.

I'm moving into the downstairs bedroom.

I have a laundry list of solid reasons. Penny's clearly unwilling to go upstairs, and she's not comfortable being alone downstairs. Spending the night on the couch has left my pregnant body aching all over. I'm going to become increasingly front-heavy as my belly expands further, and traipsing up and down steep stairs without being able to see past my stomach adds an unnecessary degree of difficulty. Besides, the downstairs bedroom is the largest. There's plenty of room for a crib and changing table in the area currently occupied by that damn chaise.

The biggest reason for the move, though, is me.

I need to move on. I need to reclaim my space and push past my pain.

I *will* push past it. I have to, for my babies.

Once dressed, I gather clothes and toiletries, sorting them into neat stacks on my bed. I'm only collecting the basics; it's not like I'll need skinny jeans or cocktail dresses anytime soon. I'll ask Tucker and Tom to haul the chaise to the garage and move the monitor for the security cameras from my bedroom upstairs down to my new space.

I eat breakfast while watching the sunrise before heading to the clinic. I'm enjoying the quiet solitude when it occurs to me how much has changed in the past couple of days.

I have a new four-legged friend.

I'm choosing to be a single mom to my twins, an idea as terrifying as it is exciting.

Most of all, I've finally gotten closure. I've accepted Mark's unwavering decision, and I'm ushering his constant invisible presence out of my home.

An old song Colonel Sherman used to sing after too many beers runs through my head.

"There was a time when I thought of no other,
and we sang our own love's refrain.
Our hearts beat as one,
and we had our fun,
but time changes everything."

CHAPTER TEN

CHARLIE

LILA POKES HER HEAD cautiously into my office. "You're here early," she says, watching me closely, but for the first time in a long time, I'm okay. I've been trying to work my way through the piles of paperwork on my desk. It's bordering on unmanageable. Tara's covering my clients so I can play catch-up.

"These things breed at night." I gesture to the stacks of papers.

She frowns. "We really do need more help, you know? Someone to fill in the gaps. Filing, answering calls, dealing with insurance companies…"

"Scrubbing hydro tubs between clients, tidying at the end of the day, helping us launder the towels and massage blankets, ordering supplies," I add in agreement.

She looks thoughtful. "There's enough to keep someone busy full-time, don't you think?"

I nod. "More than enough, especially with Stubbs coming on board, too. Besides, look at how often we have to stay late or come in early."

"Or take invoices home to work on," she says, nodding pointedly at the overflowing folders stacked beside my laptop. "Besides, it won't be long until you're not able to do as much."

I frown. "I'll keep up."

She laughs. "Sure. I can see you now. Eight months pregnant with twins, on your knees scrubbing a tub or sitting in the floor sorting paperwork."

"I sort papers like a civilized adult," I say loftily. "I'm not a floor-sorting-Neanderthal like some people."

Lila sticks out her tongue and grabs a large stack of papers from my desk. She sinks cross-legged to the floor, graceful as always, and begins sorting them into piles. She's always preferred floor-filing, as she refers to it. "How did Penny do on her first night?"

"Okay, I think. She sticks to me like glue unless I go upstairs. When I went to bed last night, she cried until I came back downstairs."

She casts a worried glance in my direction. "You were awake all night?"

I deflect her question. "I stayed on the couch. I was going to see if you, Tuck, and Tom could help me for a few minutes after work."

"Of course. What's up?"

"I'm moving downstairs. It's a larger bedroom, and it won't be long before I'm too front-heavy to navigate the stairs safely. Plus, Penny won't go upstairs, and she cries without me. But I need the guys to move that chaise out. I can't look at it," I confess quietly.

She doesn't hesitate. "We'll be there."

Tom sidles in. "Hey," he greets us, then frowns at the reams of paper covering my desk and the floor. "The damn things multiply like rabbits."

"That's what I said," I agree. "Can I borrow your muscles for a few minutes after work?"

Lila chuckles as Tom grins and flexes one huge bicep. "Of course. What's up?"

"I need you and Tucker to move a chaise lounge to my garage. It's ridiculously heavy."

"Sure. I helped Tucker bring it in while you were in Texas." He studies my face, and I know he's wondering why I'm getting rid of it. "How's Penny?" he asks instead.

"She's good, except she's terrified of my staircase, and she cried the whole time I was upstairs. I stayed on the couch last night, and now I'm all achy, so I'm moving into the downstairs bedroom, but that chaise has to go." My words tumble out in a rush.

He reads my mood and steers to safer ground. "So you're still okay with keeping Penny?"

"Yes. What do I need to do to adopt her?"

Tom beams, rubbing his hands together like a proud father. "Let me call Liz. She can come here to fill out the paperwork. She'll want to see Penny anyway. What's your schedule like?"

"Tara's covering my massages so I can deal with this." I gesture to my barely-visible desk.

I hear Tom on the phone with the shelter owner as soon as he leaves my office. Lila continues sorting papers before faxing them to physicians' offices. I keep plugging away after she heads out to meet her first client. She's talked to Tucker, and we're all meeting at my house after work.

Tom's friend Liz comes by, and I officially adopt Penny after we go next door to check on her. Penny is relaxed, settling by my leg comfortably after calmly greeting Liz. She and I return to my office where I write her a check for more than the adoption fee.

Liz smiles. "Penny needed your energy. You two are a perfect match."

I think I need Penny as much as she needs me.

After work, the four of us head to my house. Penny waits by the door, wagging her tail as I let everyone in. Tom gives her a wide berth to avoid alarming her. Penny glances at him warily once or twice, but eventually lays down in the living room, observing the proceedings from a distance.

Tom and Tucker discuss the easiest path to haul the heavy chaise to my garage while Lila and I fill laundry baskets with my belongings and carry them downstairs. It only takes a couple of trips. She helps me put away clothes and toiletries while Tom and Tucker set up the security monitor on the console table inside the bedroom door. The entire event takes less than thirty minutes. When we finish, I smile gratefully.

"I'm buying dinner. Who wants what?"

"I can't stay," Tom says. "I need to take Maya to the bakery before they close. They're having a cookie swap at school. Raincheck?"

"Of course." I give him a quick hug. "Thanks, Tom."

I turn to Lila and Tucker. "What do you guys want?"

"We need a raincheck, too," Tucker apologizes. "Joey called and asked me to come by."

"We'll come over for dinner Friday, but we're buying." Lila purses her lips as she eyes me critically. "Chinese, I think. You need 'meat with green stuff and brown sauce' to fatten you up," she says, using my nickname for Chinese food.

"The whole point was to buy you dinner to thank you," I protest.

"Yeah, well, you're eating for three, so get over it."

They've barely pulled out of the driveway when my phone rings. I look down and smile before answering. "Hey, Stubbs."

"Hey, Green Eyes. Got a minute?"

"Sure. What's up?"

"Were you serious about letting me crash with you until I found a place?"

"Of course."

"Are you sure? It might be for about a month," he says doubtfully.

I smile. "That's not a problem."

"Even though it would be over the holidays?"

I laugh. "Yes, Stubbs, it's fine. You're welcome to stay, even if you do snore," I tease him. When he visited over the summer, we'd all taken a group camping trip deep in the mountains. Our quiet nights were frequently interrupted by jarring sounds not unlike a flock of geese being sucked into a jet engine. He'd insisted that something blooming in the woods had agitated his allergies, but

I knew better. He'd snored just as loudly in the guest room upstairs on the nights leading up to the camping trip.

"Here's the thing," he says, explaining that a tenant is moving out next week, but the new owner wants to quickly revamp the apartment before letting him move in. "She's updating all the apartments to make them disability-friendly, but I don't want to wear out my welcome with you if her contractors take too long."

I laugh again. "Seriously, it's fine. You've seen my house. There's plenty of room. Besides, we need you at the clinic. How soon do you think you'll be here?"

He hesitates. "That depends. How soon can you be ready for me?"

I roll my eyes. "Even if you're calling me from my driveway, all I'd have to do is dust and make the bed."

"I can be there this weekend. Are you positive that's not too soon?"

"Stubbs," I say impatiently, "shut up and get your ass up here. You can stay as long as you want."

There's a deep breath on the other end of the line. "I do love an assertive woman," he murmurs, and I grin.

"Good thing, since you're staying with me."

He chuckles. "Okay. Let me call the moving company back."

MARK

Monday afternoon, I awaken with a blinding headache in my old room at Tucker and Lila's. I vaguely remember them bringing me here because Lila was worried I'd fall, and Tucker had refused to stay in my crappy little apartment. The afternoon sun blazing through the sheer curtains pierces my eyeballs like needles. I drag the pillow over my head, wishing I'd made better choices.

Like not drinking most of a bottle of whiskey in one afternoon.

Or better yet, not destroying my only chance at happiness by abandoning the woman I love.

Bits and pieces of last night come back to me, and I hazily recall talking with Lila. I struggle to remember her words. Something like... it's not my leg that's the problem. It's that I fixate on what's missing. And she gave me a business card for someone. A psychiatrist.

As my dulled senses clear, I have a flash of introspection between the waves of pain rocketing through my skull. I'd rather have a root canal than discuss my feelings, but when my emotions – and words and actions – were out of control at Brooke, Dr. Friedman helped me get a handle on them. Once again, I've allowed my uncontrolled emotions to drive my behavior. I'd finally opened up to Dr. Friedman after my behavior hurt Charlie. Maybe seeing someone will help me figure out how to fix the pain I've caused again.

I sit up slowly, noting with surprise that my prosthetic leg has been removed. Tucker must have detached it after he and Lila practically carried me into the house. The Allen wrench and prosthetic are on the bedside table. The business card for the psychiatrist is nowhere in sight.

I connect my artificial limb to the abutment and carefully stand, bracing myself on the headboard. I'm steady, but my head is throbbing mercilessly.

I deserve far worse.

I shower and brush my teeth, studying the mirror as I examine my black eye. It's impressive. Tucker's well-placed strike made a powerful statement. It isn't as swollen now, but the bruising has spread, and I resemble a puffy purple raccoon. At least I can open my eye. Sort of, anyway.

Thankfully, I don't get nauseous when I'm hung over, so I down two glasses of water and three aspirin before opening the refrigerator. Lila has left a plastic-wrapped plate of sandwiches under a note. "M – Eat these, hydrate, and take aspirin. L." I take the plate and sit down, trying to recollect last night around the sizeable gaps in my memory.

I remember telling Lila I'd screwed everything up and wasn't sure how to fix it, and I recall her hesitant reply that she's not sure I can.

I definitely remember Tucker telling me what Charlie said, about how I'd been very clear about my feelings and that she was done. I also recall him saying he didn't think I could undo this much damage.

Fuck.

I drop my head. Tears burn my eyes and a lump forms in my throat. I pull out my phone and text Lila. "Sorry about last night. I need the name of that psychiatrist again."

She must have been with a client, because she doesn't reply until a few minutes before the hour. "No apologies. Dr. Sid Allen. Hope your face feels better." She includes his number.

I immediately dial it and request his first available appointment. "We've had a cancellation for tomorrow at nine," the receptionist says. "Are you available then?"

I don't know if seeing him will help, but I grab the appointment like it's my last hope.

Maybe it is.

Dr. Sid Allen is a thin, birdlike fellow who moves quickly and has piercing brown eyes. He leads me into his office and gestures to a chair. I sit, and he perches opposite me. His eyes roam over my bruised face, but he doesn't ask. "I'm Dr. Allen, or you can call me Sid, whichever you prefer. You're Mark Chandler, but that's all I know. Why don't you tell me the story of Mark?"

"Uh, okay," I say, surprised. "I filled out the questionnaire." I gesture toward the waiting room.

He smiles. "You'll tell me everything I need to know. I'll look over it later."

"Oh. Well, in January, I was hit with an IED and lost my right leg below the knee. I had a lot of other injuries, too." I recount the story of my hospitalization, recovery, and subsequent osseointegration. "So now I can walk around like I'm normal, even though I never will be."

Dr. Allen studies me silently when I finish, simply nodding. The lull in conversation continues long enough to become awkward. Finally he speaks. "Is that all?"

My eyebrows pull together. "What more do you want to know?"

"You told me quite a bit. Probably more than you realize," he adds. "You see, I asked for the story of Mark – things like your thoughts, your dreams, your plans, your likes and dislikes – in short, what makes you who you are. Asking people to tell me their story reveals how they see themselves. You focused entirely on your injuries and not being 'normal'. What you've told me is that you've reduced who you are as a person to merely the sum of your injuries."

I shift uncomfortably. "Well, yeah, but that's why I'm here, right? Isn't that what you do? Deal with vets with body issues?"

He lifts one thin brow. "Who told you that?"

"My friend Lila. She got recommendations from some other wounded vets for a shrink because she said I have body image issues. No offense," I add.

He smiles. "I've been called far worse than a shrink, I assure you. Why do you think your friend said you have body image issues?"

"Because I've made some really bad decisions because of how I see myself," I admit.

"Does she say they're bad decisions, or do you?"

"Both, because they were."

"Would you like to talk about that?"

Not really, but then I tell him the whole story, about my relationship with Charlie before we became involved, about becoming intimate with her and falling for her, about breaking it off and why, about hurting her and being miserable ever since. I tell him about Lila and Tucker and even Charlie trying to convince me I was wrong, recount the VFW story, and end with fleeing from her in the parking lot.

"So you feel you don't offer her any real value because you require a prosthetic leg?" Dr. Allen asks, his dark eyes probing gently.

"I guess."

"Do you view other amputees in that same light?"

"No." I describe Stubbs and his swaggering, masculine, larger-than-life persona.

Dr. Allen scrutinizes me. "It sounds as though your self-image was unhealthy even before your injury."

My eyebrows shoot up. "I wasn't insecure before the explosion."

"Self-image isn't merely being secure or insecure. You assigned value to yourself based solely on your physical characteristics. You were healthy and strong and athletic, and that was your source of self-worth. When your physical characteristics were altered, you decided your value had diminished." He studies me, running a long finger across his lower lip.

"It isn't just my body that changed. Everything changed. I used to be in charge of a platoon of soldiers. I devised and directed field ops in a hotspot in Afghanistan. That IED stole everything —my home, my job, my future. I didn't just lose my leg, I lost my career."

He seizes on my words. "So your intrinsic value was determined by your career?"

I shrug. "When you introduce yourself to people, they ask what you do."

"Not everyone has a glamorous job. Is someone's value based on what they do for a living?"

I shake my head. "Not to me, but some people see others that way."

"You say you don't see others like that, and yet you feel your value diminished after losing your leg and your career," he points out. "A person's worth isn't determined by their job any more than it is by their physical characteristics."

I'm silent.

Dr. Allen leans forward. "I'd like to meet with you twice a week, Mark. When I see you next time, I'd like you to bring in a list of at least five valuable traits you see within yourself."

That's it?

That's all he's got?

I bared my soul to him, told him about my injuries and throwing away my relationship with Charlie, and he told me exactly what Lila did – that I don't see myself clearly because all I can focus on is my leg. And she told me for free. And now I have to come up with a list of my valuable traits. Fan-fucking-tastic. That should take me from now until my next appointment.

There's a reason this guy is highly recommended. Give it time.

I stop at the receptionist's desk and make an appointment for Thursday. I'm walking to my van when I suddenly recall Lila's words to me during my drunken plea for help.

"If you don't find a way to fully accept yourself, the parts you like and the parts you don't, things will never work out between you and Charlie. The broken part of you that's destroying everything isn't your leg. It's that you fixate on what's missing and ignore what's still there. If you want any shot at repairing things, you have to be the best version of yourself. That means becoming emotionally healthy, because that's what she deserves."

On my way home, I pick up a spiral notebook for my homework assignments.

LILA

On Tuesday, I have a free hour while Charlie's in a massage. I plop down in my office chair and reach for my cell phone. The number rings twice before a deep voice answers. "Hello?"

"Stubbs? It's Lila."

"Well, hello, Beautiful," he greets me. "What can I do for you?"

"I wanted to make sure you got the pictures of the apartment Tucker sent. Obviously, it hasn't been remodeled yet, but you can get a feel for the lay-out. The owner is replacing the appliances and furniture and remodeling the bathrooms."

"I got them. I actually called the owner this morning. She seemed nice. After we talked, I sent her my signed rental agreement."

"Awesome! Did she give you a time frame?"

"Hopefully by mid-January, but she cautioned me that it depends on the contractors."

"So when should we expect you?"

"I don't have a ton of stuff," he says. "The moving company can pack me up by the end of the week, and they'll haul the storage pod up for me. I just have to find somewhere to put it until the apartment is ready. I talked to Charlie to see if she was serious about letting me crash with her and Mark for a few weeks. She said I could stay as long as I needed to."

I freeze. *Charlie hasn't told him?* It takes me a moment to regain my voice. "You can have them leave the storage pod at our place. We've got plenty of room. But Stubbs, Mark and Charlie aren't together anymore. He left her."

Stunned silence hangs between us, followed by, "What the fuck did you just say?"

"He walked out on her three months ago. He said she deserved better than a useless cripple and moved all his stuff while she was at work. I thought he'd come to his senses, but I was wrong."

His voice shoots up two full octaves. "He dumped Charlie because of his leg?"

"He hates his body, and nothing anyone says gets through to him. It got a lot worse after his surgery. Tucker even dragged him to an amputee support group, but it didn't do any good."

He sighs heavily. "How is she?"

"Better than she was, but she's still struggling," I admit. "Things got pretty dark for a while."

"Dammit," he growls. "I knew something was up when she stopped calling and skyping. She'd text every day or two, but just pictures or funny stories." He pauses. "Will me staying with her make things better or worse?"

I consider. "Better, I think. She'll have to engage outside of work. She's been pretty withdrawn since he left, especially since Mark stayed at our house for a couple of months until he found a disability-friendly place." I hesitate. "There's something else. Charlie's pregnant."

"He walked out on her, and she's pregnant?" he growls, indignation bleeding through the phone.

"He still doesn't know about the pregnancy. The doctors at Walter Reed told her she was infertile after everything those bastards did to her. He was there when they told her, so neither of them ever dreamed it might happen. She's tried repeatedly to get him to meet with her so she can tell him, but he refuses."

"I'll drag his ass over there. He'll listen then."

I sigh. "She's past that point." I explain about the parking lot incident. "She's done, Stubbs. She's decided he can find out about the babies from her attorney. She's suing him for sole custody."

He falls silent for long moments. "I just can't believe it. Those two were meant to be together."

"They would have been, if Mark would have pulled his head out of his ass."

He blows out a deep breath. "I'll talk to him when I get there. If I can't talk sense into him, I'll beat it into him."

CHAPTER ELEVEN

CHARLIE

AFTER WORK TUESDAY, I wander through my house, bored. I got Stubbs' room ready after he called last night. It's dusted and fluffed, with a freshly scrubbed bathroom and vacuum trails in the carpet. He texted earlier to say he'll be here Saturday evening. The movers are loading his storage pod and leaving it at Tucker and Lila's place. They have more room for a pod than I do. With our clinic next door, clients sometimes park in my driveway when the lot is full.

My evening is wide open. My housework is all caught up, and I'll go to the grocery store Friday evening to ensure I'm fully stocked for a houseguest. Penny and I go for a long walk in the woods, but I'm still restless when we get back, and nothing on television grabs my interest.

Maybe some retail therapy will brighten my mood. I need to go Christmas shopping, and I actually enjoy buying things for other people. I just despise going clothes shopping for myself.

I'm not even ten minutes into my shopping trip when I regret it.

The mall is bustling with cheerful people. Couples walk hand in hand, sharing large hot chocolates topped with whipped cream and drizzled with chocolate syrup. My heart aches when one couple leans close, and the man cups the woman's face before kissing her deeply. My chest tightens as I re-member Mark holding my face that way.

Let it go. I'm moving forward.

After the mall, I stop by a photo shop, a trophy store, and the ticket booth for a local auditorium before returning home with my purchases and a pizza. I leave my bags on the living room floor and take Penny out for a quick break in the frosty air. Then I collapse on the couch with iced tea and Hawaiian pizza while another sappy Christmas movie plays on the TV.

The movie does nothing to improve my frame of mind, so I exchange it for Christmas carols and flip on my gas fireplace and Christmas tree lights, hoping to inspire festive post-dinner gift-wrapping. I pull out thick pearl-white paper and red silk ribbon and go to work. I bought a huge insulated tumbler customized with a large bear paw and a thick black hooded sweatshirt for Tom. I found a cute purse for Maya, along with trendy earrings for both her and Skyler. For Tara, I bought a gift certificate to a spa I've heard her mention, and for Stubbs, a scarf, gloves, and thick fleece jacket since he's moving from toasty Texas to the frozen mountains of Colorado. I also had the trophy shop engrave a plaque for his new office. It boasts "World's Best Therapist: Because Badass Apparently Isn't An Official Job Title". For Tucker, I purchased two tickets to an MMA event in January and a gift card to his favorite restaurant, and for Lila, a delicate silver necklace with three vertically hung sapphires and a gift certificate for a pedicure. I pile the wrapped presents beneath my tree and pause, studying the one item I have left to wrap.

Despite the parking lot fiasco, I'm giving Mark a gift, not to sway him to come back, but as part of letting him go. I've enlarged the photograph of him with his mom and placed it in a beautiful silver frame. This is their final photo together, and he deserves to have it. I'll mail it so he won't have to see or talk to me. I tuck it inside a tissue-filled box, wrapping it in the pearly paper and tying it with red ribbon. Then I slip the box into a padded mailing envelope and turn off the television. When I head for bed, Penny follows, leaping lightly onto it and curling up beside me.

Despite my productive evening, I'm still edgy. Seeing happy couples together has left me unsettled. I toss and turn in the bed, even though Mark's warm pine scent has been replaced with fresh orange oil. This room, this bed, makes me think of him. How could it not, when he and I spent every night in here, even before we became romantically involved?

Moving on would be a lot easier if I didn't still love him. Even Penny's presence doesn't help.

Tears burn my eyes. I take Linda's advice and "feel my feelings" for a few minutes. According to her sage advice, I'm allowed to have a pity party as long as I respect the guidelines. Like any other party, I can attend, as long as I leave after a brief visit. I can't stay and wallow.

I ugly-cry for twenty minutes, then decide if I'm not sleeping, I might as well accomplish something. I retrieve my laptop and purchase a crib and changing table online from a local furniture store. I'm sure Tucker will come with me to pick them up. It's after three before I finally drift off to sleep, clutching my pillow.

I'm startled by the metal door clanging behind me, ricocheting off the stone walls. I jerk my head up, glancing toward the ceiling. Barbed wire cuts deeply into my wrists, suspending me above the floor. What was once a slow trickle of blood from the gouges has developed a foul stickiness. The same foul odor emanates from the slashes and burns on my back and the cuts deep inside me. I'm hot, so hot. My skin feels like it's on fire. My brain is foggy, my limbs heavy. I find myself fading in and out of consciousness more often now.

Game face on. No weakness.

But even the voice in my head sounds frail, its determined ferocity slowly waning. Sepsis is setting in.

I'm going to die a slow death from infection, tortured until the very end.

A booted foot slams into my lower back, and sharp pain rebounds through my entire abdomen. It feels unusually taut, and I bite back a groan.

Maybe I'll die from internal bleeding first. It would be faster.

I grit my teeth as the goddamned Chihuahua steps in front of me, the short, stubby, vile bastard with the soulless black eyes. He leers at me, and my stomach churns. I'm caught off guard by the scuffle of boots behind me. My mind is hazy, and I'm fighting so hard to maintain my focus on him, I didn't even hear their approach.

I force my attention to the sawed-off asshole in front of me. He reaches into the sheath on his belt and unearths his rusty knife.

Please no. Not again.

I blink, trying to muster up the strength to steel myself against what's coming.

For once, he doesn't waste time punching or slapping me, or even cutting my breasts. He simply yanks my legs apart and shoves the knife up and into my vagina. Warm blood spills down my thighs. He does it again. And again. And again, until I finally pass out.

I regain consciousness to thick fingers digging into my hips and a large male behind me, grunting as he thrusts into my raw flesh.

I jolt awake with a chilling wail, finding myself crouched with my back against the headboard and my fists clenched. My heart pounds as I pant, tears streaming down my face. Penny pushes her face into my neck and whimpers.

I'm safe now.

Breathe. Slow and easy.

I'm safe.

Just breathe.

It takes me a long time to calm myself. It's barely five when I check the clock. My unease lingers even after I've showered and dressed.

It dawns on me once I'm at work that if Stubbs is staying with me, he's going to learn firsthand just how bad my PTSD still is.

LILA

Charlie's been noticeably paler and quiet at work this week since the incident in the parking lot. The encounter left her shaken, and though she's been more determined than I've seen her in weeks, it's still taken a toll on her. Her eyes hold the familiar shadows I've seen when her nightmares ramp up. I corner her in her office.

"You're having night terrors again, aren't you?"

She looks up from the bottom cupboard of her credenza, where she's squatting in the floor, collecting office supplies for Stubbs' new space. "What?"

I cross the room and tug at her elbow. "Stand up. You don't need to be squatting like that."

"Actually, it's good for my pelvic floor muscles," she says, but gets to her feet anyway.

"Fine. Don't do it in front of me. I have an irrational fear that your babies are going to just shoot out."

She smiles faintly. "You'd rather I do it when I'm home alone?"

"You're avoiding my question," I tell her, removing empty file folders, legal pads, and an unused scanner from the cabinet.

"They started back when I moved into Mark's old room," she admits quietly. "I haven't had them in a while, so I'm pretty sure that's the trigger. I'm seeing Linda later this week. I'm planning to talk to her about them."

"Where's your gun?"

"In the dresser under my shirts. I can get to it in an emergency, but I'm not sleeping with it."

"Good," I murmur. "I can have Tucker start keeping the laptop on to alert us if you need us to."

She shakes her head. "I'm not sleeping on the bench. I'm in the bed."

"The camera can capture that room. Well, sort of. We could see you in the floor the night Mark left."

She frowns. "You were watching me?"

"We checked on you late that night, when you wouldn't return any of my calls or texts. I was worried. We saw you in the floor in Mark's room. Once I knew you weren't getting drunk with strangers, I felt a little better." I leave out the part about Tucker keeping watch over her all night.

"If it gets worse – if I think I need the camera – I'll let you know. I just hope I get them under control again pretty quickly, because Stubbs is coming this weekend. He's never seen me have one, and I'd like to keep it that way."

I wave her off. "It's good practice. He's going to be doing therapy with vets with PTSD. He should see a night terror or two."

"He's probably seen or experienced them before," she says darkly.

"Maybe," I agree. "Either way, he won't judge you. He can help." I pause. "And I'm really proud of you for letting him stay with you. I know he's your friend, but he's also a male. A year ago, you'd never have been able to do that. Make sure you tell Linda."

Charlie smiles. "Definitely. She loves celebrating small victories."

I take the stack of office supplies from her and carry them to Stubbs' office. I really hope Charlie can finally get her feet back under her. Mark's idiotic behavior has left her reeling for months, leaving her torn between wanting him back and letting him go. But this week, despite the dark circles under her eyes, there's been a quiet strength about her that I've not seen in quite some time.

Charlie Emerson is reclaiming her life.

And it's about damn time.

MARK

Thursday morning, I show up at Dr. Allen's with my notebook in hand.

"Does this mean you did your homework?" he asks, dark eyes curious.

In answer, I open my notebook. "Five valuable traits I see within myself," I read from the page. "Leadership skills. Intelligence. Decisiveness. Loyalty. A strong sense of justice."

"These sound very career-oriented," he comments. "Are you basing these solely off your military career?"

"They were useful in the military, but they're also applicable to civilian life."

"So in the Army, you were a good leader, intelligent, decisive, loyal, and fair. Are you those things now?"

"I'm not a leader anymore. And I thought we weren't basing my value on my former career."

"We aren't, but recognizing traits that have served you in one area often reveals things you haven't realized are relevant to your self-worth." He pauses. "How old are you, Mark?"

"Thirty-five."

"That's young. What's next?"

I frown. "What do you mean?"

"You've essentially recovered. You have a lot of years left. What do you want to do with them?"

"I don't know," I confess. "I've spent all year focused on getting stronger and rehabbing so I can walk. I hadn't really thought past that."

"You could return to the military, if that's what you want. Amputees do it all the time."

I slowly shake my head. "I feel like that part of my life is done now."

"Because of your leg?"

I hesitate. "I'm not sure. Going back doesn't feel right, though. I feel like I belong here now. But I do miss leading my team."

"What do you miss about it?"

"It was like chess," I say pensively. "I could envision the big picture and anticipate the enemy's response. I instinctively knew what move to make. Some people get hung up on what's in front of them, but I could take a bird's-eye view and play things out in my head. And I enjoyed guiding younger recruits, helping them learn not just what to do, but why. I was good at that."

"There are a lot of careers that will allow you to utilize those skills. Guiding, educating, leading – that's everything from a teacher to a business manager. Being calm and decisive in a crisis is perfect for emergency management or

health care. Seeing the big picture and anticipating the next move are necessary skills for a coach. There are multiple paths someone with your strengths
could take. You've achieved your short-term goal of walking. Now you need
to decide on your next goal."

"What does that have to do with seeing myself more clearly?"

"Realizing you have more to offer the world than merely being athletic
and having two legs will change the way you view yourself," he replies. "I'd
like you to stop by the local college and pick up information on classes. Find
some that appeal to you and start considering career options. Maybe you have
a burning desire to open a bar or write the next great novel. Give it some
thought, and let's discuss it next time."

After my appointment, I visit the local community college. The ladies in
the admissions office fill my arms with catalogs and offer to take me to the
guidance counselor, but I decline, promising to call for an appointment when
I've had time to review my options.

As I drive back toward my crappy little apartment, I notice Christmas decorations and sales signs everywhere. Christmas is coming soon. I don't have
a tree. I don't have room for one even if I felt festive, which I don't. I do need
to buy gifts, though. I only have a handful of people to buy for, and I'm pretty
sure one of them won't accept anything from me. I make my way through the
traffic to the mall, eschewing the handicapped spaces in the parking garage.

I wander through various department stores and boutiques, looking for
inspiration. I choose a silk scarf for Lila in shades of blue and violet that echo
her eye color. I also find a pair of sapphire earrings to match the deepest colors
in the scarf. Lila's always loved sapphires. Tucker is more challenging to buy
for. I finally have a tank top personalized for him at a kiosk. It says "I Flexed
And My Sleeves Fell Off." I'll buy a bottle of his favorite whiskey to go with it.

A dark-haired girl with springy curls dashes past me, and for a half-second,
I think it's Maya, but it isn't. The sight of her makes me remember the group
dinners we had on workout days before I wrecked everything, and I realize I
miss Tom and Maya too, especially now that I know Tom and Charlie aren't
an item. I get a tee shirt personalized for Tom that proclaims "PT: Personal
Torturer – I Mean, Physical Therapist." I struggle with what to get Maya,
because I could write everything I know about ten-year-old girls on the head
of a pin and still have room left over. I finally settle on movie ticket vouchers
and a gift card for the theater's concession stand. I've heard her gush about
movies she wanted Tom to take her to see.

I take my purchases to a gift-wrapping kiosk and wait while they make
them look like the packages shown in movies and on commercials. I absently
watch them trim the heavy paper and transform bland boxes into legitimate
works of origami-like art, silently racking my brain. I want to give Charlie...
something. But what? When the girl hands the bags of wrapped packages

back to me, I dump them in my van and reenter the mall, looking for something that speaks to me.

I end up at a custom jewelry store.

It's the last place I ought to be, even though it's the place I *would* be if I hadn't fucked everything up. Before my surgery, I'd planned to tell Charlie I loved her as soon as I was "normal". I'd thought about the future, about how I wanted her beside me for the rest of my life.

I still want that.

I love Charlie so much it hurts. Being away from her feels like there's an enormous hole in my chest, burning with every breath. It was never that I didn't love her. If what Lila and Dr. Allen and everyone else has been saying is accurate, it was that I let my hatred for my changed body overshadow my love for her, let it convince me to hurt the woman I love. How fucked up is that?

More to the point, how fucked up am I?

I don't deserve the privilege of being able to give her a gift, but I can't not get her something. She's the most important person in my world. No one means more to me than Charlie. No one ever could.

I wander through the jewelry store, looking through case after case of beautiful and unique pieces. When I pass a sparkling display of engagement rings, I swallow against the burgeoning lump in my throat and keep walking. I've let my screwed-up psyche destroy that possibility.

I keep hunting, searching for something special. Not a ring – that's impossible. Not a bracelet, because she'll only wear stacked ones that conceal the scars around her wrists. Maybe a necklace or earrings, though she doesn't wear a lot of necklaces because they catch in her hair.

I linger for a long time at the earring counter before I see them, a beautiful dangling pair of gold and diamond ones. They fan out like delicate upside-down branches, diverging and rejoining, and each golden tendril ends in a small diamond. I purchase them, and the store presents them to me in a flourish of glossy black paper and red ribbon.

I have no idea if she'll accept them. Tucker said I'd pushed her too far and lost her for good, because I placed more significance on the missing part of my leg than on the woman I love.

Maybe I have done too much damage to repair.

I drive home and stuff the box in my dresser drawer, out of sight.

Thinking about how much I've screwed up leaves me agitated, unable to sit still. I pace my tiny apartment, but it's so small, it only frustrates me more. I head to Tucker's gym. He's finishing a training session with a client. I sit on a weight bench to wait. He joins me when his client heads for the locker room. "What's up?"

"Got a minute?"

Tucker nods. "I've got an hour. I was going to grab a sandwich. Hungry?"

When I agree, Tucker leads me next door to a small deli. We stand in silence while they make our sandwiches, then return to his office to eat. We sit at a table in the corner of his office. "What's on your mind?"

"I want Charlie back. I need her back."

Tucker examines me carefully. "Why?"

I stare, dumbfounded. My reasons should be obvious to him. "What do you mean, why?"

"I mean, why? For months, you've ignored her and treated her like shit. Why do you want her back now? What changed? Is this your ego talking because you know you finally went too far?"

His words burn like salt in an open wound. "No. I want Charlie back because I love her and I need her. She's the best thing that ever happened to me. I made a huge mistake, and I hurt her. I need to tell her I was wrong and I'm sorry."

Tucker unwraps his sandwich, staring fixedly at the wrapper. "Why couldn't you have come to this conclusion weeks ago?"

I shake my head dejectedly. "I thought she deserved someone better. You said I didn't see myself clearly. You were right. Because I had – and still have – trouble accepting myself, I didn't want her to be stuck loving someone like me." I hesitate. "Do you think she'd be willing to talk to me?"

Tucker chews a mouthful of sandwich. "Honestly? I doubt it. That shit you pulled in the parking lot was the last straw."

I close my eyes against the sudden burning. "Dr. Allen asked me to name some positive traits I saw in myself. One of the things I listed was loyalty. But I'm not loyal. I broke all my promises to Charlie."

"Who's Dr. Allen?" Tucker asks, reaching for his tea.

"The psychiatrist Lila recommended. He's working with me on changing my view of myself. I've made a lot of bad decisions because of my skewed self-image. That doesn't excuse my actions, but it helps me understand myself so I make better choices in the future. "

"It's about damn time you talked to somebody. You need to move past that 'half-a-man' bullshit," he says, taking another bite of his sandwich. Mine sits on his desk, untouched.

I nod, unoffended by his blunt assessment. "I can tell myself that up here," I say, tapping my temple. Then I touch my chest. "It's in here that it's hard, you know?"

Touching my chest makes me remember Charlie thumping her heart twice the other day in the parking lot, telling me she loved me. I very nearly responded in kind. I jerked to a stop when my brain yelled that she deserved someone better, someone whole.

And I turned and walked away, probably losing her forever.

"I don't know if Charlie will agree to talk to you or not," Tucker says slowly, "but if you reach out to her, you've got to be nonthreatening. Don't just show up unannounced. She needs to be able to brace herself."

I've hurt her so much that she has to brace herself against me.

She expects me to keep hurting her.

My gut churns, but Tucker keeps talking. "Text her. You could try to call, but I doubt she'd answer." My stomach tightens further. "I'm serious, though, Mark. You may be too late."

Please don't let it be too late.

The universe can take both my legs if I can have Charlie again.

I nod. "I'm the one who chose how things ended. If there's ever anything between us again, it will be her choice and on her terms. I just hope she'll give me one last chance."

Please, please let her give me another chance.

CHAPTER TWELVE

CHARLIE

On Thursday evening, Tucker drives me to the baby furniture store to pick up my purchases. He carries in the huge boxes containing the unassembled baby furniture like they weigh nothing and places them in one corner of my bedroom. "Lila and I will help you assemble everything whenever you're ready," he promises, kissing my forehead on his way out.

Friday morning, I run by the post office to mail Mark's gift. I'd sat at my dining room table for a long time, struggling with what to write on the note. I almost didn't include one – after all, it's not like he won't know who it's from – but moving forward doesn't preclude basic courtesy. It took me an hour to come up with seven simple words: "I wanted you to have this. Charlie."

Poetry. Sheer poetry.

I'm between clients, grabbing a quick sandwich at home, when my phone buzzes with a text. I wonder if I've looked at my schedule wrong and forgotten a massage. I thought my next client wasn't until one o'clock.

I didn't screw up my schedule. It's a text. From Mark.

"Not a single day goes by that I don't think of you."

What. The. Fuck.

My heart leaps wildly inside my chest when I read and then reread his words. My excitement rapidly turns to anger. How *dare* he toy with my emotions like this? I texted him every day for weeks. I begged him to talk to me. I banged on his door, repeatedly yelling that I needed to tell him something important. He ignored me every single time, including his most recent — and public — rejection: walking away and leaving me with my soul hemorrhaging in a parking lot. And now he has the nerve to fling romantic words around like rose petals?

My fury at him morphs into anger at myself, for being so weak that a few sweet words from him on a screen sent a brief electric thrill through me.

I throw my phone onto the counter and dump my sandwich in the trash, my appetite gone. I storm next door to the clinic, stomping noticeably. Tom raises an eyebrow as he glances up from his client. I deflate and mouth a silent apology.

Emotions boil inside me all afternoon, fighting over which one gets to bubble to the surface next. Frustration. Confusion. Sadness. Anger. Disbelief. Pain.

And fear.

That's the one that grabs my attention. The others make sense, but not fear.

That anxious, fearful feeling lingers throughout my appointment with my new custody lawyer at Goldstein & Goldstein's Family Law office.

Linda greets me with a perky smile when I show up for my appointment late and apologetic. I recount my hellish week, including my recurrent night terrors, celebrate my victory in inviting Stubbs to stay, and describe my irrational fear response to Mark's text. "I don't understand. Why would I be afraid?"

Linda whips out Standard Psychiatrist Response 101. "Why do you think you felt fear, Charlie? What is it you're afraid of?"

I sit there, stumped, until I consider how Willow, a sex therapist and intimacy specialist, might answer. "Maybe it's because he's the only person I've ever been completely vulnerable with."

She nods. "And he repaid your vulnerability with pain."

"So I'm afraid he's going to hurt me again. I'm afraid to trust him."

"Are you asking me or telling me, Charlie?" she says gently.

I hesitate. "I'm not sure." There's another pause. "I was never afraid of Mark before, not even when I was terrified of every other man on the planet."

"You never thought he would hurt you."

I shake my head.

"And yet he did."

I consider her words. "So maybe I'm afraid to trust myself?"

"Is that possible?"

"I've wondered how I could have been so wrong about him," I admit.

"Does knowing the reason behind his betrayal soften the blow?"

I frown. "What do you mean?"

"His betrayal was linked to his body image. He left because he didn't believe he was good enough for you. He believed you deserved better. That's what you've told me."

I nod.

"Mark loathes himself because he equates his changed body to personal failure."

Her words hang there, sucking all the air out of the room. My voice is barely a whisper when I answer. "Like I did."

When I first met Linda, my wounds hadn't fully healed. They were still in the process of scarring over. I wore long-sleeved silky tops that wouldn't be rough against the tender skin on my back. I covered my wrists with soft woven bracelets to hide the still-healing gouges. I took down every removable mirror in my house so I didn't have to see my chest or back.

In short, I was repulsed by my body because it was a constant reminder of what I perceived as my failure, not their brutality. And because I hated myself, I made bad choices. I withdrew. I drank. I contemplated suicide.

That's essentially what Mark has done. He abhors his changed body and views it as a failure or shortcoming on his part. And his bad choices – like pushing me away – stem from that.

I have a sudden insight. "So it isn't that he doesn't love me. It's that he hates himself." My words are thoughtful.

Linda waits as I wade through this revelation.

"So is it really a betrayal?" I ask, more to myself than to her. "If Mark did what he thought was best for me, intentionally hurting himself in the process, is it really a betrayal?"

"That's something only you can decide, Charlie," she says gently.

Even if he meant to do what he thought was best for me, Mark's judgment is skewed because of his self-image. Unless he stops hating himself, I can't trust him not to hurt me again. I love him, but I can't risk spiraling into darkness again, not with my babies to think of.

It's safer to let go and move on.

I leave Linda's office more depressed than when I went in, despite pretending I'm merely deep in thought. She sees through my façade, but doesn't call me out. She simply squeezes my arm and tells me to embrace the peace of the holiday season.

Peace. Things haven't felt peaceful in so long. A sudden, desperate longing for tranquility makes my eyes burn, but I force my tears down. Instead, I head to the grocery store to stock up for Stubbs' impending arrival. When I pull into my driveway, Tucker and Lila climb out of his huge truck.

"I hope you weren't waiting long," I apologize. "The grocery store was packed with people."

Tucker grins cheekily. "Nope. Gave me time to make out with my hot wife. In fact, if you want to drive around the block a few times, I know how we could pass the time."

She swats him. "Stop it. Come on, let's unload her car."

I open the back of my SUV and start to reach in, but Lila shoos me away. "Not an invalid," I remind her, but she rolls her eyes.

"Go unlock the house and take Penny out. We've got this."

I grumble under my breath, but cooperate. I've learned to pick my battles with Lila. Besides, Mark's text, the meeting with my new attorney, and my epiphany at Linda's office have left me feeling raw and drained. By the time Penny's done, Tucker's unpacked my canvas grocery bags and Lila's putting things away.

My phone buzzes with a message, and my stomach tightens as I reach for it. I never answered Mark's text. But when I look down, it's Stubbs, not Mark.

"Hitting the road at the ass-crack of dawn in the morning. Hope to see you by about six tomorrow evening. I'll call if that changes. See you soon, Green Eyes."

I smile and tap out a quick, "Be safe. See you when you get here!" When I look up, Lila's watching me curiously. "Stubbs," I explain. "He thinks he'll be here by about six tomorrow night. Says he's leaving at – and I quote – 'the ass-crack of dawn' tomorrow."

"I wonder if he'd work out at my gym," Tucker says. "I'll take him on as a client for free if he'll let me tell people I'm his trainer. Talk about effective advertising."

Lila swats him with a smile. "Stop lusting over his body."

He snags her around the waist and plants a kiss on her rosy lips. "The only body I lust after is yours, Sweetness. He just has impressive muscle definition." He pauses. "Very impressive." Lila swats him again.

Tucker had called in our Chinese food order while they were waiting for me to get home, and it arrives as we're putting away the last of the groceries. The three of us sprawl across my living room, eating vegetable lo mein, beef with broccoli, and sesame chicken with chopsticks, chatting comfortably in the glow of my Christmas lights and the fireplace. We've finished eating when Tucker looks my way.

"I need to talk to you, Charlie." His serious expression makes my chest tighten.

It's about Mark.

"What's up?" I ask, afraid to breathe but trying to sound casual. Lila eyes him inquisitively.

"Mark came to see me yesterday. He's probably going to reach out to you."

"He already did. He texted this afternoon. He said not a day goes by that he doesn't think about me." I keep my expression neutral. "Any idea why?"

Tucker hesitates. "He finally understands how badly he screwed up, and he wants you back."

Hot anger instantly courses through my veins. "He's the one who walked away. He's ignored me for months. Now that he's all by himself and feeling lonely, he wants me to just forget the past three months?"

Tucker's voice is quiet. "Believe me, he's very aware of my feelings on this subject."

Tucker's expression fills me with guilt. "Sorry," I mutter. "Today's not been a good day. I didn't mean to take it out on you." He waves my apology away, and I'm silent for a minute. "What's with Mark's sudden change of heart?"

"I think he's known for a long time," Lila says gently. "He just wouldn't admit it."

"So why now? What's different?"

"He's started seeing a psychiatrist about his body image issues," Tucker answers. "He's realizing that the negative way he sees himself affected the way he believed everyone else saw him, and he's made bad choices because of that."

"He's already seeing Dr. Allen?" Lila asks.

Tucker nods. "Twice a week."

I turn questioning eyes on Lila. "You knew about this?"

She raises her hands. "Not like you think." She glances at Tucker. "After the parking lot incident, Tucker had it out with him."

"What she means is that I punched him in the face and told him he'd finally lost you forever," he says calmly.

My jaw drops. "You *punched* him?"

He nods. "When I saw how badly he'd hurt you again, yeah." His expression is a blend of guilt and frustration. "For what it's worth, I held onto his shirt when I hit him. I didn't want him to fall and screw up his abutment."

It's exactly what a guy would do for his sister, and it means even more because he loves Mark like a brother. A lump rises in my throat. "Thanks for having my back, Tuck."

"You're family," he says simply, and a swell of emotion hits me. My eyes fill with tears that I blink back, but not before Tucker and Lila see them.

"So what's this about a psychiatrist?" I ask, turning back to Lila.

"After Tucker gave him a black eye and chewed his ass, Mark got completely shit-faced. He texted me, and we went over. He said he'd screwed up and wanted to fix things. I said he needed to get help for his body image issues first. I gave him the name of the psychiatrist I found when you and I talked after his surgery. I didn't tell you about it because I wasn't sure if it was drunken regret or if he was serious. I didn't want your emotions jerked around if he didn't follow through."

I stare at her. "Mark got drunk?"

"Completely hammered," she says. "Falling down, slurring his words, passing-out drunk."

I blink in shock. I don't think he's gotten drunk since my parents were killed by a drunk driver. Maybe even before then.

"He was serious about getting help," Tucker says. "He wants to repair things between you. I warned him I didn't think he could fix this. I also told him that if he did reach out, it needed to be something nonthreatening, something that let you choose whether you wanted to respond. I'd intended to prepare you ahead of time, but it sounds like he beat me to it."

I rub my forehead against the sudden throbbing behind my eyes. "For months, he's rejected every attempt I've made to reach out. The second I decide I'm done, he wants to fix things. I swear, every time I almost get my feet back under me, the ground shifts again." I look at Lila. "I was pissed when I read his text. Pissed that he thought a few sweet words could erase everything, and pissed that, for one brief moment, his words made me feel good. After my anger faded, do you know what was left? Fear."

Worry creases Lila's brow. "You're afraid of him now?"

"Not like when I was afraid of all men. It's more that I'm afraid to trust him." I pause. "Given how long we were best friends, I think that's probably worse."

"So are you going to talk to him?"

I shake my head. "I can't live at the mercy of Mark's emotional roller coaster. Just because he's lonely today doesn't mean he'll feel that way tomorrow." And when my attorney serves him with custody papers after Christmas, his roller coaster may derail completely.

"I'm pretty sure he's serious," Tucker says. "He admitted he loved you all along."

"To you, Tucker. Not to me. The night we broke up, I told him I knew he loved me. I begged him to admit it, but he wouldn't. Now that he knows he's gone too far, he told you, knowing you'd tell me." I shake my head. "He's giving me whiplash. It's safer to let go and move on."

Lila's eyes grow sad. "I'm sorry, Charlie. If you think things are too far gone to repair, we'll stand by you. And if you want to work something out, whether it's just being civil for the sake of the babies or trying to be friends again or even something more, we'll stand by you in that, too. You're not alone," she promises, crossing the room to hug me.

For the sixth night in a row, sleep evades me most of the night. I doze off in the wee hours and wake up screaming before dawn as black soulless eyes attack my sleep again. I sink onto the bench in the shower sobbing, overwhelmed and exhausted.

TUCKER

Lila and I made love twice tonight, and it had nothing to do with ovulation schedules. Now she's dozing with her silky curls spread across my chest. I'm stroking her luscious curves when my phone buzzes. It takes me a minute to locate it because it's been shoved under the pillows. I drag it out and squint at the screen.

It's Mark.

"I texted Charlie this afternoon. She didn't answer."

"Maybe no answer is your answer," I type. Did he honestly think one little text would make her drop everything and go running back into his arms?

"I bought her something for Christmas. Would you give it to her for me?"

I don't even hesitate. "Nope. You fucked up. Figure your own way out of this."

"But I don't think she'll accept a gift from me."

"Again – maybe that's your answer."

Lila raises her head and looks at me with sleepy eyes. "You're growling," she murmurs. "What's wrong?"

"Dumbasses make me cranky," I say, kissing her on the forehead. "Go back to sleep. I'll be quiet."

"Is it Mark?"

"He's the biggest dumbass we know."

She shifts in my arms and tilts my phone so she can read our conversation. Little dots dance on the screen as he types. I wait impatiently as he stops and starts multiple times. Several minutes later, his text finally lands.

"Tuck, I love her. I can't do this without her."

The rawness of his words makes me sigh heavily. It's hard to be pissed at someone who's truly hit rock-bottom. Telling him he should have thought of that before behaving like a jackass for months is neither helpful nor productive, though it is awfully tempting.

"I can't tell you what to do, Mark. I told you, I'm not sure you can fix this."

"I won't give up, Tucker. I can't."

I smile. "Then don't. Try harder."

CHARLIE

Saturday morning, I go to Tom's house to deliver their Christmas gifts. They're flying to New York Tuesday evening so Maya can spend the holidays with Chele, and I want her to have her presents before she leaves town.

Tom greets me at the door with a warm hug. "Merry Christmas," I say.

"Come on in." He ushers me inside, closing the door against the cold air. His comfortable craftsman-style home is decorated with fresh pine garlands and ornaments Maya has made over the years, and colorful lights are strung throughout the house. I laugh when Bella appears. The massive half-grown pit bull puppy has a floppy red bow around her neck, and she's grinning her happy toothless grin when she bounds around the corner to greet me. I kneel and reach into my bag, pulling out a container of soft treats. She skids to a stop at Tom's command. I offer her two treats and she wolfs them down, excitedly rooting around for more after I close the package.

Tom laughs. "Maybe I should put those somewhere she can't get them." He reaches out a hand and tugs me easily to my feet.

I pass the container to him and hand him a smaller one as well. He looks at me curiously.

"Salmon treats for Eddie," I explain. Eddie's their three-legged black and white rescue cat who twines through visitors' legs and marches across their laps, unconcernedly twitching his tail under their noses. Unbeknownst to Tom at the time, Maya named him after an "emo vampire" (Tom's words) whose movies she adored, and he hasn't yet found a good nickname.

I follow Tom into the kitchen. "Are you taking Bella with you?"

He shakes his head. "No. The pets are staying with Tracy. Bella doesn't like being boarded, and she's not Chele-appropriate." He grins. "She's too big to fit in a purse, and she's definitely not runway-ready."

"She most certainly is. She's beautiful," I scold him. Bella was mistreated, left chained to a pipe in an abandoned warehouse. When workers happened upon her, she was skin and bones, her teeth ground to the gumline where she'd chewed on rocks and concrete in her hunger. Tom brought the puppy home to foster and couldn't let her go. Her teeth had to be removed, but he fattened her up, and now she's huge and excitable and perfect.

He laughs at my defense of Bella. "She is beautiful," he agrees. "I just meant she's too rambunctious for Chele. She views pets as an accessory."

I grin. Bella's definitely a handful, all puppy energy and big feet and floppy jowls crammed into a one-hundred-pound body.

Maya comes downstairs, wrapping her arms around me while I kiss her forehead. "I've missed you," I murmur, giving her an extra squeeze. The three of us sit down in the living room to exchange gifts. An enormous Christmas tree consumes one entire corner of the room. The top half of the tree is completely covered in ornaments and tinsel, but from the center of the tree down, there are only lights – not a single decoration. I look at Tom in confusion, then realize why and laugh at the same time he explains, "Bella."

I give them their gifts, leaving Skyler's beneath their tree. Maya excitedly puts on her new earrings to model them and squeals and dances when she sees her new purse. Tom raves over his sweatshirt and personalized bear paw tumbler, holding a huge hand up next to it while Maya snaps a photo. Then he glances at her and nods. Maya dashes across the room and reaches behind the tree, producing a large flat package and bringing it to me.

"We had a little help from Lila," Tom says. I look at him curiously.

"Open it!" Maya urges, bouncing on the couch beside me.

I peel back the green foil paper and stare, mesmerized. Charcoal sketches of the 4D ultrasound pictures of my babies are matted side by side in a black frame. They're beautifully detailed, gorgeous beyond description. My hands fly to my mouth as tears fill my eyes.

"Don't be sad," Maya says worriedly.

I shake my head. "These are happy tears," I assure her. I look at Tom. "This is incredible. How did you do this?"

He smiles softly. "Lila borrowed the pictures from your desk drawer so I could take them to a friend who's an artist. I wanted you to have something to remind you of how special this time is. I know things are hard right now, but I don't want you to forget the magic of those two little miracles you're carrying."

Tears trickle down my face, and Maya slides her arm around me, concern in her warm brown eyes, the same melted chocolate shade as Tom's. "Are you sure you're not sad?"

I hug her and kiss her cheek, brushing her copper-highlighted curls to one side. "I promise. Thank you, Maya. This is the most beautiful gift I've ever gotten." She beams at my praise.

I set the print aside and cross the room to Tom. He stands, and I hug him tightly. "Thank you," I whisper, kissing his stubbled cheek.

When I get home, I know exactly where I'm hanging their portraits. There's a blank space on the wall above the bench in my foyer. This space represents a time when fear dominated my life. I spent every night on that bench, vigilantly guarding the entrances to my home, terrified of being a victim again. It's where I'd doze off and wake up terrified, firing my gun at the walls.

I'm reclaiming this space. No longer does it get to be a place of fear. From now on, it will be a reminder of my choice to move forward and heal. I hang my babies' sketches on the wall above the bench and smile.

Love triumphs over fear.

MARK

In the Army, I was a captain. I managed a platoon of soldiers in one of the hottest war zones in Afghanistan, even after it was renamed an "area of concern" when the powers that be backed away from the war. I analyzed the intelligence we collected, devised operations to accomplish our goals, and led my team on the ground. I was an effective leader because I looked at the big picture and wasn't afraid to do whatever needed to be done.

Those are some of my best traits. It's time I used them to win back the heart of the woman I love.

I know Charlie. After being friends for nearly twenty-five years, I know almost everything about her. I know how she thinks, what she likes, what speaks to her. I know the things that are important to her and the things that aren't.

I've spent a lifetime gathering intelligence on her. Now I need to figure out a way to convince her to give me, us, another chance.

And I'll do whatever it takes to prove to her I'm worth it.

CHAPTER THIRTEEN

CHARLIE

IT'S DARK OUTSIDE WHEN I hear the crunch of gravel in my driveway shortly after five o'clock. I push myself out of the deep sofa cushions and hurry to the front door. Penny barks once as I open it. I glance down in surprise. I've never heard her bark before.

"It's okay, girl," I reassure her, patting her head.

A hulking black SUV rumbles in my driveway before shutting off. The last time I saw Stubbs, he was driving some little red sporty thing that seemed entirely too small for someone who's six-foot-five. This vehicle suits him better. Penny follows me as I approach.

Stubbs hops out, the porch light reflecting off his shaved head. His eyes travel over me, pausing on my midsection, but he doesn't comment, instead sweeping me into a crushing bear hug. "Green Eyes! Good to see you!"

"You too," I say when I can breathe again. The man doesn't know his own strength. "You made it ahead of schedule. How was your drive?"

"I made good time once I got out of Texas, but I'm glad to be out of the car. Long drives make me stiff. I'm not eighteen anymore." I grin. I've never asked how old he is, but I'd place him in his mid-to-late thirties, a few years older than me.

"I see you've got new wheels." I tip my head at the SUV.

He nods. "As soon as I got back from visiting you over the summer, I ordered this baby."

"Why?"

He waves his hand in a loose circle, indicating our surroundings. "I told you, this place is peaceful. It called to my soul. Sexy little sports cars are fine for

Texas, but not for Colorado winters. I picked something more durable with four-wheel-drive."

Penny snuffles him with great interest, and he leans down to rub her ears. "I forgot to ask if you're okay with dogs," I say, just as he croons to her and makes kissy sounds. She squirms excitedly, trying to lick his face. "I'll take that as a yes. This is Penny."

"She's gorgeous. Aren't you, you beautiful girl? Just gorgeous," he purrs, cupping her soft cheeks in his huge hands and ruffling her fur. Her entire back half wags at his attention.

Eventually, Penny calms down, and Stubbs opens the back of the SUV and removes a large suitcase. I reach for a leather duffel bag, but he smacks my hand away. "You can't seriously think I'm letting you lift anything," he says with a raised eyebrow, and I know either Tucker or Lila has filled him in. I frown. "Here," he says, handing me a pillow. "You can carry this."

"I'm not an invalid," I grumble, starting to feel like a broken record as I lead him upstairs. He follows, easily carrying his suitcase, duffel bag, and a garment bag. "How does pizza sound?" I ask him as we go back downstairs.

He heads back to his car for his laptop and a backpack. "As long as it has meat, I'm good."

Stubbs grabs a quick shower while I order a pizza loaded with meat and toss together a quick salad. I'm taking the extra large pizza from the delivery guy when he returns, dressed comfortably in a white tee shirt and cutoff sweats that reveal his matching carbon-fiber legs. His rich mahogany skin contrasts with his perfect white teeth when he smiles. "I'll grab us a couple of drinks," he says on his way to the kitchen. "What'll you have?"

"Tea, please." He gets our drinks, and we settle at the dining room table. We both dig into the steamy, cheesy goodness, and I have a big salad with it. No matter how much I eat lately, I seem to be hungry again within a couple of hours. Penny sits between us at attention, and I feed her my crust. She eyes Stubbs expectantly until he chuckles and does the same.

We chat about his move, his new job at the clinic, and his road trip for the first several minutes. Only after I've finished my second piece of pizza does he pin me with his dark eyes. "So when did you plan to fill me in about you and Mark?"

I pull back from the third slice I'd been reaching for. "There wasn't a lot to tell. I told him I loved him, and he left."

He picks up the pizza slice I'd reached for and places it on my plate, nudging it toward me. "When you say he left..." he prods.

I meet his gaze without flinching. "He said he didn't love me, and that I needed to find someone who wasn't half a man."

His mouth tightens. "What did you say to that?"

I flush, recalling my sarcastic outburst. "I lost my temper and said some things I shouldn't have," I admit. "In my defense, he was being a dumbass."

He raises an eyebrow. "What did you say to him?"

I bite my lip as my face heats. "I grabbed my phone. I told him since he was so sure losing one leg made him half a man, he needed to let you know that losing both legs made you a quarter of a man. Then I said I needed to know more about the ratios. Like if a hiker lost a few toes to frostbite, what percentage of a man was he?" I meet his eyes. "I know, it was a horrible thing to say. It wasn't my finest moment."

He grins, apparently unoffended by my heat-of-the-moment retort to Mark's ludicrous rationale. "I don't know," he says. "It sounds like a perfect response to his bullshit logic."

I shrug. "It didn't work. He accused me of making a joke out of his feelings, and I told him he was being an idiot." I stare at my pizza. "Like I said, not my finest moment."

He watches me carefully. "For what it's worth, he's not the first to act this way. It's much easier to accept someone else's injuries than to accept your own. I made my own mistakes because I couldn't come to grips with my changed body, and they cost me dearly."

"You came to your senses, though."

But the big man shakes his head. "Not soon enough, Green Eyes. Some damages can't be undone."

I nod. "Mark's made choices he'll regret. And I'm not referring to myself." I hesitate before gesturing to my rounded abdomen. "I'm pregnant."

He grins. "I noticed. What did he say when you told him about the baby?"

"Babies," I correct him. "I'm having twins." Stubbs' dark eyes widen. "He wouldn't return my calls or texts. He wouldn't even come to the door when I went by to tell him. He left me standing on his doorstep in the cold, pounding on his door. He still doesn't know I'm pregnant."

"He hasn't seen you?"

"Not since he left. He's refused to. He saw me last week from across a parking lot, but I was bundled up in a coat. We held eye contact for about thirty seconds before he practically sprinted to his van and peeled out of there. He texted me out of the blue yesterday to say he thinks about me every day, but..." I sigh. "I don't trust him not to reverse course again, and I didn't cope well when he left." *Understatement of the century.* "And honestly, I can't go through all that heartache again. I met with a custody lawyer yesterday. They'll inform him about the babies, and I'll deal with the fallout."

He sighs, his eyes sober. "I'm sorry, Charlie. If there's anything I can do, just let me know."

Sudden tears prick my eyes. "Thanks, Stubbs," I say, my voice rough.

He pushes my plate closer. "Eat. Feed your little parasites." When I frown at him, he laughs. "They're taking everything they need from you. That's the literal definition of a parasite. Eat."

Once again, I'm reminded that while it might feel like it sometimes, I'm not alone.

MARK

Sunday afternoon, I'm startled by a firm knock on my front door. I turn down the volume on the football game I'm half-watching and open it, expecting to see Tucker or Lila. Instead, I find an African-American man roughly the size of a Kodiak grizzly on my doorstep. My jaw drops.

"Hey, Pretty Boy. Thought I'd swing by and visit you."

I gape at him. "Stubbs? What are you doing in town?"

He laughs. "It's too damn cold to discuss out here. You gonna let me in?"

I step aside, too stunned to speak. Stubbs steps inside and gives me a man-hug, clapping me hard on the back before stepping back to appraise me. "I've never seen you without your crutches before. Looking fine, Pretty Boy. Looking damn fine," he says admiringly.

I regain my senses and narrow my gaze. "Don't ever call me fine when you're looking me up and down like a piece of meat."

The big man roars with laughter. "Fair enough."

I close the door, and Stubbs peels off his jacket. He looks much too large for my crappy little apartment, eating up all the space as he strolls into my living room. "Avoid that end of the sofa," I warn him quickly. "It has a rogue spring guaranteed to turn you into a eunuch." He halts, eyeing the couch, then cautiously sits on the opposite end.

"I didn't know you were coming to town," I tell him.

He gives me a meaningful look. "Maybe you should return a call or a text once in a while," he says evenly. "What the fuck? You're too good to talk to me now? I was okay to get you through the rough stuff, but now that you've had your surgery, you just blow me off?"

"That's not it at all," I protest.

"Then what is it?" he challenges.

I hesitate. "It's complicated."

"I'm a simple man. Uncomplicate it for me."

I frown. "I wasn't in a chatty mood, that's all."

"You couldn't even answer a damn text for five months?"

I don't say anything, because he's got me dead to rights.

"Heard you broke up with Charlie a while back," he says, watching me expectantly.

I abruptly turn and head into my postage stamp-sized kitchen. "I'm getting a beer. Want one?"

"Sure." He pauses for a beat, then continues, "What'd you do a dumbass thing like that for?"

"It's a long story," I mutter from inside the fridge.

"Your life seems to be full of long, complicated stories. Good thing I'm free all afternoon."

"You never did tell me why you're here," I persist, desperate to shift the conversation.

"Aren't you happy to see me?"

I bring him a beer and sit down on the loveseat. "Sure. You caught me off guard, that's all. I mean, you live seven hundred miles away."

He raises the bottle to his lips and takes a long swallow before answering me. "Not anymore. I took that job with the VA," he says. "I'm going to be a counselor at Lila and Charlie's clinic."

"Congratulations," I say, surprised Tucker hasn't mentioned it. "So you're living here now?"

He nods. "Just got into town this weekend."

"Did you have any trouble finding a place to live?" I ask, remembering how long it took me to find something disability-friendly.

The huge man grins slowly, showcasing perfect white teeth as he pauses with his beer halfway to his lips. "Nope. I moved in with someone special."

I chuckle. "Such a ladies' man."

He shakes his head. "This one's not another notch on my belt. She's different. Special."

This is news. I've never seen him get serious about anyone. "Really?" I ask, curious. "Someone finally tamed you?"

Stubbs laughs. "I'm not averse to settling down. I was married once, you know."

"You were? What happened?"

He looks away for a brief second. "That's a story for another day. Living in the past does nothing but wreck the future."

"And your future is with your new woman?"

A smile spreads over his features. "She's pretty amazing."

"Tell me about her."

But he shakes his head. "I don't want to jinx things. I'll wait for the dust to settle. Then I'll tell you. In the meantime, you can tell me what happened with you and Charlie."

My chest grows tight.

What happened was that I fell in love with her, but was convinced I shouldn't saddle her with my perceived inadequacies for the rest of her life.

What happened was that I decided she deserved more than I could give her because of my injuries.

What happened was that I didn't trust her to truly love me because I saw my changed body as unlovable.

But I can't say any of that to a fellow amputee, especially not one in a happy relationship. "We wanted different things," I finally reply, which is true. She wanted me, and I wanted her to have someone better.

"You couldn't come to a compromise?"

"No," I said soberly. "There wasn't any middle ground."

"Must make your friendship awkward," he comments mildly.

I shoot him a dark look, because he obviously already knows. "We aren't friends now."

"That sucks," he says. "You guys had been friends for like twenty years, right?"

"Twenty-five. Can we talk about something else?"

"Why? Is this conversation bothering you?"

"Yeah, it is," I snap, my irritation flaring. "I'm done talking about Charlie."

"Okay," he agrees easily. "Let's talk about why you ghosted me."

I purse my lips. "I already told you, I haven't felt very chatty lately."

He tilts his head, studying me. "So you view friendships as mood-dependent? Interesting." He taps his lower lip. "That's two friendships you've decided weren't worth your time or effort. What about Tom? How long has it been since you saw him?"

My jaw tightens. "A while."

"And Tucker? Lila? Who do you actually give a damn about, Pretty Boy?"

"It's not that I don't give a damn." My tone's sharper than I'd intended, and I pause to take a couple of deep breaths.

"Friendships are a two-way street, Chandler. Just because you decide you no longer need somebody doesn't mean they don't still need you. I'm a big boy. My feelings will be just fine. But Tom and Charlie busted their asses to help you recover. It's pretty shitty of you to drop the people who cared about you because you decided you didn't need them anymore."

Tucker's words ring loudly in my head. *"You dropped Charlie like a used tissue the second you got tired of fucking her."*

Now Stubbs is accusing me of the same thing.

I open my mouth, not sure what I'm going to say, but it doesn't matter. He stands, placing his beer bottle on my battered coffee table. "Thanks for the beer. I'll see you around." He strides to my door and leaves, pulling it closed behind him.

I exhale heavily. Just what I needed. One more person telling me what I already know – that I've made a massive mistake that will haunt me the rest of my life.

CHARLIE

I didn't wake up with night terrors last night.

It's the first time since I moved into Mark's old room that I haven't woken up with them.

Maybe it's because I was legitimately exhausted.

Maybe it's because I took one of the sleeping pills Dr. Oaks gave me.

Maybe it's because Penny wrapped her furry body around mine and snuffled me anxiously every time I moved.

Or maybe it's because there's another person in the house, someone I can trust to have my back.

Whatever the reason, I wake up refreshed, and for the first time in a long time, I feel settled.

I can do this.

MARK

Living alone gives me plenty of time to think. The past few weeks, that's not been a good thing. Sometimes my head is a dark place to be. But I need to make amends for the things I've screwed up, and that requires self-analysis. I'm doing a lot of reflecting, and I'm not happy with what I'm seeing.

The airline industry uses something called the "swiss cheese model" to understand how plane crashes occur. Usually, the cause isn't a single major problem. Instead, multiple little things go wrong, and when combined in exactly the right way, they spell disaster. In short, the holes in the swiss cheese line up perfectly, and all the little problems collectively evade the safeguards, resulting in catastrophe.

My life became my own swiss cheese situation. Multiple things combined and led to my disastrous situation, and by extension, Charlie's.

For starters, when my relationship was going well with Charlie – prior to my surgery – I quit taking my antidepressant. I decided I no longer needed it since I wasn't depressed. I broke the cardinal rule of taking any prescribed medication: don't make spontaneous changes without talking to your doctor.

Here's the kicker – I'd been warned. One of the things Dr. Friedman and I discussed when I was at Brooke – before I even took the first dose – was how antidepressants should never be stopped abruptly because of the risk of intense rebound depression. But that didn't stop me. I didn't check with my doctor. I didn't even taper down my dose. Hell, no. I decided I knew what was best and quit cold turkey. Besides, I was feeling great, so what was the harm?

A lot, actually.

The reason I'd felt better was because the medication was doing exactly what it was supposed to do – reduce the sharp peaks and plunging valleys of my moods. Because I rashly stopped taking it when Charlie and I became intimate, I set myself and ultimately, our relationship, up to fail.

Had it been Charlie impetuously stopping a medication, I'd have encouraged her to talk to her doctor first. But that's not what I did. Nope. I made an impulsive decision without communicating with the other person – in this case, my doctor – and it had serious repercussions.

At my next visit, I admit to Dr. Allen how and why I quit my antidepressant, and when he urges me to resume taking it, I do.

My second "swiss cheese moment" was when I realized Charlie was in love with me.

I made a hasty decision driven by my self-loathing, convinced I knew what was best, and I never discussed it with her. Not honestly, anyway. I lied and said I didn't love her, and I refused to listen to what she – and everyone else

– was telling me. Because I'd stopped my meds, my out-of-control emotions drove my actions, and I made another impulsive, unilateral decision without honest communication: I abandoned the most important person in my life.

Another "swiss cheese" situation was my starry-eyed belief in osseointe-gration surgery. For months, I'd equated that surgery with becoming "whole" or "normal", much as I'd convinced myself at Brooke that pushing myself harder would make me normal. Both rehab and surgery helped tremendously, but they each had limitations.

Once again, I set myself up for failure by having unrealistic expectations. After surgery, when I saw the ugly abutment protruding from my shin and realized it would stare at me every night when I removed my prosthetic, I instantly reverted to self-disgust and depression. I never even stopped to be grateful for the chance to walk without crutches, my singular goal since my injury.

Other people's words and observations keep rising to the surface. Lila said I fixate on what's missing and ignore my strengths. Dr. Allen said essentially the same thing – that I've focused on my injuries to the detriment of everything else. They're right. I reduced myself to the sum of my wounds. Poisonous self-talk and believing I was a "useless cripple" created another "swiss cheese" hole.

Tucker's declared repeatedly that regardless of my injuries, my only limitations are self-imposed. He's right. Viewing myself so negatively limited my present and my future.

The worst part is that believing I wasn't good enough for Charlie because of my leg mushroomed into a self-fulfilling prophecy. Because I thought I wasn't good enough for her, I lied to her. Hurt her. Abandoned her. Betrayed her.

And that's the behavior of someone who isn't good enough for her.

I was wrong, and I fucked up. Being good enough for her has nothing to do with a man's limb count and everything to do with his heart. Charlie deserves someone who loves her more than life itself, who worships the ground she walks on and treats her like a queen.

I want to be that man.

More than anything, anything at all, I want Charlie back. I *need* her back. I meant what I said. The universe can have *both* my legs if it will let me have her again. It doesn't matter whether I have one leg, two, or none. I no longer care. The only thing that matters to me is Charlie.

But before I devote all my attention to begging her forgiveness, I've got things to take care of. I head over to the VFW to join the amputee support group. I've got to get rid of all this emotional baggage surrounding my leg. It's destroying everything. Who better to help me navigate this minefield than people who have already done so successfully?

When I walk in, Buck's already there. He grins, his eyes twinkling as he rolls his wheelchair toward me. "I'm surprised to see you. Thought you might go the way of your 'special leg' and disappear."

I smile and shake my head. "Sorry to disappoint you. I thought I'd do as my friend suggested and pull my head out of my ass, but I need some help."

He smiles broadly. "Get over here and sit down, son. We've got time and a pry bar."

LILA

I spend Sunday afternoon wrapping Christmas gifts and filling out cards while Tucker naps on the couch behind me. One stack is for Tucker's mom, Marie, and his brothers Ethan, Joey, and Shepherd. Another pile is for Tara, Tom and Maya, and Stubbs. Mark's gift is in the garage. I've ordered Charlie's gift – a gliding rocker recliner for the corner of her bedroom. It'll be perfect for rocking her precious babies to sleep. It should be delivered this week. Tucker's gifts are already wrapped and tucked beneath the tree. When I'm done wrapping presents, I stretch my aching back and snuggle in beside him. He rolls to his side, pulling me against him without waking up.

Charlie tried to convince me to spend Christmas with Mark instead of her. In spite of his mountain of bullshit, she doesn't want him to be alone for the holidays. I told her flatly that ignoring her wasn't an option. Eventually, we agreed we'd divide our time, much like children dealing with divorced parents. On Friday, we'll have the Maxwell family Christmas party at Marie's house. On Christmas Eve, we'll go to Charlie's and celebrate with our usual hors d'oeuvres, Christmas movies, and gift exchange during the afternoon and early evening. Then we'll return home and have Mark over for dinner and exchange gifts with him.

Christmas Day? That's strictly for me and Tucker. Our lives have become overly busy, and I'm longing for couple-time. I mentioned that to him, and since we're closing the clinic for the holidays Tuesday afternoon and not reopening until after New Year's, he's decided to work half-days while I'm off and spend his afternoons with me.

And I can't wait.

I'm done letting my desperation to conceive drive a wedge between us. Just because motherhood seems to be an impossibility, that doesn't mean it is. Charlie's living proof. If it's meant to be, Tucker and I will conceive, and if it doesn't happen with fertility treatments by the time I turn thirty-five, I'll look into adoption.

For now, though, I want to reconnect with my husband on a deeper level.

CHAPTER FOURTEEN

MARK

TUCKER SAID TOM AND Maya are leaving town Tuesday to fly to New York for Maya to see her mom. Monday morning, I leave a bag with the gifts for Tom and Maya at the entrance to the clinic. Tom wouldn't care if his gift was delayed, but I'd rather Maya got hers early, not late.

That's not the only thing I leave on the clinic's doorstep.

My text telling Charlie how much I think about her didn't garner any response. That's okay. I've overcome challenges in the past. I've worked out my battle plan, so to speak, to convince Charlie to give me one last chance. It's a multi-layered approach, and my second attempt is primed and ready. I leave a container of daffodils with a card at the door of the clinic, next to the bag for Tom. It's not even seven, so she isn't there yet, but they'll be coming in soon, hopefully before the cold has a chance to damage the flowers.

Charlie loves daffodils. Her mom, Grace, loved them too.

I've been thinking a lot about Charlie, not just about our intimate relationship, but about our relationship in its entirety, from the time we were kids through our teen years, military life, and beyond. I can't recall a time when my life wasn't tied to hers. Even now, we're still linked through Lila and Tucker, and because of them, we always will be.

If I want any chance at all to rebuild what I've destroyed, I need to remind Charlie of the good times. It won't outweigh the pain I've caused, but maybe it will be enough to convince her to speak to me again.

My first attempt—my text—was met with silence. I shouldn't have expected her to answer. After all, I've spent months ignoring every effort she made to connect with me. I'm sure my words rang hollow, because my actions haven't matched those of a man who can't stop thinking about a woman. For my second try, I tell her how I felt about her mom.

Charlie's mom was amazing. Aside from my own mom, I can't think of another soul in the world who was a better mother. I was devastated when I lost my mom. Cancer's a bitch. It destroys you insidiously from within, ravaging the body in secret a few cells at a time, until you're just a husk of the person you once were. When my mom died, I was at that awkward early-teen stage, more than a boy, but not remotely close to a man. I missed my mom so much it was physically painful, but I was too embarrassed to say so.

I never had to say it with Grace.

Grace knew instinctively what I needed. She nurtured me in ways I didn't fully see or understand until long after she'd passed away. She did the things my own mom would have done if she were alive, and she provided the emotional support my grief-stricken dad couldn't. She did those things moms do so well – hemming my jeans, taking me shopping for school clothes, and stroking my hair or squeezing my shoulder when she'd walk past. When my mouthguard slipped during football practice and I took a hard hit in the teeth, she took me straight to her dentist. When I needed to learn to dance, she and John demonstrated slow dancing, then had Charlie and I practice in the living room while she corrected our form. When my dad committed suicide, she brought me into their home immediately. They'd asked me if I'd consider letting them take me in permanently before they had any idea my dad had already named them my legal guardians.

The first Mother's Day after my mom died was horrible. I missed her. God, I missed her, and even at fourteen, I knew I'd have never made it without Grace. My dad was too imprisoned by grief to notice me most days. I took my saved allowance and bought daffodil bulbs, then went out before daylight to dig up around the base of her big oak tree out front and plant them. I showed up at breakfast and presented her with fresh daffodils from the florist. When she made a huge fuss over them and kissed me on the cheek, I took her outside and shyly showed her where I'd planted the bulbs so she could have daffodils every spring.

When she cried, I thought she was upset I'd dug up her yard. I apologized and promised I'd reseed the grass I'd wrecked. Instead, she pulled me close and hugged me tightly.

I can still smell her perfume when I close my eyes.

Grace was incredible, and losing her was as hard as losing my own mom, though in a different way. I think it's because she sought me out to love. She was a wonderful woman, and she raised one hell of a daughter. Grace would be so proud of Charlie, of all she's done, of her strength, her brilliance, her spirit.

And I want Charlie to know that.

I found a florist in southern California two days ago that was willing to create an arrangement to my specifications and overnight ship it for an exorbitant fee. They arrived last night. When I saw them, I knew they were worth every penny.

I just hope Charlie likes them half as much as Grace would have.

CHARLIE

I see them as soon as I walk into my office Monday morning.

A deep white dish perches jauntily on one corner of my desk. It holds a cluster of yellow daffodils bursting from soft green moss and polished brown creek rocks, and they're beautiful.

It's also December, with several inches of snow outside.

Tara pokes her head into my office, her dark hair swinging free. "Those were out front when I got here. They're lovely," she says. "I can't imagine where someone found daffodils this time of year."

They are lovely, and I adore daffodils. They hint at better things to come.

Beside the crock is a cream-colored envelope with a single sheet of heavy paper inside. I recognize Mark's handwriting, and my heart skips a beat. I unfold the paper, scanning the page.

CHARLIE,

YOUR MOM LOVED DAFFODILS, AND I KNOW YOU DO, TOO. THESE MADE ME

THINK OF HER. SHE WAS A SELFLESS WOMAN WHO MADE SURE I KNEW I WAS

LOVED. I HATED LOSING MY MOM, BUT GRACE WAS ALWAYS THERE FOR ME.

SHE'D BE SO PROUD OF THE AMAZING WOMAN YOU'VE BECOME. I HOPE

THESE MAKE YOU THINK OF HER AND SMILE.

MARK

Tears spring to my eyes as I read the note. His heartfelt words touch something deep inside me. This is the Mark I miss most – the Mark who shares his mind, his soul, his heart.

My Mark.

He doesn't mention anything about us or our issues. He simply reminds me of a shared past, of a mother's love, of a time and a person with deep meaning for both of us.

The painful contrast between this Mark and the one who discarded me like smelly garbage is so sharp, I have to sit down.

I can't do this.

I take the note and bury it in my purse before drying my eyes. It's beautiful, sentimental, and perfect, but like Dorothy in the Wizard of Oz, I've seen behind the curtain. I can't let myself get drawn in by the illusion.

I have to get rid of the flowers, but my conflicted emotions insist I take a picture of them first. I pick up the container and march down the hall to Tara. "Would you like these? I think I'm allergic to them," I lie.

Tara's dark eyes scan my face. "Your eyes are red," she agrees. She reaches for them. "My next-door neighbor's husband died two years ago. He used to cut daffodils from his garden for her every spring. He had hundreds of them that he'd planted just for her. I'll bet these would cheer her up. The holidays are difficult for her."

"That's perfect. I'm glad they're going to someone who needs them."

Lila joins me in my office a few minutes later. "Since when are you allergic to daffodils? They're your favorite."

"I can't do it, Lila. I'm can't let Mark back in only to have him snatch the rug out from under me again. There's too much at stake. It's safer to let go and move on." My eyes burn again.

Sadness flashes over her delicate features, but she nods. "Okay, Charlie. Whatever you need." She closes my door behind her when she leaves.

The softly closing door feels like one slamming shut inside my heart.

I miss the old days, when Mark was just Mark, and I was just Charlie, and we were *us*.

Inseparable.

I drop my head into my hands and cry.

MARK

I still don't hear anything from Charlie. I texted Lila to be sure, and Charlie definitely received my daffodil arrangement. She didn't say what Charlie thought of them, though.

Did you really think a few flowers would erase the hell you've put her through?

I'm disappointed, but not discouraged. I'll spend every day for the rest of my life trying to make things up to her. I love her too much to do anything else.

I've told Charlie how much her mom meant to me. For my next attempt, I want to tell her how much her dad meant to me, too.

John was a great guy. He stepped in to help when my mom was diagnosed with cancer. Where Grace filled the gaps my mom couldn't because of her illness, John supported my dad, taking care of things around our house to allow my dad to focus solely on my mom. After her death, John tried to help my dad through his depression, but he couldn't accept help. Dad died in a car crash, though I didn't realize until later that it wasn't accidental; he aimed his car straight at a concrete overpass support because his grief was destroying him. I'd been living with Charlie's family for a few months when I found out. I couldn't sleep and had my head in the fridge when I'd overheard them talking in John's office.

"I wish Jack would have gotten help. I begged him to," John said, his voice anguished. I'd straightened up and closed the refrigerator, listening. Grace had murmured something in response, but I couldn't make it out.

"How could Jack do this to Mark? He'd lost so much already when Diana died. Now he's all alone. I should have pushed him harder to get help."

"Mark isn't alone," Grace had responded quietly. "He has us. What happened isn't your fault. Diana was everything to Jack. He couldn't face a life without her."

I was shocked to hear John crying, blaming himself. I didn't blame him. I didn't even blame my dad. I blamed cancer. It wrecked everything.

John helped me through those challenging years where boys grow into men. He taught me things you can't learn in school – self-reliance, determination, and strength of character. He showed me love is an action, not merely a feeling, when he opened his heart and home to the skinny orphan from next door. He took me camping, worked with me on football moves, and helped me buy my first car. It was John I called the night I went to a party and got drunk, and he picked me up without a word of complaint. We talked about it the next day when he drove me back to get my car. I'd expected a scolding. Instead, John swore he'd always rather I called him instead of getting behind the wheel drunk. I've never forgotten that conversation, because his voice broke when he said he couldn't bear to lose me, too.

That was the last time I ever got drunk, until that day with Charlie in the parking lot.

I don't think John ever said the words "I love you," to me. Grace told me all the time. It's just the way she was, wearing her heart on her sleeve. John expressed his emotions in actions, not words. Where Grace would come up and wrap her arms around me and whisper that she loved me, John would drop a hand on my shoulder and tell me he'd ordered tires for my car because mine were looking worn, or bring home a new pair of winter gloves because he'd seen me leave the house barehanded because I'd misplaced one of mine.

I've never once doubted that he loved me every bit as much as Grace did. Love poured from everything the two of them did for me, and they did it for a boy who wasn't their own.

When I see daffodils, I think of Grace and Charlie. With John, it's cheese-cake.

John loved life. Every event was a cause for celebration – finishing final exams, the first crocus in spring, the appearance of pumpkins and vivid autumn leaves. And every event was celebrated with his favorite dessert: a chocolate chip cheesecake with a chocolate cookie crust, rich, buttery, decadent, and not too sweet.

There's a bakery in town that makes chocolate chip cheesecake. I swing by and sample a piece. It's not quite the same as the one he brought home, but it's close.

It's the first time I've eaten chocolate chip cheesecake since his death.

I arrange for one to be delivered to Charlie's house on Christmas Eve, when I know she, Tucker, and Lila will be enjoying their holiday munchies-and-movies marathon.

The woman behind the counter smiles knowingly when I hand her an envelope and ask her to deliver it with the dessert. She clips the envelope to the order ticket. "I'll take care of it," she promises with a wink.

Attempt number three is underway.

CHARLIE

Tuesday morning, Tom stops by to grab some papers he'd forgotten before going back home to finish packing for his trip. He pokes his head into the communal kitchen to find me drinking hot green tea with pomegranate. "How's it going?" he asks, taking in my pale face and tired eyes.

I sigh. "Tucker says Mark wants to talk to me."

He studies me carefully, leaning against the door frame. "He wants you back."

"I guess. He sent me a text that said he thinks about me every day, and yesterday he sent flowers and a letter talking about how much my mom meant to him. He said she'd be proud of the woman I've become."

"You got rid of the flowers," he observes, and I nod. "Why?"

I struggle to put my feelings into words. "He said all the right things. He reminded me of the Mark I've always known. Well, at least until a few months ago." I pause. "But the Mark he was back then wouldn't have behaved the way he has recently."

"The Mark he was back then hadn't been through everything he's been through this year." My eyes shoot to Tom's. "I'm not defending his behavior," he says quickly. "I'm just pointing out that he's had a lot thrown at him."

"He has," I agree. "But so have I, and I didn't take it out on him."

"True." He pauses. "So Mark wants you back. The question is, what do you want?"

I exhale loudly. "It's safer for my heart to let him go and move on, but I have to do what's best for my babies."

He pinches his full lower lip before taking a seat at the table across from me. "Your babies' needs are very important. That's why you need to do what's best for you. Trust me on this, Charlie. I knew marrying Chele was a mistake, but I thought Maya needed a two-parent home. What she actually needed was for me to be happy so I could give her my best. That's what your babies need, too." His brown eyes are serious. "If you want to get back together with Mark for yourself, do it. But don't do something solely for the sake of your babies."

I think about Tom's words after he leaves. I love Mark. Part of me always will. He's been in my life so long, it's hard to remember a time we weren't close. And I'm pretty sure I'm still *in* love with him, based on my initial reaction to him in the parking lot.

But then he walked away.

Again.

And I can't trust him not to leave me again.

So am I really in love with him?

Is it possible to be in love with someone you don't trust?

I'm not the only one whose emotions are all over the map. His are even worse than mine. He told Tucker and Lila he screwed up and says he misses me, but what happens when he finds out about the babies? Will his "half a man, you deserve better" crap apply to fatherhood?

The worst part of this is that I'm the only one who can decide what my heart really wants. And as emotional as I am these days? I'm screwed.

I don't have a lot of empty time to mope, though, which is another reason having Stubbs around is a good thing. He and I fall into a comfortable routine in the days leading up to Christmas. The clinic is closed, so I'm finally resting and relaxing. I'm sleeping well, which is a delightful change of pace. I haven't had night terrors since Stubbs moved in. He and I have worked out a deal – he cooks breakfast, I make lunch, and we either order out or take turns cooking dinner. One day I drive him all around town, something that takes no time in a place as small as Cedar Ridge. I show him the best restaurants, the movie theater, the mall just outside of town, and the turnoff for the highway to Pueblo where the VA is. We end by stopping at Lila's so he can root through his storage pod for some of his belongings, then return to my house. Lila and Tucker decide to join us for dinner when they hear I'm making chicken Alfredo, and the four of us have a relaxed dinner, with Penny slurping noodles from her bowl on the floor. The sound reminds me of that night with Maya months ago, when I was struck by the sudden desperate realization that I wanted a family – a loving husband who didn't see me as broken, a house full of kids and messy chaos, and cranky cats and big dogs that slurped noodles from the floor.

Well, she's not big, but I have a dog who slurps noodles, and I'll have two kids. That's half my dream right there.

I wonder how well Penny would get along with a cat.

Thursday morning, I awaken at four o'clock with my bladder ready to burst. One of my little butterflies is stomping all over it, or maybe both of them are. I can't be sure. All I know is that by the time I'm done, any chance of going back to sleep is gone.

I was dreaming of Mark when I woke up.

I dreamed he came to see me, swept me into his arms, and told me he loved me. Only then did I tell him I was pregnant, and when I did, he kissed me long and hard, then dropped to his knees and cradled my belly in his hands, pressing his face to it. Even in my dream, I wondered how he'd seen me and not realized I was pregnant, because the babies have made their presence obvious in a surprisingly short amount of time.

The joy in my dream contrasts sharply with reality, and it leaves me feeling raw, like he's rejected me all over again. Hot tears slide down my face.

It's okay. I'm prepared to manage without him.

Raising my babies alone won't be easy, but I'm strong enough to do it with help from my chosen family.

Lila. Tucker. Tom and Maya. Even Stubbs.

For my babies, I'll be strong enough.

When I get into the shower, I throw a scent tablet under the water – one of those discs that fizzes and releases its smell when it gets wet. This one smells like jasmine. When I'm done, I blow dry my hair to ward off the chill and dress in black leggings and a tunic-length beige sweater. Then I do something I haven't done in ages – give myself a pedicure. My ever-growing baby belly adds an entirely new degree of difficulty, but I manage to do a decent job painting my toenails a gorgeous burgundy pearl color.

Self-care.

It's something Linda has stressed for years, and I'm finally trying. Taking walks in the woods. Eating properly. Watching flames dance in the fireplace or staring at the Christmas tree lights in the dark. Drinking cocoa. Reading for pleasure. Using scented candles. Even painting my toenails – they're all things I'm doing because I enjoy them.

Progress, not perfection.

Stubbs makes omelets for breakfast, and I leave the house before nine. I have appointments with both Dr. Rose and Linda today. I see Dr. Rose first. It's a long drive for a short visit. In a nutshell, things are humming along nicely. I've gained six pounds in two weeks, and while I'm still underweight, I'm moving in the right direction. My blood pressure is good, the vomiting has stopped, I'm eating well, and I'm meeting the appropriate pregnancy milestones.

Then she puts the doppler on my belly, and I hear my babies' heartbeats. Both lub-dub rapidly, but one is slightly faster.

"Usually the boys have slightly faster heartbeats," she says, glancing at my face as she shifts the probe toward the sound.

"So that one's the boy?"

"More than likely, yes," she smiles. "And here's your daughter," she says, sliding the probe back across my abdomen to pick up a still fast, but slightly slower, swishing heartbeat.

My son. My daughter.

No, I correct myself. Our son, and our daughter. These babies are very real, and becoming more so every day. Mark and I have to come to some sort of agreement.

The court date has been set for the end of March, and my attorney will have Mark's papers served next week, sometime after Christmas but before the end of the year. Today's the twenty-third. Sometime in the next three to eight days, Mark will find out he's going to be a dad.

"Two weeks," Dr. Rose says, holding the exam room door open for me. "We'll do another ultrasound then to make sure everything's on track."

Mark will know about the babies by then. I wonder if he'll want to come along.

I wonder if he'll even be speaking to me.

Probably not. Finding out he's going to be a dad by being served custody papers won't sit well with him. Tough shit. All he had to do was open his damn door or answer his phone, and he'd have heard it from me.

I have to breathe deeply to quell my rising irritation.

My appointment with Linda goes well. I'm doing the things I'm supposed to – practicing self-care, reflecting, journaling. I fill her in on things with Mark. She applauds my choice to give away the daffodils to someone who would enjoy them rather than let them make me feel bad. Linda is a diehard believer in reinforcing her clients' good choices.

We revisit the topic of whether Mark leaving me was a betrayal if he intentionally hurt himself by doing so, believing it was for my own good. Last time, I'd decided it didn't matter, because his self-image was so skewed I couldn't trust him not to hurt me again. Today I'm less sure. Some of the things I've learned from Tucker – that he's seeing a psychiatrist to help with his body-image issues and trying not to view himself as half a man – indicate he's trying to get to a healthier place. In the end, I'm firmly in the "I don't know" camp when it comes to whether it was a betrayal. I still don't trust him not to revert back to a negative mindset, but I do believe he made his choice despite knowing it would hurt him.

When I leave Linda's, I stop at the grocery store for last-minute items for our Christmas Eve get-together tomorrow, as well as for the Christmas dinner I'll make for myself and Stubbs. He'd gone out the day after he arrived and come home with enough groceries for an army. He'd attempted to give me rent money that morning, and I'd flatly refused. When he persisted, I told him exactly where he could insert the cash he was trying to push into my hand. He'd finally said he surrendered, but the sneak found a work-around by taking over the grocery shopping and errands. He wasn't aware of our holiday plans, so I pick up deli meats and cheeses, a fresh turkey breast, green beans, potatoes, oranges, and cranberry-orange relish. On a whim, I add cream cheese and red and green colored sugar to my cart.

Stubbs snatches the front door open as soon as I open the back of my car. "Freeze," he says, and I glance up. "Lift one bag and you're in deep shit, Green Eyes."

I roll my eyes but lift my hands in resignation. "Why does everyone act like I'm helpless just because I'm pregnant? Women in other countries work in the fields right up until they deliver."

He loops the handles of all seven stuffed canvas bags over his huge fore-arms and hoists them with no visible effort. "Lucky for you, you're here, surrounded by people who care about you."

I close the back of the car and walk ahead of him to get the door. "You know, you make it hard to argue with you when you phrase it like that," I mutter, and he grins.

"Therapy 101. Poke holes in faulty arguments when it's in the client's best interests."

Stubbs insists on making dinner even though it's my night to cook, saying I need to rest after running around all day. I roll my eyes but acquiesce, because while I'd never admit it, I am pretty tired. He whips up an incredible stir-fry with chicken and vegetables spicy enough to make my eyes water, served over jasmine rice made with coconut milk and lime zest.

"Too hot?" he asks. "The chilis packed more of a wallop than I expected."

I shake my head, draining my water glass. "It's good. The rice helps tone down the heat." He purses his lips as he glances at my watery eyes.

"I'll cut back on the chilis next time," he promises.

That night, I dream of Mark again, holding me in his arms and telling me he loves me. He doesn't notice the pregnancy this time, and in my dream, I'm relieved, because I know his words are based on his feelings and not coming from some misplaced sense of duty toward his babies.

I wish I knew what his true feelings are in real life.

Then maybe I could figure out what to do with my own.

CHAPTER FIFTEEN

MARK

I'M GOING A LITTLE bit crazy.

Okay, maybe a little more than a little bit.

It's been six days since I texted Charlie to tell her I've thought about her every single day.

It's been three days since I delivered daffodils with a handwritten note, talking about Charlie's mom and how much she meant to me and how proud she'd be of Charlie.

And I haven't heard a word from her.

Not. One. Damn. Word.

The logical part of my brain tells me that I've hurt her badly, betrayed her trust on every level, and it's going to take more than a text and some flowers to fix the mess I've made. The primal part of me is desperate to get her back, scrambling to figure out my next steps. The cheesecake will be delivered tomorrow while she's celebrating Christmas Eve with Tucker and Lila. If that doesn't get her to at least talk to me?

I have no idea what to do next.

I pace back and forth in my crappy little apartment, but it doesn't do much good. Snow's starting to fall, but I ignore it. Maybe a drive will clear my head. I've been driving a lot lately, especially at night. I drive past Charlie's house several times a night. Sometimes I pause outside, staring up at the windows, imagining what she's doing. Wondering if she's sleeping on the bench again. Worrying she's having night terrors. Hoping she hasn't moved on.

She's bought a second car, a giant black SUV that looks awfully big for her. Maybe the new car symbolizes taking a new direction in her life. A direction that doesn't include me.

I grab my keys and jacket and climb into my van. Today, I drive north, deeper into the mountains, not heading anywhere in particular. I just need to get my mind on something else. Anything else.

The lull of the winding curves pulls some of the tension from my body, but my brain is still searching for a way to convince Charlie to talk to me, to give me another chance. After thirty minutes, the snow is falling harder, so I turn back toward Cedar Ridge. I'm not sure how well my van handles snow, but it's a van, so I suspect rather poorly, and I'd rather not plunge off a mountain to my fiery death today. In the parking lot of my apartment complex, I lean on my steering wheel, my head on my arms. I've screwed everything up, and I don't know how to fix it. I'm not even sure I can. A chill falls over me, and going inside my crappy little apartment does nothing to ease it.

A sharp rap on my door startles me out of my gloom. Lila's off because the clinic is closed for the rest of the week, and Tucker's taking afternoons off to be with her. Still, it's not like them to drop by out of the blue. Maybe it's Stubbs, come to chew my ass again.

I open my door to find a voluptuous woman who is most definitely not Stubbs standing on my doorstep. She's wearing a low cut white blouse that emphasizes her ample assets and a pair of jeans that appear to have been airbrushed in place. Her long platinum-blond hair has a wide streak of hot pink, the same neon color as her pouty lips and long nails. Jet-black eyes gaze at me from beneath lashes coated so heavily with mascara, they resemble spider's legs.

My scalp tingles in apprehension. Something about her makes me think of an anglerfish.

An anglerfish is a deepwater predatory fish. It has a bioluminescent appendage that dangles in front of its face. The fish wriggles it, causing its shimmering light to lure in smaller fish. When the small fish approach, mesmerized by the dazzling beauty of its iridescent lure, the anglerfish strikes, ripping them apart with horrifying fang-like teeth. That's the vibe this woman is giving off. Everything about her screams predator.

"I'm looking for Mark Chandler," she purrs.

I've never seen this woman before. Thoroughly unsettled, I meet her eyes. "I'm Mark Chandler."

She smiles, pushing her pouty lips out even further, holding my gaze provocatively. Without breaking eye contact, she reaches inside her black leather jacket and produces a manila envelope. She presses the envelope against my chest, lightly flexing her long nails over the fabric of my shirt. "Mark Chandler, you've been served."

TUCKER

I'm stretched out on the sofa, half-dozing. Lila is curled on top of me watching a romantic comedy, occasionally swatting me if I start snoring. I'm only working half days this week, spending my afternoons with her since their clinic is closed. The afternoon sun shines in my face, making me squint, so I throw my arm over my eyes.

My phone dings with a message, but it's on the far side of the coffee table. I ignore it. If it's important, they'll keep texting or call Lila.

A minute later, it dings again.

Nope. I've got a gorgeous blond wrapped around me. Whoever it is can wait.

It dings a third time.

I wonder if it might be Charlie. Maybe something's wrong.

That thought has me reaching toward it when Lila's phone buzzes. "Someone must really want you," she mumbles. She pats the floor in front of the couch until she finds her phone. When she lifts it up, she raises an eyebrow.

"Tell Tucker to answer his goddamn phone," she reads aloud. I glance at her quizzically. "Mark."

It buzzes again in her hand. "Never mind, I'm coming over. Be there in a minute." She sighs. "Something's got his panties in a pucker."

I pull her face toward mine and claim her mouth. "I'll have yours in a pucker later."

"No, you won't," she answers saucily. "I'm going commando."

My lower body twitches at the thought, and I wish Mark weren't coming over. "You could have mentioned that earlier."

She grins. "Just because I'm a sure thing doesn't mean you shouldn't have to work now and then."

I lean forward and kiss her until she's breathless. "I'll work you over later," I promise, and I feel her smile against my lips.

She sits up, stretching her arms over her head and purposely thrusting her perky breasts forward. "I suppose we should get up before Mark gets here," she says. She stands and leans over, grasping her ankles as she contorts herself into a pose like an inverted taco. My mouth goes dry at the sight of her perfect ass just beyond my reach.

The Rainman in my head starts chanting. *Definitely not wearing underwear, definitely not wearing underwear.*

She smiles up at me from her bent-over position, her voice husky. "Mmm. I needed a good stretch. It feels soooo amazing."

"Keep it up, Sweetness. I'll lock the front door and have you right here. Then we'll talk about how amazing you feel."

She straightens up. "Mark just pulled in," she says, grinning. She leans over to kiss me. I slide my hand behind her neck when she moves to pull away. "I'm not done with you yet," I mutter against her mouth. I kiss her thoroughly, until she grips my shoulders and moans into my mouth.

An angry fist starts pounding the door, and I groan as Lila squirms away. "Later," she promises, heading for the door.

"Good," I hear Mark say, his voice tense. "You're both here."

"What's wrong?" I hear Lila ask. I round the corner to see Mark in the hall, his hands fisted, a wad of crumpled papers clutched in one of them. He's breathing hard, his face deep red.

"Did you know?" he demands, glaring at me.

"Know what?"

He waves the papers. "About this."

"What the hell are you talking about?"

Lila pushes the door closed before tugging the wrinkled papers from his hand and smoothing them out. Her eyes widen. "It's a petition for sole custody."

I glance at Mark, then back to Lila. "I thought she wasn't going to do anything yet."

Mark's expression turns murderous. "So you did know," he growls.

"That depends on what you're asking," I say evenly. "If you're asking did we know she was serving you with custody papers, then the answer is no."

"How could you not tell me something this important?" he roars, and Lila's eyes narrow.

Aw, hell. Now he's done it.

"You listen to me, Mark Chandler," she says, advancing on him. "Don't you dare come into my house ranting about why we didn't tell you something Charlie's been trying to tell you for weeks."

"No, you listen," he starts, but Lila's having none of it.

"Don't you *dare*," she snarls, her tone venomous. "Tucker and I have watched Charlie go through hell because of you. You destroyed her, Mark, destroyed her, and we had to help her pick up the pieces because you were too busy wrapped up in your own little poor-pitiful-me bullshit to give a damn about anyone but yourself. She's tried to tell you over and over. She left you voicemails to call her back so you could talk. She texted you every damn day that she needed to see you. She stood on your fucking doorstep pounding on your door, telling you it was important, listening to you silence her phone calls a dozen times." Lila steps closer, her violet eyes flashing as she stabs his chest with her index finger. "Do you know why she was there that day? To show you the ultrasound pictures she'd just gotten. But you were too busy being an asshole to share those first glimpses of your babies with her. She had to share them with us, with me and Tom and Tucker, because we were there for her when the only person you gave a flying fuck about was yourself and your dainty little wounded ego. So don't you dare stomp in here behaving like a jackass when you're the one who refused to listen."

Mark's taken several steps back, retreating from her fury, and Lila's pursued him step for step, backing him against the wall. His red face has drained of all color during her tirade. His voice is barely a whisper when he speaks again. "Babies?"

Lila stares at him like he's an idiot. "What else would it be custody of? Puppies?" she snaps.

He swallows hard. "Plural? More than one?"

Mark looks like he might faint for a minute, and since Lila's still breathing fire, I step forward. "Come sit down, Mark. I'll get the scotch."

MARK

Once I saw the words "petition for sole custody", my vision swam, and I didn't read any further.

I couldn't imagine who was trying to hit me up with a fake paternity suit, until it dawned on me that this was probably Tucker's idea of a joke.

Then I scanned further down and saw Charlotte Emerson listed.

Charlie?

Charlie would never prank me like this.

I remember that terrible day when the gynecologist came into her room at Walter Reed. I'd gotten up to leave, but Charlie had grabbed my hand and begged me to stay. "The rapes, the mutilation, and the subsequent infection have severely damaged your cervix," the doctor had said gently. "I'm sorry, Charlie. It will be impossible for you to conceive." She'd added the usual speech about adoption or fostering, but Charlie had already shut down.

I held her while she cried all afternoon and into the night. Lila sat with her for days, both of us wishing we could do something to relieve that tormented look in her eyes.

But we couldn't. It was one more way those fuckers had hurt her, even after their deaths.

It wasn't that Charlie had specifically planned to have children. I don't think she'd given it any thought. If she had, it wasn't anything she'd ever talked about with me. But having the option ripped away because of what those bastards did was one more knife in her soul.

My head spins. *It's not a prank.*

Charlie's pregnant?

And she's suing me for custody of an unborn child?

Tucker and Lila's words replay in my head. Tucker telling me I didn't have any clue what I'd thrown away because I couldn't be bothered to talk to Charlie. Lila glancing at Tucker when she told me Charlie and I would always be tied together in some capacity for the rest of our lives.

I go from confused to furious in a split second. *They knew.*

They knew, and they didn't tell me.

I text Tucker, but he's not answering. I try Lila once before deciding I'm going over in person. Fuck this. I want some goddamned answers.

I'm so angry I can barely focus on driving, something exceptionally unwise given the snowy pavement. I nearly hit a mailbox and spend as much time on the shoulder as the road during the brief trip. I storm inside, so mad I can't see straight, shaking with rage, demanding answers.

That's when Lila gets in my face. Sweet, tiny Lila.

I forget how ferocious she can be because she looks so delicate, but Lila's not one to trifle with. The furious blonde backs my grown ass down without missing a beat, one finger stabbing into my chest as her eyes flash fire.

Then she sweeps my legs completely out from under me. *"You were too busy being an asshole to share the first glimpses of your babies with her."*

Babies?

Babies?

More than one?

My vision swims again, and Tucker leads me to the couch. I sit numbly, holding the glass of scotch he's brought me.

I've transformed from raging bull to silent churchmouse.

Lila and Tucker perch on either side of me on the sectional sofa. "Drink," Lila says, nudging my hand. Obediently I lift the glass to my lips. I take one sip, then another.

Babies?

I drain the glass.

Lila studies my face. "Are you ready to have a calm, rational discussion, or do you need another drink?"

"Both."

Tucker pours more scotch, eying me carefully. "Remember the day Charlie was vomiting blood?"

I nod. "She had an ulcer. You drove her to the doctor." I burn with shame at the memory of my behavior, snapping that she was merely hung over, that she needed to grow up and move on.

Tucker nods. "The doctor found several health concerns. She had an ulcer. She wasn't sleeping. She was malnourished. She'd lost twenty-five pounds –"

I stare in horror. "But she only weighed maybe one-fifteen to start with."

He nods again, his face as serious as I've ever seen it. "Dr. Oaks threatened to hospitalize her. She did a full workup and discovered along with everything else that she was pregnant."

I shake my head. "But the doctors said she couldn't get pregnant. I was there when they told her. She was devastated."

"Dr. Oaks called them miracle babies," Lila says quietly. "She's pregnant with twins, Mark. Fraternal twins."

All the air whooshes from my lungs.

Twins.

"I have to go talk to her," I say immediately, but Tucker reaches for my arm.

"No," he says firmly. "You're going to sit your ass here and listen. I don't care if I have to tie you to a fucking chair, you're going to listen."

"I have to talk to her," I repeat.

Tucker's eyes blaze. "You wouldn't listen to anybody for the last three months. You're fucking listening today."

I turn to Lila. "I have to get her back."

Lila shakes her head. "Forget it."

My head jerks back. "What?"

Tucker actually has the balls to nod in agreement. "Charlie's been very transparent about her feelings on this. She talked to me about it the morning she found out she was pregnant. Under no circumstances will she take you back because of the babies."

My jaw drops. "But she has to. She can't do this alone."

Lila turns savage again in a heartbeat. "You are *not* making this about you, Mark, not again. All this shit you've put her through has been about you, about what *you* feel and what *you* want. Not anymore. This is about Charlie and what she wants, and if you don't like it, tough shit."

My mouth drops open to respond, but Lila's not done. "Charlie was very clear. Either you came back to her because you loved her, or you didn't come back at all."

"But I do love her."

Tucker shrugs. "You should have told her before you found out about the babies."

"I didn't know about them," I protest.

Lila growls, I swear to God, growls, as she turns to me. "Whose fault is that? Who walked out? Who refused to speak with her? Who turned his back on her in a goddamn parking lot? Every single time she reached out to you, you shoved her away."

"I can't lose her, Lila." My voice comes out like a plea. "I can't."

She looks away, exhaling heavily. I hear her thoughts as clearly as if she's said them aloud.

I'm already too late.

My heart starts to slam hard inside my chest, and my vision goes dark around the edges. I feel like I can't breathe, and I squeeze my eyes shut. In the distance, I hear Tucker repeating my name, but he sounds miles away.

A sudden sharp sting on my left cheek makes me open my eyes. Lila's watching me. Tucker's looking back and forth between us.

I lift my hand to my cheek, rubbing it. "Did you – did you slap me?"

She shrugs. "I didn't have any smelling salts, and you looked like you were going to pass out."

I nod, unsure what to say. *Thanks* doesn't seem appropriate. *Thanks for not slapping me harder?* Maybe. Finally I take a deep breath. "Okay. I'm listening, Tucker. Tell me what I need to do."

CHARLIE

I awaken on Christmas Eve to the smell of bacon, the world's most delicious alarm clock. I take a quick shower and dress in leggings and a cream sweater with sparkly gold threads woven in. By the time I'm presentable, Stubbs is grinning from ear to ear as he points out his creations.

"In honor of today's festivities, I've chosen a red and white theme. Bacon, which is sort of red. Sauteed red potatoes with red peppers. Stuffed French toast topped with warm strawberry compote. And a blood orange and pomegranate yogurt parfait with toasted almonds."

I gape at the spread he's laid out on the dining room table. "I hope it takes the contractors a really long time to finish your apartment."

He laughs. "Come on. I'll help you make your hors d'oeuvres after breakfast."

Stubbs is an excellent cook, but this stuffed French toast is the best thing he's ever made. He dipped thick slices of challah bread into a vanilla-egg mixture before cooking them. Lightly sweetened cream cheese is spread between the stacked slices, and the warmed strawberry topping brings it all together in an explosion of deliciousness. I clean my plate, even licking the last of the strawberry compote off the back of my fork.

He tries to hide his amusement. "Would you like more?"

I sniff delicately. "It's your fault for being such an excellent cook. And the babies' fault, too, for sucking the life out of me. I can't be held responsible for my appetite for the next four months."

We wash the dishes together before starting on the afternoon's menu. "Cookies first," I tell him. "Cream cheese sugar cookies." I'd seen the recipe once on a cooking channel, and after making them, I won't bake sugar cookies any other way. I mix the dough while putting him in charge of fishing my serving platters out of the upper cabinets.

"Alright, Green Eyes, what am I putting on these?"

"There's a deli meat tray, a cheese tray, a veggie tray, a fruit tray, and crackers. I'll make my sweet chili meatballs and cheese puffs after I finish the cookies and then help with whatever you haven't gotten to."

Stubbs is fast in the kitchen. The meat and cheese trays are arranged, covered, and in the refrigerator before I finish making the cookies. He eyes me when I pull ingredients out for the sweet chili meatballs.

"You can't be serious," he says, staring at the jars in my hands.

I grin. "When you taste them, you'll understand," I promise. I dump bottled chili sauce, grape jelly, and onion powder into a saucepan and add a splash of water. When the jelly is melted and the sauce is combined, I add frozen meatballs. Stubbs looks horrified. "Trust me," I tell him. "It's one of my most-requested holiday recipes. They're life-changing."

I turn my attention to making cheese puffs next, rotating pans of puffs and cookies in and out of the oven and onto cooling racks while he slices fruits and vegetables and arranges them on trays like a professional. He even whips up two dipping sauces – a savory one with sour cream and chives, and a sweet one with cream cheese and honey. Penny stands beneath us the entire time, snuffling for fallen goodies. I pretend not to notice the ham Stubbs sets aside for her. Penny notices enough for the both of us.

Stubbs catches me smiling as he feeds her. "She's too thin," he says defensively.

"She is," I agree. "She had an abusive asshole for an owner until a few weeks ago. Now I'm fattening her up and exposing her to people who show animals the love they deserve."

My kitchen is back in order, the house is tidy, and the food is all prepped and ready when Tucker and Lila knock at my door. They both halt mid-step when they see the framed charcoal sketches of my babies hanging on the foyer wall. Lila gazes at them, her mouth a perfect "O" shape. Tucker takes the food they've brought to my kitchen and returns to study them.

"Oh, Charlie," Lila says, her voice full of wonder. "They're beautiful." She caresses the glass lightly with a fingertip, entranced.

Tucker agrees. "They're spectacular." Then he frowns. "Which one's which?"

"It doesn't matter," Lila scolds him. "They're both perfect."

The two of them squabble over whether it's important to know which baby is which, continuing their impassioned discussion into the living room. I roll my eyes and return to the kitchen. Tucker has placed multiple trays of food on the counter, and Stubbs has set out the food we've prepared. There's enough to feed us for days.

I'm startled when my doorbell rings. Anyone who'd visit me on Christmas Eve is already here. Well, except Tom and Maya, but they're in New York.

I open my front door to find a young woman with silky red hair and intense blue eyes holding a flat pink bakery box in her arms. "Charlie Emerson? Merry Christmas," she says, holding it out to me. There's a cream-colored envelope with familiar handwriting tucked beneath the silver cord securing the box closed.

Dammit.

"Have you got a second?" I ask. When she nods, I toss the card aside and open the box. My heart sinks.

Chocolate chip cheesecake.

I've not eaten it since my dad died. I can't.

I don't plan on changing that today.

I reach for my purse and pull out forty dollars. "Twenty for you, and an extra twenty if you'll deliver this to the VFW instead and thank them for their service."

She smiles. "That's really sweet of you. I'll take it over. Merry Christmas."

I carry the cream envelope into the kitchen to open it alone, knowing already what I'll find. Inside is another piece of the same heavy paper that arrived with the daffodils. I unfold it with shaky hands, scanning his neat handwriting.

CHARLIE,

YOUR DAD CELEBRATED EVERY SPECIAL OCCASION WITH THIS DESSERT.

JOHN HELPED ME THROUGH ONE OF THE MOST DIFFICULT TIMES IN MY

LIFE. HE SHOWED ME THAT LOVE IS AN ACTION, NOT MERELY WORDS OR

FEELINGS. HE TAUGHT ME SO MUCH BY LOVING SO DEEPLY. THANK YOU

FOR SHARING YOUR FAMILY WITH ME WHEN I NEEDED THEM MOST. I

HOPE THIS REMINDER OF HIM ADDS JOY TO YOUR CELEBRATION TODAY.

MARK

Chocolate chip cheesecake.

My dad's favorite dessert, brought home for every occasion – getting a "B" on my algebra test or Mark scoring the winning touchdown or sometimes, just because. My dad used a simple dessert to show he cared, that he was paying attention to the things that were important to us.

Once again, Mark is reminding me of our entwined past by telling me how much my dad meant to him. He's trying to use a cheesecake to tell me that he cares, too.

Tears flood my eyes. I miss my dad. I miss my mom. And dammit, I miss Mark. *My* Mark, not the one who deserted me. The one he keeps trying to convince me is still in there.

No.

It's safer to let go and move on.

Stubbs, Lila and Tucker enter as I lay the note on the counter. "What's that?" Tucker asks.

"Another note from Mark."

"Another?"

I nod. "On Monday, he sent daffodils and a note about my mom. Today he sent cheesecake and a note about my dad."

Tucker's face lights up. "There's cheesecake?"

I shake my head. "I had the delivery girl take it to the guys at the VFW instead."

His face falls. Then he looks puzzled. "Why?"

"Because flowers and dessert and a text saying he thinks about me every day doesn't erase everything he's done."

Tucker still looks confused. "I don't get it. Those all sound like good things."

I sigh heavily. "He's choosing things with a specific significance," I explain. "Daffodils were my mom's favorite flower, and he sent a note telling me how much my mom meant to him. Chocolate chip cheesecake was something my dad would bring home just to say he cared. He sent one with a note about how much my dad meant to him."

"He's reminding you of your connection," Lila says.

"Exactly."

Tucker looks from me to Lila and back again. "But you didn't keep either gift?"

"No. He still hasn't bothered to speak to me, and he's not offered any apologies or explanations. I gave the flowers to Tara for her widowed neighbor, and I gave the cheesecake to some vets who are probably lonely over the holidays. Some good should come from them."

All three of them watch me. Stubbs hasn't said a word, but he hasn't taken his eyes off me, either. I look away and pick up a plate, hoping that if I fill it with food, they'll take the hint.

I should have known better. Emotional subtleties are lost on Tucker. "So what happens now?" he asks, his dark blue eyes studying me.

"Now we get our food and watch 'It's A Wonderful Life'."

He watches me, not reaching for a plate. "So it's really over between you and Mark?"

"It was over when he left three months ago, Tucker. The only thing that's changed is that I've finally accepted what his words and actions were saying."

"But his words and actions are different now."

I exhale sharply. "Look, you've seen 'The Wizard of Oz', right? Remember when Dorothy sees behind the wizard's curtain and realizes it's all an illusion? That's what this is. Flowers and dessert and notes – they're supposed to charm me into forgetting everything else. But him leaving me, breaking his promises, refusing to even talk to me – those things weren't an illusion, Tucker. Those are real. That pain is real." My voice has risen as I've spoken, and I stop, clenching my fists.

Lila sees my growing distress and comes to my rescue, taking my hands and opening them. "Breathe. We're not going to dwell on this today. Today is about the four of us spending the holiday together. It's about a sweet dog and two tiny people growing inside their mom and eating amazing food with special friends. That's what we're focusing on today." She nudges me toward the counter. "Get your food and let's go watch movies. I'm dying for your sweet chili meatballs."

Tucker takes my plate from my hands, puts it down, and pulls me against his chest. "I'm sorry. I didn't mean to upset you."

"It's not you," I say, even as tears spring to my eyes at his hug. Then I wave him off. "It's the damn hormones. I'm fine. Let's eat."

Even Penny gives me a skeptical glance.

"Whatever you need, I'm here," Stubbs says quietly, his large hand squeezing my shoulder.

"Thanks, Stubbs."

The problem is, I'm so jumbled up inside, I have no idea what I need.

It's safer to let go and move on. I can't take a chance on him destroying me again, not with my babies to think of.

But moving on would be a hell of a lot easier if I could quit dreaming about Mark.

CHAPTER SIXTEEN

CHARLIE

It's a pleasant afternoon. Stubbs relaxes quietly on the opposite end of my reclining couch, and Lila and Tucker take the other one. I try (and fail) to suppress my grin when Stubbs goes back for a third helping of my grape jelly and chili sauce meatballs. Tucker feeds Penny turkey and crackers, and she sprawls out with her head on his feet. After a while, he moves to the floor, leaning against the sofa, and Penny drapes her head across his lap. He strokes her silky ears as she looks up at him adoringly. Lila curls up on her side, her face close to Tucker's, absently running her fingers through his hair. I smile, watching Tucker pet Penny while Lila pets him. They're completely comfortable together.

My smile fades.

Mark and I were like that once.

A sharp pang runs through me. I think of the babies, wondering if he and I can salvage anything that was once between us, even civility.

Probably not, after he hears from my attorney.

The movie forgotten, I objectively consider the past few months, like an outsider looking in.

I'm pretty sure that with time, I can forgive Mark. His reasons for his behavior are familiar – self-loathing, depression, fear. These are things I understand, not just in the context of his life, but from my own.

But trusting him?

I'm not sure I can ever trust him again, even though until he left, I trusted him with my life.

Actually, I'd still trust him with my life.

It's my heart I can't trust him with.

We finish watching "It's a Wonderful Life" and "Miracle on 34th Street" and exchange gifts. Lila loves her sapphire necklace, and Tucker is thrilled with his MMA tickets. He offers to take Lila, who rolls her eyes and suggests Mark accompany him instead. Stubbs gives them a gift certificate to a swanky restaurant in Pueblo. Lila oohs and aahs, but Tucker groans. "Black tie?"

"I've suffered through Hooters with you more times than I care to count. You'll survive one evening dressed like a grownup," Lila says dryly before winking. "Besides, we can always stay overnight in Pueblo. They have a luxury hotel with hot tubs in every room." At that, Tucker brightens.

He and Lila give Stubbs a gift card to a big box store for all those little things you discover you suddenly need when you move into a new place – lamps, more towels, wastebaskets, and so on. Their gift to me is a gliding rocker for my bedroom/ nursery, so I'll have somewhere to rock my tiny people once they make their appearance. It's slated to be delivered next week.

Like Mark's papers.

Those should be delivered next week, too.

I've filed for full custody of our babies; however, I've included a formal letter encouraging him to file paternity action papers with the courts if he wants to establish parental rights and pursue a joint custody arrangement. I'm giving him the opportunity to decide how much a part of their lives he wants to be.

I'm just not sure how much a part of *my* life I'm willing to let him be.

MARK

Nothing.

I've texted Charlie that I think about her every day, sent flowers I knew she'd love, and sent her favorite dessert, but it's still radio silence.

I didn't think this would be easy, but I never expected her to turn a blind eye toward me, even though I've completely ignored her for months.

Like a mental fortune cookie, an inspirational quote pops into my head. *With time and effort, water smooths even the roughest stone.*

I can be patient. I'll wait for Charlie forever if I have to. But can she really forgive the trust I've broken over and over?

When I swore nothing could ever make me walk away from her.

When she was pleading with me to tell her I loved her.

When I refused to answer her texts, or her calls, or her knocks at my door.

When I rejected her in a parking lot without so much as a backwards glance.

I close my eyes and pinch the bridge of my nose. And now there are babies to think of.

Babies.

I've never even held a baby before. I don't have a clue what to do with one.

Of course, if Charlie gets full custody – which given my recent behavior, my current lack of employment, and my residence that barely qualifies as a hovel, is quite probable – I may never get the chance to hold my babies, anyway.

My son.

My daughter.

I wonder if they'll have their mother's beautiful green eyes.

It's nearly eight, and I'm about to head over to Tucker and Lila's for our Christmas Eve get-together, when there's a knock at my door. I'm instantly wary after yesterday's pink-haired predator, but it's the postman. "You're working late. Don't you know it's Christmas Eve?" I say, as though he could possibly be unaware, given his line of work.

He grins ruefully, passing me some envelopes and a flat package. "The package had fallen beneath the seat and gotten wedged. It should have been delivered several days ago. My apologies. Merry Christmas!"

I thank him and shut my door, thumbing through the stack. It's mostly junk mail.

I glance at the package and freeze when I recognize Charlie's handwriting.

The envelopes fall to the floor as I rip open the padded shipping envelope. Inside is a flat box, carefully wrapped in pearl-white paper and tied with red ribbon. There's a plain white card tucked into the ribbon. The handwritten note inside is short, written in her rounded script. "I wanted you to have this. Charlie."

I hesitate for a split second before carefully opening the gift, peeling the heavy paper back and pushing aside the tissue. My heart stops.

It's the picture of me with my mom, the one with her head wrapped in her pink scarf because the chemo had stolen her long curls. I'm in profile, the camera focused on her face. The photo was taken when the cancer was assured victory over her body. She's skeletally thin and pale, but she's smiling.

It's the last picture she and I ever took together.

Her hands are on either side of my face, cupping it gently. She's gazing at me with such deep love that I can feel it through the photo, through the years, through the gaping void of death. I don't realize I'm crying until a tear splashes onto the silver frame.

I reach for the shipping envelope and glance at the postmark, and my breath catches.

Charlie mailed this before she got my flowers.

After she told Tucker she was done.

Charlie was reaching out to me again, even before I reached out to her.

Even after the hell I've put her through, she sent me this.

I close my eyes. *She still cares.*

A tiny beam of light touches my heart. There's still hope.

I have a relatively pleasant evening with Tucker and Lila. I'm on my best behavior after showing my ass and being brought down several notches by a decidedly not-so-delicate blonde yesterday. There's a ton of food. Tucker lets it slip that they brought home some of it from Charlie's house. I make sure to sample everything I know she made. It's the one way I can connect with her. I give them their Christmas gifts. Lila squeals at her scarf and sapphire earrings. Tucker laughs at the tank top and raises the bottle of whiskey in a salute.

Tucker and Lila lead me to the garage for my gift. "I know a guy," Tucker says, gesturing to a long, sheet-covered object topped with a red ribbon. "I called in a favor and worked out a deal. It's not brand-new," he cautions me, "because I wasn't sure you'd like it. If you do, you can trade up later on." I glance at him and reach for the white sheet, tugging lightly.

It's a black mountain bike. My jaw drops. I don't know much about them, but even I can tell it's nice. "It's a trail bike," Tucker says, "so it's more versatile as far as where you can ride it. This model is designed for quick handling, and it's geared for efficient pedaling. It's lightweight and has full suspension, so it will absorb the impact and allow you to ride more comfortably."

I run my hand over the bike. "Wow. You shouldn't have, Tucker. These things aren't cheap."

He waves me off. "Like I said, it's not new, and I called in a favor. But you've reached the pinnacle of your recovery, and you're ready to get back out there and start living again." He grins. "It was either this or skiing lessons."

I try to imagine myself hurtling at top speed down a steep slope with nothing more than a pair of boards and some thin poles standing between me and certain death. I shake my head. "If you want me to survive, skiing probably isn't the best choice." I gesture back to the bike. "I don't know what to say. Thanks."

Lila steps up and hugs me. "Merry Christmas, Mark. I'm really glad we got to spend Christmas Eve with you."

I hug her tightly, pulling Tucker in, too. "Dammit," he mutters, "he's getting all mushy."

Amused, I plant a noisy kiss on his cheek, and he bristles. "Cut that out, will ya? There's no damn mistletoe out here."

"I couldn't help myself," I tell him, winking. "You won my heart with your generous package."

Lila groans. "You did not just tell him he had a generous package."

Tucker grins. "I am rather gifted in that department," he says, waggling his eyebrows.

I step away from him. "Way to make it weird, Maxwell."

He laughs. "You started it," he reminds me.

I lean down and kiss Lila's cheek instead. "From now on, I'll kiss you twice, and you can give one to Mr. Generous Package."

He gives me a saucy wink. "I'll still know it's from you."

Tucker helps me put the bike in my van while Lila fills a shopping bag with leftover food and sends it with me. It's nearly midnight when I'm back in my van.

My eyes fall on the small package on my passenger seat. It's a flat box about four inches square, wrapped in glossy black paper and tied with red ribbon.

Charlie's gift.

I'd tossed it on my front seat when I left the house tonight after opening her gift to me. She gave me something truly meaningful despite our shattered relationship. It gives me hope that I can do the same for her.

After all, it's Christmas, the season of miracles, right?

I hope she's still awake.

I start my van and head for Charlie's house.

CHARLIE

After Tucker and Lila leave to spend the evening celebrating with Mark, I glance at Stubbs. "Do you have any Christmas traditions?" I ask, realizing I should have asked him before now.

"I do, actually," he says. "I watch Christmas movies. You know all those classic kids' movies? The ones using stop-motion puppet animation?"

"Like the Rudolph movie?"

He nods. "And a few others, too."

I smile. "I have an entire shelf dedicated to kids' Christmas movies."

He beams. "Then let's get cracking, Green Eyes. I'll make popcorn and cocoa. You pick the movies." He heads for the kitchen, and I start gathering DVDs.

"Bring some sugar cookies, too," I call after him as my little butterflies squirm excitedly inside my abdomen.

I've never had a Christmas Eve like this before.

I'll never have one quite like this again.

And I'm going to take Linda's advice and be fully present in this moment: Christmas Eve, five months pregnant, watching kids' movies and drinking cocoa with a friend while a sweet dog catches tossed popcorn and sneaks bites of cookies.

It's not perfect, but it's pretty damn nice.

MARK

I park in Charlie's driveway just after midnight, wondering at the wisdom of appearing unannounced on her doorstep. Christmas Eve or not, it'll take one hell of a miracle for her not to slap the shit out of me the second she sees me at her door. I shove her elaborately-wrapped gift into my jacket pocket and reach for my door handle.

A large shadow passes in front of the living room window, followed by a second smaller one that I recognize as Charlie. I pause, frowning. Tucker and Lila are at home. I left them there not five minutes ago. Tom and Maya are in New York for Maya to visit her mom over the holidays.

So who the hell is inside with her at midnight on Christmas Eve?

My eyes fall on the giant SUV parked next to Charlie's car.

The SUV that's been parked here for the last week.

The SUV I'd assumed was one Charlie bought for herself.

The one I couldn't understand why she'd have bought, because it's so big and bulky and unlike any car Charlie's ever owned.

Realization settles like lead in the pit of my stomach.

Someone's living with Charlie.

The big shadow passes in front of the window again, and I see Charlie reach up and hug the tall figure.

The tall, distinctly *male* figure.

He pulls her close and brushes her hair back from her face before kissing her forehead.

What. The. Fuck.

Charlie disappears, and I see the bedroom light flick on, followed by the bathroom light. The broad shadow moves through the living room again, then turns back toward the bedroom.

My old bedroom.

The one they're apparently staying in.

Hot jealousy roars to life inside me.

I get it. It's none of my business who she's living with. I told her she deserved better. I left specifically so she could find happiness with someone better.

But the thought of her finding someone else now that I've admitted she's the only woman I'll ever love makes my throat spasm in panic. Someone's in there with her. Hugging her. Kissing her. Encroaching on my territory. On my woman. My *pregnant* woman.

Mine, growls a primal voice from deep within my chest.

I'm out of the van and up her front steps before I've even considered what I'm going to say. A plan would be good. I'm an excellent tactician, able to coordinate multi-pronged military attacks and dark ops in my sleep. But finding out who Charlie's moved on with?

No plan. No ideas. Just raw emotion.

Probably not wise, but I have to know.

I have to.

I rap sharply on the door, waiting impatiently. My breath catches as heavy footsteps approach. Several locks click open before the door swings wide. My eyes widen as I stare at the man in front of me. "Stubbs?" The giant man looks as surprised to see me as I feel seeing him inside Charlie's house. "What — what are you doing here?"

He leans against the door frame, paying no attention to the frigid air rushing into the house. "I live here," he says.

My heart skips a beat. "What do you mean?"

"I moved in with Charlie."

My vision swims, and my throat tightens. "What?"

"She and I are living together," he repeats.

"She's the special woman you — you and Charlie — you're together?" I stammer stupidly.

Stubbs cocks his head. "Are you feeling alright? You look a little pale."

The monster in my chest rears its ugly head. "No. She can't be with you. I left because she deserved better."

At my words, he plants his feet and crosses his arms over his enormous chest, his face impassive. His placid non-reaction fuels my anger.

"I have to talk to Charlie," I tell him, starting to push past him, but he blocks me with his broad body.

"She's in the shower," he says, a slow smile spreading over his face. "And *you* weren't invited to join her."

His smug expression tells me he obviously was.

"What?" I say, the faint buzzing in my ears growing louder.

His smile widens. "Charlie's quite the sexy green-eyed goddess, isn't she? I do love a woman with curves," he murmurs.

My temper explodes, and I see red. I lunge for him, but he's expecting it. He steps smoothly to the side, and before I know it, he's spun me around and trapped me in a chokehold from behind, my neck pressed into the crook of one massive forearm while his opposite hand presses the back of my head forward. "Easy there, Pretty Boy. Let's not do anything you'll regret."

He's pulling me backwards, keeping me off balance. I struggle against him, trying to get my feet under me. "She can't be with you! I left so she could find someone better!" I spit out.

Stubbs drops the hand pressing into the back of my head, instead yanking my right arm up behind me and steering me outside. I try to jerk away from him, but fail. In the scuffle, Charlie's gift falls from my jacket pocket, thumping against my thigh before tumbling into the snow near her steps. I'm too far gone to care, though.

"You're a goddamn amputee, too! I left to spare her that!" I roar.

"No. You threw away an amazing woman because you couldn't accept yourself." He leans in close to my ear, his voice low. "Trust me, I won't make that mistake."

"I can't believe you'd do this to me!"

He herds me through the snowy gravel toward my van, and from the corner of my eye, I see him shrug. "I couldn't believe you'd do the things you've done to her." He laughs softly. "I guess I should thank you. If it hadn't been for you, she wouldn't have needed someone to lean on."

"But you're a goddamn amputee!"

He stops beside my van, turning me and pushing me back against the driver's side door, one huge hand gripping my jacket. "I am," he agrees. "I'm also man enough not to let it define me." He loosens his hold. "Are we gonna have a problem if I let you go?"

Too stunned to answer, I simply shake my head, and he releases me. I stare at him. "I thought you were my friend," I mutter.

Stubbs barks out a humorless laugh. "Funny, that's exactly what she said about you." He turns back toward the house, and the heart I thought was already broken shatters into a million pieces.

CHARLIE

I step out of the shower and feel an icy draft blowing under the bathroom door. I dry off quickly and dress, wrapping my wet hair in a towel before going to find the source of the cold air. Stubbs is coming back into the house when I step into the foyer. He closes the door.

"I wondered why it was chilly," I say. "What is it, like twenty degrees out there? Are you looking for Santa? I'm pretty sure you're on his naughty list. "

"It's twenty-eight, and I'm definitely naughty," he replies with a grin. Then his smile fades. "So I did something, and I'm pretty sure you're not going to like it."

I study his face. Now that he's not teasing, there's tension around his dark eyes, and his jaw is tight. I sigh, gesturing to my towel-swathed head. "Give me a minute. Something tells me I'm going to need to sit down for this."

He nods. "That's probably a good idea."

I quickly towel-dry my hair and run a wide-toothed comb through it before joining Stubbs in the living room. He's waiting for me on one of the couches. I sit down, facing him. "What's up?"

"Mark knows I'm living here."

I glance back to the hallway. "He was here?" He nods. My brows pull together in confusion. "Well, you are living here. What's the big deal?"

"There was a knock at the door while you were in the shower. It was Mark, and he asked why I was here. But it wasn't just like, 'Why are you here?' It was more like, 'Why are you at Charlie's house with her at midnight on Christmas Eve?' So I told him we were living together."

I absorb his words. "How did he respond?"

"He asked if you and I were together."

I eye him suspiciously. "And you told him no, right?"

He hesitates. "Not exactly."

I raise one eyebrow. "You said we were?"

He shakes his head. "I deflected his question and told him he looked pale. Asked if he was feeling alright."

"Well, that's okay. No harm, no foul." But Stubbs still looks sheepish. "What else?"

He licks his lips. "This is the part you might not like."

I frown. "What else did you say?"

"He kicked up a fuss. Said he'd left because you deserved better. Called me a goddamn amputee and said the whole reason he left was because he'd been trying to spare you that." My chest tightens at his words, even though it's not a newsflash. "Then he said he needed to talk to you and tried to push his way in. And..." Stubbs pauses and takes a deep breath. "I said last time I'd seen you, you were getting ready to slip into the shower, and that he wasn't invited to join you." I stare at him, dumbfounded, as he continues. "I called you a sexy green-eyed goddess and said I loved a woman with curves. That's when he came at me."

"He what?" I squeak.

He shrugs. "I was expecting it. Goading him, if you want to know the truth. I put him in a chokehold. I was trying to knock some sense into him. Not literally," he adds when my eyes widen. "I stopped by his apartment the other day. When he asked where I was living, I said I'd moved in with someone special. I figured he'd hear through the grapevine that I was living here, and I thought a little jealousy might be a good thing. Him showing up here tonight gave me an opportunity to say some things he needed to hear."

"What did he say?" I ask, dreading his answer.

"He mostly seemed upset to think you'd ended up with an amputee. I told him he'd thrown away an amazing woman because he couldn't accept himself. When he called me a goddamned amputee, I agreed, and said the difference was that I'm man enough not to let it define me."

I sigh heavily, rubbing my forehead.

"I'm sorry, Charlie. For what it's worth, I didn't lie. I just sort of... sculpted the truth." I shoot him a quick look, and he starts ticking statements off on his fingers. "I am living with you, albeit temporarily. You were in the shower. You are a green-eyed goddess. I do love a woman with curves. And he did throw away an amazing woman because of his skewed view of himself." He gives me a small grin. "I simply presented the information in a way that led him down the path I wanted him to take." His smile fades. "Are you pissed?"

I think about it for a minute, then shrug. "No. It might tick him off and make him jealous, but it won't change his mind. Even if it did, I won't tolerate him showing up to pound his chest and stake his claim. That ship has sailed."

He watches me for a long moment before nodding. "Okay." He gets to his feet. "I'll go by next week and correct his misconception. Not too soon, though," he adds. "It'll be good for him to think about how he's let his self-loathing affect everyone around him."

After Stubbs goes upstairs, I lie in bed, wondering how Mark's processing the idea that he left me because of his amputation, and I ended up – in his mind, at least – choosing a man who's a double amputee.

Maybe Stubbs is right. Maybe it will force him to reevaluate his own value. He needs to. Not for us – it's too late for that – but for himself. That's the Christmas miracle I'd most like to see – for Mark to accept himself as he is, scars and all.

The way I'm finally accepting myself.

CHAPTER SEVENTEEN

LILA

AFTER MARK LEAVES, I curl up on the couch with Tucker, running my fingers through his hair while an action movie plays on television. It's a mafia flick, and the accents are so overdone and the stereotypes so exaggerated that I find myself offended on behalf of actual mobsters.

I slide my hand behind his neck and pull him toward me. He comes willingly, and I kiss him, lingering. Tucker smiles against my lips, then drags me onto his lap, his hard chest pressing into my back while he nuzzles the side of my neck. "You smell delicious, Sweetness," he murmurs against my throat as he trails hot kisses to my collarbone. I tilt my head to give him better access. His hands leave my waist to slide beneath my sweatshirt and palm my breasts, squeezing my nipples until I gasp. I grind against him and feel his hardness against my ass. I pull my legs up, kneeling to straddle him, rubbing against his hard length. His chest rumbles with appreciation. Strong hands leave my breasts, skimming down my sides before sliding into my yoga pants. "Mmm. No panties. Christmas is coming early. For both of us." He scrapes my neck with his stubble, and I suck in a deep breath. One large hand slips between my legs, circling, stroking. I arch against it and moan. "So wet for me already," he whispers, his breath hot against my ear, making me shiver and arch against him again. I reach back between our bodies to stroke his hardness through his clothes, and he thrusts against my hand in response.

"Tucker," I moan as two curled fingers work their magic inside me. His thumb circles my clit, pressing just like I like it.

"That's right, Sweetness. Take what you want."

"I want you inside me. Now," I gasp, stroking his thick cock for emphasis.

"Yes ma'am," he says, and before I can blink, he's shucked his sweatpants and peeled my yoga pants off, leaving our clothes in a heap on the floor. He lifts my hips, shifting me back against him before guiding his cock to my entrance. "So wet," he murmurs. "So fucking hot."

I sink onto him and we groan together as I start to ride him. He drags my shirt off and cups my bare breasts, squeezing my nipples as I pick up speed. He surges beneath me, deepening the thrusts. His hands grip my hips, pulling me harder against him as the pressure in my body builds.

He removes one hand from my hip, slipping it between us to massage my clit between thrusts. "Oh God," I moan, arching against his hand.

"That's it, Sweetness," he groans. "Just like that."

I come screaming his name. He comes shouting mine.

We have a repeat performance in the shower, where he braces me against the wall with my legs around his waist while he drives into me, biting my neck, and a third session in our bed where he laves me thoroughly with his tongue before burying himself to the hilt, murmuring my name against my lips between slow, deep thrusts.

"Damn, woman, you've worn me out," he grins, collapsing beside me. I roll atop him and kiss him deeply until he grips the back of my neck and groans into my mouth. "So fucking hot," he breathes when I pull away.

"You're not so bad yourself," I say, nestling into his chest.

He trails his fingers through my damp hair, twining blond curls around the long fingers of his right hand while his left strokes my back. I gradually melt into him, my body sated, his deep breathing relaxing me.

When I wake, the house is dark.

Completely dark.

An icy chill runs down my spine.

I bolt upright, clutching the sheet to my chest as I strain to see in the inky blackness. My breath comes faster, rasping in the silent house.

"Lila?" Tucker's voice comes from near my elbow, gruff but alert as he slides his arm around my waist.

When I don't answer, he sits up. "It's okay," he says. "You're safe. I'm right here with you." He reaches for the bedside table, fumbling for his phone. When he finds it, he turns on the flashlight and hands it to me. "Take this. I'll go check the breaker."

I clutch his arm. "Don't leave!" My voice is high-pitched, my throat tight.

Tucker turns, pulling me close. "I won't leave you, Sweetness. Do you want to come with me, or do you want us to stay here together?"

"I need the darkness to go away," I whisper. "Please." Tears burn my eyes.

He presses warm lips to my bare shoulder. "Then let's make this darkness our bitch."

TUCKER

I keep Lila's hand in mine as I slide off the edge of the bed, feeling around on the floor. I locate my shorts and tee shirt. I pass the shirt to her and pull the shorts on as she shimmies into my shirt and scoots off the bed to stand beside me.

I listen intently, but the house is silent. Still, I'd be a fool to go snooping around unarmed without knowing for sure we don't have an intruder. I take Lila's hand again and lead her to the dresser, retrieving both our handguns. I'm thankful she's a good shot as I pass her the weapon. "Stay behind me and don't fire at me," I whisper.

I feel some of the tension leave her body as soon as she's armed. Like Charlie, Lila has intense triggers from their kidnapping. Neither of them can handle being unarmed in total darkness. The sheer vulnerability of it over-whelms them. They're also both certified marksmen who feel safer with a weapon in their hands.

We make our way downstairs slowly as our eyes adjust to the deep shad-ows. I head straight for the fuse box. It'll be easier to be certain the house is secure with lights. "Do you want to check the fuse box or cover me?" I whisper. She passes me the phone with its flashlight and nods toward the box before raising her gun, her eyes sweeping the black room behind me.

One of the breakers is tripped. I flip the switch and lights begin to come on immediately. I glance at Lila. Her eyes are wide, and she still has the gun raised. I tip my head for her to follow me. We go room by room, Lila at my back as I lead the way, clearing each area, checking every closet, every corner. It's the only way she'll feel safe tonight.

Once we've swept the entire house, I stuff my feet in shoes and step outside, scanning the snow and checking around the house. There are no footprints in the fresh snow besides mine. No one's been here.

I step back inside and lock up before rejoining Lila in the kitchen. She's breathing hard, her eyes still wild. I place my gun on the counter and reach for hers. She hands it over willingly before launching herself at me. I wrap my arms around her, feeling her trembling.

"You're safe, Sweetness. I've got you."

She drags my face down to hers, kissing me with untamed desperation. I kiss her back, but it's not enough.

She needs more.

"Tell me what you need," I whisper against her lips.

"Make me forget the darkness," she says, arching up against me.

I slide my hands beneath her hips, scooping her up, and she wraps long legs around my waist, pulling my mouth back to hers as she grinds against me.

Easy, my brain warns. *This is dangerous territory.*

Because the darkness isn't just about being in a dark house. It's about what those animals did.

I ease her down onto the kitchen counter, trying to gentle the kiss, but she won't let me. I pull my lips away anyway, kissing her neck as I reach beneath her shirt to caress her breasts. She moans, arching against my hips, pushing my shorts down before peeling off her shirt..

"Please," she whimpers.

"Tell me what you want, Sweetness. Tonight you have to tell me."

After I first came home to her, I didn't truly understand how much damage those bastards had done to her. Taking Lila from behind like earlier, on the couch? That would never have happened in a million years. Hell, the first time I stood behind her and wrapped my arms around her waist, she shattered a glass and damn near shivved me with it. It took us a lot of therapy to get to a place where sex was something both of us could fully, freely enjoy.

But when she's been triggered, I make her tell me what she wants. I won't take a chance on guessing wrong, on inadvertently hurting her. I love her too damn much for that.

"Table."

My mind whirls. She can't be serious.

"What?"

"Fuck me on the table, Tucker."

Lila and I have never had sex on a table. I've never even considered it. Those goddamned bastards chained her to one after she killed the first man that tried to sexually assault her. They kept her bound facedown for eleven days, raping her.

We've never gone here before, and saying I'm hesitant is the understatement of the century.

I lift my face and stare into her violet eyes. They're still wild, but right now, they're blazing with passion.

"The table?" She nods. "You're sure?"

She nods again. "No more darkness."

I carry her to the table, perching her on the edge. "Tell me your safeword, Lila."

For the record, we aren't into BDSM. Lila's endured enough non-consensual bondage and sadism to last a dozen lifetimes. However, for times when she's struggled with flashbacks or when we're doing something that might trigger her, we have a safeword. Willow suggested it as a way to ensure Lila could communicate the need to stop.

"Violet," she whispers. "My word is violet."

Violet, like the eyes in front of me, pleading with me.

I claim her mouth then, delving into its depths, tasting and teasing her until she's panting with desire. Only then do I ease her down onto her back, clasping her wrists loosely in my hands.

Her eyes drift closed. *Bad idea. I need her focused.* "Eyes on me," I command, and her eyes snap open, finding mine. "Good girl," I murmur, rubbing my cock through her wet folds. She moans, and I do it again. "You like that?"

"Please," she sighs. "I need you, Tucker."

I slide into her silken depths then, her walls automatically contracting, pulling me closer.

I maintain a loose hold on her wrists, using them to pull her body against me as I slowly thrust into her. Her eyes close again as she moans. "Eyes on me," I remind her, and she looks up, biting her lip seductively.

I can't afford to get caught up. I can't afford to lose myself in the moment. I've got to be one hundred percent attuned to her in this position.

But she's so fucking hot, it's taking every bit of my focus.

I set a steady rhythm, swirling my hips as I thrust, ensuring my pelvis makes contact with her clit. She's moaning, twisting her wrists to clutch at mine as I keep holding her in place.

She startles me when she suddenly sits up, tugging her hands free. "Step back," she gasps. I immediately back up to give her space, and she hops off the table.

Shit. It was too much for her.

She shocks the hell out of me by leaning forward over the table, her beautiful ass facing me as she grips the edges of the table. "Like this."

"Lila?" I ask uncertainly.

"Please, Tucker. I need to beat the darkness. Please."

Her quiet pleading rips my soul apart.

I wrap her long curls loosely in my hand and tug lightly, turning her face to one side, my body lightly covering hers as I claim her mouth. She pushes her hips against me, circling, trying to get to my cock, but I keep shifting out of reach until she groans her displeasure.

"Easy," I whisper. "I want more than just a victory for you, Sweetness. I want you to enjoy every second of this. That's how you beat it." She arches her back and pushes against me impatiently, and I chuckle.

Then I drop to my knees and lick her like melting ice cream on a hot summer day. She gasps, pushing her sweet pussy into my face. I suck on her clit and curl my fingers inside her until she's so close, she can't form coherent words. All she can do is whimper and arch against me.

Then I take her over the edge, listening to her cries, feeling the shudders ripple through her.

Only when the storm of her orgasm has passed do I stand and lean over her back again, careful not to touch her with my cock in case she's changed her mind. I nuzzle her cheek.

"Eyes on me," I whisper, and she looks over her shoulder. Her eyes are glazed with passion, and she's smiling.

I smile back. "Feel better?"

She surprises me when she shakes her head.

"Not even a little?"

She pushes her hips back against me, circling again. "You're not done yet," she says. My lips find hers again, and she sucks my tongue, moaning into my mouth. "I need you inside me this way, Tucker," she whispers when I break the kiss.

"You have to let me know you're with me," I say, my urgency building as she reaches back and guides my cock inside her.

Translation: Eyes on me and keep talking.

"Oh, God, you feel so good," she whispers. Her eyes drift closed, but she opens them again quickly, glancing back at me.

I spread her legs further apart and tug her body back closer to mine, filling her deeper. "Yes," she confirms. "Like that."

My thrusts start slow, but begin building in speed and intensity. "Tucker," she moans, saying my name over and over, letting me know she's in this moment.

Letting me know it's okay to let go.

She raises up on her forearms and begins pushing back against me with every thrust, looking back over her shoulder, those gorgeous eyes holding my gaze as she bites her lip.

"Grab my breasts," she says, and I move my hands from her thighs to cup them, squeezing them, using them to guide her body against mine.

"Harder," she whimpers, moving faster against me.

I groan, feeling my control start to slip when I look at her face. She's caught in the throes of passion. Her eyes are closed, but I have no doubt she's with me, because she's moaning my name over and over, pushing back harder and harder as I thrust into her.

"Oh, God, Sweetness, I'm too close," I mutter, trying to slow down, to wait for her, but she refuses to let me. She's teetering on the knife edge as well, moving frantically, moaning incoherently.

She comes again with a loud cry, gasping my name, her body squeezing me like a silk glove. I'm a split second behind her, emptying into her as she milks every drop from me.

God, this woman is incredible.

When I come down from my high, I drape myself over her, caging her within my arms but careful not to make her feel trapped.

"You still with me, Sweetness?" I murmur against her collarbone.

"Mmhmm," she mumbles. "I don't think I can move, but I'm with you." Then she turns her face to me, and her violet eyes are shining. "Thank you," she whispers, and for a second, I see tears in her eyes.

I scramble to get up, but she grabs my arm in an iron grip. "Stay," she insists. "These are good tears."

I study her face, unconvinced.

She slides a hand behind my neck and pulls me closer, pressing her lips softly to mine. "We exorcized demons. Thank you."

I kiss her again, slowly, tenderly. "I love you, Sweetness."

"I love you, too."

LILA

Tucker and I sleep until midday on Christmas. Even after all our years together, something shifted between us last night, bringing us even closer. After defeating my demons late in the night, we ate omelets and drank white wine before returning to bed, where we eventually drifted off to sleep in each other's arms. It was perfect.

Tucker eventually awakens to find me cooking a full holiday dinner – turkey and ham, side dishes, and two kinds of pies. He enters the kitchen, scenting cinnamon rolls fresh out of the oven. I smack his hand as he reaches toward the pan.

"They aren't glazed yet, and you'll burn yourself."

"Give me the glaze. I'll do it." His eyes wander around the kitchen. "It looks like you're cooking enough for an army."

I shrug. "It's what I do. Besides, leftovers means no cooking for a couple of days."

He dips a finger into the glaze and sucks it, looking thoughtful. "Needs something."

I frown. "I made it the same way I always do." I move toward him, reaching for the bowl, but before I can touch it, he's dragged me against him and claimed my mouth.

"This is what I needed," he says against my lips.

"Me, too," I agree, wrapping my arms around him, and breakfast is quickly forgotten.

Half an hour later, I'm rewarming the glaze and cinnamon rolls. "You're very distracting," I tell him.

He grins. "I have a special set of skills." Then he looks around the kitchen again. "How long before you're freed up?"

"Things are on autopilot right now."

"Good. It's present time," he says, catching my hand and pulling me toward the living room.

"I thought you just gave me your present," I tease him.

He winks. "That's the gift that keeps on giving. In fact, if you're really good, it might *present* itself again later."

I look at him from underneath my lashes. "Do I get to sit on Santa's lap?"

He tugs me closer and kisses me until we're both breathless. When he pulls his lips from mine, he shakes his head. "Unwrapping presents first."

"I have to admit, I'm intrigued. Delaying sex for gifts? That's not like you."

He just smiles mysteriously and pulls the packages from beneath the tree.

I've given Tucker several small things – a couple of shirts, a new pair of sneakers, and cologne. His big gift, however, drops his jaw.

"A trip to the Caribbean? But what about our animals?"

"Shepherd's going to take care of them. We're going for Valentine's Day. I've made all the arrangements."

He pulls me onto his lap and kisses me deeply before burying his face in my neck. "I can't wait to pick out your bikini. It'll fit in your sunglasses case with room left over."

I've already opened a beautiful pair of suede boots, a gift certificate for a full-day spa visit, and a gorgeous pair of diamond and sapphire earrings, so I'm surprised when Tucker produces an envelope from beneath the sofa cushion and hands it to me.

"What's this?"

He pulls me onto his lap, wrapping his arms around my waist. "Open it and see."

I open the envelope and pull out a single appointment card with a series of dates inscribed on it – January 11, January 25, January 29, and February 12. I turn the card over. It's from Dr. K's office. I look at him. "What are these?"

He nestles his head against my upper arm. "The first date is for your blood tests to check your hormone levels and start the shots again. The second one is for them to harvest your eggs while I produce my semen sample." My eyes fly to his. "The third is for them to implant our little test tube tots into your uterus. And the fourth is for a pregnancy test to make sure everything took."

My heart pounds as I spin to face him. "But I thought –"

Tucker pulls me tightly against him. "Lila, I should never have shut you down when you brought up IVF. I was being stupid. I didn't want to jerk off with an office full of people knowing what I was doing. I've decided I don't care. Hell, they can sell tickets. I want a family with you, and if that's what it takes, I'm all in."

I throw my arms around his neck. "Oh, Tucker!"

He pulls back and lifts my chin, gazing down at me with those deep blue eyes that still make my heart skip a beat. "I love you, Sweetness. Always have, always will." When his mouth meets mine, it's so tender that my heart aches.

It's a good thing my goats love burnt cherry pie.

CHAPTER EIGHTEEN

CHARLIE

CHRISTMAS MORNING, I DREAM Mark is holding me in his arms, kissing me, caressing my very pregnant belly, telling me how much he loves me and our soon-to-be-born babies. Penny and two Bella-sized dogs bounce around, hassling a hissing cat while a pot boils over on the stove. My secret longing for a loving, chaotic family invades my dreams frequently now.

Waking up and remembering the truth breaks my heart all over again.

Tears leak from the corners of my eyes. I keep telling myself it's safer to let go and move on, but clearly, a large part of me yearns for reconciliation.

It was just a dream. It's not real.

Oh, Penny and my babies are real, and I'm sure my future holds messes and barely-contained chaos, but they're something I'll have to face on my own.

I miss Mark, and I want him back, but my heart is safer if I let go and move on.

I lie in bed for a few moments, letting myself imagine what it would be like if things worked out for us. If Mark did tell me he loved me. If I told him about the babies and he were excited.

Then I consider the anger he's sure to feel when he finds out about them from a stranger serving him papers.

That's his own damn fault. If he'd bothered to answer his door or phone, he'd have heard it from me.

I rub my forehead and sigh before climbing out of bed and pushing all thoughts of lawyers, babies, and Mark out of my mind. Today is Christmas, a day for peace.

But I can't remember the last time I felt peaceful inside.

Stubbs and I enjoy a quiet day together. He makes breakfast – fully loaded omelets – and we unwrap gifts by the tree. He gives me a gift basket full of pampering supplies ("Thank God for salesgirls," he grins) and a pair of gorgeous handmade rocking horses for the twins. He even produces a basket of treats and chew toys for Penny. He opens my presents to him, proclaiming the fleece jacket, scarf, and gloves a lifesaver. He beams when he holds up the plaque for his office. "Maybe I could get a name plate for my door that says Badass Therapist," he muses.

I laugh. "Your office, your door. Most of our vets prefer a casual atmosphere anyway."

I roast a turkey breast with oranges and sage, basting it frequently with melted butter. We eat it with fluffy mashed potatoes, steamed green beans, and cornbread dressing that Stubbs makes from his grandmother's recipe. Cranberry-orange relish is the perfect complement, and I eat until I'm stuffed. Penny naps on her side, sleepy from her turkey and potatoes. I end up dozing off on the couch watching football with Stubbs. I awaken hours later to find he's tucked a blanket around me.

I'm going to be okay. I'm not alone.

The day after Christmas, Lila and Tucker come by. Tucker's carrying a large paper sack, and I smell chili when he walks in. "Thought you might like something besides turkey leftovers," he greets me. "I brought chili dogs and fries."

"And cole slaw," Lila adds, hugging me. She knows I love slaw on my chili dogs.

Stubbs grabs plates and napkins while I get us some drinks, and the four of us settle around the dining room table. We chat comfortably while we eat. Tucker bought Penny her own order of french fries, and he feeds them to her one at a time. She sits at attention, polishing them off, and when they're gone, she lays her head on his lap while he rubs her ears.

I've pushed my empty plate away when Lila turns. "We need to talk."

I groan. "Every time someone says that, it's more bad news."

"Not bad," she assures me, "just a little unexpected."

I take a deep breath. "Okay. Let's hear it."

"Mark got the custody paperwork on the twenty-third."

I stare at her. "He wasn't supposed to be served until after Christmas." I didn't think attorneys ever did things in a timely fashion. I'd paid extra for them to expedite the process, but still.

She nods. "That's why I'm letting you know. I didn't want to wreck your Christmas, so I waited to tell you. But he knows about the babies."

"You talked to him?"

"He came by," Tucker says.

"How'd that go?"

Tucker shrugs. "He showed up ranting about how we'd known and not told him, but Lila adjusted his self-righteous attitude pretty quickly." He grins. "She handed him his ass without missing a beat." He squeezes her hand. "You're sexy when you're mad," he winks, and she smiles. He turns back to me. "After she ripped him a new one, he sat down and we talked."

I look back and forth between them. "And?"

Lila's voice is calm. "He said he had to get you back, and Tucker told him he was too late, that there was no way you'd take him back because of the babies."

Tucker nods. "He didn't like that. He said he loved you, but Lila told him he should have done something about it before finding out about the babies."

"What was his response?"

Tucker purses his lips. "No matter what, he wants to be part of the babies' lives. He wants you, too, but it's finally sinking in that he may have fucked up too badly for that."

Stubbs grunts. "If it hadn't before, it probably has now." Tucker and Lila glance at him. "I answered the door when he showed up here around midnight on Christmas Eve. I may have given him the impression that Charlie and I are a couple."

Lila's eyes widen. "What did he do?"

"Threw a hissy fit," Stubbs says. "Lunged at me, so I put him in a chokehold and marched his ass to his car. Said he'd left because he didn't want her stuck with a goddamn amputee. I said that unlike him, I was smart enough not to let my injuries define me."

I drop my head into my hands. How did falling in love with my best friend turn into such a complicated, painful mess?

Lila's hand rubs my shoulder, and a second later, Tucker squeezes the other one. "It's okay, Charlie," he says. "So he knows about the babies a couple days sooner than you'd planned. Nothing else has changed. We've got your back."

I raise my head. "You're right," I admit. "Besides, if he'd answered his door or phone, he'd already have known." I sigh. "I'll give it a couple days and call him. My obstetrician's doing another ultrasound next week. Maybe he'll want to come along."

A lengthy car ride with someone who isn't speaking to me, followed by seeing the babies we've created together, then an agonizingly long drive home.

Yeah. That won't be at all awkward.

MARK

I have an appointment with Dr. Allen today. He studies my face when I walk in.

"You look tired," he observes. "Are you sleeping?"

I shake my head. "It's been a bad week."

"Tell me about it."

I hesitate. "Well, I started thinking about my goals. I haven't settled on my professional goals yet, but I'd set a personal goal to get things sorted out between me and Charlie."

"Why do you say that in the past tense?"

"I wanted to tell her I love her. I wanted to explain why I pushed her away, beg her forgiveness, and spend the rest of my life making her happy." I pause. "But things... things have changed, and now, I'm not sure I can win her back."

He watches me, his dark, bird-like eyes roving across my face. "I don't know Charlie, and I'm only familiar with your side of the situation, so I can't offer specific advice on your relationship. However, in order to truly commit to someone, whether it's Charlie or someone else, you have to accept yourself. If you don't come to grips with the man you are now, you can't fully engage in a relationship. You'll still be holding back. So I'm going to ask you what I asked in our very first session. Tell me the story of Mark. Tell me who he is."

"I'm just a man," I say simply. "I have flaws and failures, hopes and dreams. I may be the sum of my experiences, both good and bad, but I'm not limited to them. I'm a man who's desperately in love with an incredible woman, praying for a future with her."

"And if she says yes?"

"Then I'll spend every minute of my life loving her."

His dark eyes probe mine further. "And if she says no?"

I hesitate. "I'm not sure. If she agrees to rebuild our friendship, I'll accept it and hope that as I regain her trust, she might want more than that. But if she's truly done?" I swallow hard. "Last week, I'd have said I'd have to move away. I'd have told you I'm not strong enough to see her all the time and not be with her. Especially if she were with another man..." I trail off.

"A man with two legs?"

"I don't care if he's got two legs, one leg, or five." Or in Stubbs' case, a pair of carbon-fiber prosthetics. "It doesn't matter. Charlie owns me, heart and soul."

"You said that a week ago, you'd have moved away. What's changed?"

"I can't leave, even if she hates me." I take a deep breath before meeting his gaze. "She's pregnant with twins. Our twins."

He tilts his head. "You seem surprised."

I nod. "After what those bastards did, doctors said she'd never be able to conceive. I was there when they told her. She was devastated. Her pregnancy was a shock for both of us."

"How's she taking the news?"

"I – I'm not sure. I still haven't talked to her." He raises an eyebrow. "She served me with custody papers. I've been such an asshole, she decided she's better off going it alone." I pull the wadded stack of papers from my back pocket, thrusting them into his hand.

It doesn't go unnoticed by either of us that my desire to "spend the rest of my life making her happy" contrasts sharply with Charlie's decision that she's "better off going it alone".

Maybe I can't get her back.

Maybe it really is too late.

Panic rises in my chest.

No. I can't believe that.

I have to try to set things right between us.

"Is she better off going it alone?"

His words slice through me. "No, she's not."

"What makes you so sure?"

"Because I love her, and I'll always love her, and because deep down, she still loves me."

He cocks his head to one side. "You said she's suing for sole custody. Does that strike you as the action of someone who wants a relationship with you?"

My mouth opens, then closes. Maybe he's right.

No.

I stubbornly shake my head, remembering the picture of my mom that she sent even after I rejected her in the parking lot. My stomach clenches at the memory of her anguished expression. "Part of her still loves me," I insist.

Dr. Allen watches the emotions flit across my face, observing silently for some time before he pulls his reading glasses down off the top of his head and begins to flip through my legal papers.

"Why do you suppose she served you with papers, rather than speaking with you directly?"

I swallow hard. "Because I've refused all of her attempts to make contact."

"Yet she consistently continued to reach out to you despite your rejection?"

I nod, feeling worse and worse as my mind tallies my ledger full of sins.

"Then I suspect she still cares deeply for you."

My eyes fly to his. "What makes you say that?"

"Did you actually read these papers?" He holds them up.

I pause before slowly shaking my head. "I saw the phrase 'petition for sole custody' and thought it was one of Tucker's pranks. Then I saw Charlie's name and knew she'd never joke about something so painful for her. I didn't even realize it was for two babies. I went barreling over to my friends' house and threw a fit until Lila jerked a knot in my ass."

"So you didn't look through these?" he persists.

I shake my head again. "Why?"

"Because your proof she still cares is right here," he says, tapping the paper.

"What are you talking about?"

"She included a letter. Well, she and her attorney." He fishes one sheet out of the crumpled stack. "It encourages you to file paternity action papers with the court to establish parental rights and pursue joint custody." He gestures to the sheaf of papers. "She's even included the forms."

My mind spins. *Joint custody?*

"Even if you never told Charlie how you felt, even if you never apologized, she still wanted you to be part of your children's lives."

She's offering me the chance to be part of the babies' lives. Of her life.

Despite everything I've done, she's showing me she still cares.

Just like when she sent me the photo of my mom.

Charlie's been showing me she loves me the entire time I've been shoving her away.

God, I've been such a fool.

CHARLIE

Mark knows about our babies.

Knows we're having twins.

Knows I'm suing him for sole custody.

He's known for four days now.

Four. Days.

Ninety-six hours.

And he hasn't said so much as a peep.

He says not a day goes by that he doesn't think of me, but when given earth-shattering, life-altering news, he has nothing to say to me? Nothing?

It's safer to let go and move on.

That's what I keep telling myself.

But I keep dreaming of being in his arms.

I wake up Tuesday, five days after he's learned about our babies, not that I'm counting. Once again, I dreamed of him caressing my belly and kissing me senseless. Waking up to reality is extremely disappointing. I stretch as Penny half-heartedly thumps her tail. Beneath my pillow, my phone buzzes with a text. I fish it out and glance at the screen.

It's Mark.

I bolt upright – quite a feat, given the loss of my previously-taut abs.

"I was wondering if I could stop by so we could talk."

I pause, suddenly nervous. I'd been wondering why even impending fatherhood hadn't convinced him to speak to me. Now that he's ready to talk, I'm not sure I want to.

After a few seconds, common sense gives me a much-needed kick in the rump. We have to talk. We're going to be parents, and we need to figure out how that's going to work. However, I'm not willing to tolerate a tantrum about my "being with" Stubbs, nor am I particularly inclined to clear up that pesky little misconception. Finally, I type a one-word response: "Why?"

He doesn't answer.

I climb out of bed, shower, dry my hair, and dress, and he still hasn't replied.

Of course not. Why would he? It's too much fun being cryptic and toying with me.

I shove down my snarky attitude and follow my nose to the kitchen, where Stubbs is once again cooking bacon. I inhale deeply. "That smells amazing."

The big man grins. "You're as scrawny as a stray cat. I've got to fatten you up so your little parasites can grow."

I bat my lashes at him. "You say the sweetest things."

He chuckles, dropping bread in the toaster. "How do you want your eggs?"

"Scrambled," I answer, just as my phone buzzes.

It's Mark.

About damn time.

Jesus. I'm as grumpy as a cat caught in a rainstorm. I should go back to bed.

But first, bacon, because after all, it makes everything better.

I open his text. "There's a lot I need to say, things we should discuss, and I'd rather not do it over the phone. Can I come over?"

My heart skips a beat. *Breathe.*

I type quickly, before I can chicken out. "Sure. Come on. We're about to have breakfast. There's plenty." To Stubbs, I say, "Make it eggs for three."

"We?" comes Mark's quick reply.

"Yes. Stubbs and I."

There's a brief pause. "Alright. I'll be there in a few minutes."

My stomach tightens, and I glance up. "Mark's coming over."

Stubbs puts down his whisk and crosses the room to brace my shoulders. "Breathe," he says, echoing my thoughts. "This is a good thing."

"Are you sure? Because all I can see are a dozen ways this ends badly."

Stubbs squeezes my shoulders. "What's the worst that can happen?" he says reasonably. "You've already broken up. You're already preparing yourself to be a single mom. He won't act out with me here. He's the one asking to talk. This is your turf. You have the tactical advantage."

Tactical advantage. Like we're at war.

I suppose suing him is a form of war, albeit one held in a courtroom.

"Maybe," I allow.

"Besides, Mark may need to talk to you about the babies, but he wants to talk because he thinks you've moved on to another man. He wants to see it for himself."

I glance up in surprise. "You think that's why?"

He snorts. "You think it's a coincidence he wants to come here after finding out I'm living with you? He could have asked you to meet him at a coffee shop. He didn't have to come here."

"You have a point," I admit.

"Breathe," he repeats. "I'll answer the door and remind him that if he doesn't behave, I'll snap him like a twig." The image coaxes a smile from me. "You've got this, Green Eyes."

MARK

Charlie's answering text arrives not long after I ask if I can stop by so we can talk.

"Why?"

Her question catches me off guard. Responses fire through my head, machine-gun style.

Because I'm sorry.

Because I regret how I've behaved.

Because I fucked up the best thing in my life.

Because I need to explain why I did what I did.

Because you're the only thing that gives my life meaning.

Because I'm in love with you.

Because I need you to know I still care.

Because I want to beg you for forgiveness.

Because I desperately want you to give me another chance.

Because I long to share a family with you.

Because... Because.

And the longer the pause between her question and my response, the more my stress level skyrockets. There's so much I want to say, but I don't know what Charlie is emotionally capable of hearing right now. God knows I don't want to make things any worse than they already are.

Twenty minutes later, I finally compose a generic answer. "There's a lot I need to say, things we should discuss, and I'd rather not do it over the phone. Can I come over?"

She invites me to breakfast, and a thrill runs through me, even though I know Stubbs will be there. That's okay. At least she's willing to talk. That's a start. A chance.

I park my van next to the monstrous black SUV I now know belongs to Stubbs, not Charlie. I exit my vehicle, feeling a dull ache begin inside my chest.

Re-establish contact on good terms. She loved me once. Maybe some of that still lingers.

Maybe.

But seeing her and Stubbs as a couple might destroy me.

Out of nowhere, Kip Kramer's face pops into my head. Kip was an amputee I met at Charlie's clinic. He was twenty-one, just a kid, with blond hair, dimples, and a neverending stream of chatter. Losing his girlfriend due to his injuries had devastated him. He committed suicide the same day I'd ranted about how the surgery he was looking forward to had left me a freak, and how if he was counting on osseointegration to fix things, he was in for a real disappointment.

Heaviness fills my chest. I'm toxic.

Maybe I'm toxic to Charlie, too.

My inner drill-sergeant growls. *Suck it up and quit whining. You've got babies to think of.*

The voice snaps me to attention, because that's the reason I'm here. I want Charlie back because I love her, I miss her, and she's carrying my children. This is far bigger than my wounded pride or my self-loathing. It's about our babies. Our children.

Our family.

I knock on the door and wait. After a moment, locks begin to unlock. I count five of them and frown. When I left, she had three locks – a chain, a standard locking knob, and a deadbolt. My insides clench when I realize how unsafe Charlie must have felt when I left.

No.

When I abandoned her.

That's what Lila said, and it's true.

But negative thinking isn't productive. I tip my head from side to side, cracking my neck, and prepare to face the music.

The door swings open, revealing a stern-faced man with a determined set to his jaw.

"Ground rules," Stubbs says, not bothering with trivialities like "Hello," or "Good morning." "You will not act out or lose your temper. You will not hurl accusations or blame anyone else for the consequences of your actions. And if you make her cry, rest assured, I won't hesitate to do the same to you."

I meet his dark eyes without flinching. "Agreed."

"Then come in. Breakfast is ready."

I step inside, closing the door behind me. The big man strides down the hall ahead of me to the dining room table. Charlie's already sitting there. She looks up when I enter, and I stutter to a halt, unable to keep myself from staring.

Emerald-green eyes. Creamy skin. Full lips. *God, she's beautiful.* Silky brown hair shimmers with hints of red and gold, cascading over her shoulders, and a blood-red shirt hugs her full breasts. The table conceals the rest of her, but it doesn't matter. She's everything I remember.

No.

She's even more amazing than I remember.

I take another look, suddenly seeing what I missed before. The anxiety in her eyes as she watches me. The tension in her shoulders. The uncertainty as she bites her lip.

She's afraid of me.

Afraid I'm going to hurt her.

Again.

Stubbs appears not to notice, sitting at the end of the table to her left. He's claiming the head of the table, and I recognize it for the power play it is. I feel his eyes on me, waiting for me to object. I draw a steady breath. It's my own damn fault. No point taking offense. I pull out the chair beside him, across from Charlie. "Good morning. Thank you for inviting me," I say.

"You said you needed to talk." Her voice is soft, without reproach.

She'd said she needed to talk to me, too. She'd texted daily for weeks, but I ignored her.

The proof that she's a better person than I am isn't a revelation.

"Help yourself," Stubbs says, picking up a large dish of scrambled eggs. He takes a scoop before offering her the serving spoon while holding the dish. "You need to eat," he tells her.

She smiles as she serves herself some eggs. "I don't want to name names," she says in a conversational tone, "but *someone* informed me this morning that I resembled a scrawny stray cat. I informed said someone that he certainly had a way with words."

Twenty-five pounds.

Tucker said she'd lost twenty-five pounds, and now that I'm looking, I can tell. The tendons in her neck and shoulders stand out, and her wrists and collarbones are sharp and knobby.

My fault.

I close my eyes.

"Take some eggs," Stubbs says, breaking into my thoughts. His words remind me of the morning after Blake jerked away from Charlie when she revealed her scars to him. He'd come in to apologize over breakfast, too. When he'd sat there uncomfortably, I'd pointed my fork at him and told him to eat, talk, or leave.

Of course, back then, I was the hero, not the villain.

I fill my plate with bacon, eggs, toast, and orange wedges and pour coffee into a cup from a carafe on the table. We eat in silence for a few minutes – and not the comfortable kind. Finally, I speak. "I want to apologize to both of you for my behavior the other night. I said and did things that were completely out of line, and I'm sorry."

Stubbs shrugs. "Takes more than that to pucker my panties. I'm comfortable with who I am."

His words hang there, challenging me. After a brief pause, I say, "I'm trying to reach that point myself."

And that's all that's said about my outburst from a few nights ago.

The conversation picks up, though it's somewhat stilted. We talk about Stubbs' move, his new car – the one I'd thought was Charlie's – his new job, and some of the people we both knew from the amputee support group at

Brooke. Partway through the meal, I'm startled by a snuffling nose along my knee. I look down to find a gorgeous Brittany Spaniel with soft ears, big brown eyes, coppery spots on her chest, and a distinct affinity for bacon. Except for telling me she's recently adopted her new dog, Penny, Charlie is quiet, eating her food and sipping green tea. When we've finished eating, Charlie starts to clear the table, but Stubbs stops her with a hand on her upper arm. "I've got this, Green Eyes. You rest." I jump to my feet, unwilling to be outdone, and help clear the table, rinsing dishes for Stubbs to load into the dishwasher. Charlie watches us with an amused expression. When we're done, Stubbs turns to her.

"I'm going upstairs to rummage through my boxes for books and things I'll need for my new office. I'll leave the door open in case you need me." He gives me a warning look.

She smiles faintly. "Thanks, Stubbs."

I watch the huge man leave, listening to his heavy footsteps on the stairs. I glance at Charlie. "So, you and Stubbs, huh?"

I didn't mean to say it, and as soon as the words leave my mouth, I wish I could call them back. Her spine stiffens, and her eyes flash fire. "That's why you came over? I try for months to convince you to talk to me, but you completely ignore me. You find out Stubbs is living with me, and suddenly, you can't wait to talk." She looks away. "I should have known. He was right."

"I'm sorry," I blurt. "I didn't mean to say that. It just kind of came out." She purses her lips, still not looking at me. "I'm sorry," I repeat.

"Why are you here, Mark?" she asks, turning to watch my face.

"I –" My voice trails off. Now that I have her undivided attention, I don't know what to say. All the things I want and need to tell her scurry to the back of my mind, out of reach. I study her, staring at her hollow cheeks and bony wrists. "How – how are you feeling?"

She surveys me for a minute, then exhales, the fire leaving her eyes. "Better than before."

"Are you – um – still throwing up? Blood, I mean? Or – or regular, either?" *Smooth. Really smooth.*

Her lips twitch as though she's trying not to smile at my awkward attempts at conversation. "No. Dr. Oaks put me on medications for my ulcer, nausea, and sleep."

"Is he your – um –" Stress leaves me unable to find the word. "Your baby doctor?"

This time, she does smile. "No. She's my family doctor. I see Dr. Rose in Pueblo for the babies. She's an obstetrician who specializes in high-risk pregnancies."

My stomach clenches. "High risk?"

She nods. "Because of the scarring to my cervix and uterus. When it's time to deliver, I'll need a C-section."

"Surgery?"

She nods again. "The traditional exit isn't possible, given my damage and scarring."

Guilt spreads through me like heat from a furnace. "I'm sorry, Charlie."

She eyes me, her shoulders tensing noticeably. "For what?"

"I should have used protection. You're in this mess because of me."

She bristles as her eyes narrow. "Don't worry. I'll deal with this *mess* just fine."

"That's not what I meant. I – dammit, I can't say anything right today." I shove my hand into my hair and draw a ragged breath. "Maybe I should go."

"So that's it? You're walking out again?" She shoves her chair back from the table and stands. "Why bother coming over if you're going to bail the second I say something you don't like?"

All the air in the room disappears, and for a second, I can't breathe.

I can't take my eyes off Charlie. Her face is flushed, her jaw is tight, and she's pissed. But what grips my heart is the way her red shirt clings to her rounded abdomen.

I'm standing in front of her before I realize it, my hands reaching for her belly. I stop myself just in time, snatching them back. "Sorry," I mutter.

I don't have the right to touch her anymore. I lost it when I threw our relationship away.

She stuns me, taking one of my hands and pressing it palm-side down against her belly. It's surprisingly firm, like touching a warm volleyball. I stare, awestruck, then lift my other hand, spanning the width of her belly.

"My God," I murmur. "You're really pregnant. This is really happening."

She cocks her head and raises one brow. "It's not something I'd make up."

I shake my head. "That's not what I meant." I swallow hard. "I – this just got very real."

She studies my face before letting out a slow breath. "Yeah. I had that moment when I saw them during my ultrasound."

I close my eyes. I wish I'd been there.

I don't realize I've said the words aloud until she speaks. "She's doing another one next week. Would you like to come?"

I jerk my head up. "You'd let me come with you?"

Her gaze softens, and I see deep sadness in her eyes for one brief moment. Then she blinks, and it's gone. "Regardless of how our relationship ended, Mark, they're your children. If you want to be part of their lives, you're welcome. But," she adds, her eyes sharpening, "only if you're going to be consistently present. I won't let you breeze in and out of their lives. I won't let you hurt them."

The way I hurt her.

She doesn't say the words, but I hear them just the same.

"I want to be involved, Charlie, as much as you'll let me. I want to rebuild our friendship. We need to be friends to raise our children in an emotionally healthy way."

She studies me, her face carefully neutral. "Friends," she repeats.

I remove my hands from her belly. Nerves make my throat grow tight, and I swallow. "I think it's important for us to get along. For the babies," I add, hoping to nudge her closer toward letting me back into her life.

"Yes, I suppose it is," she says, her voice quiet.

"Then I'd like very much to come with you to your appointment."

Her face is impassive when she nods. "I'll text you the details."

We're on a positive note, so it's probably a good time for me to leave. I don't need to say something else stupid and lose the ground I've gained. I step back. "Thank you for breakfast. And for inviting me to your ultrasound. I appreciate it."

Confusion flits across her face, but she rapidly masks it. "You're welcome." She and Penny walk me to the door. Penny presses against Charlie's leg as though she senses distress, but though I eye her carefully, Charlie's expression doesn't change.

I'm walking down the steps when a flash of red in the bushes to my right catches my eye.

Her Christmas gift. The one that tumbled out of my pocket when I was tussling with Stubbs.

"What did you find?" she asks as I brush snow off the damp, bedraggled package.

"I dropped something the other night," I explain, shoving it in my jacket pocket and hoping she doesn't press me further. It's not like I can give her jewelry now that she's moved on to someone else. "Thanks again for letting me come over."

I drive away, pleased at my progress. Not only are Charlie and I on speaking terms again, but she's willing to let me back in, to try to be friends again, to be a dad to my unborn children.

I smile to myself. Today is a very good day.

CHAPTER NINETEEN

CHARLIE

FRIENDS.

He wants to be friends.

He's finally speaking to me. He wants to be part of the babies' lives. He wants us to be able to get along for the sake of the children.

These are good things. It's a lot more than I had twenty-four hours ago.

So why does it hurt so damn much?

I sink onto the stairs, hugging my knees as best I can around my baby belly.

It may be safer to let go and move on, but that's not an option. Mark is the father of my children. For the next eighteen-plus years, he'll be part of their lives.

And mine. He'll be part of mine.

I'm going to see him.

Miss him.

Long for him.

Love him, without being loved in return.

Mark gets exactly what he wants – a civil relationship with me, and father-hood to our babies.

And I lose.

No matter how things shake out, I lose.

Images shutter rapid-fire through my mind. Seeing Mark all the time, re-membering what we had, knowing I can never have it again. Watching him laugh and play with our kids, tousling their hair, tossing them into the air as they squeal, with Penny barking and trying to join in.

It's so close to my dream – the kids, the chaos, the dog, the man.

But it's not my dream. It's a nightmare.

Because the man I love is there, with the babies and the dog and the unbridled chaos. He just doesn't love me back.

And that one fact changes everything.

Just when I'm on the verge of despair, I gasp, my hands flying to my abdomen. Something – no, some*one* – just kicked inside my belly.

It doesn't hurt, but it gets my attention. I press firmly against the spot where I felt it, waiting. A few seconds later, there's another tiny thump against my hand.

The little kicks from one of my Tiny People, as Lila has nicknamed them, settle me down and ground me.

Yes, I have to see Mark. I knew that would likely be the case. I wanted him to be a part of our children's lives. I invited him. They deserve a dad, and he has the potential to be a great one.

They also deserve a mom who will be strong for them.

And I will be.

I've survived unbelievably hard things and emerged a stronger person. I'll survive this, too.

Yes, it's safer to let Mark go and move on, but I refuse to live a safe life because of a fear of being hurt. I spent years being controlled by my fear. Not anymore.

I choose to be strong.

I choose intentional vulnerability.

I choose to place myself in a situation that will almost certainly bring emotional pain.

Letting Mark back in for the babies' sakes, knowing he doesn't love me, will hurt. When it does, I'll bleed for a while. Maybe even for a long while.

But sooner or later, my wounds will heal. They'll scar over.

And no matter how ugly they are, scars don't hurt. Scars remain after a wound has healed.

No matter how much being around Mark hurts, I will heal.

I will be the strong mother my babies deserve.

MARK

Stubbs shows up the morning after my breakfast with him and Charlie. My college course catalogs are spread everywhere when he comes in. I stack them on my coffee table, still open, with courses highlighted and notes jotted in the margins and in the spiral notebook I use for my therapy homework.

He tips his head at the pile of catalogs. "What are you doing?"

"Goal-setting. I've achieved my goal of walking. It's time to set new ones."

"And have you?"

I shrug. My primary goal is getting Charlie back, but since they're together, I sure as hell can't say that. "I'm narrowing my options."

Stubbs sits on the safe end of my couch, avoiding the hateful eunuch-spring. "I've got coffee," I offer.

His bulky body dwarfs my full-sized couch. "Black, please," he says.

I pour two cups, hand one to him, and sit on the loveseat. "What's up?"

He takes a sip, pausing for a long moment. "I told you I used to be married, and you asked what happened," he says. "I think talking about it might be good for both of us."

"Sure," I say, trying to hide my surprise. "Whatever you need."

The huge man leans forward, resting his elbows on his thighs. "Maria and I were high school sweethearts," he begins. "She was tiny, five-foot-nothing and barely a hundred pounds, with dark hair to her waist and huge brown eyes. And a fiery temper," he laughs. "Everything they say about spicy Latino women was true in her case." He pauses. "And strong. She was strong, much stronger than I was, though I couldn't see it. We dated for two years in high school. We were crazy about each other. She was devastated when I enlisted. I couldn't make her understand why it was something I needed to do. All she saw was that it would separate us. I was eighteen when I shipped out. I didn't learn she was pregnant until after basic training. I missed Ty's birth. I came home on leave, married her, spent a day or two with her and the baby, and went back out. Every time a tour ended, I'd re-up. It felt like the right thing to do, but I missed birthdays, Christmases, anniversaries, peewee football. I missed all the important moments in both of their lives."

He stops for a moment, and I wait. "It's been seven years since I lost my legs. When it happened, I thought my world had ended. I wholeheartedly believed I'd lost everything. I was full of rage without an outlet. Maria and Ty moved halfway across the country so I could keep rehabbing at Brooke. They changed jobs, schools, houses. I acted like they owed it to me. I acted like everybody owed me. I was an ass to everyone around me, but most of all, to my family.

"Maria put up with a lot from me. A lot," he repeats with emphasis. "Way more than she should've. She tried to shelter Ty from the worst of my tantrums, and for some reason, that made me even madder."

Stubbs drops his head, and silence falls over the room. "I got drunk one night. Nothing new. I drank a lot back then. I was always angry, and drinking only made me worse. Something set me off. I don't remember what." He stops, thoughtful. "You'd think I'd remember something that changed the entire trajectory of my life, but I don't. I just remember getting mad and yelling. I jumped up, like my crippled ass was going to stomp out of the house, but when I stood, I lost my balance. Maria ran forward, trying to catch me before I hit the floor."

He closes his eyes for a full minute before continuing. "I fell against the wall, and as I did, I put my arm up to block her. I didn't want help. Didn't want to need help, especially not from a tiny thing like her. The momentum of my fall, throwing my forearm up, and her rushing to help all combined to knock her off balance. She fell into an end table." He looks at me, his eyes bleak. "I was raised to protect women. I'd have died before I'd have hurt her on purpose." He exhales heavily. "Ty came running in when he heard the noise. She'd hit a ceramic lamp when she fell, and it shattered and cut her elbow. Ty thought I'd shoved her, that I'd hurt her on purpose." He pauses. "He'd just turned fifteen. He was about five-ten, but he hadn't filled out yet. He didn't care that I was a head taller and a hundred pounds heavier. He helped his mama up and got between me and her. Got in my face and shoved me. Told me if I ever laid another hand on her, he'd bury me." He smiles sadly. "Even drunk and mad and shocked, I was proud of him for protecting his mama. He threw me out with nothing but the clothes on my back. I spent the night on a bus stop bench. I didn't argue when Maria served me with divorce papers."

He turns to me. "I wasn't there for Maria. For thirteen years, I missed everything important, and even though it was hard on her, she never complained. She focused all her energy on making sure Ty had everything he needed. When I was home, things were good. But after the explosion, I let what I'd lost take priority over everything I had left. I had my life. I had my mind. I had an incredible woman who loved me. I had an amazing son." He shakes his head. "And I threw it all away, because all I could focus on was how I wasn't who I used to be. I forgot that who I'd once been isn't nearly as important as who I choose to be now."

Silence falls over the room. After a minute, I speak. "Do you ever see them?"

He nods. "Ty's twenty now, and we've repaired our relationship. It took a long time for him to trust me again. My shrink held some family sessions with me, him, and Maria after I got my shit together. We worked through things. Now that he's older, he's able to comprehend the mindset I had and the things

I was dealing with. I wasn't dealing with them well," he quickly adds, "but when I lost my anger, so did he."

"What about Maria?"

He sighs. "We have a cordial relationship, but I irreparably damaged our marriage those first couple of years after my injury. She remarried last year. Ken's in finance. He's a good man. He dotes on her. She deserves someone like that."

Stubbs draws a deep breath. "My mistakes cost me my marriage and my family. I refused to accept my body after the explosion. I saw myself as less than, as useless, as not good enough, all because I'd lost my legs. I hated myself for not being what I once was. That hatred bled all over everyone I cared about, and it cost me every relationship that mattered."

His dark eyes pin me as he stands. "I won't ever make that mistake again, Mark. You threw away a relationship with an extraordinary woman because your focus was on what you'd lost, not everything you still had." He pauses for a half-second. "You still have a chance. So what if you aren't the man you used to be? None of us are. Life is about adapting to changes. You get to choose who you want to be now. Choose wisely."

I sit in silence for a long time after he leaves, closing my front door with a soft click.

CHARLIE

It's been more than twenty-four hours since Mark's breakfast visit, and I haven't slept a wink. I'm tired, frustrated, and cranky.

He wants to be friends.

I've accepted that having Mark in my babies' lives will bring me pain. I'm bracing myself for soul-deep wounds from knowing my perfect family is just beyond my fingertips. I know those wounds will eventually scar, and for my babies, I will be strong enough to prevail.

But rebuilding our friendship? An actual friendship, not merely friendly interactions? I'm not sure I can do that.

My relationship with Mark ended horribly, and though I think I understand his reasons, the narrative I've conjured in my head is simply supposition. He hasn't said a single word about what happened. It's as though our intimate relationship never took place. With no explanations or apologies, I'd be an idiot to blindly trust him again.

I cease my grumpy pacing and flop on the couch. Even with explanations and apologies, if I weren't pregnant, I'd tell him to fuck off.

Friends?!? Seriously? Friends don't behave the way he has.

But I can't tell him to fuck off, because I have babies to think of.

I mentally replay that day in the hospital when he was so cruel, impaling me with words in a way no one else could. Even now, the memory chills me. But once I'd gotten past my initial pain and shock, I'd reminded myself that true friendship means being there for someone even when – and especially when – they push you away because of their own fear, pain, or grief.

He'd texted from his hospital bed. *Please don't give up on me.* The naked honesty in those few words was enough. Despite fearing another eruption, I'd squared my shoulders and returned. It was the catalyst that led him to seek help, repairing and ultimately strengthening our bond.

That day in the hospital was a brief outburst – brutal, but brief.

These past few months haven't been like that. This wasn't the result of a single heated explosion. Our relationship died from a nuclear winter, a chillingly complete withdrawal of him from my life. Mark executed a cold, abrupt end to the closeness we'd developed over decades.

Now he wants to pick up our friendship like none of that ever happened, and his tone-deaf attitude pisses me off. As a result, I'm muttering under my breath and stomping through my house as Penny trails behind. Big brown eyes glance from me to the door, wordlessly hinting that I need another walk in the woods to calm down.

It doesn't help.

Stubbs spends his morning in his new office, unpacking boxes and arranging things the way he wants them. I text him when lunch is ready. The lunches I cook don't hold a candle to his breakfasts. This morning he made a bacon-spinach-tomato quiche with fried cheese-grit cakes. My lunch of creamy red pepper soup and turkey-cheddar wraps pales in comparison, but he falls on it like a starving man nonetheless. After lunch, he heads to a local nursery, citing the need for plants for his office. I curl up on the sofa with my pregnancy book and a notebook. I'll need to pick up quite a bit over the next few months, and having twins means needing twice as many of everything – car seats, sleepers, diapers. Despite Mark's proclaimed interest, I'm half-expecting to tackle parenthood alone, so the more prepared I am, the better my chances of success.

The sheer volume of information in the book makes my head spin. I set it aside a little after four, just as my phone buzzes.

It's a text from Mark.

"Would it be okay if I came by later to talk?"

My stomach knots, but I steel myself. *I'm not going to allow fear to control my life again.*

My phone buzzes again. "It's okay to say no. I know I don't deserve it."

I sigh. Mark's making an effort. Besides, dinner is safe. He won't act up with Stubbs here. I type quickly before I can change my mind. "Come over for dinner. It's my night to cook."

"I'll bring dinner," comes his immediate response.

"I'll be glad to take a night off cooking. How's six-ish?"

"Perfect. I can't wait."

His palpable enthusiasm confuses me. I'm wondering if I should remind him Stubbs will be here when another text lands. "Does Stubbs have any food preferences?"

The subtle reminder that he knows what I like to eat, that Stubbs is the outsider, doesn't go unnoticed, and I frown. Then again, maybe he's trying to be considerate, and I'm just overly tired and grumpy. "He'll eat anything with meat that isn't nailed down," I reply. "He says the Marines trained him well."

Little dots dance on the screen. "See you around six."

Stubbs thumps down the stairs a few minutes later wearing fatigues hemmed at the knee and a faded Marine Corps tee shirt. "I'm going to the VFW," he announces. I glance up in surprise. "It's a good place to meet veterans," he explains with a grin, "and since that's the clientele I'm looking to serve, it can't hurt to network."

"When will you be home?"

He pulls on his jacket. "When the crowd thins out." He tilts his head. "Is it alright for me to come in late? I don't want to disturb you."

"It's fine. I was just wondering if I should expect you for dinner."

He shakes his head. "I'll grab something."

He opens the door, then pokes his head back into the living room. "Does it snow every day here?" he asks, sounding exasperated.

I peek outside. Large flakes drift lazily down from the gray sky, and the ground is white. "It is winter, you know," I tease him. Then I frown. "Are you comfortable with driving in snow?"

Stubbs rolls his eyes. "A little late to worry about that, isn't it?" My frown deepens, and he grins. "I'll text you when I get there and before I head home, worrywart." I flip him off, and he laughs as he heads out the door.

I decide to take Penny for her afternoon walk before the sun starts to set or the weather worsens. I tug my boots on, then grab my coat and whistle for her. She bounds to my kitchen door, her tail wagging furiously as she waits for me to open it. She scrambles onto the deck before dashing through the yard to wait impatiently for me by the gate at the far corner of my yard.

Just below my backyard is a path leading into the woods. There's a slight incline, with several streams and trails leading around and up the mountain. Since Penny's arrival, I've started taking her into the woods on our afternoon walks. Linda suggested I relieve my stress and depression by doing things that bring me joy, and the woods have always been my happy place. The solitude of nature, the smell of green things, and the sound of trickling water soothe my soul like nothing else can. I've been taking Penny – and sometimes Stubbs – to explore the lower trails. I'm not dumb enough to hike straight up a snowy mountain while pregnant, but there are several easy trails that border brooks and lead to wooded areas. Last week, Stubbs brought a wooden outdoor bench, the kind you'd see at a public park. He carried it like it weighed nothing and set it up beside a stream close to my house. "Your soul craves time in the woods. It relaxes you. I want you to have somewhere to sit and listen to nature, to the water and the wind and the birds," he'd said, and I'd hugged him impulsively. He'd chuckled and kissed the top of my head.

I unlock the gate, and Penny sprints toward the trail before stopping to frolic in the snow. She nips at falling flakes and barks when one touches her nose, and I laugh before herding her toward the woods. She knows the path, and I follow behind her as she runs ahead, then dashes back to me when I take too long to suit her. In a few minutes, we've reached the stream. I sit down on the bench to wait for her to get the zoomies out of her system. I close my eyes, listening to the splashing water, the sigh of the wind through the trees, and the sound of softly falling snow. I breathe slowly, deeply, centering myself for the evening ahead.

Because with Stubbs going to the VFW, I'll be facing Mark alone.

The sun is starting to dip below the peaks, painting them with splashes of red and orange, when Penny decides she's done sloshing back and forth through the stream. As we're heading back Stubbs texts to let me know he arrived safe and sound with enough burgers to feed thirty people, though there are only a dozen or so there. That's okay, he says, because there's enough for everyone to eat their fill, including the bartender.

By the time we reach the house, my fingers are numb and my nose is runny from the cold air. "Sit," I tell Penny, pointing to the scatter rug by the back door. When she obeys, I grab a couple of towels from the hall bathroom. I toss one on the floor for her to stand on, then kneel to towel-dry her legs and undercarriage with the second. That's followed by blow-drying her long belly fur. When I stand, I'm immensely glad no one is around to witness. Pregnancy has changed my center of gravity, and me struggling to my feet isn't a pretty sight.

I glance at the clock. It's already after five. Mark will be here soon, and thanks to Penny, I reek of eau de wet dog. I pin my hair up and race through a shower, then take the time to fix my hair and apply makeup.

Yeah. I'm primping. For a man who broke my heart, then says he wants to be friends again.

A smarter woman wouldn't primp.

She also wouldn't dream of said man every night.

I curl my hair in loose waves and use warm brown eyeshadow to enhance my green eyes. Concealer hides the evidence I haven't slept, and mascara draws attention to my long lashes instead of my dark circles. I dress in my usual black leggings and add a beige tunic with rose-gold threads woven through it. I'm still too thin everywhere except my stomach, but other than that, I'm passable.

I return to the living room, growing more tense with each passing moment. At five thirty-five, I turn on the television and find a music channel. At five forty, I switch it off, annoyed by the noise. At five forty-five, I wonder if a glass of white wine with dinner will soothe my jangled nerves. For now, I down a glass of water, hoping it will do the trick. At five fifty, I close my eyes and concentrate on deep breathing.

Breathe.

Slow and easy.

Just breathe.

My body is starting to relax when I feel rapid bumping deep within my belly. I glance down, startled, and press my hand to my stomach.

One of my babies is kicking hard against my hand.

Wonder and amazement course through me. That's followed by sadness that Mark isn't here to share this moment, then frustration at him for leaving and annoyance that he wants to pick up our friendship like nothing ever happened.

I'm an emotional mess today. Maybe him coming to dinner is a bad idea.

The doorbell rings at five fifty-five.

He's early.

Panic spirals through my chest. I take a deep breath before opening the door. "Hi," I say, my voice way too breathy.

Damn, he looks good.

I'd tried not to let my gaze linger on him yesterday, but tonight, I can't stop myself. Pale blue eyes meet mine. They're framed in lashes so long, they ought to be illegal on a man. His strong jaw is dusted with warm brown stubble. His lips are soft and full, made for kissing. His sandy blond hair is longer on top than it's been in years, and the back is just long enough that I could twist my fingers in it if we were making out, the way we once did. I wonder absently if it's as soft as I remember. Jeans hug his long legs, and his black leather jacket makes me want to grab the front of it, drag him close, and kiss him until I forget everything else.

Dammit.

I shut my eyes, trying to regain control of my wayward thoughts. When I open them, his eyes are traveling over my body, too. He pauses on my midsection, and I wince, trying not to think about how unappealing my pregnant body must look, particularly to the man who rejected me.

"Sorry I'm early," Mark says, his eyes returning to mine. "I couldn't wait any longer." His words hit me square in the heart, pleasure mixed with pain.

"Come on in." He steps inside, carrying two large paper bags and heading toward the kitchen. When he passes me, I smell bacon. So does Penny, because she trots after him.

"I brought four subs and some salads," he calls over his shoulder, "because I wasn't sure what Stubbs might like best."

"Actually, he left a few minutes ago. He decided to go network at the VFW. He won't be joining us for dinner after all."

Mark stops unpacking the bags, realizing it'll be just the two of us. I can't tell if he thinks that's a good thing or a bad thing. He glances at me. "I – um – I brought you a BLT sub."

His guarded expression jogs my memory. I brought him takeout nearly every day while he was at Brooke. It was a way to help him briefly escape the harsh reality of hospital life. There was a fantastic deli nearby, and I'd stop by several days a week. We had a regular sandwich rotation – turkey with provolone, pulled pork with pineapple, Cuban paninis, and BLT subs. His favorite was the pulled pork and pineapple. Mine was the BLT.

He remembered.

I guess I said it out loud, because he nods. "To you, they were just sandwiches. Not to me. For a few minutes, I got to forget I was a patient. You brought normalcy to my life during a time when my life was anything but normal. Thank you."

My mouth falls open, and I quickly close it. "You're welcome," I murmur. My heart races as his words bring back memories of the man I once knew, before everything changed.

I turn toward the refrigerator. "What would you like to drink?"

"Whatever you're having."

I pour us both glasses of tea as he points to each item in turn. "Pulled pork – although it doesn't have grilled pineapple – an Italian sub, your BLT sub, and a club sandwich sub. I also brought fries and three chef's salads."

I turn back to the refrigerator. "I actually have a bottle of grilled pineapple barbecue sauce, if you want some for your sandwich," I offer. "It's pretty good."

"Please," he agrees.

I grab it, along with ketchup for the fries and a couple of bottles of salad dressing. We sit down with our food at the dining room table. I share my sandwich and fries with Penny, who's thrilled with the bacon and the bread that's soaked up its flavor. I pour raspberry vinaigrette over my salad, polishing off the entire thing along with the sandwich and fries. I catch Mark smiling as I lick the last of the dressing off my fork.

"I'm hungry all the time," I admit. He pushes the other half of his sandwich toward me. I shake my head. "I'm full now, but in three hours, I'll be hungry again. The babies take everything they need from me. My stores are pretty depleted, so I have to refuel frequently."

His smile falters at my words, though he tries to hide it. "There's another salad and two sandwiches. I've got you covered till morning."

After dinner, we put the leftovers in the refrigerator and relocate to the living room. Penny hops up on the sofa beside me. Her silky brown ears look auburn, and the coppery speckles in her white chest fur are more pronounced in the lamplight. Mark sits on the opposite end of the couch and reaches over to scratch her head. She promptly climbs onto his lap. He laughs, and she pushes her face into his hands.

"So what's her story? How did you two end up together?" he asks, obliging her by rubbing her cheeks. I explain about her being removed from an abusive situation and describe how her terror around Tom led him to bring her to me.

"That was one thing I missed in the Army," he muses.

"Having a dog?"

"Yeah. I mean, we had the camp dog. But it's not the same."

Sarge was a skinny brown mutt we'd found half-starved near the base. In no time, he went from skin and bones to fat and sassy. Everyone doted on Sarge, even Colonel Sherman. Dogs were against the rules, but with the way Sarge boosted morale, neither the Colonel nor Mark gave a damn. He was a friendly, furry reminder of life back home.

"Little things mean more when you realize what you've taken for granted," Mark says quietly.

I know he's talking about more than a dog, but I can't discuss anything emotional, not today. My moods are vacillating way too much. I change the subject. "Do you miss being over there?"

He pauses. "I miss feeling useful. Feeling needed. I miss teaching and guiding and leading. I miss knowing what I'm supposed to do and having a sense of purpose. I miss some of the people. But I don't miss getting shot at and having to get you to patch me up, and I definitely don't miss the dust and the heat and the noise."

"That's why I moved somewhere green and quiet. I needed the woods and the peace."

"Yeah. This place is definitely the opposite of the Sandbox."

I study his expression. "What did you mean when you said you miss feeling useful?"

Something dark crosses his face, and he laughs, but not with humor. "Isn't it obvious?"

"Not to me."

"I had a job. A purpose. Missions. Things to do, objectives to accomplish, and I did them well. I was needed. I'm not needed now."

That's not true. I need you, and our babies need you.

I squelch those thoughts and redirect the conversation again. "Have you thought about what you want to do now that your leg is healed?"

He hesitates. "I was talking about that with my doctor." I wonder if he's referring to his psychiatrist, but don't ask. He's not shared that information with me. "I've been browsing college catalogs. I'm not sure what I want to do. Maybe teaching. Maybe coaching."

"You'd be good at that. I'd never have made it through algebra or chemistry without you. And coaching is just another form of teaching."

He looks away. "I'm not sure about coaching."

"Because of your amputation?" I ask bluntly. "Because you know that's bullshit, right? Or do we need to have that discussion again?"

He's silent.

I can't keep the pain out of my voice. "Are you ever going to stop seeing yourself as half a man?"

"I'm trying, Charlie, I swear," he says softly. I exhale heavily and close my eyes. This is why I can't let myself trust him, because I can't be sure he won't flip back into that "useless-cripple" mindset. When he changes the topic, I let him.

We spend the evening reminiscing about military life, about people we knew and little things that made deployment more enjoyable. It's familiar and nonthreatening, and I let myself relax as the evening goes on. "Do you remember right before Tucker and Lila started dating, when he kept mouthing off at her and she stole his clothes while he was in the shower?"

Mark starts laughing. "I remember the catcalls when he was trying to cover himself with his hands as he ran barefoot for his quarters."

I giggle. "He finally flipped everybody off with both hands and strolled through the camp, buck naked."

Mark chuckles. "She wanted to get his attention."

She got it. She and Tucker shared their first kiss later that night.

"You'd think Tuck would be more well-behaved by now. He knows Lila will get even."

"I don't know," he replies. "Tucker's pretty well behaved. He's got everything he wants. He's not going to screw things up." He pauses. "He's smarter than I was."

I stay silent, mostly because I'm not sure what to say, and agreeing hardly seems appropriate.

Mark breaks the awkward silence. "I remember getting you to patch me up the night I broke up a fight between a pair of drunk privates and got caught in the crossfire."

I glance over. "When one of them split your eyebrow?" He nods. It looks pretty good, if I do say so myself. There's barely a hint of a scar. "I'm surprised it didn't scar more. It was deep."

"You did a good job," he said.

The split was two inches long and all the way to the bone. I'd cleaned it, sutured the inner and outer layers, and secured it with adhesive skin tape. He'd ended up with one hell of a shiner, but he fared far better than the privates. He'd flung them into opposite corners after a fist caught him in the face when he jumped in to separate them.

"You have a gentle touch. You were always very tender with me." He pauses again. "Even when I didn't deserve it."

Once again, I don't answer, unsure what I'm supposed to say or read into his words.

"Do you miss military life?" he asks, picking up on my discomfort.

"I loved being a medic," I admit. "What I did made a difference."

"You make a difference now."

I snort. "I used to stand between soldiers and death. Now I rub sore muscles."

"Maybe it's not as dramatic as the battlefield, but you're still helping soldiers heal. You're relieving pain and helping them look past their wounds and reclaim their lives."

Maybe, for some of them. But I couldn't help Mark look past his wounds.

I change the subject as my throat tightens. "Sometimes I miss the structure of military life, but then I remember I enjoy sleeping late and eating food that wasn't canned or freeze-dried."

He chuckles. "The food wasn't great, but there was plenty of it."

"I got an email from Colonel Sherman. He's retiring in the spring."

"The old bird's going home?" he asks, surprised. "What's he going to do with himself?"

"He's bought a place in Montana, a big farm with horses near his son and grandkids."

"That sounds relaxing. He deserves it."

"He has to go to D.C. for a while after he leaves the Sandbox, but I asked him to stop by Cedar Ridge on his way to Montana. I'd love to see him."

We chat a while longer, and I'm shocked when I look at the clock on the wall. We've talked till almost eleven, but I still have no explanation and no apology.

I guess we're talking, at least.

He follows my gaze to the clock. "I should let you get your rest. I didn't mean to stay so late." He gets to his feet, and so do I. "I've had a good time tonight. Maybe we can do this again?"

"I'd like that," I hear myself say, surprised to find I mean it. My reluctance to trust him has waned slightly over the course of the evening. Maybe it's because the Mark I saw tonight reminds me of the Mark I once knew as well as I knew myself.

I walk him to the door, and he looks at me, his eyes softening. "G'night, Baby Girl."

The tender nickname hits me hard, like a kick to my gut. I hug myself tightly, instinctively protecting my vital organs, backpedaling away from him as my tightly-held emotional control unravels. I feel myself breathing fast. Too fast.

He lifts a hand toward me, his expression startled. "Charlie? Are you okay?"

I scuttle further backwards, and something inside me bursts. "No, I'm not okay! Why would you call me that now, after –" I break off, my throat tightening. "Do you get off on hurting me? Is that it?" Tears blind my eyes, and I turn away.

"I'm sorry, Charlie. I didn't think –" He stops. "I didn't mean to hurt you. I never want to hurt you again." He pauses. "I'll go. I'm sorry," he repeats. I hear the door open, followed by a rush of cold air and a quiet click as he closes it behind him. Bleak emptiness overwhelms me, and I sink onto a step as my tears begin to fall in earnest.

Damn him.

I associate Mark calling me Baby Girl with trust and deep emotions. Hearing his tender name for me after months of silence and apathy crushes my heart in a fist. Casually tossing out a familiar nickname feels like one more way he's trying to erase the pain of the past few months.

About ten minutes later, my phone rings. When I see it's him, I don't pick up. He calls again and again until I turn the phone off altogether. I curl up on my bed, hugging my pillow, crying until my eyes are puffy and Penny's fallen asleep against me.

CHAPTER TWENTY

MARK

I'M AWAKE ALL NIGHT after upsetting Charlie. Her tear-filled eyes haunt me, her words resounding in my head all night. *"Do you get off on hurting me?"*

Fuck. All I do is hurt her.

I spend the entire night belittling and berating myself, going to dark places in my mind again.

By morning, I'm thinking more clearly. I'm pushing too hard. I need to approach her like I would a wounded animal – with gentle words, cautious movements, and plenty of space. I called her over and over last night, but she never answered. I need to apologize for calling her Baby Girl. I didn't mean to – it just slipped out. That's how I think of her, as my Baby Girl. But I know that name holds significance for her, one I destroyed with my toxic behavior.

Toxic.

"I think I'm one of those toxic people," I say. It's early afternoon, and Dr. Allen is still closing his office door after asking me how I am.

"What makes you say that?" he asks, taking a seat.

I sit across from him, watching as he crosses his legs and leans back in his leather chair. "I read a few articles about toxic people online this morning."

He smiles faintly. "Researching on Dr. Google?"

"There were several traits of toxic people listed that I definitely exhibit."

He tilts his head. "Could you give some examples?"

I tick them off on my fingers. "Inconsistency. Frequent mood swings. Broken promises. Wanting attention, but only on my terms. Behaving in ways that damage others."

He studies me, his dark eyes roving my face. "Many of those traits you listed apply to the majority of the human population at some point. Inconsistency peaks in late January every year as people abandon their New Year's resolutions. People have mood swings as stressors in their lives increase. They break promises. They act out. It's part of the human condition."

"I wasn't like that before," I argue.

"So your behavior changed following your combat injuries," he says. "That's a normal physiologic response to a head injury. That doesn't make you toxic."

Kip would disagree.

I stare down at the floor. "There was a kid," I say slowly, and begin telling him about Kip, about how he lost his leg and how it cost him his relationship.

"Let me stop you for a moment," Dr. Allen interjects. "Why do you say it cost him his relationship?"

"Because that's what she told Kip." I pause. "Or maybe it was what her best friend told him afterwards, I can't remember. Someone said it, though, and Kip believed it."

"Do you believe that's what led to the demise of his relationship?"

I snort. "No. She was using him. He was trying to find a way to buy her a new car to persuade her to come back before he died." I pause again. "No. Before he committed suicide."

"Can we talk about that?"

It takes a moment for me to gather my courage, to steel myself. "He was excited. I was having a shitty day. A shitty week. I wasn't doing well emotionally. I was –" I stop for a second. "I was drowning in self-pity. I hated myself even more than I did when I first saw my leg after the explosion. I felt like a freak. I hated my abutment –" I gesture to where my prosthesis connects to the metal rod protruding from my residual limb – "even more than I did my amputation. I'd thought the surgery would make me normal, but..." I exhale in a huff. "I'd been trying to convince myself it wasn't real, I guess. I insisted on wearing my prosthetic all the time and concealing it with pants, so I'd look like I still had two legs. I decided I'd sleep in it one night. Charlie tried to talk me out of it, but I insisted. The next morning, it got tangled in the blanket, and I fell on my ass. She jumped up to make sure I was okay. I was humiliated, and I acted out. I yelled and then didn't speak to her for a couple of days. I just withdrew."

My insides twist with guilt. I've treated her like shit so many times.

Focus.

I glance over at Dr. Allen. "Like I said, I wasn't in a good place. That's when Kip came in for PT with me." I stop talking, unable to continue for a full minute. "He was all excited. He'd found out he could have the same surgery

I'd had. He was convinced he would be normal, that the shallow woman he was so crazy about would take him back. And I lost my shit on him."

Dr. Allen watches, but doesn't speak. When I realize he's going to wait me out, I shake my head. "I told him the surgery had turned me into a freak, and if he was counting on the surgery to get his life back, he'd be disappointed, because sooner or later, he'd take his prosthetic off, and he still wouldn't be normal. Still wouldn't have a damn leg. I was yelling. I stormed out and left him sitting there, looking shocked." I swallow. "Those are the last words I said to him. They might be the last words anyone said to him. He went home and blew his brains out that night."

Dr. Allen studies me. "And you blame yourself?"

I stare at him. "Well, yeah. Weren't you listening?"

"So if you hadn't said anything, if you'd just listened, do you believe he'd still be alive?"

His words give me pause. "I'm – I'm not sure."

"Why not?"

"I talked to the investigating detective," I admit. "Told him what I'd said. Told him I thought it was my fault. He told me Kip had been buying thousands of sleeping pills. And he said he'd been writing and rewriting a suicide note since he'd been in the hospital."

Dr. Allen's voice is mild. "So you think you know more than the detectives?"

"He shot himself," I point out. "If he'd taken pills, he'd have had a window of opportunity to change his mind and call for help. Shooting himself was an emotional reaction."

"I'd say it might be a more conventional response, actually. A soldier fresh out of combat will instinctively reach for a firearm. It's second nature."

I think of Charlie, more comfortable with her weapon than without it since her return from Afghanistan. "Maybe," I concede.

"So if the detective said he'd been planning to commit suicide, why do you blame yourself?"

"Because I pushed him into it."

"Did you tell him he'd be better off dead?"

I frown. "No."

"Put the gun in his hand?"

I shoot him a look. "Do you seriously expect me to believe there's no cause and effect there?"

"It's no one's fault that Kip killed himself," he says firmly.

I raise an eyebrow in a wordless challenge.

He shakes his head. "Suicide is rarely an impulsive decision. Suicides happen because someone is in a great deal of pain for a very long time. They usually can't see any other way out of that pain." He purses his lips. "I'm actually familiar with Kip's case."

That gets my attention. "You are? Why?"

"He'd had an appointment scheduled with me. The information was jotted down on a slip of paper that the detectives found while searching his home. The police questioned me briefly, but he'd committed suicide four days before his initial appointment was scheduled. I shared the information given to my secretary when he was referred to me, and they revealed information they'd turned up as well. Kip had attempted suicide twice previously."

"With pills," I recall, remembering what the detective had said.

He nods. "Correct. And he hadn't taken a lethal amount either time. From the number of pills he'd accumulated, he didn't intend to make that mistake a third time."

That's basically what the detective told me.

Dr. Allen continues speaking. "Kip had a history of suicide attempts, Mark. That means that at some point in his life, he'd decided it was a viable option to deal with his pain. Once a person has classified suicide as a potential solution, it lingers in the subconscious mind until he or she finds a clear reason to make it unacceptable. There has to be a strong motivation to remove that option from the table permanently." He pauses. "When someone is in tremendous pain all the time, sometimes all they can think about is making the pain stop."

I look away. I remember feeling like that. Wanting the pain to stop. Being so full of self-loathing that I wished I'd died, rather than survived, broken.

His voice is quiet. "Do you still feel that way?"

I glance up, shocked.

Brown eyes watch me steadily. "I've seen that expression on the faces of a lot of veterans who've come through my door."

I swallow. "No. Not now. There was a time," I admit. "But not now."

He nods. "So if we can agree that Kip was in terrible emotional pain, and that he saw no other way to make that pain end, can we agree that you were not at fault for Kip's suicide?"

I consider his words. "I feel responsible."

"Just because you feel something doesn't make it true."

I raise an eyebrow.

"Kip felt that a prosthesis or a new car would convince his ex-girlfriend to come running back. Was that true, in your opinion? Would she have come back?"

I shake my head. "She was shallow. I don't think he could have done anything to get her back, nor should he have. She'd already moved on to the next guy within a few days of dumping Kip."

"So even though he believed it, it wasn't true?" he asks pointedly.

I narrow my eyes.

"In med school, I took care of a man who believed he was Moses. He wore a red bathrobe and leather sandals. He carried two stacks of newspapers that he'd duct-taped into his very own Ten Commandments tablets." He grins. "To the dismay of the nurses, he kept his robe untied and refused to wear anything beneath it. He was convinced he was Moses. Did that make it true?"

I sigh. "Fine. You've made your point."

"Just because you believe you are responsible or toxic doesn't make it true. In fact, I would argue that worrying you're a toxic person proves the opposite. Toxic people don't give a damn about how their actions affect others. They only care about themselves. I believe seeing yourself as a toxic person is merely another manifestation of your lingering self-loathing."

I pause. "I hadn't considered that."

"Then that's your homework for this weekend. Examine yourself for any areas in which your self-loathing is still present. Write them down, and we'll discuss them at our next visit."

Maybe I need an outside perspective to get a better look at my internal issues.

When I get home, I text Charlie.

CHARLIE

I wake up hours before dawn, headachy from crying. When the sun comes up, I throw on boots, a scarf, and a warm coat. I pass Stubbs in the kitchen as Penny and I head out for a long walk. His eyes linger on my face, but all he says is, "Morning, Green Eyes."

"Morning," I respond, trying to sound cheerful, but based on his frown, I'm not successful.

Outside, the snow is deep enough to cover my ankles and halfway up Penny's legs. She's bouncy and excited. I love snow, but today, its damp heaviness matches my mood, and the greyness of the day matches my spirit. We head to our usual spot, and I wait on the bench while she splashes in the stream. It takes ages for her to decide she's done so we can head back.

I'm chilled to the bone when I return. Stubbs is gone, but there's a plate of pancakes and sausage waiting for me with a note telling me he's gone to the clinic to set up his files. I blow dry Penny's fur and eat breakfast before crawling into my deep tub upstairs to soak, draining it as it cools and adding more hot water. It fails to soothe me. I'm wrinkled as a prune when I finally climb out and dry myself on a plush white towel.

I dress in leggings, thick socks, and a brown and cream sweater as though cocooning myself against my dark mood. My head pounds ferociously, and I curl up on the couch. Sensing my mood, Penny presses against my side. The bright sun glaring off the snow makes me close my eyes, and I fling my arm over my face. Tears trickle as I recall last night, and the fact I'm crying yet again annoys me. I'm overly emotional, and I'm not sure whether it's from fatigue, hormones, or Mark. Probably all three.

Eventually, I calm enough to be objective about Mark's inadvertent use of my nickname. He and I had been reminiscing, reliving a time during which I'd called him Big Guy and he'd called me Baby Girl. We'd been recalling memories made when we were close, and a tentative peace had settled between us. It's understandable that his nickname for me slipped out. That name doesn't hold the pain for him that it does now for me. He wouldn't have expected my outburst.

Based on the twenty-one missed calls from him last night, he knows not to call me that again.

Penny and I take two more walks in the snow as the day drags on. I make a pot of chili, then bake two dozen blueberry muffins and a pan of honey-jalapeno cornbread. I scroll absently through numerous motherhood websites, jotting notes and making lists, but my mind keeps wandering.

Around five, I give up and push my laptop away just as my phone buzzes with a text.

It's Mark.

"I apologize for upsetting you last night after such an enjoyable evening. That certainly wasn't my intent. If I promise to keep my foot out of my mouth, could I come by this evening? I could really use your insight on something."

There's a short pause before he texts again. "I understand if you don't want me to. I know I screwed up."

A third text lands almost immediately after the second. "Again."

I sigh heavily. We're going to be co-parenting in a few months. I've got to be able to talk to him without dissolving into a puddle of emotions. Seeing him regularly is the only way to make that happen. Besides, after last night's fiasco, I'm betting he'll be on his best behavior.

"Come over for dinner. I made chili and honey-jalapeno cornbread," I type, ignoring the flutter in my chest at the thought of seeing him. That flutter has nothing to do with fear and everything to do with the way he's been in my dreams, and *that* scares the crap out of me.

"Sounds delicious. What can I bring?"

"Dessert?"

"Any cravings?" he answers.

You, I think, and butterflies rush through my stomach.

No, dammit. I squelch down my traitorous body's lusty response. "Chocolate pie?" I type instead. "Or really, anything chocolate."

"What time?"

"The chili's been simmering all afternoon, so anytime is fine."

"Be there around six."

"See you then," I type.

"Can't wait," he texts. Tiny dots dance on the screen as he continues. "Thank you, Charlie."

Charlie. Not Baby Girl.

He's trying.

"You're welcome."

Stubbs returns from the clinic a short time later, disappearing upstairs briefly before coming back down. "I'm going to the VFW again. Do you need anything?"

He won't be here for Mark's visit.

Again.

"I'm good," I tell him. "How's networking going?"

He beams. "I've got six clients already lined up. I figured I'll spend the first couple of days re-introducing myself to your regulars and learning the documentation and billing programs."

I nod. "I'll work with you. It shouldn't take more than a few hours to get you comfortable."

The huge man glances around my living room, pausing as Penny comes over. He leans down and scratches her ears as she wags excitedly. "Are you okay being here alone at night?"

Stubbs knows about my night terrors, and I'm touched by his concern. I wave my hand at the security systems and camera. "I was alone for a few months before you moved in. I'm fine. But I won't be alone tonight. Mark's coming over."

He frowns. "He came over last night."

I raise an eyebrow. "And?"

"And you looked like hell this morning. Your eyes were all red and puffy."

I smile wryly. "You truly have a gift for flattery."

He scowls. "Do I need to have another word with him?"

I shake my head, picturing Stubbs physically removing Mark from the house a few days ago. "No. We're talking, trying to reestablish some semblance of friendship. I'm just overly emotional." I gesture toward my belly. "It's the damn hormones."

He doesn't look convinced. I keep talking in an effort to redirect his attention. "Do you have plans tomorrow? I always host the New Year's Eve get-together. I'd love for you to join us."

He smiles. "I'll be here." He eyes me on his way out. "I'm going to the store tomorrow morning. Leave me a list of what you need."

I roll my eyes, knowing he's got me over a barrel. If I don't give him a list, he'll just keep stuffing my fridge, freezer, cabinets, and closets with whatever he sees fit. The other day, he came home with two hundred jars of baby food.

Two. Hundred.

When I pointed out to him that (a) my babies haven't been born yet, and (b) it'll be several more months before they're able to eat solid food, he'd smiled placidly and told me the food wouldn't expire for another two years. I'd pursed my lips before thanking him. The next day, he'd made several trips in and out of the house, carrying in six cases of diapers from a big box store. Each case held ninety-six diapers.

I'd stared at him as he'd opened my hall closet. "Six hundred diapers?"

"You'll go through eighteen or twenty a day with twins," he'd said. "You know, it would be easier if you'd just take rent money from me."

"No," I'd said, gritting my teeth. "We've been over this. You're my friend. I'm not taking your damn money."

He'd grinned and stacked the boxes in the closet. "Then get used to me showing up with random shit."

After Stubbs drives off, I flip on my Christmas tree lights before stirring the chili. I slice jalapeno and green onion and pull out shredded cheese and sour cream. The doorbell rings. I look at the clock. It's not even five-thirty. He's early. I glance in the hall mirror and sigh.

Glamorous, I am not.

My brown and cream sweater tents over my pregnant belly. My hair is twisted up in a clip, though several tendrils have worked themselves loose over the course of the day. I'm not wearing makeup, either. I'd planned to at least slap on some foundation and lip gloss before Mark got here – though I don't really want to think about why.

Too late now. Besides, it's not like he hasn't seen me barefaced before.

Bare-everything, actually.

I hurriedly shove that thought from my head.

Penny beats me to the door, prancing impatiently. When I open it, Mark stands there, a sheepish expression on his face. "Sorry I'm early. I – I really wanted to see you." He thrusts a box into my hands. "French silk pie," he says. "The girl at the bakery let me sample some from the case, and it was fantastic. I hope you like it."

He's talking too fast, twisting his hands. He's nervous, and somehow, that relaxes me.

Penny's practically climbing him, trying to reach his face as her tail thumps against the door frame. He laughs and leans down to pet her, and she whines, trying to get closer. It's a feeling I'm all too familiar with. I open the door wider. "Come on in."

He steps through the door and glances around. "Where's Stubbs? I didn't see his car."

"He went to the VFW again to drum up business."

Mark keeps his expression neutral. "I kind of expected him to show up and beat my ass for upsetting you last night. I can't believe he's letting you see me again."

I frown. "No one 'lets' me do anything. I make my own choices."

He hesitates, looking uncertain. "Then thank you. Do you need help with dinner?"

I lead him to the kitchen, talking over my shoulder. "Everything's ready. Help yourself."

We sit down at the table with fully loaded bowls of chili and squares of sweet-hot cornbread. Conversation revolves around trivial things, mostly the weather, Tucker and Lila, and Penny. "This is fantastic," he says, helping himself to a second bowl of chili. "I haven't bothered with anything quite so fancy."

My lips quirk up in a smile. "I'm not sure chili counts as fancy."

He shrugs. "No point in cooking just for myself."

"There's plenty left. Feel free to take some home."

There's a short lull in the conversation while I wonder what exactly he wanted my insight on. He's not mentioned anything so far. Maybe he's waiting until after dinner to begin a potentially unpleasant conversation.

"I saw they're having fireworks downtown tomorrow night. Are you and Stubbs going?"

I shake my head. "I'm having a low-key New Year's Eve celebration here. Tuck and Lila will be here, and so will Tom and Maya. Would you like to come?"

His eyes flick to mine. "Yes," he says immediately. "Very much. What can I bring?'

"I've got dinner covered, and Tom and Maya are bringing dessert. Tucker and Lila are in charge of cocktails, but if there's anything specific you want to drink, bring it."

Mark shakes his head. "I don't plan on drinking. My van handles very –" he pauses, trying to select the right word "– interestingly on slick roads. Adding alcohol to the mix won't help."

"I let everybody stay here," I explain. "I don't like people driving on New Year's Eve. Too many drunks on the roads. And after my parents, well... anyway, I host a grownup slumber party. It's a tradition."

His brows pull together. "You have a sleepover every year?"

I nod. "I have five bedrooms. I'd rather have everyone stay here and be safe." I hesitate briefly, letting myself look at him. His white button-down shirt stretches across his broad shoulders and muscled chest. The familiar scent of his cologne makes my chest ache, and I swallow. "You're welcome to stay, too."

Something flickers in his eyes. "Thanks. I'll think about it."

Mark insists on cleanup duty, so I take Penny out. When I return, he's waiting on the couch in the living room with a spiral notebook, chewing his lip.

He's nervous.

I sit down at the opposite end of the couch, pulling my feet beneath me. Penny hops up, settling on the cushion between us. I tip my head toward his hands. "What's with the notebook?"

He takes a deep breath before meeting my gaze. "I've been seeing a psychiatrist," he says. "After that day in the parking lot –" he breaks off, looking down. I wait until he raises his eyes to mine again. "That was a turning point for me," he confesses. "Tucker and Lila showed me some tough love, and Lila gave me the name of a psychiatrist that specializes in wounded vets with body image issues. I've been seeing him twice a week since then, and I'm making progress."

He stops talking again, and I sit quietly. I wonder if Mark's body image issues and the resulting demise of our relationship are what he wants my insight on, and my stomach tightens at the thought of having my pain laid bare.

"I had a bad night last night," he finally says. "I know you did, too, and I apologize for that. When you asked if I enjoyed hurting you, it hit me hard." Guilt rises in my chest. "I realized that my behavior over the past few months has given you every reason to believe that."

"I'm sorry," I interrupt him. "I shouldn't have said that. I was upset, but that's no excuse."

He shakes his head. "I hurt you, and you reacted. But it made me start thinking about things. I had an appointment today with Dr. Allen. I told him I thought I was a toxic person."

I tilt my head, confused. "Why would you think that?"

"Because I've hurt you. A lot," he adds, "not just last night. I've hurt other people, too."

I draw in a slow breath. "I was upset last night," I agree, "but I've done a lot of thinking since then. We'd been discussing good times. I can understand why you slipped and called me Baby Girl. You wouldn't have known that it doesn't hold the same connotation for me now as it does for you. You didn't say it to hurt me, and I apologize for saying so."

Some emotion I can't read flits across his face. "What connotation does it hold now?"

I wrap my arms around my chest without realizing it till I've done it. "Pain."

There's a long pause. His voice is rough when he speaks. "Why?"

I hug myself tighter. "From the time we were teenagers, when you'd call me that, it was –" I hesitate. "It was special. It told me I meant something to you, that I mattered. After things ended – after you left – I didn't matter anymore." He opens his mouth, but I hold up my hand, and he closes it. "In San Antonio, the day you blew up on me, that was like Mount St. Helens blowing her top. It was brutal, but brief, and then it was over. This situation, though? The past few months?" I gesture between the two of us and shake my head. "It was more like a nuclear winter. You withdrew from me more and more for weeks after your surgery, and then you left me altogether, with no end in sight." I meet his gaze. "I understand your struggles with your body image better than most people. But having you cut me out of your life so completely –" my voice breaks, and I swallow. "Hearing you call me that name now reminds me of everything I've lost."

I can read the shame in his expression, the pain in his eyes. His jaw tightens, and he shoves a hand through his sandy hair. "I should go," he says. "All I do is hurt you."

'No," I say firmly, and he looks up, startled. I exhale heavily. "Look, you and I have to figure out a way to co-exist if you're going to be part of these babies' lives. To do that, we've got to work through some difficult things, and it's not going to be easy on either of us. I'm not trying to lay a guilt trip on you. I told you, I understand why you slipped back into calling me that last night. You asked why it was painful for me, and I've explained. Now we move on."

He casts me a skeptical look. "Can we move on? Really?"

I gesture toward my abdomen. "If you're going to be involved in their lives, we have to. I refuse to saddle them with tension every time we see each other. They don't deserve that."

He doesn't say anything at first, but after a moment, he nods. "You're right."

There's a brief pause. I square my shoulders and dive right back into the messiness. "So tell me more about why you said you're a toxic person."

He draws a deep breath, letting it out slowly. "Like I said, I was having a bad night. I started reflecting on the people I've hurt. I went online, searching for answers, and the term 'toxic' kept popping up. Toxic relationships. Toxic personalities. Toxic people. And I had a lot of the traits they described regarding toxic people. Inconsistent behavior. Being someone people have to walk on eggshells around. Sharp mood swings. Not keeping my promises. Wanting attention, but only on my terms. Creating drama. Behaving in ways that damage others." He looks up. "I think we can agree that I've certainly exhibited those traits over the past year."

I pause, taking the time to consider his words. "I don't think it's fair for you to judge your entire personality based on the past year. The last year is only one segment of the timeline of your life. To be accurate, you'd need to assess your life as a whole. I don't believe you're toxic, because those aren't behaviors you've shown long term."

"But I have acted like that over the past year," he persists.

"Fine. Let's look at your past year. I think we'd both agree it was spectacularly shitty." I hesitate briefly before flinging caution to the wind, naming off everything he's been through – as though he could possibly have forgotten. "The explosion. Nearly dying. Losing your leg. Spending months in a hospital. Coping with the after-effects of your head injury. Dealing with depression. Struggling with your body image. Losing your career. Losing brothers on the battlefield. Leaving your men behind without getting to say goodbye. Leaving the only home you'd known for years. Going from being fiercely independent and controlling the world around you to having to depend on others and not feeling like you're in control of anything. Pinning all your hope on a surgery to fix things and being disappointed with the results." I pause before continuing. "Any one of those things would be enough to cause mood swings and bad behavior, and you've had to deal with all of them."

His face has grown more bleak the longer I've gone on, and I wonder if I've overstepped and dredged up too many bad memories. He sits in complete silence for a full minute. "That doesn't excuse my behavior," he finally says.

"True," I nod. "But it helps explain it."

He meets my gaze. "I need to tell you something," he says. "It's about Kip." My chest tightens as the face of the sweet kid with blue-green eyes and an infectious smile pops into my mind. I listen as he tells me, with several stops and starts, about the last time he saw Kip, about his excitement about having the osseointegration surgery. About exploding on him and storming out. About me coming home to tell him Kip had killed himself that night. About going to the detective, and what the detective had told him. By the time he's finished, I'm in tears, wishing I'd realized how despondent Kip truly was behind that cheerful smile. Mark watches me with miserable eyes. "That's why I say I'm toxic, Charlie. Everyone I touch, I hurt."

I dry my eyes, absorbing everything he's disclosed. Then I shake my head. "You aren't toxic."

He stares at me in disbelief. "How can you say that after what I just told you? After everything I've done to you?"

I study his face. "Let me rephrase that. The person you're actually toxic to is yourself, and when it overwhelms you, it spills out onto other people." He eyes me doubtfully, and I push on. "Think about it. What you said to Kip was you spewing your own self-hatred. The way you behaved with me was essentially the same thing, all that 'half a man' garbage, telling me I deserved someone whole. It was all about your poisonous self-loathing. It's not that you're intentionally toxic to others. You aren't manipulating people or creating drama in their lives for your own enjoyment. It's that your hatred of yourself leaks out onto other people."

He sits there silently, running a long finger over his beautiful lips. He's actually considering my assessment instead of dismissing it. "Dr. Allen said something similar," he says slowly. "He said seeing myself as toxic is a manifestation of my self-loathing."

"What do you think?"

He blows out a breath. "I think you know me better than anyone. He wants me to write down any areas where I still struggle with self-loathing so we can discuss them." He lifts the notebook. "That's what I wanted your insight on."

"Last night you told me you didn't feel useful anymore, and that you weren't sure about being a coach because of your amputation."

"The lack of usefulness is because I don't have a purpose. No one needs me."

"Bullshit," I blurt. "I need you, and our babies need you."

My chest tightens when I realize what I've just said, and his eyes fix on mine. I scramble for something to say, to cover my oversharing. "I need you to get your shit together, because our children need a dad. You want a purpose? There's your purpose, and those babies won't care whether you have one leg or two. They need you to love them and guide them and be there for them." My tone is sharper than I'd meant it to be, probably because I've inadvertently bared my feelings, and I'm desperate to distract him before he can reject me again.

"And if your leg is the only thing keeping you from pursuing a career as a coach, write that down in your notebook, too," I say, tipping my head at it. "There's two areas for you to talk about with him already."

"We've been talking about them," he says, his eyes on me. He hasn't broken eye contact since I said I needed him. "That's why I'm looking through college catalogs."

"The fact you're uncertain if you can coach means you're still struggling to accept yourself." I point at the notebook, and he finally looks down, flipping it open and finding a fresh page before jotting down "being needed/ useful" and "coaching".

"What about your physical appearance?" I ask.

He looks up. "What about it?"

"Are you comfortable with it, or do you still hate your changed body?"

He hesitates, and I point to the notebook. "Write it down."

He draws a deep breath and writes "body".

"What about dating?" I ask him, trying to sound business-like, even though my heart is in my throat.

He stiffens. "What about it?"

"Are you comfortable meeting women and discussing your amputation?"

He shakes his head. "I'm not interested in meeting women."

My heart skips a beat, but I try to maintain a neutral expression. "If your prosthesis is a factor in not pursuing a romantic or sexual relationship, write it down."

He doesn't write it down.

Does that mean he doesn't see himself as half a man now?

"How about your depression? How are you doing?"

He snorts. "What if I'm depressed, but not about my leg?"

I chew my lip thoughtfully. "Is it a result of something related to your leg?"

He puts pen to paper again, though he's tilted the notebook so I can't see what he's written. I wonder if what's depressing him has to do with me.

With us.

Of course, I don't ask. I can't handle him saying no, that he's perfectly happy without me.

But I'm not sure I could handle a yes, either.

"What about fatherhood?"

He glances at me in surprise. "What about it?"

I'm blunt, but he came here for honest insight. "If any of that 'half a man' crap is still on your radar in any way that makes you question your ability to parent our children, write it down."

He doesn't write that down, either.

At that moment, a flurry of kicks drums the right side of my abdomen, and I gasp, pressing my hand to it. I glance up, meeting his startled gaze. "Come here and give me your hand."

He scoops up a sleeping Penny, deposits her on the floor, and is next to me with his hand outstretched in under a second. I take it and press it where I felt the kicking. He watches my face, and I watch his, waiting. Several seconds pass, and then it happens again – one kick, followed by another. His mouth drops open, and he brings his other hand up to place it on my belly, waiting expectantly. Another pair of kicks lands, but further over from the first few, and I laugh.

"Does it hurt?" he asks, his voice full of wonder.

I shake my head. "It's sort of like a little poke from a knuckle, but from the inside."

We sit like that, his big hands cupping my belly, for a couple more minutes, but my little kicker has apparently gotten comfortable and gone back to sleep. He pulls his hands away reluctantly, then meets my gaze, his pale blue eyes sad.

"I've missed so much," he says quietly, and I try to ignore the pounding of my heart. "I'm sorry you've been alone in all this."

I shake my head. "I haven't been. I have a very strong support system. Tucker was with me the day I found out. I swore him to secrecy. I needed to sit with it for a bit before I could tell Lila. I told her a couple of days later."

He stares at me in amazement. "You told Tucker before you told Lila?"

I chuckle. "Yeah. She's still mad at him. But he'd driven me to the doctor, and he kept asking what was wrong." I chuckle again. "To be honest, I think he was even more excited than Lila, and that's saying something."

"I'm sorry I wasn't there, Charlie."

"Stop," I say sternly. "Regrets don't fix the past. All we can do is move forward."

I watch the struggle play over his face before he takes a deep breath and nods. "So how did you break the news to them?"

"Tucker and I were waiting for my medications, so he and I went to lunch. I was pretty shell-shocked, and he kept asking what was wrong until I told him. He was so excited," I grin, shaking my head. "But I was terrified, and I told him so. I had no idea how I'd manage twins. He said he and Lila would move in and help raise their nieces or nephews if necessary."

I study his face, and I can see the guilt in his eyes, but I don't mention it.

"I didn't tell Lila until a couple of days later," I say to distract him. "They came by with a Christmas tree for me. Tucker pulled out an ornament with two pairs of baby footprints, and I started to cry. And then I told Lila and she cried, and then we were all hugging and laughing and crying." I grin. "We were kind of a mess."

He tilts his head. "Is that why you came to my apartment? To tell me about the babies?"

I nod slowly. "I'd just gone for my first visit with the high-risk obstetrician in Pueblo, and she'd done an ultrasound." A wave of sadness rushes over me, but I push it down, willing the expression off my face. "Seeing them was incredible. I wanted to share that moment with you, even if you and I never worked things out. They printed pictures of the babies from the ultrasound, and I came by to show you."

His eyes grow immeasurably sad, and he looks away. Then his gaze darts back to mine. "You have pictures?"

I smile softly. "I do. Would you like to see our babies?"

MARK

Would I like to see our babies?

"Very much," I say, my voice gruff.

She starts to get up, but I place a hand on her arm. "What do you need?"

"My purse. It's on the foyer table."

"I'll get it." I jump up, retrieving it and waiting with baited breath until she produces an eight-by-five white envelope and passes it to me. She pats the cushion beside her, and I sit, conscious of our closeness, of her soft jasmine scent. I reach into the envelope with shaky hands. When I pull the pictures out, she leans close, her head pressing into my shoulder, her thigh touching mine.

Exactly where she belongs.

I stare at the top picture, a black and white photo that's shockingly clear. A baby is turned to one side, presenting a perfect profile with one hand up to its mouth. The detail in the tiny face is incredible – the shape of the nose, the rosebud mouth, the curve of the head. Even the tiny hand and thin arm are captured perfectly. The quality of the image is amazing, especially considering it was taken from outside Charlie's body.

Her voice is soft. "This is the one I've decided is our daughter. It could be either one, of course, because it's just a closeup of her face and arm."

My fingers lightly touch the photo, tracing the image of her face before halting. "Is she sucking her thumb?" I ask, mesmerized by the tiny figure. I study that perfect rosebud mouth again and agree with Charlie – this is our daughter.

She nods, watching my reaction. Astonishment washes over me, and I trace my fingertips over the tiny face, my hand trembling. "My God," I breathe, utterly overcome. "She's beautiful."

"She is," Charlie agrees quietly.

After another minute or so, I slide the top photo to the side and examine the second one. "This is the one I've decided is our son, but again, it could be either baby," she says. The infant is facing forward, one tiny fist clenched beside his head as if he's frustrated. The determined set of his mouth makes him look irritated, as though he's on the verge of a tantrum.

"He looks grumpy," I say, bewildered by his expression. I trail one finger along his jawline, then touch his fisted hand.

She chuckles. "He does, doesn't he? I can't imagine why. He's cocooned, warm, and fed. All he has to do is sleep and grow."

I smile. "Maybe he's feeling crowded. You don't have a lot of room for them," I observe, casting a downward glance at her belly.

She smiles wryly, smoothing a hand over her abdomen. "Trust me, they're making room. I had to buy new clothes because nothing fit. They've changed my shape."

The next two pictures showcase what the technician has helpfully labeled "boy" and "girl," with tiny arrows pointing at what are presumably the appropriate parts. "Gratuitous nudity," Charlie says, grinning.

I rotate the pictures, frowning as I try to make sense of the varying blobs of gray. "How can they tell what that is?" I ask, pointing to the region labeled "boy". "I don't see anything that looks remotely like a penis."

She tries to hide a smile. "I don't either," she admits, "but if you looked at tiny penises all day long, you'd get good at identifying them too."

I smile broadly. "No son of mine will be saddled with a tiny penis." She smiles, too, then glances away.

The final picture is one of Charlie's cramped uterus, with both twins visible. One is lying sideways in the foreground, giving a full-body profile; the second sits upright in back, facing forward. The air whooshes from my lungs as these babies become very, very real.

"Twins," I whisper.

She nods slowly. "Twins."

I lay the photos aside gently and reach toward her rounded abdomen again, skimming it lightly, reverently.

Twins.

We're having twins.

And soon.

"So what else did your doctor say? The obstetrician?"

"I have to go for visits every two weeks. Later on, it will be weekly visits, to be sure everything is on track. She said I need to gain weight and eat more." She laughs. "That's not a problem. I'm always hungry. And like I said, I'll need a C-section."

I swallow hard, and she lays a hand on my arm, sending trails of fire blazing up my body.

She's not mine anymore. She's Stubbs'.

"It'll be fine, Mark," she says, and it takes me a minute to remember that we were talking about her having surgery. "Women have this done all the time." Then she hesitates. "Do you want to be there for the birth?"

"Yes," I answer quickly. I hear the nervousness in my own voice and hope she doesn't notice a battle-hardened soldier growing queasy at the thought of childbirth.

She smiles reassuringly. Of course she noticed. This is Charlie. "It's okay. If it's too much for you, Lila, Tucker, and Tom have all offered to be birthing coaches."

I shake my head. "I'll manage." I was there for the conception. I'll be there for the delivery, even if I have to keep smelling salts in my shirt pocket.

Charlie stands then, catching me by surprise. She startles me even more when she reaches down and takes my hand. "Come with me," she says.

She's walking toward my old bedroom.

Our bedroom.

Where we slept, and laughed, and made love.

My cock twitches, even as I know that can't be where she's headed.

Sure enough, she veers to the right just outside the bedroom door, stopping in front of a large sketch hanging on the wall. When I look up, my mouth drops open.

"Tom had an artist friend do these charcoal sketches from my ultrasound pictures. He gave it to me for Christmas. He said even if things were challenging right now, he didn't want me to forget this miracle."

It's all too much – her pregnant belly, seeing the pictures of the babies, recognizing the miracle and realizing I threw it all away. It hits me hard, and without thinking, I move behind Charlie and wrap my arms around her upper body, dropping my head to her shoulder. She stiffens at first, then relaxes back against my chest, reaching up to hold my forearms.

"It is a miracle," I murmur, my voice rough.

Heaviness soaks into my soul. It's a miracle, but it's a painful one, because my stupidity has cost me dearly. I'll always be on the outside looking in, seeing the family that would have been mine if I hadn't been such a damn fool.

When I leave, I go to Tucker's gym. It's open twenty-four hours, and I've got a surplus of energy from my desperate need to win Charlie back. I lift weights for an hour, but it doesn't muffle the berating voice in my head, reminding me of everything I've lost.

No.

Everything I threw away.

That's when I look at the row of treadmills.

I shuck off my sweatpants – I'm wearing shorts underneath – and climb onto the treadmill, studying the buttons. I guess I stare a little too long, because before I know it, a blond guy pops up by my elbow. "Need some help?"

He's wearing a nametag that says Corey. I've seen him here before.

I gesture at my prosthetic leg and watch his expression. He glances down briefly before looking back to my face. It doesn't seem to bother him at all that I have an artificial leg. In fact, he seems confused about why I felt the need to point it out.

Huh.

"I've only had this prosthetic a few months," I say, still waiting for a negative reaction that never comes. "I've only been fully weight-bearing for a few weeks, but I'm doing fine with walking. I want to try a slow jog and see how it goes."

Corey nods and reaches for the controls, expertly adjusting the numbers. "If you want to increase your speed, use this," he says, gesturing to a dial on the right. "Here's the start button and the emergency stop button. It's going to start off at walking speed, just to let you get used to how it feels with your prosthetic. When you're comfortable with your cadence, you can increase your speed." He gestures over his shoulder. "If you need me, just yell."

I jog three miles.

It isn't fast, and it definitely isn't graceful, but I do it.

I even watch myself in the mirror, and for the first time ever, I appreciate my prosthesis. Yeah, the abutment is kind of awkward looking. A titanium rod protruding from the tip of my residual limb isn't exactly attractive, but functionally, it's perfect. I lock my carbon-fiber space-age prosthesis into place every morning with an Allen wrench, and it won't come off unless I manually unlock it with the wrench. It's not going to slip if my leg gets sweaty or changes shape throughout the day. It's mechanically connected to me in a way slip-on prostheses can't match.

I haven't jogged in almost a year. I haven't been able to since the explosion. Jogging is one of those things I took for granted, assuming it would always be available to me.

Kind of like my relationship with Charlie.

The day I found out about the babies, Tucker and Lila said some things that were really hard for me to hear. Not just about me not being there for her. I've been beating myself up over that for a while now. I'm familiar with that tune. I sing it all the time.

But they brought up things they hadn't before.

Like how even after I dumped Charlie, I expected her to be waiting in the wings.

How I just assumed if I changed my mind, she'd be ready to let me back in.

I tried to deny it at first, but Tucker pointed out that until he'd punched me in the face and told me I'd finally lost her forever by being such an asshole, I'd not wavered.

He's right. That's what finally broke me.

Deep down, part of me believed if I wanted her to, she'd always come back.

I treated Charlie like she was only there for whatever I needed and wanted. If I didn't want or need her, she should stay away, but if I did, she should come running back. Even when I sent her flowers and a cheesecake, I was surprised when she didn't immediately respond.

My sheer arrogance appalls me. My disgust turns to a sick feeling in the pit of my stomach when I remember what's at stake.

Not just the woman I love, but our babies. Babies I never knew about. Babies neither of us expected, under the circumstances.

A family.

So much at stake, and I may have lost it forever.

As Lila and Tucker both emphasized, Charlie needed to hear how I felt about her *before* I found out about her pregnancy. Otherwise, she could never trust that I came back because I love her and can't live without her, instead of due to a sense of duty to my children.

Once again, my selfishness got in the way. There's no damn reason I couldn't have picked up the phone and called her. No reason I couldn't have gone to her and told her I love her with every fiber of my being. No reason I couldn't have told her I'm lost without her and that she's the only thing that gives my life meaning.

No reason, but I chose not to.

And my stubborn selfishness may have cost me everything I never knew I needed.

CHAPTER TWENTY-ONE

CHARLIE

IT'S SHOCKING HOW MUCH spaghetti seven people can eat. Technically, nine, if you add the twins.

Maya and I turned four pounds of ground beef and two pounds of Italian sausage into what I was sure were enough meatballs to feed an army. I made a giant pot of spaghetti sauce and cooked four pounds of angel hair pasta. Lila brought two huge bowls of salad and four loaves of garlic bread.

There might – might – be enough meatballs and sauce left for Stubbs and I to share for dinner tomorrow, but we'll need to make more salad, pasta, and bread.

We're all stuffing ourselves with pasta when Mark clinks his water glass with his fork. When everyone turns to look at him, he clears his throat, looking nervous.

"Since we're all together, I wanted to apologize for my behavior over the past few months. It's no secret that I struggled a lot after this last surgery, but that's no excuse for acting like an a–" he breaks off, his eyes flitting to Maya. "Sorry. For acting like – uh –"

"A pain in the rump?" Maya suggests, and he smiles.

"Yes. I was definitely a pain in the rump, and I'd like to say I'm sorry."

Maya grins. "We all mess up. Dad says admitting you messed up is brave, and that forgiving people is a mark of good character."

Stubbs lifts his glass. "Wise man," he says to Tom, and then to Mark, "No sweat off my bal– er – my rump," he corrects himself with a quick glance at Maya. "It's all good here." He gestures around the table.

Mark meets my gaze and holds it, and I'm reminded that as far as the deterioration of our relationship goes, he's still not offered explanations or apologies.

Maybe this group apology is all I'm going to get.

Does it really matter in the long run?

Besides, a wise man said forgiving people is a mark of good character.

We finish our late dinner, and Tucker and Tom assume dish duty, a task I'm more than happy to relinquish. Afterwards, music chosen by Maya thumps loudly from my living room speakers. Mark, Tucker, Tom, and Stubbs stand in the far corner of the living room. From their slow, exaggerated movements, I'm pretty sure Tom and Tucker are comparing MMA moves. Stubbs watches in amusement, no doubt considering showing them how he'd take them down in a flat second. Lila and Maya are dancing in the middle of the living room, arms swaying over their heads as their hips roll with the beat of the music. Just watching them exhausts me. I stretch out on the couch waiting for midnight, far more tired than I ought to be.

"Come on, Sleepyhead," purrs a voice at my ear. "I'll walk you to bed."

My eyes fly open to find Mark kneeling beside the couch, his face inches from mine.

"I'm waiting for midnight," I protest, startled by his closeness.

He chuckles softly. "You dozed off almost an hour ago. You missed it. Happy New Year."

He smells good, so good I close my eyes to remember his scent all over my skin.

But that was before.

I open my eyes and struggle to sit upright, feeling like a turtle on its back. He slides a strong hand behind me and boosts me into a seated position. His touch sends shivers down my spine, and my breath catches. I glance around. The living room is empty except for us, and the music has been turned low. The others' voices drift in from the kitchen, but Mark and I are alone.

"Happy New Year," I stammer.

Mark brushes a lock of my hair behind my ear, his hand grazing my cheek before dropping to his side. My heart slams in my chest.

Am I dreaming again?

If I am, I don't want to wake up.

"Happy birthday," he murmurs.

My eyes flick to his. "You remembered."

He nods, warm eyes holding mine. "I'd like to take you out for a late lunch, if that's alright."

My mind whirls, feeling a half-step behind the conversation. It takes me a moment to answer him. "That sounds... nice."

He stands smoothly, his movement graceful. If I hadn't known he was wearing a prosthetic, I'd never have been able to tell. My eyes rake over his body, long and lean, firm and muscled, and I miss him so much, it hurts. He reaches a hand out to me. I take it, and he tugs me to my feet, though I don't really need the help now that I'm upright. He releases my fingers when I'm standing, instead guiding me toward my room by my shoulders.

"How's three o'clock?" he asks, and I'm so distracted by the feel of his hands that for a moment, I have no idea what he's talking about.

Lunch.

Right.

"Three o'clock is good," I hear myself say.

He stops at the door to my room – his old room – *our* old room – and lifts his hands from my shoulders. I turn, unable to tear my eyes away from him. "I'll see you this afternoon, then. Happy New Year, Charlie. Pleasant dreams."

I watch, unable to speak as he shrugs into his leather jacket and slips out my front door with a soft smile.

Something's shifted between us, and I have no idea when it happened.

MARK

Seeing those pictures of our babies has clarified everything for me. I have to get Charlie back.

Have to.

Not because she's pregnant.

Because the love for her that flooded my entire body as I stared up at those charcoal sketches was more than I can put into words. I wrapped my arms around her, knowing I love her more than life itself, knowing I already love these babies I haven't even met.

I have to get her back. I love her, and she's the only thing that gives my life meaning.

And while Stubbs is a great guy, he'll never love Charlie the way I do.

So my one New Year's Resolution? My singular goal?

To win back Charlie's heart.

To convince her to give me another chance.

To tell her I love her and that I'll do anything to make her mine again, even find a way to accept myself as I am now.

When the ball drops on New Year's Eve, I glance over at Charlie, her soft lips parted and her emerald eyes closed in sleep, and pray to the heavens above to give me just one more chance.

I'll do anything.

CHARLIE

I awaken at ten o'clock on New Year's morning, officially thirty-four years old. The scents of cinnamon and sausage tease my growling stomach. I dress quickly and pull my hair into a messy bun before following my nose to the kitchen, where Tom and Maya are making breakfast.

Maya scurries over and wraps her arms around my waist. "Happy birthday," she says.

I kiss her soft cheek and return her hug. "Thank you. Happy New Year's. What's all this?"

"Everybody slept over except Mark, and since Dad and I woke up first, we decided to make breakfast."

I glance toward the stove. "It smells amazing. What's on the menu?"

"Cinnamon-bread French toast, sausage, eggs, fried potatoes, and fruit," Tom says, coming up to drop a kiss on my forehead. "Happy birthday."

"You forgot the cocoa," Maya reminds him.

"And lest we forget, cocoa, courtesy of Maya," he says dryly.

The back door opens, and Tucker and Lila enter in a swirl of snowflakes and soggy dog. Penny scampers toward me at top speed, but Tucker lunges after her, dragging her back to be toweled off. He kneels down, and Lila grabs the blow dryer I've been leaving at the back door thanks to Penny's determination to play in the ice-cold stream.

The six of us sit down to breakfast, and conversation flies fast and furious around the table. Food is followed by a flourish of unexpected birthday gifts: a digital photo cube from Tom and Maya, a gift certificate for a full-day spa treatment from Tucker and Lila, and a gift card to a baby superstore from Stubbs. Tucker and Lila clear away the dishes when we're done, and I end up alone on the couch with my thoughts, wondering if I imagined the tenderness in Mark's voice and eyes last night when he woke me up and ushered me off to bed.

After a few minutes, Tom joins me, and I nestle into his side. "Thank you for the photo cube and for breakfast. The twins loved your French toast."

"I noticed," he teases, and I blush. I was hoping no one noticed I ate three pieces.

"They were hungry," I say loftily, and he laughs.

"So how was your trip to New York?" I ask, glancing up at him.

He sighs. "Chele was Chele. She was all excited on the phone ahead of time, but once Maya got there, she kept finding other things to do. Mostly Maya and I did a lot of sightseeing. I took her to the Museum of Natural History, the Bronx Zoo, and ice skating at the Rockefeller Center."

I frown. "How much time did Maya actually spend with Chele?"

I feel his body tense, and he almost growls his answer. "We met for dinner the first night, and Chele brought her newest boyfriend. Everett something-or-other. Maya hated him because he wouldn't stop talking about his money. Apparently he owns his own island."

I raise an eyebrow. "That's pretty rich."

He shrugs. "I'm pretty sure he's one of those Ponzi-scheme money shufflers. Maya was completely unimpressed, and that annoyed Chele. She didn't see Maya again until the fourth day, when she'd promised to take her to lunch and then a spa for a girls' day. Maya said she stayed on her phone the entire time they were at lunch. When they left the restaurant, Chele posed for pictures with Maya, telling a reporter how rewarding it was to spend time with her daughter. As soon as he left, she canceled the spa trip and dropped Maya off at our hotel." He pauses. "Maya said Chele made her feel like nothing more than a prop to boost her social image."

Anger ripples through me. "Do you have sole or joint custody of Maya?"

"Sole," he answers. "But I don't want to keep Maya from her mom."

"So why not let Maya decide when she wants to see her mom?"

He sighs heavily. "Because Chele will accuse me of refusing to let her see her daughter."

"That's bullshit. Planes fly both directions. Tell Chele she can see Maya anytime she wants to fly here."

He glances down. "Chele hasn't been here since the divorce."

"That's my point. All the burden of maintaining Chele's relationship with Maya falls on you. That's not your job. It's Chele's. Yours is to make sure Maya has a healthy, well-adjusted life."

"But Maya needs her mom."

I frown. "Does she really? Because it sounds like visiting her does more harm to her than good. At least from a distance, she can pretend her mom gives a damn. She can't do that when they're together and Chele can't be bothered with her. It's time Chele took responsibility for maintaining her own relationship with her daughter."

He considers that. "The problem is, she won't make the effort, and I don't want Maya hurt."

"How is that any worse than you and Maya traveling halfway across the country so she can be ignored by someone on the other side of the table?"

He exhales heavily. "I guess it's not. I just can't stand the thought of Maya feeling rejected by her own mother."

I wrap my arm around his waist. "I think she already does."

He's quiet for a moment. "So what am I supposed to do?"

My anger at Chele's blatant dismissal of Maya fuels my bluntness. "Chele's going to hurt Maya either way, so give Maya the choice. Would she rather go to New York or invite Chele here? She's old enough to have a say in things."

He sits there for a minute, considering. "We could try it over Spring Break," he muses. "Extend the offer to Chele, but have a pre-planned backup vacation. That way, if she declines or backs out at the last minute, we still have fun things planned." Tom gives my shoulders a one-armed squeeze and drops a kiss on my head. "Thanks for letting me vent."

I hug him back, wondering how someone so sweet ended up marrying someone so shallow. "Just remember, Lila and I will kill Chele for you in a flat second, and our rates are surprisingly reasonable."

I dress carefully for my lunch with Mark. Part of me wants to remind him what he's missing. One look in my full-length mirror puts that notion to rest. My previously sexy-ish body – at least, he once found me sexy – has changed dramatically, and not in a good way. I settle on wearing a red wrap dress that clings to my rounded belly, paired with black tights and calf-high black boots. My hair looks good – I've styled it in loose waves and swept the sides back in a clip – and I spent extra time on my makeup, emphasizing my eyes. I look nice, but with the new physique I'm sporting, the "sexy" ship has sailed.

I'm picking up my coat when my phone buzzes. "Still on for lunch?"

Mark's text makes me wonder if he's worried I've changed my mind.

Maybe I didn't imagine the difference in him last night after all.

"Headed out now," I type, then pull on my coat and step outside. A gust of wind ruffles my dress, and I tighten my coat, trying to pretend the flutters in my stomach aren't because I'm looking forward to seeing him.

MARK

I'm already at the restaurant when Charlie pulls in, fifteen minutes early.

Maybe she's as excited as I am.

Or maybe she just left early because the roads are still icy in spots, and she wanted to take her time.

Negative thinking isn't productive.

I'm parked in the far corner of the lot, as far away from the handicapped spaces as it's possible to be. I'm crossing the lot to take her arm when she gets out of her vehicle, and I watch her look from my parking spot to the handicapped spot and back again, then shake her head. I should have known she'd notice.

She waits by the front of her SUV for me, a goddess in a black coat. Her exquisite legs are clad in sheer black fabric, and her silky hair cascades over her shoulders. She eyes the arm I hold out to her. "I don't want you to slip. There are icy spots," I say.

She takes my arm without complaint. "Thank you, but I don't want to pull you down, either."

"If one of us is going to fall, it needs to be me," I say firmly. "You're the one carrying precious cargo." She doesn't argue, and I breathe a sigh of relief when we make it inside the restaurant without incident.

She doesn't release my arm when we're inside, and my chest swells with hope as we wait for the hostess to approach. I've reserved the back dining room for us. I've decided it's time to bare my soul. Charlie deserves to know the truth about my feelings, both then and now.

I help her out of her coat, my eyes instantly drawn to her luscious curves. I lean down close to her, aware of the heat of her body so close to mine. "You look incredible," I murmur.

She blushes, then drops her eyes as she whispers, "So do you."

My heart thuds so hard, I'm certain she can hear it.

The hostess appears, leading us to a dimly lit room with a single table in the center. She takes our drink orders before promising our server will be with us shortly. After she leaves, Charlie raises one eyebrow. "A private dining room?"

I shrug. "It's quieter."

She narrows her gaze, and I chuckle. "Fine, I reserved a private dining area. Happy?"

She eyes me suspiciously. "That depends on why you want privacy. I may not look it anymore, but I still know thirteen ways to kill a man with a fork."

A small cough to one side tells me our waitress both heard and approves of Charlie's dark sense of humor. "Good evening," she says, trying to hide her smile. "I'm Kayla, and I'll be taking care of you this evening." She sets ice water and tea before each of us, then hands us menus. "I'll let you look this over and be back in a few minutes." She turns her attention to Charlie and winks. "The steak knife is more effective than a fork if you need a weapon."

Charlie grins, waiting until the server closes the door before replying, "True, but it's so much more intimidating to pull a man's eyeball out with a fork. After that, he's putty in my hands."

I can't help laughing, and when I do, she joins in. For a split second, it feels like old times, until her smile fades. "I miss this, you know? Laughing with you."

My smile fades, too. "Yeah. I've missed it, too." I pause. "I miss all of it." An awkward silence falls, and we busy ourselves reading the menu and making our dinner selections.

The waitress returns to take our order, making it a point to examine me as though looking for blood. "No knife wounds, I see."

"Not yet. I need my utensils," Charlie says, gesturing to her stomach. "I'm eating for three. Otherwise..." She glances at me and drags her finger across her throat in an unspoken threat.

To Charlie's delight, Kayla pulls another set of utensils from her apron and places them on the table next to her. I shake my head and grin. "I'm feeling ganged up on, when all I've done is take a beautiful woman to dinner."

And betray her.

And break her heart.

And leave her, alone and pregnant.

I stop myself in my tracks and take a deep breath. *Stop. Negative thinking isn't productive.*

That's my new mantra, courtesy of Dr. Allen. I'm having to repeat it to myself several times a day, whenever I catch myself reverting to pessimistic thoughts.

We order our meal, making small talk as our courses arrive, one at a time. The soup is French onion, topped with broiled crusty bread and baby Swiss cheese. The salads are crisp and green, with shaved Parmesan, homemade croutons, and Italian dressing. When our steaks are served, they're perfectly seasoned and medium rare, just the way we both like them. She has hers with potatoes au gratin and green beans, while I've chosen a baked potato and grilled asparagus.

The food is incredible. Watching the woman I love enjoy it is even better. Charlie's newfound appetite astounds me. I've known her most of my life, and I've never seen her eat like this. It takes my breath away – in a good way. When she licks butter from her lips, my heart skips a beat, and I have a strong urge to trace the path her tongue took with my own.

I can't stop staring at her plump pink lips after that, at least, not until she catches me and raises one perfect brow. "Enjoying the view?"

I can't tell from her expression whether she's intrigued, angry, or pleased. My face heats, but I ignore it. "Immensely."

Charlie dabs her mouth with her napkin before returning it to her lap and folding her hands on the table. She holds my eyes without looking away for several seconds. Then she drops her gaze. "You're a very confusing man, Mark Chandler," she mutters. I don't say anything, and after another moment, she looks back up. "Alright, spit it out. What's really going on?"

My stomach clenches as I study her carefully neutral expression. "I wanted to take you out for your birthday."

She eyes me skeptically. "In a private dining room?"

"I wanted to talk to you. Alone."

She glances pointedly around the otherwise-empty room before letting her gaze fall on me.

Deep breath. Here we go.

"I meant what I said earlier, Charlie. I've missed you. I miss seeing you, hearing your voice, watching you smile, talking to you. I've missed the way your eyes sparkle when you laugh and flash fire when you're angry. I've missed the way you bite your lip when you're nervous."

She stops biting her lip immediately.

"I don't understand," she says, her voice barely audible, eyes fixed on her empty plate.

"What don't you understand?"

"Any of it." Her words tumble out in a sudden torrent of frustration. "I don't understand why you dumped me and snuck out of my house like I was nothing more than an embarrassing one-night stand." My gut clenches at her comparison. Is that how I made her feel? "I don't understand why you cut off all contact with me after everything we've been through. I don't understand why the second you found out Stubbs had moved in, I was suddenly worth talking to again. And I don't understand why you tell me you just want to be friends for the babies' sake, but then look at me like —" Her voice breaks, but she soldiers on. "Like I matter."

My heart twists into knots inside my chest, shame filling me at the reminder of my horrible behavior. "You do matter, Charlie. You matter more to me than anyone." I hesitate, then plunge ahead. "And I don't want to be just your friend."

Tears fill her beautiful eyes, and she blinks them back as she looks away. She doesn't believe me. Why would she, after what I've put her through?

Negative thinking isn't productive.

I draw a slow breath. "I told you a couple of days ago that the parking lot incident was my breaking point. From what Tucker and Lila said, it was yours, too." She nods, still avoiding looking at me, and I recall Tucker and Lila's dire reproaches. That I'd pushed Charlie too far. That I'd done too much damage to repair. That I'd finally lost her for good.

I push on, ignoring the dark voice in my head that agrees with them. "That night was when I truly hit rock bottom. That's when I accepted that Lila was right, that I needed help to work through my issues. That's when I decided that no matter what, I'd spend the rest of my life trying to win you back, to make you mine again."

She looks up, her eyes wary. "Why?'

"Because I'm in love with you, Charlie."

I'm not sure what I was expecting at my declaration of love, but it wasn't silence and a dubious expression.

Well, she didn't storm out yet. Keep talking.

"I started seeing Dr. Allen two days later. I told him my self-loathing had shattered everything important to me. I decided I'd try to show you I loved you. The flowers. Cheesecake. Earrings." Her brows furrow. "I didn't give them to you," I admit. "I stopped by on Christmas Eve and – well, you already know what happened," I say, hoping to distract her from thinking about Stubbs while I'm baring my soul. "I'd been hoping I hadn't destroyed everything you ever felt for me. And then the mailman brought me a package on Christmas Eve."

She sucks in a sharp breath. "I wasn't sure you'd gotten it."

I nod. "When I looked at the postmark and realized you'd sent it to me after the way I acted in the parking lot?" I study her face. "It gave me hope that some part of you still cares about me. I can't believe you'd have given me something so important if you didn't. Thank you."

"I didn't keep the daffodils," she suddenly blurts. "The cheesecake, either."

"Why not?" I ask, trying to keep the hurt out of my voice. I'd put a lot of thought into giving her things that would hold significance for her, things that would mean something.

"It felt like you were playing on my emotions to buy my forgiveness. Tara took the flowers to a lonely widow, and I sent the cheesecake to the VFW." She hesitates. "I kept your notes, though." She blushes at those words and drops her eyes, though I'm not sure why.

"I wasn't trying to buy your forgiveness." I study her face. "You kept my notes?"

She nods, her eyes sad. "They reminded me of the Mark I used to know."

"I'm still that guy, Charlie," I say quietly. "I just got all screwed up inside. I know you can't forgive me, but I swear I'll spend the rest of my life trying to make it up to you."

Emerald eyes spear me. "Why would you think I can't forgive you?"

I stare at her, unable to speak or even breathe.

Charlie traces a finger along the base of her water goblet. "You apologized last night, and like Maya said, that took a lot of courage."

I shake my head. "That apology wasn't for you. It was for them."

She looks sharply at me, and I hurry to clarify my statement. "What I mean is, I owe you a lot more than a basic apology in front of a roomful of people. You deserve an explanation. I just —" I shove my hand into my hair. "I don't even know where to start."

My clarification settles her, and her expression softens. "Just speak from your heart."

I nod, my heart hammering wildly at the weightiness of this moment. I stare at the white linen tablecloth, rubbing the fabric between my fingers. My words are slow, deliberate. "At Brooke, when I first woke up after the explosion, I couldn't believe this had happened." I gesture down at my body. "I mean, I know it happens, but I never thought it would happen to me. Dr. Paxton was very direct, and I appreciated that. But it was hard to — to accept that I was broken. Really broken. That I couldn't be fixed. And when it finally sunk in, I was angry."

I raise my eyes. She sits patiently, her eyes on my face. "I was angry all the time, like a volcano on the verge of erupting, with hostility always boiling inside me. It slipped out a little at a time, releasing some of the pressure, but it always built right back up. You bore the brunt of my rage, and I'll always regret that."

"Dr. Friedman told me once to take it as a terrible compliment," she says thoughtfully.

I must look as confused as I feel, because she tilts her head to one side as she explains. "He told me to remember that you weren't angry with me. You were angry with your situation. He said you knew you could take your pain out on me because you trusted me. You knew I'd still be there for you. That's why he called it a terrible compliment."

"I'm sorry, Charlie," I say honestly. "It's only one in a long line of things I need to apologize for, but I'm truly sorry for how I behaved toward you after the explosion. God knows I'd never have survived it without you."

She shakes her head. "I learned long ago that pain causes more pain. Sometimes it's directed at others, and sometimes it's aimed internally. I think the majority of yours was turned inward, on yourself." She smiles gently. "I'm well-versed in that concept. And the thing about loving someone is that we're there for each other even when — or maybe especially when — the other person is pushing everyone away because they're hurting or afraid."

My heart thuds at the emotion in her voice. There's forgiveness behind her words, forgiveness I'm not entitled to. "You amaze me, Charlie," I say quietly, and her cheeks turn pink.

God, I love this woman, but I damn sure don't deserve her.

Focus.

I take another deep breath and press on. "I did better at handling my emotions when I finally opened up to Dr. Friedman and took the antidepressant, but I had subconsciously created unrealistic expectations. I struggled after my discharge because I'd believed that by pushing myself in rehab, I'd be – I don't know. Better. But when I came home with you, I felt like an invalid. Not because of anything you did," I hasten to add, "but because I didn't want to accept needing a handicapped toilet or rails in the shower or sweatpants with one leg cut off. It's one thing to see those things in a hospital setting, but with you, it felt much more final. And I felt sorry for myself," I admit. "I'd always seen myself in a certain light and expected my life to play out a certain way, and an amputation and medical discharge wasn't part of that plan."

She nods in understanding. Charlie's plans never included the hell she went through, either.

"I always thought I'd retire from the Army after my twenty years and settle down. Maybe coach, maybe teach. Maybe get married. Maybe have a family. My injuries snatched that rug out from under me. All I saw when I looked at myself was a useless cripple with all those doors slammed shut. The strange thing was, I never saw other wounded vets that way. I mean, Stubbs is the embodiment of masculine strength. No one could ever see him as useless."

As soon as the words leave my mouth, I want to kick myself. *Stop complimenting the man you're trying to steal her back from, dumbass.*

"I'm willing to bet he saw himself that way in the beginning," she murmurs.

He'd said as much to me the other day, and I nod before continuing. "I was doing better at accepting myself when you and I – when we changed the nature of our relationship," I say awkwardly. "I was happy, happier than I've ever been in my entire life. Things were so good that... that I thought I didn't need an antidepressant anymore, so I quit taking it." Stern eyes glare, and I lift my hands in surrender. "I know. I screwed up. The reason I wasn't depressed was because the medication was working, and stopping it abruptly caused the sharp rebound effect Dr. Friedman had warned me about. My emotions started fluctuating wildly, but I didn't make the connection to it being from stopping my meds. I chalked it up to pre-surgical nerves.

"Then I had my surgery." I pause for a long moment, sighing heavily. "I'd hung all my hopes on that surgery, telling myself I'd be normal afterwards. When I woke up and saw that peg sticking out of my leg, I felt even more like a freak than before. All my feelings of being a useless cripple came roaring back worse than ever, because this was it. This was the best I'd ever be. All the things I'd hoped for, for my future, for our future, just... evaporated." I swallow hard before admitting the dark truth. "I hated myself, Charlie. I wished I'd died in that explosion."

"Why didn't you talk to me, Mark?"

The anguished look on her face guts me, and my throat tightens. "I couldn't, Charlie. If I hadn't had you, I might have done something stupid. But you'd already lost so much. I couldn't –" I stop for a minute, trying to get a handle on my rising angst. "I started distancing myself from you, pulling back. I believed you deserved to be with someone as perfect as you." I struggle to force the rest of my words past the lump in my throat. "But part of me was pushing you away so it wouldn't hurt as much when you decided you didn't want to be saddled with a useless cripple."

She jerks back as though I've slapped her, tears filling her eyes and spilling down her cheeks. "How could you ever think that about me, after all you and I have been through together?"

"It wasn't about you, Charlie. It was about me, about how I see myself," I insist, closing my eyes against her tears. "I wanted you to have the best, and I didn't believe that could ever be me. That last night –" I hesitate as memories invade my mind. "The night before I said we should see other people, I poured my feelings for you into my touch, but I couldn't allow myself to say the words. You said I made you feel cherished. You were. You still are." I stop, staring at the table. "But when I realized you were in love with me, I panicked. I hated myself too much to accept your love, and I made a terrible, impulsive decision because of my self-loathing."

Neither of us speaks. I chance a glance at her. She's breathing deeply, slowly, trying to calm herself, hands flat on the tabletop and eyes closed. I wait, watching as her shoulders slowly relax.

"I'm sorry I'm upsetting you," I say quietly. "Do you want to take a break?"

I'm startled when she gets to her feet. "Yes. I need a few minutes to pull myself together. Let's go back to my house. We can talk more there."

CHAPTER TWENTY-TWO

CHARLIE

Mark walks me to my car and waits for me to start it before turning to his own. We stayed in the restaurant until after seven, and it's dark, with tiny snowflakes swirling in the chilly breeze. I drive silently through the scant traffic on autopilot, my mind reeling from his revelations.

That after his osseointegration surgery, he'd wished he had died in the explosion.

After his surgery, when he and I were a couple.

And he'd distanced himself from me because he thought I'd tire of being with a "useless cripple".

My heart aches at his painful confessions. Guilt plagues me. I'd called him my best friend. I'd have sworn I knew him better than I knew myself. I knew he was struggling, but I'd had no idea how truly miserable he was. A small voice in the back of my mind whispers that I simply wasn't enough to make him happy, but after years of therapy, I recognize that whisper as my own insecurities, not truth. Someone who hates himself can't be happy, and Mark hated himself then.

I wonder if he still does.

The babies have detected my distress, because they're both kicking and squirming. I wrap one arm around my abdomen, trying to pretend my stomach isn't doing somersaults and that I'm not on the verge of a meltdown. To distract myself, I ponder what Willow, an intimacy specialist, might say about Mark's disclosures. I decide she'd probably point out that he's opening up, choosing to be vulnerable with me. She'd likely encourage me to respond in kind.

I pull into my empty driveway. Stubbs' huge SUV is nowhere to be seen. Mark parks his black van next to me. I feel his questioning gaze, but I don't speak. I'm still too unsettled. He trails me silently up the steps and into the house. I head to my kitchen, where I find a note propped on the counter. "Green Eyes – Gone to VFW. Call if you need me. S."

I turn on my heel and head to the living room, taking a seat on the sofa. Mark sits on the end opposite me. Penny snuffles us both, but as though she's aware of the gravity of my mood, she settles quietly atop my feet instead of clambering all over both of us like she usually would.

Dead.

He wished he were dead.

While he and I were still together.

After a few minutes, I remind myself that sometimes, you just want the pain to stop, no matter what form that takes. The important thing is that unlike Kip, Mark didn't act on his feelings.

I glance over and find Mark watching me. His eyes are tight, his hands knotted. "Please tell me what you're thinking," he says softly.

"It hurts that you wished you were dead while we were together, and I'm upset at myself for not seeing it," I answer honestly. "I'm not saying I don't understand your feelings, because I do. But it's difficult to hear you were hurting that badly when we were together and I didn't see it."

His gaze narrows, his tone sharp. "What do you mean, you understand my feelings?"

"You're not the only one who survived a horrible experience and found the pain afterwards to be almost unbearable," I say stiffly, feeling chastised.

"Oh," he says. "I thought you meant..."

I don't respond, because I know exactly what he thought I meant, and while I won't lie, I have no intention of telling him how poorly I handled his leaving. Not yet, anyway. Maybe never.

"I'm calmer now, if you want to keep talking," I say instead.

He looks surprised, but takes a moment to gather his thoughts. "Well, like I said, I wasn't in a good place. Eventually, I agreed I needed to talk to someone about my body image issues. Lila gave me Dr. Allen's information."

"Do you like him?"

He surprises me by smiling. "I do, actually. I was desperate, though, so maybe that helped."

My chest tightens. *He wished he was dead, and he was desperate?*

I try to keep my voice steady but fail. "Desperate?"

He follows my train of thought and shakes his head quickly, reaching for my hand, his pale blue eyes unwavering. The touch of his fingers on mine feels so good that pain seeps into my heart. "I'd never do that to you. There's a difference between wishing my misery would end and doing something to permanently end it. Because of you, I wasn't willing to cross that line."

I nod slowly, and he releases my hand. The pain in my heart worsens when he lets go.

"I was desperate to change, to get better," he explains. "I finally started listening to what people had been saying. Lila saying I have to accept myself, the good and the bad, to become emotionally healthy. Tucker telling me to stop putting limitations on myself. An entire room of disabled vets calling me a dumbass for the stupid decisions I made because of my self-loathing. I've got to let go of this emotional garbage. It's destroying me. So I started seeing Dr. Allen. And from the first visit, he understood. He asked me to tell him the story of Mark," he explains, "so I told him my whole explosion, hospitalization, osseointegration story. I finished by telling him that I looked normal now, even though I wasn't. But he wasn't asking about my injuries. He was asking me to share who I am, but I could only see my physical shortcomings. He pointed out that I'd reduced my view of myself to merely the sum of my injuries. When that clicked with me, things started making sense. Because I viewed myself as a useless cripple, I decided I wasn't good enough for you. It became a self-fulfilling prophecy. I didn't think I was good enough, so I abandoned and betrayed you. Someone good enough for you would never do that."

I exhale heavily. "I wish you could see yourself clearly."

"I'm really trying to change my view of myself, Charlie. It's not easy," he says hesitantly, "because there's a lot of negative chatter in my head. But I'm determined. I'm trying to look forward, not backwards. I can't change my past, but I can choose my path."

"And have you? Chosen a path?"

His eyes pin me. "I have."

"What is it?"

His gaze never wavers. "Whatever it takes to win you back."

My heart leaps in my chest as my brain simultaneously screams to pump the brakes and proceed with caution. Maybe Mark does care for me, but it doesn't change the fact that he didn't come back until he knew about the babies and thought I was involved with Stubbs.

I study his expression. "Why?"

He blinks. "Why what?"

"Why do you want me back?"

"Because I love you."

I close my eyes as he says the words I wanted to hear from him for so long. I want to believe him, but I'm afraid to.

I don't realize I've said that aloud until he nods. "God knows, I gave you more than enough reason to be afraid of me."

I meet his gaze and hold it. "I'm not afraid of you."

A sad expression flits across his face. "You should be."

I swallow hard. If he can bare his soul, so can I. "I'm afraid of your demons. I'm afraid your hatred of yourself will still be stronger than your feelings for me. I'm afraid I'll let you back in, only to have you leave me. And I'm afraid I won't survive you walking away a second time."

Mark reaches a hand toward my face, pausing to give me time to pull away, but I don't. He caresses my cheek lightly with his thumb, his palm cupping my jaw loosely. I nestle my cheek into it, closing my eyes. He shifts to face me, brushing my hair back, then takes my face between both hands and gently kisses my forehead. He lingers, his warm lips pressed to my skin, his head pressed to my own, breathing deeply.

My heart thuds loudly in my chest at the palpable emotion in his actions.

He does love me.

He did all along.

The huge fist crushing my heart opens, and the protective walls I've erected inside me crumble into dust. For the first time in months, I feel like I can breathe.

He releases me, and when I open my eyes, miserable blue eyes watch me. "I owe you so many apologies, Charlie. I'm sorry I distanced myself from you after my surgery. I'm sorry I blindsided you with a breakup because I couldn't accept myself. I'm sorry I made you think I was seeing someone else. I'm sorry I lied and said I wasn't in love with you. I'm sorry I snuck out of your house like a coward and made you feel like I thought what we'd shared was a mistake. I'm sorry for every time I didn't answer your calls or texts or come to the door. I'm sorry I rejected you in a parking lot." He draws a ragged breath. "But most of all, I'm sorry for making you believe you didn't matter to me." He pauses, swallowing hard as his jaw flexes. "I wanted you to have someone as perfect as you are. I thought you deserved someone better than a guy who has to bolt on an artificial leg every morning. I believed that because I couldn't be the man I thought you needed, I should love you enough to let you go. I thought it might be hard for you at first, but I figured you'd get over me. I knew I'd never get over you, though. I just didn't know giving you up would destroy me."

The raw anguish on his face breaks my heart.

And I kiss him.

I don't hesitate, kneeling up and leaning toward him, slipping my hands behind his neck and tugging his face to mine. His lips are soft and warm, and he slides one hand into my hair while the other cups my jaw. "Oh, Charlie," he sighs, his voice barely a whisper against my lips. I move a hand to his face, stroking his soft stubble. I tilt my head, deepening the kiss, and he groans as my tongue slides across his lips. Our mouths taste each other, teasing, caressing, at once both new and familiar, and it's like coming home.

He eases his lips from mine, pressing his forehead against my own. "I'm so sorry I hurt you." He swallows hard, then meets my gaze. "I love you, Charlie. I am completely, madly, passionately in love with you." My heart skips a beat. "I've known I was in love with you since before my osseointegration surgery. I knew then that I wanted forever with you." My heart hammers erratically at his words. "I'd planned to tell you after my surgery. When things didn't turn out the way I'd expected, I decided you deserved more than I could give you. It took me a long time to admit I was wrong, but after that day in the parking lot, I knew I'd do anything to get you back."

I study his eyes, wide and honest without a trace of deception. "Really?"

His palm grazes my face. "Charlie Emerson, I love you with every fiber of my being. All I want is a chance to prove myself to you." He pauses, then shakes his head. "Stubbs is one hell of a guy, Charlie, and I mean that from the bottom of my heart. If you're truly happy with him, I won't interfere, but he won't ever love you as much as I do."

The mention of Stubbs clears my emotional overload, and I make the time-out signal with my hands. "I need to clear something up. I'm not dating Stubbs. He's living with me for now, but he and I aren't a couple."

Mark frowns. "But he said —" his voice trails off.

"He told me he'd phrased his responses to imply we were together. He was trying to make you jealous, to get you to rethink things. I didn't know he'd done it until after the fact. I'd tried to make you jealous with Tom months ago, and that was an epic failure. I knew better than to try that again." I pause. "But I didn't correct your misunderstanding the morning you came over for breakfast, and that's on me. I should have, but I didn't, because thinking Stubbs and I were involved was the only thing that got your attention." I swallow. "Not even being served with custody papers had done that."

He cocks his head, and I can't read his expression. "Now it's my turn to set the record straight. First, you've always captured my attention. You consumed my thoughts, even when I believed you were better off without me. I came over on Christmas Eve to give you a gift. It was only afterwards that I thought you and Stubbs were together. Second, trying to make me jealous with Tom was definitely not a failure." I lift startled eyes to his, and he nods. "The only reason I didn't rip his head off was that I'd already convinced myself he was the perfect guy for you."

I stare in disbelief. "Tom? You thought I should be with *Tom*?"

He nods. "He's protective of you. He's good-hearted, handsome, kind. You have a strong friendship, and you trust him. He'd treat you like a goddess. And Maya worships the ground you walk on. You'd have a ready-made family. He's perfect for you."

I shake my head. "I love Tom, but he's like a brother to me. There's zero chemistry."

He snorts. "You could have fooled me, watching you two cuddling on the couch."

I raise an eyebrow. "That was kind of the point."

"Touché," he says, then continues. "Third, I didn't come see you when I got the custody paperwork because I didn't want you to think I was only showing up because of the babies."

My heart drums a staccato beat inside my chest. "Aren't you?"

Mark shakes his head forcefully.

I hesitate. "I know you, Mark. You'll say whatever it takes to be there for your children. You're too honor-bound to do anything else."

He studies my face. "I'm not a praying man," he says slowly. "I've come to terms with the fact that I've killed people without remorse. Wartime or not, men died by my hand, and I'm okay with it. That seems like something a Higher Power would frown upon, so I don't waste His time with my prayers." He pauses. "The day I finally admitted I'd do anything to get you back, I told the universe it could take both my legs if I could have you, and that was long before I knew you were pregnant." He meets my stunned gaze. "I won't deny I'm obligated to take care of our children, but I'm not obligated to be with you to do it. I don't want you back because you're pregnant, Charlie. I want you back because I love you more than life itself."

Time freezes, and I stare into serious blue eyes that soften as he scoots closer to me on the couch.

"And just to be clear," he says quietly, "I'm really glad you aren't with Stubbs. That way, I don't have to feel guilty about trying to win you back."

MARK

I've just told the woman I love how I feel about her – for about the fifth time this evening – and I think she's finally starting to believe me. Her eyes are wide, and she's biting her lip. I'm reaching out to touch her face when a furry brown and white body pushes between us, whining.

"Potty?" Charlie asks, and Penny scrambles toward the kitchen before pausing and looking back in our direction.

"Apparently, that's a yes," she mutters.

"I can take her," I offer, but she shakes her head.

"I don't mind. I like the night air. But you can come along."

I stand first, taking her hand and tugging her to her feet before releasing her. I hold her coat for her and pull my jacket on before opening the back door for Penny. The light breeze is cold on my face, and tiny snowflakes glitter like diamonds as they fall. There's about four inches on the ground, maybe a half-inch of fresh powder since I followed Charlie here from the restaurant. Penny scampers off the deck and bounds through the snow, heading straight for the gate at the far end of the yard. She sits beside it, looking expectantly at Charlie.

"I don't think so," she laughs. "Go potty."

Penny deflates visibly, her expression mournful. Then she sniffs a circuit around the yard before squatting in a far corner.

"We go hiking in the woods every day," Charlie explains. "The path we take has a little stream, and she loves to play in the water, no matter how cold it is. Stubbs carried in a bench for me to sit on while I wait for her. She wants to go splash in her stream."

She leans against the house, waiting for the dog to finish. My breath stutters as I drink in her gorgeous body. Her black wool coat stops just below her hips. It covers her lush curves, but can't conceal them. Black tights hug long legs beneath her red dress, and a memory flashes into my mind, those exquisite legs wrapped around my hips. Her light brown hair shimmers under the porch light, falling in loose curls around her shoulders, framing a face that haunts my dreams. Stunning eyes make my heart pound as she stares up at me, her expression uncertain.

Uncontrollably drawn to her, I brush a lock of her hair behind her ear. "God, you're beautiful," I whisper. My thumb lingers on her cheek, and she pushes her face into my hand again as her eyes drift closed.

It's all the encouragement I need.

I take her face between my hands and step forward, claiming her soft lips. She responds tentatively at first, but in seconds, her lips part beneath mine, opening herself to me and deepening the kiss. She clutches my leather jacket, dragging me closer, and I go willingly. Her body molds against me as her tongue dances with mine.

God, I've been such a fool.

The heat between us ends abruptly as a snow-covered nose shoves beneath my shirt, rooting up my bare back. I jump, barely managing to contain an extremely unmasculine yelp.

"Penny," Charlie scolds, and the dog retreats to sit innocently on the deck. She's covered in snow, apparently having rolled in it while Charlie and I were busy. I try to brush her off, but her body heat has already melted it, soaking her fur. I hide my grin at Charlie's groan. "Seriously?"

I kiss her adorable upturned nose. "I'll blow dry her. Let's get you inside where it's warm."

Penny bounces into the kitchen, her entire body wagging. I kneel beside her, drying her while dodging excited puppy kisses. I manage to keep my lips out of her reach, but by the time I finish, one whole side of my face is slobbery. Charlie tries not to smile while I wash up at the sink.

"Afraid of men, my ass," I grumble, mock-glaring at the dog, who wags and lolls her tongue out of one side of her mouth, not the least bit sorry.

Charlie grins. "She's certainly not now. She even went to Tom to be petted last night, and she used to be terrified of him."

"She's allowing people to show her she can trust them." I meet Charlie's eyes. "That's all I want, too, Charlie. A chance to prove you can trust me again." I pause, studying her. "I know you're afraid. I know I've hurt you badly. All I'm asking for is a chance. Will you give me that?"

Green eyes examine my face before she slowly nods.

I move toward her, dropping a kiss on her soft pink lips, then another longer one. "I love you, and I'll do whatever it takes to earn your trust." I step back, holding her gaze. "I'll call you tomorrow."

"Tomorrow," she repeats, her expression hesitant. She's still not sure.

But she's giving me a chance.

And I'll *prove* I can be the man she deserves.

CHARLIE

He loves me.

Mark says he loves me and wants me back.

And I believe he means it... today.

But just because he means it today doesn't mean he won't leave again.

He says he told the universe it could take both of his legs if he could have me back. But if his amputation became an issue, if he had to give up his prosthetic due to injury or illness, would he discard me again?

I honestly don't know. I've experienced his reaction when his body image takes a hard hit, first after the explosion and then again after his surgery.

I desperately want to believe him, and that desperation terrifies me. My blind faith in Mark meant I barely survived him leaving me.

I do believe him when he says he loves me. I believed it before he left me, even though he denied it outright.

But I'm not convinced his love for me is stronger than his hatred for his changed body.

That hatred – and the actions he took as a result of it – nearly destroyed me.

And until I'm certain he's accepted himself, scars and all, I can't let myself trust him.

Because it's not just my heart at stake.

It's our children's, too.

CHAPTER TWENTY-THREE

CHARLIE

MONDAY MORNING, I HELP Stubbs get acquainted with the charting and billing systems at our clinic. We don't officially reopen until tomorrow, so he has time to explore the features of the programs. I hand him a cheat sheet I created with our most frequently used codes and shortcuts. "This should get you started, but if you get stuck, Lila, Tom or I can help you."

I glance around his newly-decorated office. A bookcase to the left of the entrance is filled with books ranging from clinical guides and medication references to coffee-table art volumes, military biographies, philosophy, and poetry collections. His large L-shaped desk is clear except for his computer and phone. Office supplies are neatly stowed out of sight within the desk and plant-covered credenza beneath the picture window. Floor-length sheers frame the picture window, showcasing the pristine mountain view. The seating area contains a beige couch and two matching chairs, all situated on a colorful ikat-patterned rug. His framed degree hangs respectably on the wall beside his desk. Directly below it is his Badass Therapist plaque. He's added a matching nameplate outside his door that reads "Stubbs Mackey, Badass Therapist Extraordinaire." His business cards proclaim the same, along with his phone number, email, and a quote that states, "Scars are not a sign of weakness. They reveal battles hard-fought and won."

He sees me eyeing his business cards. "Put one in your wallet."

"You live and work with me. I'm pretty sure I can find you."

He rolls his eyes. "Keep it handy for the quote. For those days when you need a reminder."

I relent and tuck a card into my pocket. "Actually, I'm doing much better."

He leans back, studying me. "Do tell."

I shrug. "It's something I've been working on. Have you heard of kintsugi?"

"Is that some kind of sushi?"

I laugh and shake my head. "No. Come to my office." He follows me around the corner and down the hall, and I lead him to my own credenza which functions as both sofa table and storage. I take a black saucer with a wide rim off its display stand, feeling the weight of the cool porcelain in my hands. Veins of gold masterfully streak across the piece. "Kintsugi is a form of Japanese art. When pottery breaks, they glue the pieces back together and accentuate the repair lines with gold. They take something others consider damaged beyond repair and create something beautiful. Linda introduced me to the concept of celebrating one's scars as a sign of victory over brokenness." I pause, stroking a thin line of gold before handing it to him. "I bought this to remind myself that being broken didn't lessen my value. I have a similar piece on the table in my bedroom."

Stubbs runs a thick finger over the gold line through the center of the saucer. "Highlighting the intention and care that went into repairing the damage has elevated this to a work of art," he murmurs. "Had it not been broken, it would be ordinary. Flawless, perhaps, but without real depth or character." He smiles. "I may steal your metaphor to use with some of my clients."

"Feel free. I stole it from Linda. You can borrow the piece to show any of your clients you feel it might help."

He turns it over in his hands. "I think I'd like one of my own. Where did you get it?"

"From an artist in Japan. I'll get you his information."

Later in the day, I hold the saucer in my hands, tracing the gold veins that turn an ordinary piece into something uniquely beautiful. One of these days, perhaps I can share my metaphor with Mark. Not yet, though. Despite his promises, I don't think he's able to accept the concept behind the words, and watching him dismiss them would frustrate me.

And I don't want any frustration between us. Not right now. I've agreed to take things slowly, to let him prove to me that I can trust him. He came over again last night, and we spent a drama-free evening assembling the babies' changing table while watching a movie and snacking on popcorn. At the end of the night, I walked him to the door and he kissed me – a leisurely kiss with just enough heat to make me crave more before he pulled away. "See you tomorrow," he'd murmured against my lips. When he closed the door, my pulse was pounding.

Tonight, we're going to assemble their crib.

MARK

I'm frozen in place, staring at the black-and-white screen in front of me.

Two babies. My babies.

No. *Our* babies.

They're squirming, and the red-haired tech in pastel pink scrubs points to the one facing the screen. "This is your son," she says cheerfully. I watch, transfixed, as he pulls his tiny fist to his face and then thrusts it down, as though swatting something away in frustration.

My son.

The detail in his tiny face is incredible, and as I watch, he wrinkles his mouth in a pout, then repeats the punching motion with his fist again.

The ultrasound tech adjusts some knobs, and a rapid swishing sound emanates from the machine. "Hear that? That's his heartbeat," she says.

I blink, then glance at her. "It's fast. Is it supposed to be that fast?"

She smiles reassuringly. "Babies' hearts beat much faster than adults because they're smaller. Your heart rate is probably sixty or seventy beats per minute. His is more than double that. A hummingbird's heart beats about three hundred times per minute. It's all relative."

She presses a few more buttons, recording data, then slides the probe across Charlie's rounded stomach. "And here's your baby girl," she says.

No. My Baby Girl is the one on the exam table.

But I can't call her that anymore, because I fucked everything up.

Stop, my brain says sternly. *Negative thinking isn't productive.*

I turn my attention back to the screen and gape at the beautiful infant there. Her perfect rosebud mouth is making suckling movements, and she's opening and closing the fingers of her left hand. She pulls the hand to her mouth and starts to suck her thumb.

Dear God. *My daughter.* I've never seen anything so perfect as these two babies.

Our babies.

My son.

My daughter.

I'm going to be a father. *A father.*

My throat tightens sharply as a tidal wave of emotion overwhelms me.

When the tech wipes the jelly off Charlie's abdomen and steps out of the room, I kneel beside the exam table, cupping my hands around her belly and pressing my face against it, my breathing quick and shallow. I hear her surprised intake of breath before her fingers slide into my hair. I stay that way, with Charlie gently stroking my head, until the doctor returns to the room.

CHARLIE

The drive back from Dr. Rose's office in Pueblo takes place in total silence.

I'd picked Mark up at his apartment this morning so we could ride up together. It's been snowing off and on all day, and my SUV handles bad weather fairly well. Neither of us were sure about his van, though, so I'd opted to drive. I'd thought it would give us time to talk about how we're going to handle parenting, especially once he saw our babies in real time.

But he's not said a word since the tech finished my ultrasound. Not to the doctor, not to the receptionist who made my next appointment, not to the expectant couple who smiled and said hello as we passed them on our way out, and certainly not to me.

Not. One. Damn. Word.

And because I don't know why he's shut down, I'm struggling not to panic.

Maybe the reality check of seeing our babies has renewed his body-image issues. Maybe he's questioning his ability to parent as an amputee. My temper flares briefly at that ridiculous notion. Then my stomach clenches. *Or maybe he's about to leave me again, only this time, for good.*

I grip the steering wheel so tightly that my knuckles turn white and my hands cramp. I try to clamp down my emotions and focus on the road, because it's snowing again, big wet flakes that cling to my windshield and turn the pavement white. I'm relieved when we get back to Cedar Ridge. The temperature is dropping, and the roads will be getting slippery. But instead of worrying about road conditions, I'm questioning whether letting Mark back into my life is the dumbest thing I've ever done.

I pull up outside his apartment without turning off my engine. He glances at me, the first time he's made eye contact since the doctor left the exam room. "Do you want to come in for a minute? You haven't seen my crappy little apartment yet."

I study his expression. His eyes are tight, his face drawn. "Do you want me to come in?"

He certainly isn't acting like he does, but he holds my gaze. "Yes. Please," he adds.

I still can't read his emotions, but I nod and shut off the engine, following him into what Lila calls his nicotine-scented plaid nightmare. It doesn't smell like cigarettes, but the living room is definitely dated. Beige wallpaper is old and water-stained, and the ancient gold shag carpeting is worn threadbare in spots. The blue plaid sofa and loveseat are old and misshapen, and I recall Lila's warning about a wayward spring. I keep my expression neutral as I glance around.

"Hovel, sweet hovel," he mutters. "It's not much, but I only signed a six-month lease."

"Tucker said the owner's granddaughter is remodeling all the units."

He nods. "I'm the newest tenant, so I'm pretty far down the list. She's starting with the disabled tenants who've lived here the longest. If this place is any indication, they deserve top priority." He spreads his arms wide. "So this is my living room," he says unnecessarily. "If you sit on the couch, don't sit at the end facing the TV."

"Lila did mention something about a eunuch-spring."

He turns, and I follow him into a small but clean kitchen. The counters are wiped, the trash is empty, and the sink is free of dishes. "My combination kitchen and dining room. The refrigerator only has one section that cools properly. The top shelf keeps the beer room temperature, and the crisper freezes the produce, so I'm limited to using the middle shelf. The stove only has one working burner. The table is fine, but all three chairs wobble, so I usually eat on the loveseat."

A loud rattle to my left makes me jump. He smiles faintly. "That's the heater. When I first moved in, it smelled like dead rats every time I turned it on, so that's an improvement." He leads me past a seventies' gold washer and dryer with black dials and push buttons, down the narrow hall that ends in a bedroom barely big enough to hold a bed, dresser, and nightstand. The double bed is crisply made with a simple gray comforter and white pillows, and clothes hang in neat rows in the closet, which lacks its bi-fold doors. An ancient television sits on a worn dresser. The only other furniture in the room is the battered nightstand.

I inhale sharply at the framed photograph beside his bed. It's the picture of us that Tucker snapped last summer when we were hiking. Mark and I were resting on a fallen log. I'd grabbed the front of his shirt and pulled him close for a long kiss.

It's the picture I kept on my nightstand when Mark and I shared a bed.

The picture he took with him when he left.

He follows my gaze to the photo and nods. "I kept it facedown in a drawer under my shirts when I was at Tucker and Lila's. I wanted a reminder of the best days of my life, but it hurt too much to look at it and remember what I'd lost. Hiding it in my drawer didn't help. Every time I closed my eyes, I saw you as clearly as if you were standing in front of me."

I pick it up, studying our faces, not just the kissing, but the joy, the love.

I put the picture back down, avoiding Mark's eyes. Even then, he loved me, and I loved him.

But he still left me.

He walked away without looking back.

I swallow hard, my throat suddenly tight, then turn and move past him toward the living room. I have to get away from that picture.

It's just the damn hormones.

And because I'm not sure why he shut down after seeing our babies.

Or why he invited me in without explaining his ninety-minute silent treatment.

I sigh inwardly. His swiftly changing moods today have unsettled me. He's gone from excited to silent to nervous, all in the space of a couple of hours.

"I need to go," Mark says from behind me. "I have an appointment with Dr. Allen."

I glance over my shoulder. "I have an appointment with Linda, too. I'm picking up pizza for dinner. What kind do you want? I know you won't eat Hawaiian."

Mark looks determinedly at the floor, avoiding my gaze. "Actually, I'm kind of tired. I think I'll just crash here tonight. I'll call you tomorrow."

The sick feeling in the pit of my stomach haunts me the rest of the evening.

MARK

Babies.

My babies.

No. *Our* babies.

But they won't be babies for long.

Babies become toddlers. Preschoolers. First-graders with gap-toothed smiles. Middle school kids dealing with bullies and mean girls. High schoolers with hormones and heartbreaks.

And I know nothing, nothing, about being a parent. Hell, I've been an adult for so long, I barely remember being a kid. Most of the stuff I do remember was from high school.

Not terribly helpful with a pair of newborns.

I don't even have anyone to ask. Every parental figure in my life is dead. My mom. My dad. Charlie's parents. All dead.

I'm used to teaching new recruits what they need to know. Who the hell is going to teach me?

I go to my appointment with Dr. Allen, telling him about Charlie giving me another chance, about telling her I love her. He praises me for being open and vulnerable, but cautions me to set reasonable expectations.

He's seen the same thing I have before – guys like Kip that take the slightest positive encouragement and inflate it to something of epic proportions in their mind. But I know how much damage I did to Charlie, and I know it'll take a miracle to truly win her back.

I don't mention the ultrasound to him.

I'm not even sure why I don't. After all, he's there to help me work through my feelings.

The thing is, I'm not really sure *what* I'm feeling.

So when he asks if anything else is going on that I'd like to discuss, I tell him no. Instead, we focus on further ways for me to explore my future career path.

When I go home, I sit alone in the dark in my crappy little apartment, wondering how the hell I'm going to learn to take care of not one, but two babies in a few short months.

CHARLIE

Mark doesn't text or call after his appointment with Dr. Allen, nor does he text while I'm at work Friday. Lila walks into my office as I'm swallowing two acetaminophen tablets.

"What's wrong? Are you okay?" she asks immediately.

"Just a headache," I tell her. "I've been staring at these invoices for too long." She crosses the room and stops behind me, dropping small but surprisingly strong hands on my shoulders. Her fingers immediately find my tense muscles and start working out the knots. There are definite perks to working with another massage therapist.

"How was your ultrasound yesterday? Did they print any more pictures?"

I slide a folder aside to lift a sheaf of black and white images. I start to pass them to her, but she shakes her head. "Hold them up for me. Your neck and shoulders are one giant tangle. No wonder your head hurts."

I flip through the pictures, and she oohs and aahs at the appropriate moments. "What did Mark say?"

I drop the pictures onto the desk. "Nothing."

Her tone sharpens. "What do you mean, nothing?"

"Remember the night I showed Blake my scars, and he didn't say a damn word the whole drive back to my house? Imagine that from the time the ultrasound tech left the room until I pulled up to his apartment."

"He didn't say anything the entire trip back from Pueblo?" Her voice is indignant, her fingers digging harder into my muscles, and I shift away from her. "Sorry," she apologizes, easing up. "What did he say when you got back to his place?"

"He invited me in to see his nicotine-plaid nightmare, which you were right about, by the way. Five minutes later he said he needed to leave. I asked him over for dinner and he declined."

Her hands stop moving. After a moment, she resumes massaging. "Yesterday was Thursday, right? So he would have had an appointment with Dr. Allen. He goes Mondays and Thursdays."

I nod. "He was heading there when I left."

"Maybe he just needed to sort it out with Dr. Allen before talking about it," she suggests. "I wouldn't worry. Have you talked to him today?" A gentle hand presses my head forward, and I groan as sore muscles between my shoulder blades protest.

"Not yet."

"Is that why you're so knotted up?" she asks pointedly.

I sigh. "I can't help feeling like he's going to bail again the second I trust him, only this time, it won't be just me his actions affect."

And despite my determination to be strong for my babies, letting Mark back in only to lose him again would destroy me in a way I'm not sure I would recover from.

Small fingers worm between layers of muscle, and I groan again as Lila finds another knot and works it into submission.

"Mark means it when he says he loves you, Charlie. I don't think he's going to do anything to screw things up again. Maybe he was just overwhelmed."

"Maybe," I concede, remembering him kneeling by the exam table, cupping my belly with his face resting against it. My heart had felt indescribably full when he'd reacted that way.

His emotional distance immediately afterwards had left me reeling as badly as if he'd physically shoved me away.

"It was a shock for you when you first saw them," she reminds me. "It probably just took the wind out of his sails."

"I understand being shocked. It's a lot to absorb. But I won't tolerate any of his 'useless cripple' bullshit again or listen to him claim our babies deserve a dad with two legs."

Lila finishes working the knots out of my neck and upper back before squeezing my shoulders. "Go home and take a hot shower. Those muscles need it, and it might help your headache."

I push my chair back. "I think I will. It's nearly five. These invoices can wait till Monday."

When I emerge from my shower twenty minutes later, I've got a string of texts from Mark.

"Sorry."

"My phone battery died and I can't find my charger."

"I ran out and picked up a new one..."

"But I had to wait for it to charge enough to text you."

"(face palm) I just realized I could have used the charger in my van."

"Didn't think about that. Sorry."

"I know you had pizza last night..."

"So it might be too soon for more Italian food."

"What if I stop by with Chinese?"

"Is that OK?"

"And if it is, should I bring enough for Stubbs, too?"

I'm no expert, but the sheer number of texts he's sent in the last twenty minutes combined with their tone reeks of anxiety. I wonder if Lila called and yelled at him.

As I'm standing there in a towel, tiny dots bounce on the screen.

"Never mind. I got enough for all of us. If you don't want to see me, I can leave it by your front door. There's enough to have leftovers for your next meal."

"Which I'm given to understand will be about three hours after that one."

I frown. *Smartass.*

On the other hand, at least he's talking again.

I start typing. "Yes to dinner. And it is both rude and dangerous to comment on a woman's appetite, pregnant or not."

His response lands almost immediately. "I'm really glad you said yes, because I'm almost at your house."

Aaaaaand I'm wearing nothing but a towel.

I very nearly type that, but don't. First of all, I'm not sure where our relationship stands right now, and second, big-belly-and-wet-hair-in-a-towel is not a look I want him to picture. Instead I type, "Stop texting and driving."

"I'm using speak-to-text."

I should have known. Ever since my parents died in a car accident, he's been a very safety-conscious driver. I sigh. "If I don't answer the door, let yourself in. I'll be out shortly."

He wasn't kidding. By the time I've sent the text, I can hear his tires crunching in my gravel driveway. I towel-dry my hair and body, then hear Stubbs and Mark talking in the foyer. Good. Let them amuse each other.

I rub texturizing cream in my hair to give it loose waves before blow-drying it, then eye my reflection. I can't put on makeup. Well, I *could*, but the blow dryer will have clued Mark in that I just got out of the shower. If he sees me with a full face of makeup, he'll assume I did it for him.

Which I would be.

Dammit.

I never used to care if he saw me without makeup. There's a distinct downside to going from best friends to lovers. Even after a breakup, physical appearances matter. And since I don't know exactly where he and I stand, I don't want to appear overly eager.

I compromise by dabbing on concealer to hide the dark circles under my eyes – I slept less than an hour last night – and add mascara and a soft peach lip stain. Then I don my wardrobe staple: leggings and a long-sleeved tee shirt.

I check my reflection and decide I look very girl-next-door-ish.

Assuming, of course, that the girl next door is knocked up with twins.

I follow the sound of voices and find Mark and Stubbs at the dining room table. They've already set out plates, forks, and chopsticks and poured glasses of tea. I shake my head. "You guys could have started without me. No sense letting good food get cold."

The huge man on one side of the table snorts. "I was not raised in a barn," Stubbs says.

"Nor was I," Mark says, standing to pull out the chair at the head of the table, seating me between them. "You look incredible," he says, leaning down to brush his lips over the shell of my ear. He lingers, humming softly as he inhales against the curve of my neck. *Dear Lord. Where was this man yesterday?* Electricity sparks along every nerve ending from my neck to my core, and I suck in a breath. "You smell incredible, too. Definitely worth the wait," he murmurs.

Stubbs rolls his eyes as Mark sits down. "I thought you had game, Pretty Boy. That's all you've got?"

Mark picks up a container of lo mein and scoops some onto his plate before passing it to me. "I assume you have a much wider repertoire, since you're obviously older than I am."

Their witty banter gives me time to internally fan myself from Mark's closeness. After a moment, I'm able to settle back and witness the inevitable trading of male insults. I take some noodles, then pass the lo mein to Stubbs and take the beef and broccoli container from Mark.

Stubbs adds a pile of noodles to his plate. "Really? Age jokes? That's all you've got? Baby, I'm like a fine wine, and I'm smoooooooth when I go down." I hide my smile at his comment. "Women adore the way I play their body like a master strumming his instrument."

"I don't want to hear about you playing with your instrument," Mark says dryly.

"No one is discussing anyone's instrument," I say firmly. Lila's right. Boys are stupid.

Conversation eventually leaves the land of juvenile male oneupmanship and turns to Stubbs' first week at work. "I love it," he tells Mark. "This is what I'm meant to do." He reaches into his back pocket and withdraws a business card from his wallet, handing it to Mark.

Mark grins. "I already know how to find you," he says.

"Maybe you need more than just my contact information," Stubbs says meaningfully.

Mark reads the card, and his eyes tighten almost imperceptibly at Stubbs' quote, but all he says is, "Badass Therapist Extraordinaire, huh? I'm pretty sure that's not an official title."

"Sure it is," Stubbs counters. "I have it on a plaque and my nameplate."

"I can call myself Her Majesty, Queen of England, but that doesn't make it true," Mark teases, "even if I print it on a dozen plaques and a thousand business cards."

The two of them bicker goodnaturedly all through dinner. Meanwhile, I replay Mark's tense expression when he read Stubbs' quote about scars and recall his distance since the ultrasound. By the time I stand to clear the table, my stomach is in knots again.

"I'll get those," Mark says, taking the leftovers from me and tucking them into the fridge. I turn to gather the dinner dishes, but Stubbs is already at the sink, rinsing them.

"I've got these," Stubbs says. "Thanks for dinner, Pretty Boy. Next time, it's on me." He loads the dishwasher before drying his hands on a towel. "Ladies, I'm headed to the VFW again."

Mark rolls his eyes at Stubbs' comment, but I grin. "Still drumming up business?"

"Helping soldiers is my purpose," he replies. "We're just fighting to survive on a different battlefield now."

Stubbs grabs his jacket and heads out, and Mark and I drift into the living room with Penny on our heels. "You've been quiet this evening," he observes.

I pause, unsure how to respond. "I've been fighting a headache, but I took something for it, and Lila rubbed my neck and sent me off to a hot shower."

"Does it still hurt?" he asks, his brows furrowing. "Do you need an icepack? I'm not as good as Lila, but I'll rub your neck if it will help."

"It's better than it was."

"Was your blood pressure high? I read that blood pressure can increase during pregnancy and cause headaches. If that happens, we're supposed to notify your doctor."

I look over, puzzled. "You've been reading about pregnancy?"

His face reddens, but he nods. "I don't know anything about it, and it seems like something I should be familiar with, given the circumstances."

I pause, digesting that. "I don't think my blood pressure was high, but I didn't check. If it happens again, I'll start monitoring it. I think it was mostly from not sleeping last night."

He looks away, and silence falls again. He doesn't ask why I had trouble sleeping. I'm pretty sure he can connect the dots. My annoyance flares. Screw it. He wants me to trust him? He can damn well tell me what his deal was yesterday.

I watch his face. "Speaking of me not sleeping, let's talk about the way you shut down on me yesterday. What was that about?"

His smile fades. "I didn't shut down."

I raise an eyebrow. "In that weather, it took me an hour and a half to drive from the doctor's office to your apartment, and you didn't say a single word until we got to your driveway."

"I didn't shut down," he repeats.

"Then what would you call it?"

He pauses. "Absorbing things."

I wait, but he doesn't continue. Finally I ask, "Was Dr. Allen able to help with that?"

He frowns. "I didn't talk about it with him."

I stare, nonplussed. "Why not?"

"Why would I?"

My spine stiffens. "That's what he's there for. To help you sort through emotional situations."

His expression turns unreadable. "So because I needed time to figure out my feelings, I should have run straight to my shrink?"

My hackles rise. "You still haven't figured out what you're feeling. One minute you're cradling my belly with your face pressed against it, and the next you're giving me the silent treatment. You ask me to come into your apartment but then refuse to have dinner with me. You ignored me all day today, then fell all over yourself apologizing and asking me to have dinner tonight. I dare to ask what was up yesterday, and you immediately get defensive. I've been hurt by your emotional roller coaster before, and this – " I gesture back and forth between us "– isn't inclining me to trust you again. I don't have the emotional energy to deal with your mood swings." I get to my feet, pressing the heel of my hand against my forehead, which is now throbbing fiercely again. "I'm taking Penny outside. You should go. Lock the door behind you."

I stay outside on my back deck long after Penny is done, until I hear his van drive off. Only then do I go back inside, curl up on the couch, and cry until I fall asleep.

Saturday morning, I text Lila and beg for a weekend shopping trip to Pueblo.

CHAPTER TWENTY-FOUR

TUCKER

"I'M STILL NOT SURE why you're here," Lila says as I follow her down the hall of Dr. K's office. "Nothing exciting happens today."

"I told you, Sweetness, I'm all in. Besides, I have more questions about the process." I've been researching IVF, learning everything I can from multiple websites of varying degrees of expertise. I want to know which hormone shots Lila will be started on, how restricted her activity will be the day of the harvesting, and when it's safe for her to work after the implantation process. The more I read, the less I feel like I know.

The nurse stops at the restroom and motions Lila inside. "You know the drill," she says with a smile. Lila steps inside.

"You do that every visit?" I ask the young nurse.

She nods. "It's standard. Urinary tract infections are very common and can affect a woman's ability to conceive, and in pregnant women, we want to catch any infections before they become serious enough to harm the baby. We also monitor for glucose, protein, things of that nature."

More things I didn't know. More things to worry about.

Lila exits the restroom empty handed. "Wait. I thought you had to pee in a cup."

She looks at me like I'm insane. "They have a two-way door. You leave the specimen on a tray."

"How do they know it's yours?"

She raises one eyebrow. "Because my name is on the cup."

The nurse leads us a bit further down the hall before pointing toward a chair. Lila slides into it and rolls up her sleeve while the nurse gathers supplies to draw her blood and ties a rubber tourniquet on her arm.

"That looks like an awful lot of tubes," I comment.

Lila gives me an exasperated look. "Tucker, honestly, this happens every visit. Relax."

"I think it's sweet," the young nurse announces. "We have some patients whose significant other has no interest whatsoever. It's nice to see a doting husband." While the nurse is searching for a vein, Lila rolls her eyes at me. I stick out my tongue like the doting husband I am.

Once Lila's been poked, weighed, and had her blood pressure checked, we're shown to an exam room. The nurse gestures to a pair of chairs. "This is just a consult, so you won't need to put a gown on today. Dr. K will be in as soon as she can. One of her patients gave birth early this morning, so she was late getting to the office. The good news is that we should have your lab work finished by the time she's ready for you."

By the time Dr. K finally comes in, Lila's ready to throttle me. I've studied every poster on the walls, looked up everything mentioned in all of the pamphlets in the small room, played with the model uterus with a fetus on the desk, and asked Lila a dozen questions about her cycle, menstrual cramps, and ovulation. I've pulled up statistics on egg delivery with a single fallopian tube and recurrent ectopic pregnancy rates and shared them with her. I finally glance up when I hear her gritting her teeth.

My excitement deflates at her expression. "I'm sorry. I'll shut up." I hesitate. "Maybe I should wait in the car."

She sighs. "No, Tucker, it's fine. I'm glad you're enthusiastic. It's actually very sweet. It's just—you know IVF usually takes a few attempts, right? I don't want you to get your hopes up and be disappointed if it doesn't work right away."

I squeeze her hand. "I won't be. It'll just be an excuse for more sex, I mean attempts."

She shakes her head and smiles. "You're hopeless, you know that?"

The door opens and Dr. K enters. I jump to my feet and stick out my hand, and she greets us warmly. "Hello, Lila. Hello again, Tucker. Sorry to keep you waiting."

Lila smiles. "We don't mind. It sounds like you've had a busy morning."

The petite, dark-haired woman returns her smile. "My schedule is dictated by my tiniest patients." She takes a seat at the corner desk and reviews the labs in front of her, pursing her lips as she flips pages back and forth.

"So you made this appointment to resume the hormone treatments, correct?" She continues looking at the papers in front of her.

"Yes," I answer.

"And it's been three months now since your ectopic pregnancy?"

Lila opens her mouth, but I answer again. "Yes."

"And you wanted to discuss IVF?"

"We want to get started with it as soon as possible," I say.

Dr. K raises her eyes, trying to hide a smile. "Someone's eager."

"Well, she would have been here sooner, if I weren't – uh – weirded out by the thought of – uh –" I feel my face reddening.

She does smile then. "Most male partners share your concerns. If it's any consolation, we have soundproof rooms and a two-way door to leave the specimen so you don't have to do the walk of shame with your cup through the lobby."

Walk of shame. The same term I'd used in my head.

"So she'll start back on hormone shots today, and then come back in two weeks for our – uh – for my specimen and her eggs?"

Dr. K places the papers on her desk and steeples her fingers, studying the both of us carefully. "Actually, after reviewing your lab results, we're going to hold off."

"But I thought..." Lila trails off. "Hasn't it been long enough yet?"

Dr. K smiles at the two of us. "You don't need the shots, Lila. You're pregnant."

I gape at her. Lila clutches my thigh, digging her nails in.

"I'd say you're just under three weeks pregnant, based on your hCG levels and the dates of your cycle."

I jump to my feet and grab Lila up in a hug, swinging her around as she laughs and then bursts into tears. I dart my eyes to hers, reading the fear there.

She's afraid of losing another baby.

"Sweetness, don't cry." I set her back on her feet. "Everything's going to be fine."

Lila pokes her head around me to look at Dr. K. "When will I know if it's in the right place?"

"We should be able to tell by ultrasound in a couple of weeks."

"Should she be on bedrest?" I ask quickly, and Dr. K smiles again at the same time Lila gouges my ribs with an annoyed elbow.

"No, she doesn't need to be on bedrest. She can keep doing whatever she normally does. And of course, she should eat right, avoid alcohol and caffeine, and get a good night's sleep."

"What about sex?" I blurt out, and Dr. K's musical laughter fills the room.

"Yes, she can have sex. Have all the sex you two want to have."

"It won't hurt the baby?"

She smiles. "No. Just imagine you're rocking him or her to sleep." She gets to her feet, placing a hand on each of our arms. "Congratulations to you both. Keep the appointment you have for the twenty-fifth and we'll do your ultrasound then."

When she leaves the room, I take Lila by the hands. "You did it, Sweetness."

She laughs. "I'm pretty sure this is a 'we' thing, not a me thing." She pauses for a moment before her eyes widen. "The timing. Almost three weeks? We were exorcizing my demons, Tucker."

It comes back in a rush.

That night the power went out.

The kitchen table.

Lila battling her fears.

Defeating her demons.

That's when we conceived – when we defeated her demons.

There couldn't be a more perfect conception story for us if we tried.

I suddenly know with complete certainty that this pregnancy is going to go perfectly.

MARK

"I saw my babies on that screen, and I just –" I break off, then look at Dr. Allen. "I love them already. But I don't have a clue how to be a dad. I've never even held a baby before."

"What was your father like?"

Pain slices through the center of my chest. Sometimes I'd swear Dr. Allen can read my mind, because he instinctively knows exactly where to probe. I draw a slow breath. "He was a decent guy. Took me fishing and played ball with me and did all the things a dad's supposed to do with his son. Things were good until I was twelve."

Dark eyes study my face. "What changed when you were twelve?"

"My mom was diagnosed with cancer. Stage four. My dad pushed her to try chemo. She knew it was too late – we all did – but he insisted she try it, so she did. All it did was weaken her enough for the cancer to destroy her."

"Did your mother's illness alter your relationship with your father?"

I swallow. "Cancer stole my mom from me when I was thirteen. My dad committed suicide two years later. He abandoned me because he couldn't stand being without her. She fought a losing battle. He just gave up."

"Is it possible he fought a losing battle as well?"

My jaw tightens. "No. She fought to live. He chose to die."

He studies me carefully. "When you and I talked about Kip, we discussed how suicides happen when someone doesn't see any other way out of their pain."

I shake my head. "It's not the same."

"Why not?"

"Because he had me, and I didn't have anyone else. My grandparents were dead, my mom was dead. My dad was the only person I had left. He had a responsibility to me."

"And you've struggled with this anger since his death?"

I blow out a harsh breath. "No. I wasn't angry before. I thought I understood how he felt. The anger hit when I saw my babies on that ultrasound screen."

"Why do you suppose seeing them made you feel this way toward your father?"

"They aren't even born, and I'd do anything for them." I pause. "And it makes me angry that even after fifteen years of being my dad, he didn't feel the same way."

He watches me for a moment. "You moved in with Charlie's family after your father's death. How did that come about?"

I shrug. "We lived next door. Our parents were best friends. Charlie and I were best friends. Her parents stepped in when to help my mom was sick and – and afterwards, when my dad wasn't coping. When he killed himself, Grace and John asked me to move in with them. That was even before they knew he'd already named them my guardians."

"It sounds as though your dad took steps to ensure you'd be well taken care of."

My gaze narrows. "What he should have done was get help. I overheard John crying after the fact, blaming himself for not pushing my dad to see someone."

"Do you blame John?"

I frown. "Of course not. You can't make someone get help if they don't want it."

"But you blame your father for not being strong enough to reach out?"

I fall silent, mostly because my temper is rising, and this newfound issue of anger toward my long-dead father isn't helping me sort out my strained relationship with Charlie.

Once again, Dr. Allen reads my mind. "Let's set your anger aside for a moment and look at your worries about being a good father. What about fatherhood concerns you?"

I laugh without humor. "All of it. I've never held a baby, and we're having two of them. I don't know how to change a diaper or give a baby a bath. I don't have a clue what to do when they cry, and babies cry a lot."

He smiles placidly. "There's a wealth of information available. Books, on-line videos, parenting classes. I suspect you can find any number of people who would happily share their experiences with you. What about your social circle? Do any of your friends have children?"

"Tom has a daughter, but she's like –" I raise a hand to chest height, realize how stupid that makes me look, and try to remember Maya's age. "I think she's ten." She was last spring when I met her. She may be eleven now, if she had a birthday during the months I was brooding with my head up my ass. "And Stubbs has a son who's twenty. Neither of them are babies."

His smile widens. "You know, all children start out as babies. I suspect they'd be able to give you pointers."

I consider that for a moment. Stubbs told me he wasn't around much when his son Ty was young, but Tom... from what Charlie and Lila have said, Tom's ex-wife walked out and left him to raise Maya on his own when she was just a baby. He's got a sister with a bunch of kids, and I'm sure she helped out, but the majority of the burden fell on Tom. And I've seen him with Maya. He's a good dad. I'm sure he'd be happy to talk me off the fatherhood ledge.

"What is it about being a father that worries you?"

"Screwing up," I say immediately.

Dr. Allen tilts his head. "Define screwing up."

"Doing something stupid that ends up driving my kids into therapy."

"Because being in therapy indicates some sort of parental failure?"

I frown in exasperation. "Not necessarily, but sometimes."

"I've been a psychiatrist for twenty years, Mark, and not one of my patients has ever come to me complaining their father didn't know how to change diapers properly," he says, his tone wry.

"I'm not worried that not knowing how to change a diaper will send them into therapy. It's the rest of it. Me."

"Your leg?" he asks bluntly. "Your self-loathing? What is it specifically that worries you?"

"All this emotional garbage," I say, my tone growing sharp. "I allowed my inner bullshit to destroy my relationship with Charlie. I hurt her badly. What if I do the same thing to my kids?"

"You hurt Charlie when you left her," he says, and I nod my assent. "And your father hurt you when he left you – first because he was too consumed by grief to be there for you, and again when he abandoned you through suicide."

I sit there, stunned, seeing the parallels for the first time.

Is that why I'm afraid? Because my own father failed me?

And I'm afraid I'll do the same thing again? Abandon the people I love because of my stupid inner bullshit?

Dr. Allen follows my train of thought. "You are not your father, Mark. You're seeking help. You're trying to work through your emotional wounds and get to a place of self-acceptance."

I sit with my emotions for several minutes, "letting myself feel my feelings," as Charlie puts it. My father suffered a tremendous emotional loss. Cancer destroyed him as much as it did my mother. And yes, he abandoned me, because he was in more pain than he could bear.

I suffered a loss as well, first in the explosion, then again after restorative surgery left me disappointed. I allowed my pain and self-loathing to consume me, and I abandoned Charlie and made the biggest mistake of my life. Now I'm fighting to prove to Charlie I won't do it again, and distancing myself from her after the ultrasound and acting pissy when she asked about it hasn't done a damn thing to help.

The problem is, I haven't yet proved to myself that I won't abandon her again. I tell myself I'd never do that to her again, but isn't that exactly what I did when we left the doctor's office?

Trying to bury my self-loathing hasn't done a damn thing. As long as I allow it to linger and fester beneath the surface, the risk remains that, like cancer, it will rear its ugly head and consume me.

The only way to eliminate it is to cut it out, like a tumor.

And to do that, I have to truly accept myself, stump, scars, and all.

LILA

After leaving Dr. K's office, I head straight to Mark's. Someone needs to jerk a knot in his ass, and his idiotic behavior has dampened my exuberance over my pregnancy.

When Charlie called Saturday requesting an overnight trip to Pueblo, I knew she was struggling with Mark's recent behavior more than she'd let on. She needed a distraction, and asking me to go shopping is always a safe bet.

She didn't say much while we drifted from one baby store to another, picking out sleepers, onesies, crib sets, and blankets. Her pregnancy has forced her to actively participate in our shopping trips instead of following me around like a caddy. We ended the day at our favorite Mexican restaurant for tacos and iced tea instead of our usual margaritas. We were halfway through a platter of tacos when she looked up. "I threw Mark out last night."

I kept my expression carefully neutral. "Do tell."

She sighed. "I don't know. As soon as I got home, he started texting me like a teenaged girl, one after another after another. He brought over Chinese food and we ate dinner with Stubbs. As soon as Stubbs left, he started acting weird again."

"Weird how?"

She paused. "Hovering at first, when he found out I had a headache. When I said I hadn't slept well the night before, he clammed up, or at least, he tried to. I didn't let him. I asked him why he'd shut down on me after the ultrasound."

"What did he say?"

"He denied it, then got all defensive. And I got frustrated," she admitted. "I told him I didn't have the emotional energy to deal with his mood swings, and his behavior wasn't doing a lot to inspire me to trust him."

"How did he respond to that?"

She blushed. "I didn't give him a chance. I said I was taking Penny outside and he should see himself out. I stayed on the deck until I heard him drive away."

I'd studied her pale face, the shadows under her eyes. "And then?"

She exhaled heavily. "I cried myself to sleep." Tired eyes met mine. "On the plus side, I slept for a solid four hours before Stubbs came home. Then I moved to the bed and slept another five."

I stirred my tea with my straw. "How's your headache today?"

"Gone. I think I was just tired and stressed."

"So what now?"

"With Mark?" she asked, and I nodded. She shook her head. "I don't know. He told me he wants to earn my trust back, but as long as he's all over the map with his emotions, that's not going to happen. Part of me thinks I should just cut my losses."

I'd studied her carefully. "If you could have anything you wanted, what would it be?"

She'd slumped back into the booth. "I'm not sure it matters." She'd paused before meeting my gaze. "The night I got the call from Colonel Sherman about Mark, I'd had dinner with Tom and Maya. She was pissed at Whitney –" Charlie grinned at my eyeroll "– and she'd said she wanted me to be Tom's girlfriend. I told her he and I were just friends and said I wasn't good at relationships because I couldn't let people get close." She continues in a halting voice, describing a previously unrecognized longing for a man who loved her wholeheartedly, for kids and dogs and cats and the utterly messy chaos of a rich family life. "I'd never wanted any of that before, and when it hit me, it was so out of the realm of possibility that it eviscerated me."

"But it's possible now," I'd pointed out. "You have the babies, the dog, the man..."

She'd shaken her head. "That's just it, Lila. I don't have the man, not really. I have a man who claims to love me, but lets everything else get in the way. I don't know if he loves me more than he hates himself, and unless he does, I can't let him back in."

I speed from Dr. K's office to Mark's nicotine-nightmare, determined to do my part to make Charlie's secret dream her reality. I park next to his van, pleased he's home. I stride to the door and knock. He opens it a few seconds later.

"Hey, Lila. I didn't know –"

"I need to talk to you," I interrupt, pushing past him and marching to his living room.

"Okay," he says slowly. "What did I do?"

"Why don't you tell me what you think you did, and we'll go from there," I snap, and he closes his front door. He gestures to the loveseat, but I don't sit. This won't take long.

"I shut down after the ultrasound and made Charlie think I might abandon her again," he says, his light blue eyes meeting mine.

I nod. "Keep going."

"I got defensive when she asked me about it, and we haven't talked since."

My gaze narrows. "You haven't spoken to her in three days?"

He studies my face. "She asked me to leave, and then went out of town. I thought that's what she wanted."

Idiot.

"So you abandoned her. Again," I add. "No wonder she's afraid to trust you."

"I would never abandon her again," he protests.

I snort derisively, aiming straight for the jugular. "Says the man who bailed on her when he saw their babies and hasn't spoken to her since she called him on it."

His mouth drops open as I turn on my heel and stalk from his house.

CHAPTER TWENTY-FIVE

MARK

I SIT IN MY apartment, staring at the faded gold carpet without seeing it.

Lila's right. After the most intimate moment Charlie and I have ever shared – seeing our unborn children together – I abandoned her.

Again.

Maybe I'm not that different from my father after all.

Stop. Negative thinking isn't productive.

I need to talk to Charlie. I call, but her phone goes to voicemail, so I send a text. "Can I come over this evening? I'd really like to talk to you." I follow that with, "If you aren't comfortable talking with me alone, I'm okay with Stubbs watching me grovel."

She must have been in a massage, because she replies about five minutes before the hour.

"That's fine. I'll be home around five."

She's not exactly bubbling with enthusiasm. My brain chimes in, *Whose fault is that?* Ignoring it, I type, "I'll bring dinner. Enough for Stubbs, too, in case he's home."

Italian food, a glass of wine, chocolate, and a lot of groveling. That's my entire gameplan.

When I pull into Charlie's driveway, my phone buzzes with another text. "Come on in. House is unlocked. Be out in a minute."

I wonder if she's in the shower, like the last time I came over. I picture her, water sluicing over her curves, green eyes wide as I lift her, bracing her back against the tiles before burying myself deep inside her, and my cock twitches.

Down, boy. I've screwed things up too much for that. I grab our dinner and head inside.

The house is quiet, and I don't hear water running. I do hear muffled jazz music drifting down the stairs, though. Stubbs must be home. That's alright. It's no secret that I was an ass to Charlie. I can beg forgiveness with an audience. I carry the food into the kitchen, leaving the insulated bags of hot food on the counter and sliding the dessert, salads, and wine into the fridge. When I turn, Penny's waiting for me, tail wagging.

I kneel, rubbing her soft ears. "I think you're the only female I know who's happy to see me."

"I'm not exactly happy, but I'm not unhappy either, if that helps," comes a soft voice from the doorway. I hadn't heard Charlie approach, probably because of the pants and whines of the excited dog angling closer to me.

I stand, studying her expression. "What are you, then?"

Green eyes rake over my body as I cross the room, and she bites her lip and closes her eyes. I stop, barely a foot from her, smelling her coconut shampoo and jasmine body wash. She opens her eyes, and our gazes lock, the sudden sexual tension palpable. Despite everything else, she still wants me. I'd give anything to pull her close, tell her I love her, and carry her to the bedroom for a night neither of us will ever forget. It's all I can do not to reach for her.

But I don't. I don't have that right anymore. Not now. Maybe never again, if I can't quit screwing up. A slight feeling of panic bubbles up, and I squash it down.

"Hmm?" she suddenly asks, blinking.

My mind goes blank as I scramble to recall what I'd been saying. "You aren't happy to see me, but you aren't unhappy. What are you?"

She takes a deep breath, and the sexual tension fades, replaced by an altogether different and decidedly less pleasant kind. "Worried."

Afraid.

She doesn't say it, but it hangs in the air between us just the same.

"Tell me what you're worried about," I say, needing to quell her concerns.

She hesitates. "I guess deep down, part of me still believes you'd only come back because of the babies. When you shut me out after seeing them, I didn't know what to think. I don't know why you're here, and I don't know what you want, so I can't protect myself."

From me. She's protecting herself from me.

It's reasonable, given my behavior, but it still hurts.

So I change the subject without reassuring her – probably not wise, but her answer has left me off balance, and I need to regroup. "How about you and I take Penny for a walk?"

She glances at me in confusion before looking toward the window. "If we hurry, we can make it to her stream, but we'll end up walking back in the dark."

"I don't mind if you don't," I offer.

There's a pause, and she nods. "I'll grab my coat."

CHARLIE

I wish I knew why Mark was here.

I wish I knew what he really wanted.

I love him. It's become clear to me, based on my dreams and my reactions to him, that I always will. I can admit that to myself. The problem is, even though Mark says he loves me, his behavior doesn't always reflect that, and I can't lose myself in his vortex of emotions again. Even if I ultimately decide I need to let him go, having babies together means he's going to be a big part of my life from now on.

And being near him all the time, knowing my dream lies just beyond my fingertips, will shatter my barely-held-together heart.

I have to be strong for my babies.

And if being strong for my babies means stopping things in their tracks and not letting him back in, then that's what I have to do.

Mark and I silently follow the path Penny and I have worn in the snow over the past few days. We reach the little stream soon enough. I brush the fresh layer of snow off the wooden bench with a gloved hand before sitting down. He joins me, and we sit side by side, our legs not quite touching. I feel his body heat radiating from him just the same, and it sends a different sort of heat sizzling through me, which only heightens my anxiety.

I force my attention to Penny and her antics. She bounds back and forth, a brown and white blur splashing in and out of the stream, running from bank to bank. Her legs and belly drip with icy water, but she doesn't care. She pounces at a dry leaf rattling beneath a bush edging the water, and we both chuckle. Mark's laughter reminds her she has an audience, and she lunges toward him, excitedly shoving between us. Mark holds a hand out and she noses it, pushing her head into his hand. He laughs and runs long fingers through her soft fur, stroking her silky ears. She revels in his attention, climbing onto his lap with her wet front legs, soaking his jeans.

"Get down, Penny." I nudge her off his legs, but she immediately tries again. In the end, she clambers onto the bench, forcing us to slide apart and make room for her. She drapes her upper body over his lap, covering both of us with eau de wet dog. I can't even scold her, because despite our fractured relationship, I'd love to crawl on top of him, too.

Mark grins as she squirms further onto his lap. "I think she likes me."

I focus on his words, trying to forget the way I'd straddle him on the couch during heavy makeout sessions and later, in his shower, when we were intimate without penetration.

Damn hormones.

Penny. He's talking about Penny.

Focus. "She's a sweet dog. I'd like to beat the hell out of the asshole that abused her."

His expression darkens as he strokes her. "She's too thin. I can count every one of her ribs."

I chuckle. "I don't think that will be a problem for long. She's a big fan of people food."

We sit quietly as darkness falls, listening to the trickling water and the soft sound of tiny snowflakes ticking against leaves and branches. I shut my eyes and inhale deeply, concentrating on the scent of fresh pine until Penny hops down and pushes her head into my lap.

I lift her chin so our eyes meet. "Home?" She barks once, then scampers toward the trail.

Mark looks impressed. "She's smart." He reaches for the spotlight flashlight I brought along and turns it on to illuminate our path before stretching his other hand out to me. I take it automatically, pained by how right it feels to have his fingers wrapped around mine.

What does he want?

Why is he here?

Much to Penny's dismay, we trek home more slowly in the dark. She darts ahead and back, encouraging us to go faster. When we get home, I slip my hand out of his, missing his touch immediately. We kick our boots against the wall, knocking off the snow before going inside.

"I need to blow dry her," I say, glancing up at Mark. "Make yourself comfortable."

I definitely need a glass of wine this evening.

MARK

Tiny specks of snow spiral around Charlie and I in the dark. I glance sideways at her as we're walking back. The spotlight on the snowy path reflects just enough of a glow for me to see her profile. She licks her lips, unaware I'm watching.

I could drown in this woman. I want to haul her against me and never let her go.

She's having my babies.

Despite seeing them on the screen, despite the obvious changes in Charlie's body, it still seems unbelievable, like a beautiful dream. Part of it is the sheer unexpectedness. Because she'd been told she was infertile, neither of us ever thought our lovemaking might lead to pregnancy.

But now that I know, I can't picture anything else. In my mind, I see Charlie's belly growing heavy with our babies. I see her holding them skin to skin against her chest after giving birth, nursing them at home by the light of the fireplace, and lifting them up in the air, laughing.

God, I want that.

I want all of it.

When we get back, Charlie hooks a finger through Penny's collar. "I need to blow dry her."

I look down at Penny and grin. Water still drips in rivulets from her belly. Charlie sinks gracefully to the floor, guiding Penny onto a towel. I lean back against the counter to wait, admiring the view.

She moves the dryer with one hand, running the other through the dog's fur. As she leans closer to Penny, her hair sways, catching the light. Red and gold strands shimmer in her warm brown waves. Long lashes frame her gorgeous eyes, and her cheeks are still slightly pink from the cold. She bites her lip, concentrating, and she's absolutely breathtaking.

It takes several minutes to dry Penny's underside. When she's done, she braces one hand on the floor to push herself up, but I'm across the room and at her side in an instant.

It happens in a heartbeat.

Charlie takes my offered hand. Her left boot is planted on the tile, but her right one is on the towel. As she stands, the towel slips, and for one heart-stopping moment, I think she's going to fall. I grab her waist, pulling her against me. She inhales sharply, and her eyes widen.

But it's not desire she's feeling as her body presses against mine.

It's panic.

CHARLIE

I slipped.

Mark was helping me up, because getting to my feet after sitting cross-legged on the floor is ridiculously awkward now. As I stood, Penny's towel slid sideways. My right leg shot out, and I had a sudden horrible vision of performing an unplanned split in the middle of my kitchen. I panicked at the thought of falling and injuring my babies. But he caught me, his strong grip holding me securely.

He steadies me, releasing me only when I'm off the towel and on solid footing. I look up to thank him and stop at the look in his eyes.

Pain.

Without a word, he steps back, then turns and disappears into the living room.

I'm confused until it dawns on me that he's misread my fear of falling as fear of him.

Dammit.

When I pause in the doorway of the living room, he's on the couch with his head leaned back, pinching the bridge of his nose. I cross the room and sit down beside him.

"I told you, Mark, I'm not afraid of you."

He snorts. "That's not what your eyes said."

"I was scared, but not of you. I was falling, and I panicked. All I could think about was what would happen to the babies. But you caught me."

"I'll always catch you," he says, his voice soft. "Always."

"I want to believe you," I confess, my voice breaking.

"You can," he promises. "You can trust me."

I swallow hard. "You don't scare me, Mark. Your skewed self-image does. I'm afraid if I let you back in, your self-loathing will overpower whatever you feel for me again. And I'm afraid I won't survive you leaving again." I hesitate, meeting his eyes. "I barely survived the first time."

He studies me carefully before lifting a hand to cup my face. "Talk to me, Charlie. Tell me what happened. Please."

I shift toward him, trying to gauge whether or not hearing this is something he can handle. I don't want to make him feel guilty about things we've already settled, but at the same time, he needs to truly understand why I'm scared to trust him. I take a deep breath, organizing my thoughts. His hand drops from my face to take mine, warm and reassuring. "When you – when you left," I say haltingly, "I didn't cope very well. I couldn't sleep. I didn't eat. I drank. I drank a lot," I admit, looking down, "but just for a few weeks. I yelled at the walls and hit pillows and paced and cried and drank. I threw myself into working because I didn't want to be at home. Everywhere I looked, I saw you, and it hurt."

His expression turns guilty immediately. "I'm sorry."

I shake my head. "I'm not trying to make you feel bad. I forgive you. I just need you to understand my mindset at the time."

Disbelief rings in his voice. "You forgive me?"

The expression on his face softens my heart. "Yes, Mark. You apologized, and I forgive you."

"You can forgive that much pain? Just like that?"

I place my hand against his cheek, meeting his stunned eyes. "Yes. Just like that. And if I can forgive you, then you need to forgive yourself."

He pales. "I don't know if I can do that."

"I need you to. I can't spend my life terrified you're quietly loathing yourself and wishing you were dead. We have more important things to focus on than something we've already resolved."

"Resolved?" he asks, dumbfounded.

I nod firmly. "Yes. It's resolved. You made a decision – a series of decisions – because you thought it was best for me, even though it hurt you. We've agreed it wasn't good for either of us. You've apologized, I've forgiven you, and we're moving forward." I hold his gaze. "We can't change the past, but we can choose a new path, remember?"

"I – I –" He stares, too stunned to form coherent thoughts. "God, I love you." He hauls me against him and kisses me fiercely, his mouth needy, insistent, desperate. His tongue sweeps into my mouth, and I whimper as heat builds between us.

Too soon I pull back, placing a hand on his chest as we both catch our breath.

"I'm sorry," he apologizes.

I tilt my head. "For what?"

"I interrupted you."

I smile. "I rather enjoyed your interruption."

"I'll behave while I listen to what you need to say," he promises.

My smile fades. I look down at my hands and pause before glancing up uncertainly. "Sorry. This is difficult."

He takes both my hands, linking our fingers. "Take your time."

His calmness spreads to me, and I take a deep breath. "Well, like I said, I wasn't dealing with – life – very well. I was depressed, and I drank a lot, trying to forget. I started having problems with my stomach. It hurt whenever I ate, and I was vomiting a lot. I felt so awful that I quit drinking. I needed to quit, because it's a terrible coping mechanism," I add, "but giving up alcohol didn't help, and with no way to numb the pain, my depression got worse. Things…"

My voice trails off, and I stare into space. "Things got really dark for a while. I was in a bad place. My stomach hurt all the time. I couldn't eat, couldn't sleep. I looked... I looked bad. Lila made me call my doctor." I pause. "Most of the rest, you know. I had an ulcer. I was exhausted and malnourished. And pregnant," I add. "But I went back to Linda, too, because... because the emotional pain was dragging me under, and I knew I had to get help."

His eyes pin me. "That's what you meant when you said you understood about me wishing I'd died."

I swallow hard. "I wouldn't have committed suicide. I couldn't do that to the people who love me. But... but having that option taken from me as a way to escape my pain left me trapped in it." I squeeze his hands, hating myself for the broken look in his eyes. "I swear, I'm not trying to make you feel guilty, Mark. I told you, I understand why you made the choices you made, and I forgive you for leaving. I just need you to understand why I'm scared to death of you abandoning me again if I let you back in. I can't go through that again. I'm not strong enough."

"I love you, Baby Girl," he says, his voice a growl. "Leaving you was the biggest mistake of my life, and it's one I'll never repeat." His hands tighten around mine. "I barely survived losing you twice before – once to those bastards, and again to my stupidity. I wouldn't survive a third time. You own me, heart and soul. Without you –" He searches my face before whispering, "Without you, I have nothing."

The truth of his words settles in my soul, anchoring me. The tension that's been in the pit of my stomach for months melts away, because I know, *know*, Mark means it.

He won't leave me again.

My words pour out without hesitation. "I love you, Mark. I never stopped."

He hauls me close, his lips finding mine, firm, seeking, hungry. I thread my fingers through the curls at the nape of his neck, and he pulls me across his lap so I'm straddling him. His hardness presses against my core, and I groan.

A door closing upstairs reminds me we aren't alone, and I slide off Mark's lap and straighten my clothes as Stubbs thumps down the stairs, sticking his head in the living room. Mark tips his head toward him as though he and I have been discussing the weather. "You hungry, man? I brought enough food for all of us," he offers.

Stubbs grins. "I appreciate it, but –"

"Let me guess," I interrupt. "You're going to the VFW."

"Are you insinuating I'm predictable?" he teases. "I'll have you know you're only partially right. I'm going to an amputee support group meeting first, then having dinner with someone."

I straighten up. "Really? Who?"

He laughs. "Let's see how dinner goes first." He whistles as he pulls on a jacket, jingling his keys as he waves. "See you later, Green Eyes. You too, Pretty Boy."

Mark turns to me and opens his mouth to speak when my stomach growls like a Kodiak grizzly, and he chuckles. "Hungry?"

"Apparently," I mutter, my cheeks growing warm.

"Good thing. I brought enough Italian food for an army."

My face lights up, all embarrassment forgotten. "Italian food? Why is this the first I've heard about it?"

He grins. "Should I be concerned at your overwhelming excitement for pasta?"

"You're exciting, too," I assure him with a grin. "I seem to recall devouring you until Stubbs came downstairs. This is your fault for tempting me with Italian food."

He laughs, getting to his feet and pulling me up into his arms. "I'll try not to be jealous of your obsession with pasta."

Mark loves me. He's loved me all along.

Maybe my life will end up like one of those sappy romantic movies after all.

MARK

On the outside, I'm calmly pulling out still-hot pans of pasta and garlic bread from the steaming insulated bag, but on the inside, I'm turning backflips, torn between outright shock and overwhelming ecstasy.

Charlie still loves me.

I can't believe it, after everything I put her through.

She's incredible.

While I open the wine and set out pans of food, Charlie pours ice water and lights candles. Then she pulls out her phone and puts on music while I collect plates, bowls, and flatware.

She still loves me. I'm grinning like a fool, and I don't care.

We each pile an assortment of food on our plates. I see chicken parm, broccoli alfredo, and spinach-stuffed meatballs in marinara on her plate, along with her favorite cheesy garlic bread and salad. I'm having the same, plus a cup of Italian wedding soup, and we each have a glass of white wine, though Charlie's only taken a few sips of hers.

"Not a fan of the wine?"

"I'm limiting my consumption." She grins and gestures to her plate. "Don't worry. The same won't be said for my appetite."

I can't take my eyes off her during dinner. She's so beautiful, it almost hurts to look at her. She licks alfredo sauce from her lips, and my body tightens.

Not yet.

After dinner, I clear the table and send her to relax by the fire with her wine. "You invited me. I'm doing the dishes."

"Technically, you invited yourself, and you bought dinner," she protests.

"Irrelevant." I wave her away. "Go relax."

She smiles and goes into the living room. From the sink, I watch her gather throw pillows and settle comfortably on the floor facing the fireplace. Penny curls up in front of Charlie, her head draped across Charlie's lap.

When I've started the dishwasher and put leftovers away, I join her, bringing my glass of wine. We sit cross-legged on the floor, listening to the hiss of the fireplace and the sound of the wind outside. She stares into the fire, a faraway look in her eyes.

I reach over and brush a lock of her silky hair behind her ear. "Penny for your thoughts?" Two brown eyes open, gazing up sleepily at me from Charlie's lap. I chuckle and rub the dog's head, and she stretches before getting up and padding across the room to flop in front of the couch.

"I'm afraid this is all too good to be true," Charlie says quietly.

"What do you mean?"

"You. Us. Babies."

I study her face. She looks nervous again. "I still don't understand exactly how it happened," I admit. "The pregnancy, I mean. The doctors at Walter Reed said there was too much scarring. I was there. They said it was impossible."

She nods. "Dr. Oaks called them miracle babies."

I close my eyes as my heart stutters. "Miracles," I agree, and when I open my eyes, she still looks nervous. "After all we've been through, I think you and I deserve a couple of miracles."

Without warning, Charlie starts to cry, and my heart lurches in my chest. "What's wrong?" Has she changed her mind about me? About us? "Don't cry, Charlie. Talk to me."

"Promise me you aren't here just because of them. Promise me," she sobs, and my heart breaks.

I wipe away her tears before tipping her face up to mine. "I'd decided I'd do whatever it took to win you back before I ever knew you were pregnant, Charlie. Ask Tucker and Lila. They can confirm it, because I'd already told them. Even if you weren't pregnant, if it were just you and me and Penny, there's nowhere else I'd rather be. You're the one who gives my life meaning." I wipe her tears again before kissing her tenderly. "I love you."

She watches me when I pull back. "You're happy? Really happy?"

I kiss her again, longer this time, then murmur, "Baby Girl, I've never been happier."

Her tears start to flow again, but they're happy tears, and she laughs and then hiccups. I reach for her belly, cupping it in my hands, and feel firm bumping beneath my fingertips. I stare at her stomach, riveted by the magic of the moment. When the tiny kicks stop, I press my face to her belly. Charlie wraps her arms around me, and we stay that way for a long time, just me, the woman I love, and our unborn babies.

CHAPTER TWENTY-SIX

MARK

Dr. Oaks is right – this is nothing short of miraculous. I stretch out beside Charlie in front of the fire, tucking one of the throw pillows under my head. My eyes travel down her body, lingering, taking it all in. Her shirt clings to her breasts – which look even more full than before – before flaring out over her belly. Black leggings hug her long legs. I smile when I notice her thick cream-colored socks patterned with dozens of tiny brown sock monkeys.

God, I love this woman.

The only thing that would make this moment any better is to make her mine forever.

But I can't ask her to marry me.

I want to. There's nothing I want more. But Charlie would turn down my proposal. She isn't secure in my feelings for her yet, and until she is, she'd see a proposal as an attempt to do the honorable thing by our children. But honor has nothing to do with why I want to marry Charlie. I love her, and I don't want to spend another moment apart from her.

But because I spent months with my head up my ass, positive I was right and everyone else was wrong, marriage isn't an option. I didn't just fuck up our past relationship – I fucked up our future, too.

I'll damn sure keep working on regaining her trust. I refuse to give up. Maybe in time, she'll realize the depth of my feelings for her and understand that I'll take her any way I can get her. I hope so. In the meantime, I'll do everything I can to prove I love her more than life itself.

If only I hadn't been such a fool.

A chill has fallen over the room, and Charlie hugs her arms to her chest. I tug a fuzzy red throw blanket from one of the couches over us, shielding us from the cool air radiating off the snowy windows. I lie facing her, my left hand bracing my head, my right one resting protectively on her belly. She smiles briefly before it fades, leaving a worried expression in its place.

"Not to kill the mood or anything, but can we talk about last week?"

I lean over and press a soft kiss to her lips. "If you'll stop looking so nervous." She relaxes then, smiling slightly. "Ask me anything," I say, giving her my full attention.

She studies my face. "Why did you shut down on me after the ultrasound?"

I take a slow breath. "I was overwhelmed," I confess. "I've never had a baby. I've never even held one. I don't know how to change diapers. I don't know what to do when they cry. I'm completely clueless."

"Wanna know a secret?" Charlie crooks her finger toward me, motioning me closer. I lean forward, and she whispers into my ear, "I am, too." Her hot breath sends tingles racing down my spine. She leans back and winks. "But making them was supposed to be impossible, and we managed that. I'm betting we can figure this out together, too."

I grin. "Interesting logic." After a moment, my humor fades. "But they won't always be babies, Charlie. They grow into toddlers. They get into things. What if they get hurt?"

She raises an eyebrow. "All kids get hurt, Mark. That's part of life."

My anxious rant picks up speed, my stress increasing exponentially. "Then they go from toddlers to preschoolers to elementary school. What if they have to deal with bullies? I don't think I can handle that."

Charlie grins. "You dealt with Corbin Holmes just fine. He never bothered me again."

I snort. "We were kids. I can't go around beating up little kids now."

She purses her lips thoughtfully. "I don't know. You're pretty tough. I'd put my money on you against any ten-year-old bully."

I glower. "Be serious. What about when they're teenagers, with all those raging hormones? Girlfriends and boyfriends and breakups and proms?"

Charlie lays a hand on my chest. "Relax, Mark. You and I have dealt with all those things before. It's going to be fine."

"How can you be so calm?" I ask, a hint of hysteria leaking into my voice.

She struggles into a sitting position before I can help her, shifting to sit cross-legged. "Well, we have two choices. We can take this time before they arrive to prepare, or we can work ourselves into a lather over it. The babies are coming either way." She eyes me with an amused expression. "Since you seem to have the panic option covered, I thought I'd take on the role of calm, collected adult."

And just like that, my hysteria deflates.

Charlie pulls the blanket over her lap. "I've been reading mommy blogs, and I picked up a couple of parenting books they recommended. We can read them together if you like."

I stare at her. "What the hell is a mommy blog?"

She laughs. "Exactly what it sounds like. Blogs written by moms, describing their daily lives and how they deal with things like – I don't know, babies not sleeping at night or potty training or whatever."

I blink. That's another worry to add to my list. Potty training.

Apparently I've said that out loud, because Charlie laughs again. "Yes, potty training. And it's a good thing, unless you want to be changing diapers forever."

I rub my hand through my hair. "I guess."

"Think of this as a mission," she encourages me. "You can plan missions in your sleep. We've got four months to get ready. Assess our needs. Look at our resources. What do we have? What do we need? Come on, Big Guy. We've got this."

She called me Big Guy again.

"Okay," I say, feeling my insides relax. "You're right. They're not showing up unannounced. We've got time to get ready. We can do this."

"That's the spirit." She studies me. "So is that what was bothering you?"

My stomach immediately tightens again. "Part of it."

She waits. When I don't speak, she raises an eyebrow. "And the other part?"

I sigh. "I talked to Dr. Allen about being worried about being a father, so of course, he asked about my dad." She nods. "The thing is, after the ultrasound, I got – well – really angry at my dad." I meet her eyes. She doesn't say anything, but she lays her hand on mine.

"It's stupid," I continue. "He's been dead for twenty years. Why get mad now? All these years, I felt like I could understand why he'd killed himself. I blamed the cancer for wrecking everything. But when I saw our babies..." I exhale heavily. "They aren't even born, and there's nothing I wouldn't do for them. And I got pissed because my dad didn't feel the same way." Charlie slips her fingers inside my fisted hands, and I loosen my grip instantly, locking eyes with her. "My dad abandoned me. Dr. Allen pointed out that he did it twice, once when he left me to deal with mom's cancer on my own, and again when he committed suicide." I drop my gaze in shame. "And I abandoned you, too. I'm no better than he was."

Small fingers tighten around mine. "Stop," she says firmly. "That's been resolved. We can't change the past, but we can choose our path."

I swallow. "I let my inner emotional bullshit spill out and hurt you. I can't let that happen again. Not to you, and certainly not to our kids. You were right all along. All of you were right. I have to accept myself, all of me, the parts I like and the parts I don't."

Charlie's eyes shoot to mine. "Do you mean that?"

I nod slowly. "I mean it, but... I don't know how to do it."

She tilts her head to one side. "Do you have a negative voice inside your head that whispers mean things to you? Awful things, things you'd never say to someone else?"

I examine her expression, trying to decide if she's teasing. "Are you asking if I hear voices in my head telling me to do bad things?"

She laughs. "No, but if you do, we should probably discuss it. I mean a toxic voice." She pauses. "I have one. Everyone does, I think. Mine tells me I'm too broken for anyone to love."

I bolt upright, startling her as I grip her shoulders. "That's not true," I say fiercely. "You can't believe that."

Memories of the night I told her that people who are scarred and broken don't deserve love fill my mind. I can still see the pain in her gorgeous eyes, the tears she fought to hold back. I wasn't talking about her – I was talking about myself, about not deserving her love. But I unintentionally gave voice to the words she'd believed about herself.

She nods. "I know it's not true. Well, I know it now," she amends. "But even though I know, when I'm vulnerable, when I'm overly tired or having a string of bad days, that toxic voice still whispers to me. The only way to defeat it is by speaking truth. Not out loud," she adds quickly, smiling. "Not in public, anyway. When my toxic voice says I'm too broken for anyone to love, I insist I'm worthy, that I am loved." I watch as she tilts her head again, studying me. "Your voice tells you that you're a useless cripple, that you're half a man. You've listened to its lies for a year. It's time to kill your toxic voice."

I give her a skeptical glance. "You want me to kill an imaginary voice in my head."

She grins. "Yep. And you kill it with kindness."

I drop my head and groan. "Seriously?"

She ignores me. "The goal is to interrupt it before it completes the thought. As soon as it starts in, you tell it that you are loved. You tell it your value is determined by your heart, not your body. You tell it you deserve love and happiness. You turn it into a mantra."

I scowl, but then realize she's describing the same exercise Dr. Allen assigned me. Telling myself, "Negative thinking isn't productive," every time I start mentally berating myself is the exact technique she's describing.

I purse my lips. "I'm actually doing something similar already," I admit, and explain how I've been instructed to respond to the hypercritical voice in my head.

She nods. "That's it. You already know what to do. You just have to adjust the response based on what it's saying. 'Negative thinking isn't productive,' is perfect for you beating yourself up about the past, about things you can't change. Now you need to add a new response for your negative self-image chatter. Keep it short and easy to remember. How about, 'I am worthy'? Or, 'My tribe loves me', or 'I am valued'? Do any of those resonate with you?"

Not really. But maybe I can create my own. "How about, 'I have a purpose'?"

She eyes me thoughtfully. "As long as it's strong enough to stop your negative chatter."

I take her hands in mine. "I'm sorry I shut you out the other day. I didn't mean to. Maybe... maybe you can help me not do that in the future?"

"Tell me what you want me to do," she says immediately.

I pause, and then it hits me. "Your safe word. Tell me your safe word if the way I'm behaving makes you uncomfortable. That'll get my attention."

Her brows furrow. "You mean daffodil?"

I nod. "We used it before, when we were doing things that might be challenging for you," I remind her.

She raises an eyebrow. "Yeah, but not for talking."

"Uncomfortable is uncomfortable. If what I'm saying or doing is bothering you, tell me. You can call me out if you prefer, but if you're worried I'll get defensive, use your safe word." I brush a lock of hair out of her face, lingering against her soft skin. "I don't ever want you to be uncomfortable around me again, Charlie."

She leans forward and kisses me, and when I go home a long time later, the only discomfort I'm feeling is the uncomfortable tightness in my jeans. The rest of me is floating on cloud nine.

Charlie still loves me.

CHARLIE

The next few weeks are the most magical of my entire life. Mark and I were best friends for more than two decades, but we're learning things about each other we never knew before.

We reconnect in a way I'd never have believed possible, working through hurt feelings and clearing up misunderstandings and misconceptions. I tell him secrets I'd planned to take to my grave, like how dark things really got for me after Afghanistan while he was still overseas. He shares in kind, letting me into the shadowy recesses of his mind, telling me his deepest fears and darkest thoughts. We talk about missing his mom, his dad, and my parents. We discuss the military – the pain, the sadness, the bonds, the fulfillment. Except for my time at work, we only leave the house for groceries, appointments, or long walks with Penny. We spend our time cocooned in honeymoon-like bliss, talking, laughing, and curled up together.

Thursday afternoon, I'm at his apartment, nestled into his side on the loveseat. We've just gotten back from my appointment with the obstetrician, where Mark was extremely attentive, asking her lots of questions about what I needed and how he could help. Unlike the last time he went to an appointment with me, this time, he talks the entire way back from Pueblo. He's decided to get the guys to help him move all of his rehab equipment from my office-turned-weight-room into the garage so he can turn that room into a nursery.

My heart is so full, it hurts.

"I have something for you," Mark says, reaching into the pocket of his jeans. A moment later, he presses something warm and metal into my hand.

"A key?"

He smiles. "Not that I think you'll want to spend a lot of time here," he says, gesturing to the plaid couch with its eunuch-spring, "but you're welcome anytime."

I pull his head down to mine and kiss him. When I let go, he captures me in a second, longer kiss. I sigh when he lifts his head. "I'm kind of here now all the time anyway," I tease.

When he and I talked about coming up with a mantra to combat his toxic negative thoughts, he'd mentioned having a purpose. Apparently, that wasn't a strong enough phrase. A couple of days later, he'd shown up and taken a ridiculous number of pictures of me, as well as borrowed my old photo album and our ultrasound pictures of the babies.

Only today did I learn why.

Mark's entire apartment is covered with pictures of me. Pictures of us as kids, in the military, me alone, us together. Old pictures, current pictures, our ultrasound pictures – they're everywhere, hung on the walls with poster putty, and they all have the same caption: **SHE LOVES ME AS I AM**, neatly written in black permanent ink.

He was worried I didn't like it when I saw what he'd done and burst into tears. Only when I threw my arms around his neck and whispered that I loved him did he relax and wrap his arms around me.

"I like having you with me all the time," he murmurs. "That's where you belong."

"If only there weren't pesky things like work and appointments," I agree. At that, he lifts his wrist to check his watch. "Is it time? Do you have to go?"

"In a minute," he says, then pulls me onto his lap, facing him.

I grin. "It seems like we used to fit better." I look down. At twenty-five weeks pregnant, I appear to have a basketball beneath my shirt, wedging us apart.

He smiles slowly. "I suspect certain parts still fit just fine," he murmurs, cupping my face in his hands and kissing me until we're both panting.

"Two more days, and we'll have my house to ourselves," I promise.

Because Stubbs is moving out in two days – on Mark's birthday, no less. We're all going to help him move into his new apartment and go out to dinner together in honor of his new place and Mark's birthday. After that, Mark's coming home with me. I've already asked him to spend the night because I miss waking up next to him.

He kisses me again before lightly swatting my rump. "You're going to make me late if you keep looking at me like that." He eases me off his lap, then stands and pulls me to my feet before wrapping me in my coat and kissing me again.

I smile to myself all the way home. Life is good.

MARK

The steakhouse is packed, but Tucker (of course) has managed to reserve us a private room in the back. The service is good, the food is excellent, and the company is exceptional. Lila and Tucker look cozier than I've seen them look in some time. Tom presents both Stubbs and me with resealable plastic containers. "Maya and Skyler made you both cookies," he says.

Stubbs makes a chef's kiss motion. "Tell them they were fan-tas-tique."

Tom grins. "Have you had cookies baked by eleven-year-old girls before?"

Stubbs frowns. "I don't think so."

Tom's grin widens. "I hope you like pink."

I peel up the lid of my container and blink at the blinding contents. "That's a lot of pink."

Charlie takes it from me and peeks inside. "Sugar cookies?" She glances at Tom, who nods. "With pastel royal icing and hot pink sugar sprinkles. Ooh, and edible pearl candies. Tell them I stole most of Mark's cookies." She glances at me. "If you're good, I might let you have one."

I lean close so only she can hear me. "Oh, trust me, I'll be very, very good."

When I lean back, she's the same shade as the sugar sprinkles.

Moving Stubbs to his new apartment didn't take very long at all. With Stubbs, Tom, Tucker, and myself carrying in furniture and boxes and Lila and Charlie unpacking his kitchen and setting up his bedroom, we were done by midafternoon. I stopped by my crappy little apartment to shower and pack an overnight bag. Then I headed to Charlie's, where we took Penny for a long walk. I listened to some music in her living room while she showered and got ready for dinner. When she came out, my cock thrummed in anticipation.

Damn.

Charlie was dressed in some sexy little wraparound dress the same exact color as her eyes. The soft fabric hugged her full breasts and perfect ass and clung to that amazing baby belly. Black leather knee-high boots showed off shapely legs. Her thick hair cascaded over her shoulders in silky curls, and as I gawked at her in open admiration, she'd bitten her plump lower lip. "Do I look okay?" she'd asked.

I'd wanted to rip her clothes off and show her just how fucking gorgeous I thought she was. Instead, I'd shaken my head. "You've never looked more beautiful," I'd answered honestly, and she'd beamed even as her cheeks grew pink.

She's had her hand on my thigh all through dinner, and though I love these people, I can barely concentrate on the conversation. All I can think about is getting Charlie home alone.

I receive birthday cards from everyone, with gift cards to local restaurants and one for the movie theater (courtesy of Tom and Maya). Stubbs receives several gift cards as well for housewarming gifts. I'm trying to find a polite way to excuse myself and Charlie so we can escape when Tucker clinks his wineglass with his knife.

"I'd like to propose a toast," he announces, and everyone stops talking and turns to him. "Family isn't just the group you're born into. Family is about love, and friendship, and having each others' backs. It's about being there through thick and thin. It's about knowing who you can trust, who will be there when the chips are down. And each and every one of you –" Tucker pauses, making eye contact with each of us in turn "– are family. I love you guys."

"Here, here," says Stubbs, raising his glass, and the sentiment echoes around the table as we clink glasses.

"To family," I agree, and Charlie repeats, "To family."

I'm glad Charlie drives us home, because snow is falling, and I'm in too much of a hurry to get there. It seems to take an eternity before we're parked in her driveway. I wrap my arm around her, taking the key from her to unlock the house. When we get inside, I peel her coat off her and have her pressed against the front door with my lips on hers in seconds. I reluctantly pull away at the sound of pawing and scratching below me.

Penny apparently needs to go out.

I kiss Charlie again, murmuring against her lips, "I'll take her. You stay here." When I start to straighten up, she grabs the front of my jacket and drags me back.

"Hurry back. I have something for you to unwrap."

"You can count on it."

CHARLIE

Mark steps back from me, straightening his black leather jacket, and my mouth dries as I study him.

Dear God, he looks good.

His jeans hug his lean body perfectly, and he's wearing my favorite shirt, a deep blue that contrasts against his pale blue eyes. His sandy hair curls slightly at his nape, long enough to tangle my fingers in when we kiss. His jaw is shadowed with soft stubble, and I remember its tickle along my neck.

And my inner thighs.

It's been so long.

Too long.

No more waiting.

I'm all in – heart, soul, and body.

When he's safely outside with Penny, I remove my boots. Then I brush my teeth, check my hair, and dim the lights in my bedroom.

We've waited long enough.

CHAPTER TWENTY-SEVEN

MARK

PENNY SCRAMBLES AHEAD OF me to the back door, dashing into the yard as soon as I open it. While she takes care of business, I'm thinking about Charlie, about kissing her all over, tasting every inch of her, and burying myself deep inside her until she screams my name.

Then I frown. I've never had sex with a pregnant woman. Is that even allowed? I mean, I'm pretty sure it is, but there's probably a few things I need to know.

Thank God for the internet. I lean on the wall beside the door, browsing webpages on my phone while I wait for Penny to finish.

I learn that the missionary position is limited because women in mid-to-late stages of pregnancy can't lie flat on their back for more than ten minutes or so at a time. However, a simple shift to one side or the other will relieve the pressure the uterus puts on the large blood vessels in their abdomen. There's lots of information about pillows – where and how to place them and why. One article says pregnant women are often multiorgasmic because of increased blood flow to the pelvis and elevated hormone levels, a theory I'm hoping to test. I'm scrolling through one site with cartoonish illustrations of the best sex positions during pregnancy when the door opens and I nearly drop my phone.

Charlie's eyes zero in on the screen before looking to mine.

I'm totally busted. "I, uh –"

That's it. That's all I can come up with.

Her lips twitch. "Researching for academic purposes?"

"I was waiting for Penny."

She raises an eyebrow, looking pointedly at the dog currently lying atop my boots.

I study Charlie's face. She doesn't look upset, merely amused. "Is there any answer I can give that won't get me in trouble here?"

She smiles. "Get in here before you both freeze."

I push off the wall. "I've been researching for academic purposes. I've found a few ways we can keep warm."

She laughs and pulls me inside, locking the door before turning to me. Emerald eyes meet mine boldly. "Then get over here and show me what you've learned."

My cock twitches as I drink in the sight of the goddess before me. I widen my stance and pull her close, smiling as her rounded belly pushes against me. I dip my head toward hers, stopping just above her soft lips. Charlie closes her eyes and sighs.

"You're sure about this?" My voice is low, needy.

"Positive," she whispers.

She stretches up on tiptoe to kiss me, her hands sliding up my chest to clutch my shoulders. I lean in, my lips capturing hers again and again. One of my hands leaves her waist, slipping into her hair to cradle her head. My tongue slides across her lips, and she opens for me immediately. I taste her, sweet as honey, exploring the depths of her mouth, and she does the same, arching up against me with a soft whimper. My body tightens in response, remembering past whimpers. Moans. Cries.

"You taste so good," I whisper against her lips. My hand moves to her ribs, stopping there, but Charlie tugs my hand higher, pressing it firmly against her breast, and I growl with pleasure.

Her fevered response fires my blood. I scoop her into my arms, carrying her to the bedroom without breaking the kiss, depositing her carefully on the large bed. She scoots to the center, watching in anticipation. I carefully remove my boots and socks. My confidence wavers when my prosthetic foot is exposed.

"Please," she whispers, reaching for me, drowning out my insecurities with a single word. I kneel beside her, cupping her face as I devour her mouth. Her fingers memorize my face before twisting in my hair. I move to her neck, trailing steamy kisses down to her collarbone. She tilts her head to give me better access, gasping when I find the hollow of her neck. I kiss and nuzzle my way back up her neck, rubbing my stubble over her soft flesh, and she moans. She reaches for the side tie on her dress, but I stop her with a quick nip of her lip.

"Let me."

"You're taking too long," she complains against my mouth, reaching for my hands.

I shake my head and smile before untying her dress. I peel it open slowly, one inch at a time, pausing to lave her creamy flesh as I expose it. I skip over her breasts, instead kissing her belly, from just beneath her bra to the top of her lacy panties. She groans and reaches for my shirt. I take her hand to move it, but she swats me away. "Let me," she replies cheekily, pushing herself upright and racing through the buttons. She slides her hands up my chest and shoves the shirt off my shoulders. "Please. I need you."

With her dress lying open on the bed behind her, I cup her breasts, feeling their weight in my hands. She arches forward against my palms, her eyes drifting closed. Her nipples harden beneath the lace of her bra. I slip my thumbs inside the cups, brushing over her nipples, teasing them, and she moans and unhooks the front clasp of her bra. Her breasts tumble free, ripe and lush, begging to be tasted. I toss her bra somewhere behind me before easing her down onto the bed, tucking a pillow behind her hip so she's not flat on her back. My mouth claims one of her nipples while my hand teases its twin, sucking, squeezing, caressing. I alternate the pressure and intensity, listening as her breathing gets faster and more erratic. She bucks her hips, seeking friction, and I push my thigh between her legs, sucking one nipple as I tug at the other, continuing my relentless assault. She grinds against me, whimpering, and my jeans grow uncomfortably tight. She wraps her arms around my neck, pulling me chest to chest, skin to skin.

It's been so long. Too long, and that's my own damn fault. It's different, too. Her breasts have gotten more full, her nipples darker. And her belly – my God, that beautiful pregnant belly. It's so sensual. I'm hit by a primal desire to stake my claim, caveman-style.

Charlie turns her head as my teeth graze her jawline, her lips seeking mine, insistent, demanding. I grip her hips, drawing her closer. She wraps a leg around my waist, pulling me against her core, and my cock surges against her in response. "Yes," she moans. My tongue delves deep into her mouth, and she meets me stroke for stroke, her hands digging into the muscles of my back. She rolls her hips against me, whimpering with need.

My fingers tighten on her hips. My control is tenuous at best right now, and Charlie's responsiveness is making it even more challenging. I move one hand from her hip to caress her swollen belly, but Charlie grabs my wrist and instead guides my hand beneath the waistband of her panties. My hand brushes over her mound, and she sucks in a breath and rolls her hips again. I slide my fingers into her silken folds, groaning when I feel how wet she is, how ready. She moans as my fingers curl and thrust inside her and my thumb rubs slow circles around her clit. Her breathing grows more rapid as I adjust the pace and pressure, watching her respond to my touch. Her hips move against my hand, and as her movements become more frantic, I lower my head to her breast and lightly bite her nipple. She clutches my shoulder, gasping, as my fingers fill and stroke her heated flesh until she cries out. The sight of her coming, biting her lip, her cheeks flushed and her head thrown back, nearly makes me join her. My cock aches to be inside her, feeling her heat surround me, pulling me in.

Not yet.

She's still panting when I kneel above her, peeling her lacy panties down her body, kissing my way from her thighs down to her ankles. I sit back and survey her from this angle, naked and gorgeous. Lush curves, soft skin, eyes I could drown in, legs for days.

Legs I plan to have around me in the very near future.

"You're wearing too many clothes." She's raised up on her elbows, watching me memorize her body.

"Just enjoying the view," I murmur, then slowly lick and kiss my way back up her legs, pausing occasionally to nibble her soft flesh and graze it with my stubble. Charlie moans and whimpers, writhing before I reach the sweet nectar at the apex of her thighs.

I pause, guiding her legs over my shoulders. "Easy, Baby Girl. I want to savor you all night."

Then I taste her, all of her, lapping her sweet juices, sucking and licking, pushing my face into her folds, driving my tongue so deep into her that her entire body trembles. I take her to the edge twice, backing off both times, until she clutches my hair and moans.

"Please, Mark."

I give her what she needs, sucking and swirling my tongue, my face buried in her. She climaxes with a scream, her thighs clamped tight around me, her hands fisted in my hair.

So. Fucking. Hot.

When her thighs finally stop shaking, I crawl up her body, hovering above her. She pulls my face to hers, kissing me fiercely before raising up on an elbow and pushing me to my back. She sets my body on fire with her touch, her lips leaving a blazing trail as she scorches her way down my body. She strokes me through my jeans, and my cock surges almost painfully against the denim as though reaching for her.

"I want you inside me, Mark. I need you inside me." Her voice is barely a whisper, but it reverberates through my head like a shout.

My inner Boy Scout starts kicking me for my lack of preparedness.

It's not exactly a quick process to remove jeans with a prosthetic leg. I sit up and scoot to the edge of the bed, then pull the allen wrench from my back pocket before unbuttoning and unzipping. I push my jeans and boxers below my knees before disconnecting my prosthesis. Then I shuck my clothes and tug the prosthetic free from the jeans before glancing over my shoulder at her.

"Prosthetic on or off?"

She looks at me like I've lost my mind. "I don't care. However you're comfortable."

Right.

I grab the allen wrench, reattach the prosthesis as fast as my fumbling fingers will move, and make a mental note to wear shorts or sweatpants for easier removal for the foreseeable future.

I rejoin her on the bed. "Where were we?"

She smiles and shifts further onto her side, raising up on one elbow and sliding her small hand behind my neck, pulling my face to hers. "You were right about here," she murmurs against my mouth. Lazy, gentle kisses quickly turn urgent. Her hands explore my body, reacquainting herself with my chest, shoulders, and back, skimming over my lower abdomen before reaching for my cock. I groan when she strokes my length. She does it again, and I reach for her wrist as my body surges toward her. I'm too close, right on the edge.

"Give me a minute," I say, my voice ragged.

"We have all night, remember?"

"Not if you keep that up." Instead I lean in, kissing her deeply until she whimpers again.

I wrap my arms around her and roll onto my back, pulling her on top of me. She gasps in surprise, her hands gripping my shoulders. I arch my hips up. "You take me."

Her eyes fly to mine. "Why?"

"Because I need to know you're sure about this. About us."

She doesn't hesitate. She leans over me, kissing me, her full breasts barely caressing my chest as her firmly rounded belly nudges my abs. When she straddles me, I steady her with my hands on her hips, bending my knees behind her for support and balance. She lifts her hips slightly, holding my gaze as she reaches between us to grasp me. When she lowers herself slowly onto my length, I groan with pleasure.

It's like being gripped with a wet silk glove. She begins to move, her damp heat wrapping around me, squeezing as she gradually takes me in deeper. My hands cup her breasts, kneading them, rolling her taut nipples between my fingers as she moans. She picks up speed, her breasts bouncing splendidly. I grip her hips to slow her as my control begins to slip.

"No," Charlie says. "No more control. Just feel."

I slide a hand between us to stroke her clit as she rides me harder, her moans coming faster.

I'm so close to losing it. I arch upward when she comes down, grinding against her. Charlie's on the edge too, biting her lip, crying out as she moves faster. The tension within my pelvis builds, starting to spread outward. I fight to hold out longer. I grip her thighs, surging against her, rolling my hips with each thrust.

When her body spasms and tightens around me, I let go, pulsing deep within her, lost in the most intense orgasm of my life. Her body squeezes me, milking me dry as she cries out my name and I growl hers. She collapses above me, both of us glistening with sweat, sated and happy.

When we can both breathe again, I tilt her face up to mine and claim her lips in a slow, tender kiss, pouring into it all the emotions I don't have words for. When she brings one hand up to cup my face and gaze at me with those gorgeous emerald eyes, I know she understands.

God, I love this woman.

CHARLIE

I'm sprawled half on top of Mark, as boneless as a jellyfish. My God. The things that man can do with his body.

The things he can do with *my* body.

My face presses into his chest as I listen to the rapid pounding of his heart slow to a steady drumming. Long fingers trail slowly up and down my spine. I trace absent circles on his ribs. Our bodies, our hearts, are completely in tune for the first time in months, and it's incredible.

A loud growl from my stomach shatters the mood.

Mark's chest rumbles beneath me as he chuckles. "Sorry," I mutter, my face growing hot.

He reaches beneath my chin and tilts my face to look up at him. He's grinning, his pale blue eyes playful in the lamplight. "For what? Growing two humans takes a lot of energy. Besides, we've just burned off all of your calories from dinner." He plants a soft kiss on my lips, then a longer one before lightly smacking my ass. "Come on. Let's go feed the Tiny People."

Mark watches in amusement as I eat rice, green beans, and leftover chicken and dumplings, courtesy of Stubbs' grandmother's recipe. "Quite the late-night snack."

"I worked up an appetite."

His eyes lock on my mouth as I lick my lips. "You're certainly working up mine."

Heat immediately sizzles between my thighs.

I'm rinsing my dishes when he approaches from behind, sweeping my hair to the side and nuzzling my neck. "I think we should christen your upstairs tub."

We spend hours soaking in my garden tub until we're way past pruny. He's changed to his shower prosthetic, leaning against the wall of the tub. I'm nestled between his thighs, my back to his chest, his arms curled protectively around my belly. We add hot water as needed, laying in each others' arms as we discuss the past few months. I mostly listen, because until I found out I was pregnant, my life after Mark was a gray blur of alcohol, depression, and pain. He describes the Pink-Haired Predator who served his papers and his ensuing discussion with Tucker and Lila. He tells me about his discussions with Dr. Allen and things he's learning about himself. He talks about his career options and how they would affect our family life, because we have a future together, even if neither of us has said it out loud. I don't know what it looks like, but I know that no matter what my future holds, this man will be in it.

"Have you ever said 'I love you' before? Romantically?" he asks me suddenly.

"To you," I say with a raised eyebrow.

"To anyone else, I mean. Have you ever been in love with anyone else?"

The sudden shift in topics confuses me. "No. They guys I dated in high school and college were mostly just interested in sex, and the ones I went out with in the military weren't much better." I hesitate. "To be honest, whatever guy I was seeing... you were the yardstick I always measured them against. And if they didn't treat me as well as you treated me, then they weren't worth my time or my heart, and I'd end things. I wasn't going to settle for anything less."

He swallows hard, and I know he's uncomfortably remembering how he's treated me over the past few months.

"What about you? Have you ever loved someone?"

"Once," he says slowly. "I didn't tell her how I felt, though."

"Why?"

"I was afraid."

"Of what?"

"That she didn't feel the same."

I have a hot, unreasonable flare of jealousy. Why is he sitting naked in a bathtub with me, talking about some other woman he was in love with? The conversation stalls as my mood sinks.

I've just decided to get out of the tub when Mark speaks. "I've slipped and called you Baby Girl on accident a few more times. I'm sorry. I know you asked me not to."

I glance back at him. "It's okay. You did it when you were telling me you loved me. It doesn't hurt now because I feel like I matter again."

"You asked me once why I started calling you Baby Girl."

"Yes. And you wouldn't tell me. You said it was classified." I roll my eyes.

He rests his chin on my shoulder. "Do you still want to know?"

I whip my head toward him. "Really?"

He chuckles at my excitement, and a soft smile crosses his face as he tightens his arms around my waist. "We were teenagers. You were fourteen and a freshman. I was sixteen and a junior. You were having trouble with algebra and I started helping you with it in the afternoons."

"I know this part, Mark – I was there," I remind him impatiently.

"You don't know the half of it," he counters, his voice gentle. "I'd sit there, day after day, with you in your strappy little camisoles and your short denim shorts, your dark hair hanging down to your waist. I'd sit close so I could smell your shampoo and watch you bite your lower lip when you were struggling with the equations."

My brain stutters to a stop. *Wait. What?*

"I was crazy about you, Charlie. I fell for you, and I fell hard. There was a song from a couple of years earlier... 'I'll Be,' by Edwin McCain. It was about a guy who was captivated by a woman with emerald eyes, knowing he belonged with her. Every time I heard it, you were all I could think of."

Goosebumps start at my scalp and travel down my entire body.

"I was hopelessly in love with you, Charlie. You were the girl I loved but never told."

"Why?" I whisper.

"Because you were fourteen, and your parents might have freaked out with us living under the same roof. And if I'd told you and you didn't feel the same, I'd have been devastated. You're the only one I've ever loved, and I told you the only way I could. I started calling you Baby Girl. It was my way of telling you I loved you without saying the words." He pauses, pressing his lips against my neck. "And every time I've ever called you Baby Girl, it was an 'I love you'."

I realize I've started to cry at the same time he does.

"Please don't cry, Charlie."

"I never knew."

"You weren't meant to. I hid it. I have a bad habit of hiding my deepest feelings from the ones I should share them with. It's a habit I'm trying very, very hard to change."

He's loved me all along.

I never knew why he called me Baby Girl, but suddenly, specific times he's called me that pop into my head.

When he rescued me out of that cell in Afghanistan, he called me Baby Girl, over and over.

When I was emotionally broken in Walter Reed, and he flew stateside to be with me, he called me Baby Girl and broke through my haze of pain.

When he first regained consciousness in the hospital, he called me Baby Girl.

When he's held me while I've cried, more times than I can count.

When he helped me through my night terrors.

And all along, each time he called me Baby Girl, Mark was telling me he loved me.

I twist in his arms, pulling him toward me, pouring the love overflowing my heart into my kiss. He responds immediately, an insatiable fire building between us. He pulls me back against his chest without breaking our kiss as his hands find my breasts just above the water, cupping their fullness, teasing my nipples. I arch backward, feeling his hardness pressing into my back. I slip one hand behind me, gripping his firm length, and he groans, moving against my hand.

"Bend your knees," he says breathlessly, and when I do, he lifts my hips, guiding me down onto his hard shaft. I gasp when he fills me completely.

Tub sex is highly underrated. Extremely messy, but underrated.

When I've adjusted to his fullness, I begin to move. He guides my hips, slowly at first. We adjust our rhythm for the buoyancy of the water. The cool air on my wet skin makes me even more sensitive, and when he cups my breasts again, my nipples are peaked. His hand slips below the water, stroking between my thighs, and I moan as the pressure inside me builds deliciously. One hand cups my ass, lifting me faster, while the other works its magic between my legs.

"Don't stop," I beg, and his hips rise to meet me, skin to skin.

I see stars, literal stars, crying out his name when my body detonates around him. I'm only vaguely aware of his teeth sinking into my collarbone as he thrusts deep inside me one more time, growling his own pleasure as he holds me in place. Our bodies pulse together, humming as one, caught in that glorious union of bodies, hearts, and souls.

I collapse back against his heaving chest, still breathing hard. His arms come up to wrap around me, pulling me tight against him.

"I love you, Charlie Emerson. I've always loved you, and I'm going to spend the rest of my life showing you just how much."

I tilt my face up to his. He kisses me tenderly before leaning his forehead against mine, those pale blue eyes searing into my soul.

"I love you, too."

MARK

I'm spooned behind Charlie, one arm wrapped around our babies, listening to her breathe. She sighs softly in her sleep, nestling closer, and a feeling of utter peace washes over me.

Mine.

As I lie there waiting to fall asleep, my mind drifts to my sessions with Dr. Friedman at Brooke. Dr. Friedman was the (mandated) psychiatrist I saw after the explosion. I ignored him for the majority of our sessions because I didn't want to need antidepressants or therapy. Once again, I was so convinced I was right that I ignored the wiser voices around me. Much like with my current situation, it was only when I listened to others that things started falling into place.

During the last few weeks of my therapy with him, we talked about two specific principles: neuroplasticity and nocebos. Neuroplasticity is the ability of the brain to learn newer, healthier thoughts and behaviors through repetition. A nocebo is the opposite of a placebo. Both nocebos and placebos are the physical manifestation of the phrase, "What you think about, you bring about." A placebo is the positive effect seen after someone believes something positive – for example, that the pill they take will relieve their headache. It is the belief, not the medication itself, that disrupts the pain path in the brain.

Conversely, a nocebo is the negative effect that follows negative thinking. My life after my osseointegration surgery is a prime example of the nocebo effect. I believed the lingering results of my physical injuries made me unworthy of Charlie. Because I believed I wasn't good enough for her, I left her. My self-fulfilling prophecy came true, because someone good enough for Charlie wouldn't have behaved as I did.

There's more to both concepts, but I definitely need a refresher.

And since I promised Charlie that I'd find a way to change the negative chanting from my toxic inner voice, I'd better find the books Dr. Friedman gave me and reread them.

CHAPTER TWENTY-EIGHT

CHARLIE

I AWAKEN TO THE smell of bacon. By the time I brush my teeth and pull my hair up, Mark has bacon piled on a platter next to a stack of pancakes and a dish of scrambled eggs.

He greets me with a kiss and a hug, followed by another longer kiss. "I was going to bring you breakfast in bed."

He pulls away too soon, and I lick my lips. "If I get you back in bed, those eggs will be cold before we get around to eating them."

My eyes roam over his firm body, wanting to touch instead of look. He's foregone jeans, opting instead for sweatpants that can be slipped off without unbolting his prosthesis. Black sweats ride low on his narrow hips, and a gray Army tee shirt clings to his muscled chest. Broad shoulders vee into narrow hips, and I have an urge to run my tongue over his rock-hard abs.

And other things.

I'm torn between devouring him and devouring the bacon and pancakes. A sudden flurry of small kicks makes my decision. I reach for Mark's hand and press it against my belly. He smiles, waiting expectantly. He's rewarded by two more kicks in rapid succession, followed by a third.

"The Tiny People are hungry," he declares, pulling me toward the table. "Food now, bed later."

I bite my lip, gazing up at him. "Promise?"

His pale eyes darken as he catches me against him. "I promise." He kisses me again, his lips lingering, before releasing me. "But first food, then your present."

"Present?"

"I still owe you your Christmas present."

"But —" He silences me with another kiss, and I moan. "Keep kissing me and we're going back to bed now."

My stomach growls then, embarrassingly loud, and he chuckles and nudges me into a chair.

"Feed our Tiny People," he says, filling me a plate with entirely too much food.

At least, it looked like too much food.

Somehow, I eat every single bite, minus the bacon and eggs I share with Penny. Mark gives her bites of his pancakes, too, and before long, she's stuffed, flopping on her side. Mark watches me clean my plate with an amused expression, but doesn't comment.

When I'm finished, he makes us each a second cup of hot tea and leads me into the living room. Penny gets slowly to her feet, yawning and stretching before padding over to a patch of morning sunlight and settling in for a long nap.

Mark sits down sideways on the couch and pulls me into his arms. I curl against his firm chest and snuggle in.

He strokes the side of my face gently with the back of his fingers. "I love you, Charlie Emerson, more than I could ever put into words." Then he leans back, studying me. "I wanted to give you these for Christmas, but I wasn't sure you'd accept them. I went to a jewelry store as soon as I left my first appointment with Dr. Allen, before you mailed the photo of my mom." His eyes cloud, and he looks away. "The display case full of engagement rings nearly broke me. I knew I'd destroyed any chance of that." Something deep inside me twists ferociously at his words, but he continues. "I knew you wouldn't wear an expensive bracelet, because you prefer these stacked ones to cover your scars." He lifts my wrist, stroking the underside lightly. "And you rarely wear necklaces because they catch on your hair." I didn't know he'd noticed. "So my options were limited. But I found something that showed how interconnected we are, how intertwined I hoped we'd always be." He pulls out a flat black box tied with red silk ribbon, placing it in my hands.

I unwrap the box and lift the lid with shaky fingers. Nestled in white cotton is an exquisite pair of earrings. Feather-light gold tendrils spread down like the roots of a tree, weaving in and out of each other, connecting in spots. Each tip ends in a small diamond.

They're breathtaking.

Mark points to the top of one of the earrings. "It all begins when two separate pieces join and become one, and everything flows from there."

When two become one.

When two souls join for all eternity.

Tears fill my eyes, and I throw my arms around his neck. "Thank you," I whisper against his chest.

He lifts my chin. "Why are you crying?"

"Because my heart is full."

"Mine, too, Baby Girl."

When we reach the bed, we take our time. Slow kisses. Lingering touches. His body bowing over my swollen belly as he whispers to me. Languid thrusts, maintaining eye contact as our bodies unite. The heat builds, but there's no race to the finish line. Only when he has me clutching his thighs and crying out his name does he pump faster, groaning with pleasure, spasming deep inside me. Even then, his mouth seeks mine, still fusing us together.

Two souls.

Joined together.

Becoming one.

MARK

Charlie and I spend the rest of the day barely leaving each other's side, almost always touching. We share a quiet dinner of sesame-ginger chicken over jasmine rice with steamed broccoli. After dinner, she settles on the couch and pats the cushion next to her. I give her a slow smile, turn on some music, and pull her to her feet.

"Dance with me."

She raises an eyebrow before looking pointedly at her expanding belly. "I'm not sure slow-dancing is going to work quite the way you've envisioned."

Instead of answering, I step behind her, molding my body to hers as I rest my hands on her hips. "We just need to make a minor modification."

She swirls her hips in a figure-eight in response, then peeks up at me over her shoulder. "What should I do with my hands?"

I nuzzle the side of her neck. "I'm sure we can come up with something."

Charlie moans appreciatively, tilting her head to give me better access. "You know, someone once told me slow-dancing was foreplay."

I nibble the soft flesh of her throat. "If you insist."

Three songs later, I'm ready to scoop her up and carry her to bed, but she turns to me with an unreadable expression. "I – I want to try something, but I'm not sure what you'll think about it."

Her seriousness gives me pause, and I stop, taking her hands in mine. "What is it?"

"I've been thinking," she says hesitantly. "That night in Pueblo, when I was struggling with my scars, you asked me to let you challenge my fears and show me how you felt about my body. Do you remember?"

How could I ever forget? It was the first time we were ever naked together, the first time I tasted her all over. I'd kissed every one of her scars and told her over and over how beautiful she was. We didn't have penetrative sex – we weren't at that point yet – but we did have an extremely pleasurable evening. The things she did – Jesus. So fucking hot.

"I remember." My voice is gruff.

"We've talked about you accepting yourself, scars and all. Would you –" she hesitates, then captures me in her clear green gaze "– would you let me do that to you?"

My blood turns to ice in my veins. When Charlie and I have sex, I keep all my attention on her. I don't want to think about my physical flaws, and I certainly don't want her focused on them.

I open my mouth to say no, but stop. She was afraid when I'd asked her the same thing, yet she'd let me challenge those fears, even though I'd felt her trembling at first.

Dr. Allen's words echo in my head. *If you don't come to grips with the man you are now, you can't fully commit to someone. You'll still be holding back.*

She steps closer, placing her hands on either side of my face. "It's okay. We don't have to. I just – I thought it might help you, the way you helped me."

"Yes," I hear myself say. Then I nod. "Yes."

Her eyes widen in surprise, then soften, and she raises up on tiptoe, pulling my mouth to hers in a slow, tender kiss. "If it's too much, all you have to do is tell me," she murmurs. Then she takes my hand and leads me to the bedroom.

Charlie pushes me down on the edge of the bed, then turns away to light candles she's scattered around the room. She turns off the lights when she's done – a big deal for her, because darkness is one of her triggers.

I'm not the only one whose fears she's challenging tonight.

She crosses the room to stand in front of me, meeting my eyes before giving me her back. She bends forward, slowly pushing her leggings down her exquisite legs, baring her perfect ass to me. She's not wearing panties, and my mouth waters. She straightens, grasping her shirt at the waist and pulling it over her head, exposing the scars that run from the base of her neck all the way to her hips. She peeks back over her shoulder, wearing nothing but a lacy black bra, then slides the straps down. She turns, squeezing her arms together, pushing her full breasts forward, and I can't stop myself from reaching for her. "Wanna help me with the clasp?" she purrs.

I immediately free her from the confines of her bra, and her beautiful breasts tumble free. I reach up, tweaking her rosy–brown nipples before taking one in my mouth. She sighs appreciatively before pushing me back. My mouth slips off with a wet pop.

"Your turn." She slides warm hands beneath my shirt, skating her fingers over my skin before peeling it over my head and tossing it to the floor. "On your back, soldier."

I like this side of Charlie very much.

I lay back, and her fingers slide inside the waistband of my sweatpants. She rakes her nails lightly over my skin, teasing, before dragging my pants down and off my body. Like her, I chose to go commando after our earlier lovemaking, mostly because I had every intention of enjoying another round this evening.

Charlie fishes around in my sweatpants before finding the Allen wrench I stowed in the pocket. Everything in me slams to a halt as an iron fist grips me, and I snap from fully engaged to anxious in the blink of an eye. "Slide up the bed," she murmurs. "To the pillows."

I swallow hard but do as instructed. I fold a pillow under my head, hating the hammering of my heart. *Don't be stupid. This is Charlie.* She was there when I took my prosthetic off to sleep last night. She was there for it dozens of other nights last summer. She's seen my stump – my stomach clenches at the word – hundreds of times. There's no reason to feel like this.

But my breathing picks up speed nonetheless.

She glances at my face, and her eyes soften. "It's okay not to be ready yet, Mark. There's no schedule for healing." She presses the Allen wrench into my hand and stretches out beside me, pressing her soft lips to mine. My hand comes up to cup her head, and I take her mouth savagely, angry that she read my panic accurately.

Angry that I panicked in the first place.

Stop.

Stop taking your anger out on her.

Charlie loves you. Don't fuck this up.

It's that last thought that gets through to me and instantly gentles my touch. I lift my mouth from hers, panting. "Sorry."

Her lips are swollen from the force of my kiss, but her eyes are bright with passion. "For kissing me like I'm cold water in a desert? No apology needed."

"I love you." I slide my hand behind her neck and pull her forward, tracing along the seam of her lips with my tongue, enjoying her honey-sweet flavor when she opens for me. I kiss her tenderly, slowly, a silent plea for forgiveness.

This time, when I lean back, I tilt her chin to hold her gaze, swallowing hard. "To keep things simple, my safe word is daffodil, too."

And I hand her the Allen wrench.

"We don't have to do this tonight, Mark."

I shake my head. "I need to."

She pauses, then takes a deep breath. "Okay. Do you want to remove your prosthetic, or do you want me to?"

"Go for it," I tell her, closing my eyes. "Like ripping off a bandaid."

With a turn and a click, the prosthetic is off. I hear her deposit the wrench on the bedside table, hear the quiet thud as she places the prosthetic on the floor. She wriggles closer to me on the bed. Her belly nudges my abdomen just before her lips brush mine. "Doing okay?" she asks, her lips just above mine. I raise my head and take her lower lip between my teeth, then pull it into my mouth, and she moans. I smile and feel her do the same.

She braces her hand against my chest and pushes into a sitting position. "A gorgeous man once told me he'd take a round trip and taste every inch of me. I'm planning to do the same. Is that alright?"

"Every inch?"

She looks down at my thick cock and winks. "Every one."

I tuck my hands under my head. "My body is yours."

She slides down the bed, kneeling over me. Her full breasts hang down, brushing my cock, and I suck in a breath. "That's where you're starting?"

She gives me an innocent look. "Your waist?"

"That doesn't feel like my waist," I say, then gasp as she shifts position. She stares up at me, leaning forward so that my cock nestles between her breasts. When she squeezes her arms together again, pushing her breasts together and forward, using them to surround my cock, I groan, unable to stop myself from arching into them.

"Mmmm," she sighs, then moves her arms away, dipping her head down to my —

Waist.

Her tongue traces from one hip to the other. As she moves, her breasts graze my cock, an unintended – I think – teasing. She kisses my stomach, licking a path up to the scar spanning the width of my abdomen. Her soft lips find each and every one of the scars on my upper body, scars from the shrapnel, chest tubes, and even the surgery to repair my ribs. She straddles my stomach, intentionally seating herself beyond my length, and tugs my arms from beneath my head. She massages my muscles as she tastes me, licking and kissing and touching. She makes eye contact with me often, and it's so fucking hot, I long to bury myself inside her, but I fight it. Tonight is about more than sex. It's about trust, and healing, and acceptance.

When she reaches my neck, she nips and nuzzles, and my cocks thrums in excitement against her thigh. "You like that?" she whispers against my skin.

"Very much." I pull her up and take her face between my hands, plunging my tongue deep inside the depths of her mouth, not stopping until she's as needy as I am. She whimpers when I release her, then draws a deep breath and slides off me to kneel beside me on the bed.

"Roll over," she says in a husky voice, and when I do, her magic hands immediately go to work. She massages as she works her way down my body, licking and tasting, nibbling and kneading. Her mouth finds every scar, every wound. Sharp teeth graze my buttocks, and if I weren't already hard enough to cut diamonds, that would have done it. She nudges my legs apart and licks my inner thighs, just behind my balls, and I nearly come on the spot. I arch and hiss out a breath, fisting the covers in my hands.

"Hang on," I gasp.

She stills instantly. "Too much?"

"Not the way you mean." I exhale. "My – entity – is a little overexcited."

"I could move down and give you a foot rub," she suggests. "Work my way up."

"Okay," I say breathlessly.

She moves to massage my left foot, and I manage to get myself under control. It slips a bit when she sucks my toes, and I grunt. She chuckles, returning her attention to my ankle and calf, resuming her massaging-kissing combination as she continues to move north. When she reaches my thighs, she massages my hamstrings while planting soft kisses on my skin. She avoids my inner thighs this time, something that relieves and disappoints me in equal measure.

"Okay, Big Guy, roll over for me," she murmurs.

Sex. Goddess.

Her lips are swollen, her cheeks flushed. Her nipples are peaked, and as I gaze at her, she bites her lower lip. Without breaking eye contact, she picks up my left leg, placing my ankle on her shoulder, and proceeds to work her way north with her lips and hands.

Fuck me.

By the time she's reached my knees, I'm panting. My stomach tightens as she glances at my abutment, but she continues exploring my left leg, all the way up my thigh, tracing the cheese-grater-textured skin graft from my burns with her tongue, flicking it over the skin. I can't feel it – the graft doesn't have sensation – but the visual impact is profound.

Charlie moves to my balls, lightly licking the side of my sac, and I groan her name. She drags her face across my cock, pausing to lick the pre-cum from the tip, then moves to my right thigh. I'm panting, desperate for release, and she knows it, but she keeps going, searing a path along the numerous scars on my thigh. I fist the covers in my hands and fight not to lose control.

Her hand closes around my cock at the same time her lips reach the fleshy skin around my abutment.

I want to be disgusted with my stump, want to stop her from putting her mouth there, but I'm too distracted by her hand around my shaft. She strokes me, slowly at first, matching her licks across my stump to the speed of her hand. When she swirls her tongue around my remaining limb, she matches the motion with her hand on my cock, and I buck my hips and groan. "Mine," she growls. "All of you. You're mine."

"Please," I beg. "I need you."

Her mouth envelopes me before the words have left my mouth, and I hiss out a sharp breath as her scorching heat slides down my shaft. She takes me in fully, all the way to the back of her throat, and I thrust toward her. She moans, reaching beneath me to dig her nails into my ass, and proceeds to give the same intense attention to my cock as she did to the rest of my body. She licks and sucks and swirls her tongue, and I'm on the verge much too soon.

"Charlie, stop now if you don't want me to come in your mouth," I gasp. In response, she grips my ass more tightly, pulling me in deeper with each bob of her head.

It hits me like a tidal wave, rolling forward from the base of my spine, drowning me in pleasure. I see stars, and my entire body spasms. I growl out her name as I explode into her, and she takes every drop, licking me clean.

When I can breathe again, I haul her to me and kiss her senseless, tasting my saltiness mingled with her honey-sweet flavor. I ravish her mouth until she whimpers, then return the favor, using my lips and tongue and hands to bring her to climax after climax, until her legs are shaking. Only then do I kneel up and enter her, staking my claim on her, just as she did on me.

Mine.

CHARLIE

Things are going so well with Mark. He's at my house most of the time I'm not at work now. We spend as much time as we can together, talking late into the night about anything and everything. Touching. Bonding. Healing.

And making love.

There's a *lot* of lovemaking. We have a lot of missed time to make up for. The tub features in a few more sessions, although the next time, we're smart enough to throw down towels beforehand. There's the bed, naturally, but also the sofa, a kitchen chair, the dining room table, and the bathroom sink. My favorite, though, is on a pile of quilts in the living room floor by the light of the fire, slow and tender and ever so sweet.

That's a memory I plan to carry forever.

A close second is the night I wake up to find him studying my pregnancy book, determined to learn what he's missed so far and what's still to come.

God, I love this man.

CHAPTER TWENTY-NINE

MARK

I'M COMPLETELY LOVING MY life right now.

Things are amazing between me and Charlie. Something shifted between us once I began making an intentional effort to accept my body the way it is. She's right about replacing my toxic voice with something kinder. Having my apartment plastered with reminders that she loves me the way I am is actually working. I can catch my negative thoughts and stop them. It's another example of neuroplasticity. I'm changing the pathways in my brain through repetition. And my tentative acceptance of my body means Charlie's more comfortable, too, telling me she loves me without hesitation. Her reticence and the fears she was harboring about me leaving again seem to have melted away. She's relaxed, which in turn, relaxes me and makes me feel more comfortable leaving my prosthetic off. She never judged me because of my amputation anyway. That was all me. But accepting myself means I don't feel pressured to keep it on when I don't need to.

And that includes when she and I make love.

That night when she decided to show me how she felt about my body – *all* of my body, scars, stump, and all – that changed something. I can still hear her fierce growl claiming me as hers as she stroked me and kissed my residual limb. Her actions loosened something inside me.

Because if she can accept and love me after all I've done, then maybe I can accept myself.

My appointments with Dr. Allen are going well. He and I discussed neuroplasticity and placebos and nocebos at length, and he echoed what Dr. Friedman and Charlie had said about toxic voices. I'd shared Charlie's assessment that the person I was truly toxic to was myself, and that it overflowed onto everyone else. He agreed with her assessment, pointing to my interaction on that fateful day with Kip as well as to the reasons why I left Charlie. It wasn't that I'd wanted to hurt either of them – it was that my poisonous self-loathing boiled out and wounded others. He's also spent time working with me on recognizing other negative thought patterns within myself so that I can stop them before they have time to take root. I refuse to take a chance on fostering any negativity that might impact Charlie or our children.

Despite the fact that we spend most of our waking hours away from her clinic together, I can't get enough of Charlie. It seems to be mutual. The first weekend in February, I'm waiting for her when she gets home from work, and we stay cocooned together until she has to return to work Monday morning. The only time we're apart is when she sends me out Saturday with a grocery list. When I kiss her before leaving, she slips her hands into my back pockets and squeezes my ass before telling me to hurry back.

I take longer than she wanted on my errand run because there's a jeweler in this small town who does custom work. I find something close to what I want and describe the modifications I'd like. There's a huge fee to have it completed in less than a week, but I don't care. She's worth it.

Late Thursday afternoon, Charlie and I drive separately into town. She's seeing Linda and I'm seeing Dr. Allen. When I finish, I stop by the jeweler's and pocket Charlie's Valentine's Day gift before picking up Chinese takeout for the two of us and chicken nuggets for Penny.

When I enter the house, Charlie's by the back door, bent over with her perfect ass up in the air, her legs clad in those black leggings that leave nothing to the imagination. My mouth dries and my cock comes to life.

She's drying Penny, who's apparently been splashing in her stream. As soon as the dog sees me, she wriggles free from Charlie and scampers toward me at top speed, toenails scrabbling over the wood floor. I manage to put the Chinese food down before she reaches me. Her entire back half wags furiously. I squat down, and she clambers onto my lap, her sodden fur soaking my jeans.

Charlie turns off the blow dryer and straightens up. "Someone was lonely today. She's been a bundle of energy since I got home, even after a long walk."

Penny's trying desperately to lick me in the face, but I can't take my eyes off Charlie. Her cheeks are still pink from the cold wind, her hair has that sexy wind-blown look, and her lips are plump, perfect for kissing.

A wet tongue swipes across my lips, and it's not Charlie's. I jerk my head away and end up falling backwards on my ass with a very excited wet dog sitting on top of me. I hear giggles right before I see Charlie tug at Penny's collar.

"Down, Penny. Sit," she says sternly, and to my utter amazement, Penny gets down, moving to sit beside me, her tail swishing rapidly across the floor.

Charlie's trying unsuccessfully to hide her smile. She offers me a hand, but I wave it away, gesturing to her rounded belly. "Not with that precious cargo."

"Are you alright?"

"The only thing injured is my dignity. I've never been french-kissed by a dog before."

I stand, shifting my weight from side to side. My prosthetic seems undamaged. "I brought Chinese food. If you want to finish up with Penny, I'll go change and we can have dinner."

Her eyes light up. "Chinese food?"

I chuckle. "Just for you, Baby Girl."

"Come on, Penny," she says, and the dog immediately returns to stand quietly on the towel. Charlie bends over to pick up the blow dryer again, and it's all I can do to walk away from that gorgeous ass. I manage to, though, because the Boy Scout in me realizes that (a) I need to scrub the dog slobber off my lips before I kiss Charlie, and (b) I need to change into sweatpants for easier removal.

Because I definitely plan to remove them, right after I peel Charlie's clothes off her creamy skin and taste every inch of her.

I manage to pull down my wet jeans, disconnect my prosthesis, yank it out of the jeans, reattach it, and tug on a pair of sweatpants in record time. They do little to hide the hard-on that's only grown as I've thought of all the things I want to do to Charlie later. I shake my head to refocus before washing my face and brushing my teeth to remove any hint of Penny.

Dinner, then Charlie for dessert.

But all thoughts of food dissipate when I enter the living room and see Charlie's perfect ass again, bending over Penny by the back door. I can't stop myself from approaching. She glances up, but doesn't straighten. My hands settle on her hips from behind, pulling her back against my erection.

She rolls her hips to push her core against me, and I groan.

She turns off the blow dryer and pushes against my erection again, and my cock surges toward her. I lean over her, reaching inside her shirt to cup her lush breasts. My mouth finds her collarbone and she moans, arching back against me.

"Couch," I mutter against her neck. She reaches for my hand and pulls me into the living room. I grab squishy throw pillows to make a cradle for her rounded belly before guiding her to lean forward over the arm of the couch. I step behind her, sliding my hands into her leggings.

No panties. My cock throbs in anticipation.

I slip the leggings down and off her body, kneeling behind her. I stroke my palm up her right leg and over her firm buttock, lightly squeezing. My left hand does the same to her other leg before kneading her ass. She moans again, and I gently ease her legs and buttocks apart. Her beautiful pussy glistens for me, hot and wet, begging to be tasted.

"So fucking hot," I murmur, massaging her ass as I spread her cheeks, exposing her pussy further.

The first flick of my tongue makes her gasp with surprise. I press down lightly on her back, bending her further forward, opening her core to me. I consume her sweet nectar, working her over with my lips and tongue and teeth. She moans and arches back, and I push my face into her, finding her swollen clit, sucking and swirling. Her hips thrust against me, and I give her everything she wants as soft whimpers turn to heated gasps. Her fingers claw at the fabric of the couch as she teeters on the edge of pleasure. "Not like this. I need you inside me. Please, Mark."

I stand, shoving my sweatpants down before dragging my cock through her dripping folds. "Oh, God," she whimpers. "Please." I pause at her entrance before pushing in slowly, an inch at a time, burying myself inside her tight depths, feeling her body stretch to take all of me. "Yes," she moans. "Yes."

I try to move slowly, but she won't allow it. She pushes back against me, taking me to the hilt again and again. My fingers grip her hips as I thrust into her, giving her what she wants, what she needs. Charlie throws her head back, her long hair flying over her shoulder as she looks back at me, holding my gaze while moaning my name.

It's my undoing, that sex goddess look, those huge green eyes and flushed cheeks, biting her bottom lip. My self-control dissolves and I pump faster, my fingertips blanching as they dig into her hips. Her pussy squeezes me, drawing me in deeper. Her muscles tense as her cries echo through the room. Her body clenches tight around me as she wails one final time. Her orgasm rips through her, triggering my own. It starts at the base of my spine and rushes forward, a tsunami of pleasure that swallows us both as I growl her name over and over.

When I'm spent, I collapse against her back, careful to support my weight above her. My lips find her collarbone again. "You are a sex goddess."

She snorts. "Yeah. I look like a goddess."

I bite her collarbone just firmly enough to get her attention. "You're the only woman who's ever made my dick rock-hard by blow drying a dog. Trust me. That over the shoulder eye contact, biting your lip? Pure sex goddess." I nudge her with my nose. "I couldn't have held out any longer if my life depended on it."

She glances back at me, her cheeks pinking again. "Really?"

I capture her lips in a firm kiss. "Really. You're the sexiest woman I've ever known, and you're mine."

She leans her head into my shoulder. It's quiet except for the sounds of our breathing.

"I wonder if I could get that on a tee shirt," she murmurs. "Pure sex god-dess."

We both laugh. Then I grab a damp washcloth to help her clean up before we sit down to dinner.

CHARLIE

Despite a wonderful, sex-filled weekend, the challenges are waiting as soon as I get to work Monday. Lila and I find Tara red-eyed and pale, and she reaches for tissues. "There's no easy way to say this, but I'm resigning. My son-in-law has brain cancer, and I need to be with my daughter." Lila and I rush to her, and she dissolves in tears. "Brock's only twenty-eight, and Brooklyn is twenty-six and pregnant." She glances at my belly. "I'm so sorry to do this. I know you need me here, but –"

I shake my head firmly. "No. Your family comes first. What can we do to help?"

"I've already listed my house," she says, startling us both. "My son and his girlfriend came this past weekend and helped me pack a few things and put the rest in storage. As soon as – well, as soon as I'm done here, I'm flying out to California. Brock's starting treatments next week to shrink the tumor before surgery." Tears fill her eyes. "I can work through the end of this week, but I'm moving in with my daughter this weekend."

Lila lays a hand on her forearm. "We understand. Do you need to leave us sooner?"

The dark-haired woman shakes her head. "I can't leave you like that. It's bad enough I'm giving you so little notice. Besides, working gives me a distraction. There are still loose ends to tie up before I leave town, so I'll be here this week anyway. If I'm working, at least I'm not worrying about Brock and Brooklyn."

When she leaves, I turn to Lila. "Let me reach out to a few people this morning and see what I can come up with."

She purses her lips. "We really need two massage therapists," she muses. "A full time and a part time who might be willing to go full time later. In a few months, you'll be giving birth. And we still need an office person to fill in all the gaps."

I turn to my laptop. "Today was going to be an office day for me anyway. I'll start making calls."

By lunchtime, I've scheduled three interviews, all of whom assure me they can start immediately. In a small community like Cedar Ridge, that's unheard of. My first interview arrives by mid-afternoon.

"I'm sorry," she apologizes. "I haven't unpacked everything, and these were the only clean clothes I had."

Contessa Maddox, who goes by Tess, is dressed in clean jeans and a crisp navy blouse with navy flats. Her shoes and coat are worn but clean. Fiery red hair curls like flames around her pale face, and her pale seaglass-green eyes hold a familiar sadness.

"It's perfectly fine," I assure her. "We're very informal around here. Come back to my office and we'll talk." She follows me down the hall, gazing at the nature prints and quietly trickling fountains.

She gasps when she reaches my office. "I love this room," she breathes. "It's so peaceful."

"It's designed to be my little retreat," I admit. "Soothing colors, warm wood tones, plants, lots of light. Nature and peace in an office environment."

"It definitely isn't a typical office space."

I shake my head. "I've dealt with my share of personal challenges over the years. One way I cope is by trying to keep my environment soothing, both for myself and our clients. Please, have a seat." I gesture to the sofa. She perches nervously on the edge of one cushion, and I join her. "Why don't you tell me a little about yourself, Tess?"

She shifts uncomfortably, looking down. "There's not a lot to tell. I'm a single mom. I have a nine-year-old daughter named Kai. I'm not afraid of hard work and I'll do whatever you need me to do."

"The position is for a receptionist, but it's really more of an office manager. We need someone to help fill in the gaps. Lila and I have been doing every-thing ourselves for a few years, but we need more help. Plus, as you can see," I gesture downward, "I'll be on maternity leave in a few months, so I'd like to have someone in place to keep things moving smoothly. We need someone to answer the phone, but also to file with insurance companies, send up-dates to physician offices, deal with medical records, and scan and fax client information. There's also more hands-on type work, such as scrubbing the tubs between hydrotherapy appointments, laundering towels and massage blankets, tidying up at the end of the day, and ordering supplies."

"I've never dealt with insurance companies before, but I'm a fast learner. The other things, the cleaning and stuff, that's no problem. I've worked in a hotel as a housekeeper before. And I worked as a secretary in Seattle, so I know how to scan and fax and file paperwork. All I need is a chance." She looks at me eagerly, though I still see something in her eyes. Fear?

Maybe she's just nervous. Something about her makes me sure she's right for us.

We move to my desk, where I start filling out employment paperwork. My good feeling dissipates when she produces her license. It's the worst fake ID I've ever seen.

I hear Lila saying goodbye to her client. I reach for the phone and dial up front, knowing she'll answer. "Can you come back here? I have a candidate for the receptionist position."

Lila comes back immediately. "This is Tess," I explain as Lila looks her over and shakes her hand, smiling warmly. "She's a single mom who's eager to be our receptionist. She's worked as a housekeeper and a secretary before, so she'd only need to learn the insurance piece." Then I finger the license lying on top of the paperwork, knowing Lila will look down.

She doesn't disappoint.

Lila leans with her hip against my desk, gazing at the redhead. "You sound like exactly what we're looking for." Tess' eyes light up. "But what's up with the fake license? I mean, seriously, I can see the stickers from the label maker under the laminate."

Tess's eyes close and her face falls. She reaches for the license. "I'm sorry to have wasted your time."

I clamp my hand over hers before she can pull it away. "We didn't say no. Just help us understand."

Her pale green eyes widen hopefully, and I release her. "I gave two hundred dollars to a couple of teenagers who swore they could get me a false ID. I should have known better. And they'd insisted on payment up front, so there was nothing I could do. It's not like I could ask for a refund or go to the police."

"But why do you need a fake ID?" Lila probes gently.

Her story comes out haltingly, an all too familiar tale of an impressionable young woman and an older man who said all the right things and then showed his true colors. She tolerated his abuse until he threatened their child, the child he'd already signed away all parental rights to. "He never even wanted Kai. He still doesn't. He just wants to hurt me. We've been running for the last eight years. It's not really even a fake name. My first name is Jacquelyn, and I went by Jacqui, but Contessa is my middle name. I started going by Tess a few years ago. And he insisted I name Kai Ella after his mother, but her middle name is Kaivalya. He can't even remember it, let alone spell it. I called her Kai as soon as we escaped him. That's the only name she's ever known. Maddox is my brother's last name. Well, foster brother. We aren't related. But he was at the last foster home I was in, and we stayed close. He's the only reason I have a phone."

"Why don't you stay with your brother?" I study her eyes, but there's no trace of deception or fear now, simply sadness and weariness, aged beyond her years.

But she shakes her head. "He's a Navy SEAL. He gave me a phone in his name so he'd always be able to reach me. He doesn't know... well, he doesn't know how Evan was. He only knows we aren't together now."

"Where did Evan find you last?"

"Vegas. We'd been there for a year and a half. It's the longest I've stayed anywhere. I got complacent, reached out to a friend from a few years back. Word got back to him about where I was, and he turned up a week or so before

Christmas." She looks down, rubbing a worn spot in her jeans. "After that I started bouncing from town to town through Arizona and New Mexico. I drove here from Santa Fe looking for a small town, somewhere he'd never search. We've been here for ten days." She looks up, her eyes pleading. "All I'm asking for is a chance to prove myself. I need this job. I'll work hard. I'll do anything for Kai. She deserves a decent life."

Lila pushes a pad of paper toward her. "Write down your number. We'll call you this evening either way."

When she's gone, I do an online search for the address she provided. "She's at the homeless shelter," I tell Lila.

"Shit," she says. "Now I really want to hire her. That's no place for a kid."

"How would we even pay her? She can't open a bank account with that ID. They'd call the police."

"Pay her in cash? And set up a bank account online, maybe?" She looks thoughtful. "I bet Tucker knows a guy who could help her with that ID."

I bet he does, too. Tucker knows a guy for literally everything.

I call her before she's even made it across town and offer her the job. She'll start the day after tomorrow.

My interviews with the massage therapists go equally well.

Cassidy Winters is in her late twenties. She's been a massage therapist for eight years. She's cheery and matter-of-fact, with sparkling brown eyes that match her thick hair. She's been working with a temp agency recently. Prior to that, she worked as a massage therapist in a spa on a cruise ship.

"That sounds fun," I say, picturing turquoise water and white sands, but Cassie shrugs and wrinkles her nose.

"They'd book seven fifty-minute massages for us in an eight-hour shift, and you never got a day off. It doesn't matter how exotic the locale is if you never get to enjoy it."

London Quinn is a fair-skinned blond with grey eyes. She's quietly confident, exuding an air of dependability. "Part-time work is fine," she assures me. "I'm a freelance writer as well, so my hours are flexible. When you need me to work more, I should be available."

Lila and Tom meet them both, and we're all in agreement. I offer them positions, effective immediately.

In order to facilitate a smooth transition, Tara takes London and Lila takes Cassie, showing them the ropes and introducing them to our documentation systems. I work with Tess, teaching her how to run the front desk, introducing her to clients, and showing her our stringent cleaning requirements. On Friday, we have a going-away party for Tara. It's sad, given her circumstances, though we try to remain upbeat. Stubbs gives her his card and makes her promise to call him when her spirits need bolstering. She smiles and pats him sadly on the cheek before tucking his card into her pocket. Tom folds her in a huge hug that leaves her misty-eyed. Lila and I hug her as well, promising she'll always have a job here if she wants it. We send her off with a sizable check for "severance pay", telling her to use it for whatever she or her family need.

Change.

There's no escaping it.

So much has changed over the past twelve months. The explosion. Mark's hospitalization. Tara joining our clinic family. Mark coming home with me. Our intimate relationship developing. His second surgery. Our breakup. Meeting Kip. Losing Kip. Bringing Stubbs into our chosen family. Penny. Learning to accept myself. Eradicating my night terrors. My pregnancy. Lila's conception struggles. Now Mark and I have rekindled our relationship, and we've brought new members into the fold – Tess, Cassie, and London. My babies are due in less than four months. So much change is still on the horizon.

My eyes fall on an art project Maya brought me. I framed it and hung it in my office. She's drawn a field of flowers filled with colorful butterflies. Beneath it, she's written, "If it weren't for change, there'd never be butterflies. Embrace the uncertainty. No one wants to be a caterpillar forever."

Out of the mouths of babes.

Time to embrace my inner butterfly.

CHAPTER THIRTY

CHARLIE

On Valentine's Day, I wake up to Mark's hands caressing my breasts and his head buried between my legs, offering a special gift. I celebrate twice in spectacular fashion before showing my appreciation and returning the favor. That's followed by a lengthy shower for two with more celebrating on both our parts.

Best. Valentine's. Ever.

After hot tea and pancakes with fruit, we take Penny for a walk. It snowed another couple of inches last night, but the trails we've worn are easy to recognize. I manage to keep her out of the stream this time, much to her chagrin. We return to the house and Mark and I curl up on the couch together, sipping cocoa. I'm mulling over something I want to discuss with him. I think he's ready, but I'm not sure how to broach the topic.

"You're quiet," he observes. "Everything okay?"

I put down my mug and take his hand. "I want to talk to you about something." His light blue eyes flicker. "It's nothing bad. It's just something Linda and I talked about that's really resonated with me."

He puts down his mug and shifts toward me, giving me his full attention.

"Have you ever heard of kintsugi?"

His brows pull together before he slowly shakes his head. "I don't think so."

"It's an ancient Japanese art form. Basically, when a piece of pottery or ceramic breaks, instead of being discarded, the pieces are cleaned and glued back together. Once it's repaired, they apply thin layers of lacquer and gold powder over the crack lines to accentuate them instead of hiding them. Essentially, it's a way of honoring what was broken and restoring its beauty."

Recognition flickers in his eyes. "Like that blue bowl you have on the table in the bedroom."

I nod. "Linda helped me see that it's kind of... well, a metaphor for life. The beauty only occurs because the object was broken. What happened to me – I wouldn't wish that on anyone, but it changed me for the better in the long run. I didn't know how strong I was until I had no other choice. I didn't know who I really was until everything I thought I knew was stripped away. If I hadn't been broken, I'd never have known who I am and what I'm capable of." I pause briefly before meeting his eyes. "I've decided I'm done hiding my scars. All of them. They aren't something to be ashamed of. They're proof I'm stronger than I thought I could be." I slide the stacked bracelets off both my wrists and drop them on the coffee table.

Strong hands cup my face, tilting it up to his, and gentle lips press against mine. "I always knew you were strong, Baby Girl. The only one who didn't know was you."

I rest my hands on his shoulders and study his face before continuing. "I think the same metaphor applies to you. You believed you were strong, but you thought your strength was physical. You never knew how strong you were until you had to be strong in a different way." I pause, and he cocks his head at me.

"Even with us, with our relationship... if you and I had continued down the path we were on and declared our love without going through the painful parts, we wouldn't know the true depth of our feelings. I think the beauty of our relationship is more intense because we were broken apart and intentionally repaired, and now things are stronger and deeper and more meaningful than before. We aren't together because we drifted closer; we're together because we chose to put the broken pieces back together, because we realized how much we loved each other."

Mark smiles down at me before kissing me again. "That's a beautiful metaphor."

My lips curve up as I shrug. "I can't take all the credit. Linda brought it up. I just ran with it."

"More beautiful because it was broken," he muses, resting his forehead against mine. "I like that. And I'm glad you've accepted your scars. They're part of your strength." He hesitates. "Like I'm accepting that my scars are part of mine."

He draws me against his chest, and I listen to the steady thudding of his heart. "I have a concept to share with you, too," he murmurs. "It's called neuroplasticity." I listen as he explains how the brain can create new pathways through repetition, as well as eliminate old, harmful ways of thinking by replacing them with something new.

"Like you've been doing with the pictures all over your apartment," I say, glancing up at his face.

He nods. "I remind myself how you see me every time my toxic voice tries to chime in."

"It's working, too." I can tell, because when we go to bed at night, he removes his prosthesis altogether before we make love. It no longer seems to bother him to be intimate with me with the abutment exposed. If we aren't making love in bed – if we're in the shower, for example, or somewhere else in the house – he'll leave his prosthetic on, but it's so he can walk afterwards, not because he hates his residual limb.

He hugs me tighter against his chest. "I have something for you," he says. I tilt my head up as he reaches into the pocket of his hooded sweatshirt. He places a small velvet box in my hand.

A ring box.

My eyes widen.

"It's not what you think," he cautions me, "so don't freak out. I know I haven't been back long enough to earn your trust, and you're still not totally convinced I'm here because I love you, not just because of the babies."

Actually... I think I might be.

"So this ring represents my promise. It's a placeholder, and whenever you're convinced I love you with all of my heart, say the word, and I'll replace this ring with a diamond. But in the meantime, I wanted to show you I'm serious. I love you, Charlie Emerson, and I'll spend the rest of my life showing you just how much." He opens the ring box for me, and I gasp.

On a blue velvet cushion is a gold band, encircled with light blue topaz and deep green emeralds.

His eye color and mine, interlocked.

A circle, representing eternity.

"It's beautiful," I murmur, breathless.

He plucks it from the box and slides it down my finger. "Now, traditionally, promise rings are given between young virginal couples promising to save themselves for each other." He grins down at my belly. "Clearly, the virgin ship has sailed." I grin back at him. "But I promise you, Baby Girl, you own me, heart and soul, forever. I love you. And if you're never ready to marry me, then this here, you and me, it's enough, as long as I have you."

"I love you, too." I throw my arms around his neck, and as I do, a flurry of tiny kicks explodes inside my belly. Even Mark can feel them, and he pulls back enough to cup his hand against my abdomen.

"I have something for you, too," I tell him when I'm able to speak again. I hand him a small white box. He looks at me curiously, then lifts the lid. I watch his face as he removes a key from the box.

He looks at me, puzzled. "Your key to my apartment? You're giving it back?" He tilts his head. "Why?"

"I don't want it anymore. I want – I want you to move back in with me. To stay. If you want, to, I mean." My face grows warm.

"Are you sure?" Light blue eyes probe mine, searching for doubt that isn't there. When I nod, he tightens his arms around me. "Yes. God, yes. I want to spend every night of the rest of my life holding you in my arms."

My heart is so full, it might burst.

MARK

Perfect.

My life is utterly, completely perfect.

Every morning I wake up with Charlie nestled in my arms, watching her pregnant belly grow larger and larger, feeling our Tiny People moving and kicking. That's what we call them – our Tiny People. I've gone to all her doctor's appointments and even got to see another ultrasound of them. It was so incredible, I couldn't even speak. All I could do was grip Charlie's hand and blink back the moisture in my eyes.

Her belly is huge. She's almost thirty-two weeks pregnant now, and I have no idea how she's going to make it another six weeks. Her abdomen is completely taut and hard, and her belly button magically flipped from an innie to an outie. It wasn't gradual, either – all of a sudden, there it was, pressing outward against her shirt. And her breasts? They were full before she got pregnant. Now they're popping out of her larger bras.

Not that I'm complaining.

Last night, one of the babies had the hiccups. I don't even know how that's possible. They're surrounded by fluid. How the hell do they get hiccups? But they did, and her entire belly jumped every few seconds for a solid fifteen minutes before they eased off.

It's amazing.

She's dealing with the pregnancy stuff fairly well. Her back hurts, and her feet swell, and she's always hungry. I've known Charlie for twenty-five years, and I've never seen her eat so much. She's having to eat smaller meals more frequently, though, because there's no room for her stomach to fill up thanks to our Tiny People. They're taking up every bit of space.

Her appetite for food isn't the only appetite increasing. Charlie's libido is off the charts. Again, I'm not complaining, not by a long shot. I'm thrilled, because her pregnant body is the sexiest thing I've ever seen, and I can barely keep my hands off her. Luckily, that's exactly what she wants – my hands all over her. And my mouth. And my cock.

My life is perfect.

CHARLIE

Mark's moved back in with me, and we've put up a sign in the rehab gym offering his apartment for anyone willing to take over his lease. One of our clients, Jake Barnes, stops by the desk to ask me about it. Jake's a left bicep-level arm amputee, working toward rebuilding his upper body muscles enough to undergo osseointegration surgery himself.

"It's not much," I caution him. I'd helped Mark pack up his meager possessions the night before. Once his personal items were out of the space, I realized how generous Lila had been when she called it a dive.

Jake shrugs, his gray-green eyes indifferent, and his dark hair falls into his eyes. "I just need to get out of my sister's place. She's sweet and all, but she's married, and I'm kind of a third wheel. Plus, they're newlyweds, and it's a small apartment with thin walls."

I laugh out loud. "I can see your point." I call Mark and ask him to stop by, and within a couple of minutes, he's coming in the front door. My face lights up as soon as I see him. His pale blue eyes zero in on me, and he comes behind the desk to kiss me thoroughly.

Jake chuckles. "I see why the apartment's available." His dark hair falls into his eyes again, and he brushes it back.

Mark straightens up and grins, stepping back around the desk to introduce himself. He offers to drive Jake to the apartment to show it to him, and Jake agrees. An hour later, Mark's making plans to help Jake move in the following day.

Work. Home. Lovelife. For once, everything in my life is falling into place.

LILA

Life is perfect.

Our ultrasound showed that implantation took place exactly where it should have – the wall of my uterus. But we were still in for a surprise.

I'm having twins. Fraternal twins. And just like Charlie, I'm having a boy and a girl.

Tucker nearly passed out when he heard the news, but the next thing I knew, he had me off the table and up in a bear hug. The ultrasound technician giggled as he smeared ultrasound gel all over his clothes, but he didn't care, and neither did I.

I'm getting my own miracle.

It's a good thing we went on that cruise in February while I still didn't look pregnant, because it's April now, and that's all changed. I'm nearly four months pregnant, and I definitely have a bump. I may never again get into that tiny scrap of a black bikini Tucker had me wearing in the Caribbean, and I don't give a damn. All I want is for these babies to be safe and healthy.

Charlie's passed along her early maternity clothes to me. Much like her, I've opted for leggings and loose tunic-type tops. We're both working. She's only doing two or three massages most days now. I'm still doing about five, but on days where I'm too nauseous or tired, London or Cassie take some of mine. I'm so glad we have the extra hands. Charlie's due in May, and I'm due at the end of September. She might be coming back to work around the time I'm heading out on maternity leave, but with both of us having twins, we've talked about sharing one position between us and hiring another massage therapist. We're also going to need another physical therapist. Our business has grown so much that Tom's having to work multiple clients at a time all day. He's got a friend moving to the area that he says will be perfect, so I'm crossing my fingers.

We're also working on baby names.

Tucker and I have decided that our son's middle name will be Chandler, after Mark. We don't have a first name yet. Our daughter's name will be Emerson – Charlie's last name. We're going to call her Emma. We haven't told Mark and Charlie, because they'd try to talk us out of it, but the truth is, I can't think of anyone else I'd want to name my kids after. Charlie is as much my sister as if we'd been born that way, and Mark will always be my big brother, the one who never stopped looking for me and Charlie until he found where they'd taken us. Family is so much more than blood. It's heart.

Charlie and Mark are still fine-tuning their babies' names. They're giving them each hyphenated middle names, combining their mothers' names and fathers' names. First names are still being batted about. At the moment, their son will be Ryker John-Jackson Chandler, and their daughter will be Sophia Diana-Grace Chandler. Only the middle and last names are set, though; Ryker and Sophia may yet be something entirely different.

She's thirty-four weeks pregnant now. In four more weeks, Charlie's miracle babies will be born, and four months after that, our miracle babies will join them. Life couldn't possibly be any more perfect.

CHAPTER THIRTY-ONE

MARK

I CAN SCARCELY BELIEVE that Colonel Harry Sherman is sitting here with me and Charlie in our living room.

He may be small in stature, but the Colonel still maintains an imposing presence. He's officially retired now, trading in his uniforms and wings for perfectly pressed khaki twill pants and a white dress shirt. His white hair may make him look like a kindly grandfather, but his brown eyes are sharp, and he doesn't miss a trick. He's also a straight shooter, which is why he's truly one of my favorite people. His plane from D.C. landed in Pueblo earlier today, and he's staying with us overnight. He'll fly out to Butte, Montana, in the morning. Tucker and Lila joined us for dinner and dessert, and the Colonel hugged Lila tightly and patted her rounded belly before she and Tucker left. He joined me and Charlie in the living room for coffee and conversation, and it's nearly eleven p.m.

Charlie scoots to the edge of the couch to stand, but I'm in front of her offering my help before she can push herself up. She's thirty-four weeks pregnant now, and her belly is the size of a beach ball. It's so taut and swollen, I can't imagine it's not painful, but she insists it's not. Her back is another story. Her center of gravity has shifted forward and down due to the twins, and by the end of the day, her lower back aches terribly. Every night I give her a backrub after she takes a hot shower. For the last month or so, I've also ended up rubbing her calves during the night. She awakens out of a dead sleep with cramps seizing her lower legs, clenching in rock-hard knots. Dr. Rose suggested adding more potassium-rich foods and doing gentle stretches before bed, so I'm religiously ensuring she eats two bananas and half a cantaloupe every day and stretching her calves every evening.

Yeah. I'm the father-to-be version of a Bridezilla.

Thirty-four weeks pregnant.

In six weeks, we'll be welcoming our babies into the world.

Actually, Dr. Rose says we're aiming for thirty-eight weeks. Of course, if everything's still going well for Charlie and the babies, she's willing to let them go closer to forty weeks since we already know Charlie has to have a cesarean section. The longer the babies can safely stay in utero, the more their lungs can mature.

Just a few more weeks until my entire world changes forever.

Maybe that should scare me, but it doesn't. I think it's because I've almost lost Charlie three times now — once to the bastards, once to sepsis, and once to my own stupidity. I won't ever make that mistake again. Now that I've got her back, I'll never let her go, and as long as we have each other, we can handle anything, whether it's dirty diapers, three a.m. feedings, colic, or earaches. It doesn't matter, as long as we're together.

I tug Charlie to her feet and she smiles, pulling me down for a quick kiss. "I'm going to make up the guest room and take a shower. I'll check on you guys later."

"I can make up the guest room."

She rolls her eyes. "Pregnant, not an invalid," she reminds me. "I'm still doing massages. I can make a bed."

Despite my protests, she's still working. She limits herself to two or three massages a day, and she rests in between, but she's still on her feet far more than I'd like. But trying to convince Charlie to rest is an exercise in futility. I can occasionally coerce her into cuddling with me on the couch or staying in bed to watch a movie, but her raised eyebrow and pointed glances tell me she knows exactly what I'm doing.

I'm trying to take care of the mother of my children. It's not a crime.

I wait until I hear Charlie rummaging in the upstairs linen closet before I turn to the Colonel. "So what's this visit really about?"

He raises his coffee mug to his lips, studying me over the top of it before taking a sip. "An opportunity," he says finally.

I cock my head at him, curious.

"I'm not the type to go quietly into the night, to leave a lifetime of strategizing and fighting behind to play bingo on Tuesdays and tennis on weekends. I may have left the battlefield, but there are still battles that need to be fought. Smaller, crucial battles. Quiet ones." His dark eyes study mine. "I think you'd agree with me."

"You're right. You're much more of a poker guy." I stare, waiting for him to make his point.

He grins. "I'm partnering with a fellow to open a private security company, and I'd like to bring you on board."

I raise an eyebrow. "I'm not a security guard."

He chuckles. "This is more... clandestine. Operations where the government can't be officially involved."

"What sort of operations?"

He scrutinizes my face before answering. "Breaking up human trafficking rings."

Now I understand the lack of government involvement. Anytime two or more countries have to agree on the terms of an operation, egos get in the way. Desk jockeys thousands of miles away try to dictate how you should behave in a scenario they can't imagine and then Monday-morning-quarterback you to death when it's over.

"So your company would do what? Gather intel and do search and rescue?"

He nods. "Among other things."

"And the traffickers?"

He's quiet. "We would obtain useful information from them," he finally says. "Information to follow this all the way to the top."

Neither of us uses the word torture, but we both know that sometimes the only way to get answers from violent people is by speaking their language. We're not dealing with upstanding citizens. These bastards attack those they should be protecting, kidnapping and selling women and children into modern-day slavery. Most of them end up as sex slaves, even the children. My jaw tightens. My entire adult life has been about safeguarding people from opportunistic oppressors. Still, running black ops in third world countries, off the books, with no backup?

"This sounds more like something for the CIA."

He shakes his head. "Ever since 9/11, when we found out the hard way that agencies wouldn't openly share information among themselves, politicians have bulldozed their way in. They've demanded transparency and open sharing of information. There may be a place for that, but you know as well as I do, the more people who know a secret, the less chance there is of it remaining one, especially when politics are involved."

"You suspect politician involvement?"

"Human trafficking is the fastest growing criminal industry in the world. Last year alone, it generated over fifteen trillion dollars. Trillion, Mark, not billion. I think we have people in both politics and governmental agencies that are being strongly encouraged to look the other way. They may not know exactly what's going on, but they know something isn't right. That's all the leeway these cockroaches need to slip under the radar. Money buys a lot of blissful ignorance."

"So what is it you want from me? I'm not exactly black-ops material anymore," I say, gesturing to my leg.

"I'm looking for a leader, Mark, someone to coordinate the operations. I need someone to collect the intel we gather and sort through it and find their weak points. I need someone who can take the bird's-eye view and plan the long game. It's great to go in and bust up one ring, but if the men go in without restraint and kill everyone, the trail stops there. I need someone to lead the operation, to guide them, to make the tough calls, and you're my top choice. Actually," he says, looking at me, "you're the only one I'll even consider."

I'm baffled by his admission. "Why?"

"Because this is what you do best," he says simply. "You excel at taking a group of men and turning them into a team. You have a gift for seeing the big picture and knowing when and where to push and when to hold. I need someone who can analyze on his feet and make split-second decisions. That's who you are. That's what you do, what you've always done."

I don't know how to respond. His praise makes me uncomfortable, but at the same time, it pleases me. I have a deep admiration for the Colonel. He may have been military brass, but he was every bit a battlefield warrior.

I shift topics. "Tell me about your partner."

"His name is Logan Randall. Former SEAL. His brother is some financial whiz who turned Logan's average income into a lot more."

"A trust fund kid?" Ugh. Rich pretty boys playing soldier. The first to run their mouths and usually the first to panic when the shit hit the fan.

But the Colonel shakes his head. "I told you, he was a SEAL. The money came later."

"Why is he so interested in human trafficking?"

He purses his lips before sighing heavily. "His sister and her family went to Haiti on a disaster relief mission. While they were there, her two children were kidnapped, a seven-year-old boy and a five-year-old girl. They were taken across the border to the Dominican Republic and sold as sex slaves. Logan was deployed, so by the time he was able to get to her, the trail had gone cold. They found the boy's body. The girl was sold to some men in Indonesia. It took a year to find her. From what I understand, she doesn't speak now and she's terrified of men, even her father and Logan."

I close my eyes, horror washing over me. Dear God. A five-year-old child, her innocence stolen forever. And her brother, enduring God knows what before being slaughtered.

Every time I think people can't get any worse, some animal proves me wrong.

"So how would this even work?"

"Logan's started a company called ShadoWolf Protection Services. The plan is to offer bodyguard services for high-profile individuals as a cover. He'll have dedicated team members for that. The human trafficking operations obviously won't be publicized. For all intents and purposes, the business will look like a bunch of bodyguards for starlets and spoiled rich people."

"What's your involvement?"

"Logan would decide which ops we take. My role would be to help plan the operations. If you take the job, I'd be a consultant, more or less. A second set of eyes to help once you've worked out the details. I'd remain stateside to coordinate anything you need during the ops themselves. You'd be the leader on the ground. The only people you'd answer to are me and Logan."

"And if we should get caught in a third world country?"

He purses his lips again. "We'd launch rescue ops. Off the books. But I'm not gonna blow sunshine up your ass. You don't want to get caught sneaking into a third world country on a mission to break up a crime ring that's quite lucrative for the local officials. Their government will deny there's anything going on and throw your ass in prison, and ours will say you're acting independently and wash their hands of you."

I rub my hand over my face. "I need to think this over, Colonel. If it were just me, I'd say yes right away, but with Charlie and the babies…"

He nods. "I understand. Take your time. We're still in the planning stages. If you decide to take me up on my offer, I'd like your input on potential team members. There's a fine line between the ability to follow orders and think independently, and we need people with the right balance of both."

He gets to his feet, rubbing his hands together. "I think I'll turn in, if you don't mind pointing me in the direction of my room. The time zone changes are wreaking havoc with my sleep."

I nod and get up as well. "Last door on the left upstairs. You're welcome to join us for breakfast before I drive you to the airport."

"I appreciate it. Tell Charlie good night for me, if you don't mind, and think about my offer."

Once Charlie falls asleep, I can't think about anything else.

CHARLIE

The Colonel joins us for breakfast in the morning. He shares the cantaloupe I only eat to appease Mark, along with scrambled eggs and toast. Mark watches me like a hawk, making sure I eat every bite. When I give Penny half a piece of my toast, he frowns.

"You need to eat."

I laugh. "Mark, all I do is eat. Relax."

Penny noses against him, rooting for his fingers, and he finally rewards her with a scratch behind the ears and a scoop of eggs on a saucer. Colonel Sherman chuckles.

"Son, I hate to break it to you, but these women are calling all the shots."

Mark grins. "Yes, sir, but it's worth it." He leans over and plants a noisy kiss on my lips, and the Colonel laughs again.

"My suitcase is upstairs. I'll go wash up and be back down whenever you're ready to leave," he says to Mark. As soon as he's up the stairs, Mark's lips are on mine again, insistent and needy. He leaves me breathless and whimpering, my fingers clutching at his shirt, eager for more.

"When do you have to go to work today?" he murmurs.

"Not until after lunch. Hurry home." I pull his head down, finding his lips again.

"If the Colonel didn't have a flight, I wouldn't leave at all. I'd take you back to bed and not stop until you make all those sexy little sounds and come all around my cock." My eyes close and my lower body throbs in anticipation.

"You're a tease," I mutter as I hear footsteps on the stairs.

"I'm not teasing, Baby Girl. It's a promise."

I can't wait for him to get back home.

I turn as the Colonel enters the room, crossing it to hug him tightly. He leans down and cups my rounded belly. "Now you two take good care of your mother until I see her again. That's an order." He straightens up and smiles. "Charlie, I look forward to seeing you again soon."

I walk the Colonel and Mark to the door, locking it behind them, then take Penny out to the backyard for a quick potty break. She's overly excited this morning from having the Colonel in the house, so I let her run off some extra energy. When she's done, we go back inside, where she scampers through the house, running laps through the entire downstairs.

I wish I had that kind of energy.

Instead, I drag myself upstairs and strip the sheets from the Colonel's bed, then wipe down his bathroom. When I turn, Penny is slowly creeping through the doorway, her tail between her legs.

My jaw drops. Penny's finally come upstairs.

"Good girl." I bend over, and she approaches cautiously, her belly low to the ground. Her eyes dart wildly around, searching for any hint of danger. I've never figured out why Penny doesn't like stairs, but this is the first time she's climbed them in the four months I've had her. I stroke her ears reassuringly. "Good girl," I croon.

She backs out of the room and into the hall, staring at the staircase. She made it up the stairs, but she's clearly regretting her decision now.

I gather the sheets in my arms and head toward the hall. "Come on, Sweet Girl," I say in a singsong voice, descending the stairs. Halfway down I turn and glance up. She's sitting on the top step, trembling.

"Come on. It's okay," I coax her, but she still won't move.

I turn to continue down the steps. Maybe from the bottom I can convince her to come down for some treats.

That's when I hear the sudden panicked scrambling of toenails on hardwood. Penny's bolting down the stairs at top speed. As she rushes past me, she knocks me off balance, and my hand slips from the rail. I turn and tumble backwards down the remaining eight steps, slamming hard into the floor.

The last thing I'm aware of is excruciating pain in both my head and my abdomen.

MARK

Thankfully, the Colonel's flight was on schedule, and I was able to drop him off without having to wait around. I speed back to Cedar Ridge, my mind focused on spending the morning in bed with Charlie. I whistle as I climb the front steps. I'm going to taste every inch of her creamy skin and not stop until her legs are shaking and she's screaming my name.

Then I open the door, and my world shatters.

Penny's whining, lying beside Charlie on the floor. Charlie's legs are bent beneath her, her eyes are closed, and she's horribly pale.

Everything goes into slow motion.

I call the clinic and yell for Tess to get Lila here now, that there's an emergency with Charlie. Then I call for an ambulance. I kneel beside Charlie. She's breathing. I don't know what else to do. I'm reaching to pick her up when Lila's voice stops me.

"No!" she says sharply. "She may have a neck or spine injury." Lila drops to her knees. "Did you call 911?" I can only nod. Lila's gone into medic mode, opening Charlie's eyes to check her pupils, palpating the back of her head and neck. She's checking her abdomen when Charlie moans.

"Baby Girl? Can you hear me?" I lean over her, and she moans again.

"Charlie, it's Lila. Can you open your eyes for me?"

The sight of her emerald eyes is the most beautiful thing I've ever seen. They drift closed again almost immediately. "Hurts," she mumbles.

"Tell me where it hurts." Lila's voice is commanding.

"My head. And – oh!" She gasps suddenly, her hands coming up to clutch her stomach. "The babies. Something's wrong –" she gasps again. "It hurts, Lila. Something's wrong."

"Look at me, Charlie. Your babies are going to be fine. You're going to be fine. We're going to roll you onto your side to help them out a little, okay?" I follow Lila's directions, carefully straightening Charlie's legs and rolling her like a log onto her side before propping her back with my jacket and leaning her against it.

Charlie sucks in a sharp breath, fisting her hands tightly before gripping my forearm. "Something – something's wrong. It hurts. The babies," she moans. "The babies."

Lila's eyes widen. I follow her gaze to the sudden rush of crimson spreading across the floor from between Charlie's legs.

"Baby Girl?" I say, but her eyes are drifting closed again. Her grip on my arm goes slack, and her hands fall away. "Baby Girl?"

A siren wails in the distance.

"Mark!"

"Baby Girl!"

"Mark!" Lila shakes me fiercely. I look up at her violet eyes. I've never seen her more frightened or serious. "Go outside and flag the ambulance down."

"I can't leave her."

"Now, Mark! Go! We can't let them waste time going to the clinic. We need them now."

I get to my feet and stumble outside.

Blood is bad. Blood means something has ripped loose inside. It means my babies are dying, second by second, and so is Charlie.

Flashing red lights round the curve, and I wave my arms frantically. Two medics hop down from the cab. "Please," I babble. "She's pregnant. She fell down the stairs. There's blood, a lot of blood." They move like a well-oiled machine, tossing a tackle box of equipment onto the stretcher and dashing inside.

My legs give out, and I collapse to my knees on the ground.

I had everything I ever wanted, and it's fading.

Dying.

Lila drags me into the ambulance with her, and she and I ride in the back with the medic. She's rolled up her sleeves and jumped into action, starting a second IV while the medic is taking Charlie's vital signs. He raises an eyebrow but doesn't argue with her. Lila asks about the blood pressure and when she hears it, she rips open another bag of IV fluids and starts them without asking. I keep my eyes on Charlie, on the paleness of her face, the rise and fall of her chest.

Lila turns to me. "Charlie's in shock from blood loss. They'll take her straight to surgery to deliver the babies. I'm not sure if they'll let you see her or not."

I hear what she's not saying.

To tell Charlie and my babies goodbye, because I may not get another chance.

I hit my knees beside her head. Her eyes are still closed, and I'm not sure she's conscious, but I remember hearing Charlie's voice when I was unconscious in the hospital, so I talk to her, repeating myself over and over as I run my fingers through her silky hair. "Baby Girl, listen to me. You're going to be fine, and so are our babies. I just need you to be strong one more time. Don't you dare leave me, Baby Girl. I love you. Be strong for me. Keep fighting." I press my lips to her cool cheek, leaving tears on her ghostly white face.

The hospital is a blur.

As Lila predicted, they rush Charlie straight back where I can't follow. A nurse comes to me for basic information, but I can't think. Lila answers the questions. How many weeks pregnant, who's her doctor, any allergies, any health concerns. The nurse says something about a CT scan, and Lila speaks to her as one professional to another. All I can do is stand there, completely helpless.

A doctor in green scrubs comes out to tell me Charlie's been taken to emergency surgery. Her uterus ruptured from the fall, and she's hemorrhaging. They have to deliver the babies immediately. Once they deliver them and stop her bleeding, they'll do trauma scans to assess her head injury and look for fractures.

I may lose Charlie and my babies.

I grab his arm. "Please." I try to say more, but that's the only word my numb mind can come up with. "Please."

He squeezes my shoulder. "She's in good hands. We'll do everything we can."

At some point Tucker shows up. I hear Lila telling him to take care of me, but there's nothing to take care of. Tom and Stubbs arrive, too, sitting on either side of me, but I'm silent.

Scared shitless.

I can't lose her again. I can't.

I know I won't survive this time.

I don't know how long I sit there. Lila's dragged a chair in front of me. She's got a death grip on my hand, and Tucker's behind me, squeezing my shoulders. They're talking to me, and Stubbs and Tom are talking, too, but I can't hear anything. All I can hear is Charlie, moaning in pain and gasping before she lost consciousness.

I can't lose her again. I can't.

I can't.

CHARLIE

The first thing I become aware of are piercing bright lights. Really bright, stabbing my eyes, and I squint. I raise my head to look around, and a sharp pain shoots through my skull. I lay my head back on the bed and shut my eyes as a duller pain echoes through my abdomen.

My abdomen.

The babies!

I gasp and try to sit up, groaning. I settle for propping myself up on my elbows before opening my eyes and scanning the blurs around me.

"Easy, Baby Girl, You're okay."

"The babies!"

"Our babies are fine," Mark says. "They're both fine."

The room starts to come into focus. Mauve wallpaper. An adjustable bedside table. Bedrails.

A hospital room. I'm in a hospital bed. I strain to remember what happened, how I got here.

A hand brushes my face, and I look up into anxious blue eyes. Mark is pale, with deep circles under his bloodshot eyes. His hair is messy and his clothes are rumpled. He looks worried and exhausted.

I lift a hand to his face. "You look awful. Are you alright?"

He laughs shakily. "I'm much better now. How do you feel?"

"My head hurts." I look at him. "The babies?" I repeat.

He takes my hand between both of his and sits on the bed beside me. "Our babies are both fine. Ryker weighs four pounds and six ounces. Sophia weighs four pounds and three ounces. They were born yesterday morning at nine forty-five. They're both healthy. They're keeping them in the newborn ICU for observation because of your fall, but they're doing fine, and we should all be able to go home in a couple of days."

The fall. It comes rushing back. The stairs. Losing my balance when Penny bumped me. Crashing into the floor, my head bouncing and striking again.

Then I realize what he's said. "Yesterday? What time is it?"

"A little after one in the morning."

"I've been out that whole time?"

He swallows hard. "You had a tough time yesterday."

"What does that mean?"

"You lost a lot of blood. They had to give you multiple transfusions. You have a concussion and a hairline skull fracture, but no bleeding in your brain. Lots of bumps and bruises, but no other broken bones." He hesitates. "They had to do a hysterectomy. Your uterus was ruptured and they couldn't stop the bleeding. I'm sorry, Charlie."

No uterus.

That means no more pregnancies.

No future babies.

I'm okay with that. I wasn't supposed to have had these two. I'll take my two miracle babies and call it a win.

"Can I go see the Tiny People?"

He chuckles. "I don't think we can call them that anymore. They have real names now."

I smile. "So do we, but you're still my Big Guy, and I'm still your Baby Girl."

Mark leans down and presses a gentle kiss to my lips. "You scared the hell out of me, Baby Girl. I can't lose you again. I'm not strong enough to survive it."

"I'm not going anywhere," I murmur.

"I love you," he says, stroking my cheek with long fingers. I watch emotions swirl in his eyes. Anxiety. Fear. Need. Love.

"Marry me, Mark."

Pale blue eyes widen. "What?"

"Marry me. You told me to let you know when I was ready. I love you, and I'm sure. I'm ready."

"Now?" I watch the wheels turning in his mind. "The hospital probably has a chaplain."

I grin. "Not right this minute. Lila will kill me if she doesn't get to plan a wedding. But soon."

"So you mean it? You'll marry me?"

I reach for him, pulling his mouth down to mine for a soft kiss. "As proposals go, that needs work," I tell him.

He grins. "Technically, I think you proposed to me, and 'Marry me, Mark,' is a little on the nose, don't you think?"

"Fine. You can show me how it's done."

The words are scarcely out of my mouth before he's kneeling beside me and taking my hand. I stare in shock. His gaze pins me in place. "Charlie Emerson, I love you with every fiber of my being. You own me, heart and soul. Will you do me the honor of becoming mine forever?"

My mouth drops open. "That's a much better proposal than 'Marry me, Mark'."

He smiles slowly. "I've had it ready for a while." He leans close, kissing me, and I sigh contentedly and wrap my arms around his neck.

"Is that a yes?" he murmurs minutes later, still in my arms.

"That's a yes."

EPILOGUE

CHARLIE

WE'RE MARRIED JUNE TWENTY-NINTH, one year to the day after our first kiss. It seems only fitting to honor the date, especially since our twins were born on April twelfth, the one-year anniversary of the day Mark first came home with me. That's the date my house became a home, and a year later, we became a family.

It's a small wedding, just our chosen family gathered in my backyard. Lila's set up an arbor wrapped in green vines and sweet-smelling white flowers. Tucker and Tom are the groomsmen; Lila and Maya are my bridesmaids. Stubbs is corralling the twins in a small playpen. The huge man is completely in his element, cooing and tickling my babies until they squeal with delight while Penny supervises with an eagle eye, ready to intervene at the first cry.

Colonel Sherman is officiating our wedding. He's been staying with us for the past week while he and Mark hammer out details for a job Mark's accepted with him. It's dangerous work – covertly breaking up underground human trafficking rings – but he's spent his life standing up for those unable to protect themselves. Leaving the military didn't change his need to take down bastards who revel in inflicting pain on others. The new job is still in its planning stages. Right now, they're sorting through applicants for their team. Tucker's expressed an interest, too, but not until after he and Lila's babies are born.

Lila spends hours fussing over my hair and makeup. I'd rolled my eyes when she'd broken out a makeup case to rival that of any Hollywood makeup artist. "You know he saw me with bedhead this morning, right?"

"Shut up and close your eyes," she says. "I've been planning this for weeks. Don't ruin my fun."

It's true. Lila picked my colors, my flowers, my wedding cake, my reception food, and my photographer. She decided how to style my hair and do my makeup and what jewelry I would wear. She chose the men's tuxedos and the bridesmaid's dresses. The only choices I made were my groom and my dress.

And though I'm not much for clothes, I do admit, this is a beautiful dress, a long white sheath of satin and lace. The halter-style neckline forms a narrow vee that hints at cleavage without being risque, and the back plunges to my hips, curving just above the dimples at the small of my back. It leaves my scarred back displayed for the entire world to see.

I've chosen to embrace my scars.

They're a part of me. I'm who I am because of my past, and though it was painful, that experience shaped me into the woman I am today. I'm not ashamed of my scars any longer. They don't signify some failure on my part. They're evidence that I fought, that I rose above the pain. They prove that even though savages may have shattered my body, my spirit prevailed.

The ceremony is simple but elegant. The men wear black tuxedos, and Lila and Maya wear black dresses with halter-style necklines similar to my dress. Maya's is fitted to the waist before flaring out slightly. The black satin sets off her perfect caramel skin. Her copper-streaked curls spring free, and Lila applied the barest hint of makeup to accent her beautiful melted-chocolate eyes, so much like her father's. Lila's dress cups her full breasts before cascading over her perfectly rounded belly. She's six months pregnant, literally glowing, blond curls tumbling over her shoulders and violet eyes shining. She's stunning, upstaging me without even trying. But I don't care. All I care about is the man waiting for me at the end of the aisle.

I step out onto the deck, and all I can see is Mark. He's gorgeous. The tux clings to his broad shoulders before tailoring down to his narrow hips. He's in a wide stance, his hands clasped behind his back. My eyes find his, and he smiles broadly.

Tucker takes my hand, gripping it tightly. "You ready for this?" he whispers. When I nod, he grins. "About damn time you two got hitched. Let's get this show on the road." He tucks my hand into his elbow and we walk slowly down the aisle, with Penny shepherding me, pressing against my left leg. Just before we reach the front, Tucker turns and kisses me on the cheek. "Love you, Charlie. I told you, you two were meant to be." He releases me at the arbor and takes his place between Mark and Tom. Before Colonel Sherman can utter a single word, Mark steps forward, pulls me into his arms, and kisses me swiftly. "I do," he mutters. "I do."

I smile against his lips as laughter erupts around us. "Hold your horses," the Colonel scolds him. "We're not there yet." We break apart and assume our places, and he steps in front of us.

"I'm not fooling with that 'Dearly beloved' nonsense, because we all know why we're here. We're here to join these two hearts in wedded bliss and unite their souls for the rest of eternity. I understand you've written your own vows. Mark, if you'd like to proceed."

Mark accepts a gold band from Tucker, and I hand Lila my bouquet of white roses before Mark steps forward and takes my hands. "Hi, Baby Girl," he says with a grin.

"Hi," I say, staring into his light blue eyes, so clear and full of promise.

"Get to the good stuff," Tucker says under his breath, and Lila glares warningly.

Mark lifts my finger and slides the ring into place as he speaks. "I was sixteen when I first fell in love with you. I was supposed to be helping you with algebra, but all I could think about was how soft your skin looked and how good your hair smelled. But I never told you, because I was afraid you wouldn't feel the same. I resigned myself to just being friends. And we were friends, best friends. You've been my best friend for so long, Charlie. You were there for me when my mom died and my dad committed suicide. You were there when I was injured. You stood by me when I needed you, and you forgave me when I was a dumbass and didn't deserve it."

"Amen!" Tucker's voice rings loud and clear, and everyone laughs except Lila, who hisses, "Shut up, Tucker!"

Mark smiles before squeezing my hands gently. "I've loved you for as long as I can remember, Charlie Emerson, but until I lost you, I never knew how much. I don't ever want to be apart from you again. I don't give a damn about losing my leg anymore. It was just a leg, and I'm more than that. You, though... you're everything I need, the only one I want, my life, the air I breathe, the one that makes me whole. I promise to love you every day for the rest of my life. I promise to always stand with you, no matter how hard things are. I promise to be your guiding light, your comfort in hard times, and your shoulder to lean on. I can't promise to be the man you deserve, because you deserve someone much better than me, but I promise to devote every second of my life to making you happy. I will cherish you until my dying breath, Baby Girl."

My eyes burn with tears as a lump forms in my throat.

Colonel Sherman turns to me. "Your vows, Charlie?"

"I love you," I say, gazing into Mark's eyes, and he smiles, leaning forward to kiss me.

"I told you to hold your horses," the Colonel reprimands him in an exasperated tone.

Mark pulls away, grinning and not the least bit sorry as he waits for me to speak. My mind goes blank for a split second, and I look down at his hands. Lila nudges me and hands me his ring, and it all comes back as I look at his face again.

I slide the ring onto his waiting finger. "I love you, Mark. We've been part of each other's lives for so long now that it's hard to recall a time you weren't there. You were always there for the big things, but you were there for the little things, too. We've endured tremendous pain and loss, but we've also had our share of triumphs and miracles." I pause and glance toward Stubbs, who's cradling an infant in each of his massive arms, gently bouncing them. I look back up at Mark, drowning in the depths of his gorgeous eyes. "I promise to stand beside you through thick or thin. I promise to call you on your bullshit and tell you when you're being a colossal dumbass." Mark grins as Tucker snickers and Lila gasps. "I promise to love you whether you're being sweet or stupid. I promise to love you enough to fight with you when necessary, and to fight for us always. I love you more than life itself, Mark Chandler, and I can't wait to spend the rest of my life as your wife."

Colonel Sherman clears his throat. "Do you, Charlie, take Mark to be your husband, to love, honor, and cherish, as long as you both shall live?"

Pale blue eyes lock on my green ones. "I do."

"And do you, Mark—"

Mark seizes me by the waist and drags me forward. "I do," he says against my mouth. "Forever and ever, I do." His firm mouth claims mine, and my lips part instantly for him. His tongue sweeps inside as he kisses me until I'm breathless and weak in the knees.

I become aware of cheers and whistles around me as Colonel Sherman shouts over the noise. "I now pronounce you man and wife. I'd tell you to kiss the bride, but you can't seem to keep your damn lips off her!"

"Get a room!" bellows Tucker, laughing.

"Believe me, there's more to come later," Mark finally murmurs against my lips, and a deep ache stirs low inside me.

Photographs are next, more than I can count. Tucker's brother, Shepherd, puts us through the paces, snapping shots from every angle. One of my favorites is me in Mark's arms, looking back over my shoulder with my scars on full display.

Beauty from brokenness.

Lila's had my favorite Italian restaurant cater the meal, because hello, pasta. When photos are finally done, I slip into the bedroom to change out of my wedding dress into something I won't be terrified of splattering with tomato sauce, and I've encouraged everyone else to do the same. We're one big family, and there's no need to stand on ceremony. Lila's commandeered the weight-room-turned-nursery as a dressing room, and everyone's brought extra clothes. When I announce I'll be back in sweatpants and a tee shirt, Lila looks like she's going to faint. "I'm kidding," I say hastily. "Relax. I'll be presentable."

I'm in the bathroom, getting ready to slip out of my dress, when I hear the bedroom door open and close, followed by the soft strains of a familiar song. I tilt my head, listening, and smile. It's "I'll Be", by Edwin McCain. The song Mark said always made him think of me.

The song he's now playing in a loop on his phone.

Moments later, my husband is standing behind me, gazing at me in the mirror.

My husband.

"Oh, no, you don't," he says as my hands reach for the clip at the neck of my dress.

"What? I have to change. I can't eat pasta in this."

"You're mine to peel out of this dress." His eyes darken as he holds mine in the mirror.

I reach behind me, finding his hands and pulling them to my breasts. "Peel faster."

He groans. "Our first time as man and wife should be slow, something we savor. We've got a houseful of guests. There's no time for savoring."

I turn in his arms, standing on tiptoe to capture his mouth in a searing kiss. "How about this? First *night* as man and wife is slow and savoring, but the first time in the bathroom as man and wife is hard and fast."

We don't even make it out of our clothes.

The top of my gown is undone to the waist, my breasts bouncing, my nipples teased into hard peaks. His bowtie is undone, his jacket off, pants around his ankles. I'm bent over the bathroom counter as he slides deep inside me from behind, giving me time to adjust to his length before pulling back and slamming into me again. I bite my lip to stifle my moans as he pounds into me, his fingers gripping my hips as I stare into the mirror at the intensity on his chiseled face. The pressure builds inside me and I push back against him, eager to find my release. I'm so close.

He pulls out then, startling me as he scoops me up and seats me on the counter facing him, lifting my gown out of the way. He kneels in front of me, sliding me forward to stroke my core with his tongue, burying his face in me, sucking and swirling over my clit. I don't last a full minute before climaxing, my fingers in his hair, whimpering when I'd rather scream his name. He's standing before the aftershocks have faded, driving into me again as I cling to him, my face in his neck, my legs around his hips. "Oh, God," I murmur, arching closer, feeling the delicious pressure building inside me again.

"That's right," he mutters. "Come for me again, Baby Girl. Come all over my cock like you did all over my tongue." I gasp, teetering on the precipice between exquisite agony and thrilling ecstasy.

He thrusts again, grinding his pelvis against my clit, giving me what I need to push me over the edge again. My walls clench tightly around him, squeezing his length, and I feel him spasming deep within me as he shudders, panting. My head falls against his chest; his chin rests on top of my head. We breathe hard, locked in each other's arms.

"You're amazing, Mrs. Chandler," he murmurs, claiming my mouth in a scorching kiss.

"Keep that up, Mr. Chandler, and we'll never get back to our guests."

"Promise?" His pale eyes lock on mine as he hovers above me.

"I do." I smile, and he kisses me again, slowly, tenderly.

Only when we're dressed do I notice the large white box on the bed. "What's this?"

"A wedding gift," he says.

"Really?"

Mark nods, suddenly looking shy. "I wasn't sure it would arrive in time. I commissioned it as soon as we got engaged."

"You commissioned it?"

He nods again. "Would you like to open it?"

"Is that okay?"

He chuckles. "Of course." He sits down on the bed, pulling me onto his lap.

The box is heavy, tied with a simple black silk ribbon. I untie it and lift the lid, pawing through the layers of tissue paper.

When I see it, I gasp. It's a huge platter, nearly two feet wide and at least eighteen inches across the middle. It's oval in shape, with a hanger attached to the back.

"It's an art piece, made to my specifications. I had them make it black on the back and use pale blue and emerald green glazes on the front, sometimes separate, sometimes blended," he says, pointing to different portions of the platter. "The black is for the darkness. The pain. The things we went through. It's in the background, unseen unless you search for it. The green parts are you, the blue parts are me, and the parts where they blend together are us." Long fingers trace the gold veins across the platter. "I had them shatter it into pieces, the way your life was shattered, the way my life was shattered." He pauses. "The way I shattered us." I reach for his face, running my fingers over his cheeks, pulling his lips to mine for a brief kiss. He smiles, kissing me again before continuing. "Then they did their magic with the lacquer and the gold and put it back together." His arms tighten around me. "They restored what was broken and made it something more than the sum of its parts. They emphasized the breaks and scars instead of trying to hide them, and that gives it beauty."

"More beautiful because it was broken," I whisper, looking at the man I love more than life itself.

"Yes," he agrees, dipping his head to kiss me gently. "More beautiful because it was broken."

FOLLOW ME FOR UPDATES!

Thank you so much for taking the time to read about Charlie and Mark's individual journeys to self-acceptance. It means more to me than I can put into words.

If you're enjoying my novels, **please visit my website and sign up for my newsletter.** When you sign up, you'll get a free bonus intro to the characters in my Shattered trilogy, complete with fun facts and photos! You can sign up here: https://phoenix-wolfe.com/ The same page has **links to follow me on Facebook, Instagram, and Twitter!**

Pop in and say hello! **I'm considering telling Tom's story... and maybe a few others', too!** Let me know if that's something you'd like to read!

If you're enjoying this series, please stop by and leave a review on Amazon. As an indie author, **reviews are the best way to get my story out to other people**, and to be honest, **there are entirely too many women (and men) dealing with the aftermath of not only sexual assault, but the struggle of self-loathing.** I'd love to put this story in the hands of as many people as I can because I truly believe the message is something most of us need to hear on some level. **If you're willing to help, I'd appreciate it.**

Warmly,
Phoenix Wolfe

LETTER FROM THE AUTHOR

DEAREST READER,

As an author and survivor of sexual assault, I felt it was important to show a realistic portrayal of the lingering aftereffects of such a traumatic event. The road to recovery is long. It is not linear, and no two people's journeys look exactly the same. It took me many years – decades – to reach what I would consider "recovered", yet even now, specific triggers can catch me off guard and cause me to struggle temporarily.

I understand that not everyone can read about such events without re-living his or her own trauma. As such, I strongly recommend reading the trigger warnings page to see if Charlie's story is a fit for where you are in your situation. You may also view a sample chapter at the following link: **https://phoenix-wolfe.com/sample-of-chapter-one**

For those who have survived sexual assault, I stand with you and support you. What happened to you was not your fault, and despite the lies your inner critic may whisper, you are never too damaged to be worthy of love. For those whose lives have not been shattered by rape, perhaps this book will provide insight into the long-term struggles survivors face.

I urge anyone who has survived any type of traumatic event to seek help, even if your trauma is not recent. Many people cope by trying to forget what happened, rather than dealing with it. I'm one of them. I tried to forget, and in the end, I still had to unearth the past and address it. Repressing and burying pain is merely a stop-gap measure. Eventually, you have to deal with the pain of your past. Talk to someone – a counselor, your health care provider, a psychiatrist, support group, or spiritual leader. You can also contact the **National Sexual Assault Hotline** 24 hours a day by calling **1-800-656-4673**. If you prefer, you can go to **online.rainn.org** and chat with someone online.

Additionally, if you or someone you know is considering suicide, I urge you to reach out for help. **You can call, text, or chat with someone from the Suicide and Crisis Hotline by dialing 988.** You can also **text the word HOME to 741741 for free, confidential support** from a Crisis Counselor 24/7. You can also reach out to the **American Suicide Prevention Foundation at 1-888-333-2377.** Please, seek help. Your life is valuable, and **you matter**.

Recovery is a journey, not a destination. You are not alone.

Standing alongside you,
Phoenix Wolfe